National Heroes and Achievers

Ray Filby

National Heroes and Achievers

Publisher : Midhurst

Published by Midhurst

Midhurst,
2, Freers Mews,
Warwick,
Warwickshire
CV34 6DP

978-1-916894-7-8

http://midhurstpublishing.uk

Contents

All of us have our own ideas about what makes someone a Hero. We may think about exceptional people in sport or public service, or about ordinary people doing extraordinarily brave things. We must accept that the concept of Hero has changed over time and differs between cultures. Our modern understanding may not have been recognised by ancient people, writers or philosophers. Odysseus, the adventuring Hero of Greek myth, was wily and brave, but not necessarily in pursuit of honourable ends. Carl Jung said that 'Hero' is one of the fundamental archetypes, representing the struggle to overcome obstacles by self-sacrifice. Shakespearean scholars talk of the Tragic Hero, such as Hamlet whose intent was decent or virtuous, but whose fundamental character flaw prevented him from acting on this intention.

In our culture now, we may see a Hero as someone who is admired by others for his or her honourable qualities of compassion, courage and self-sacrifice, qualities that are employed to help other people, or fulfil some other noble goal. Other qualities such as cleverness, strength, determination and reliability may also serve valued goals as we see in celebrated military or political leaders. There is a clue here – perhaps a key issue is the idea of a 'noble goal'. Across time, and between cultures, and within societies, there may be wildly different beliefs about what constitutes a noble goal, or valued objective. So a Hero is a Hero in the eye of the beholder, whose values are of their time and place.

In Europe in this decade, Volodimir Zelensky has been hailed as a Hero, for his strength, determination and resilience in defending his country, and the rest of Eastern Europe, against the ravenous appetites of Putin and his regime: one small figure, speaking to the rest of the world with great passion, resolve and fortitude. But his noble goal of protecting an autonomous Ukraine is not shared by his neighbour, Russia, and even some of those living in parts of Eastern Ukraine may disagree.

In 1955 in the USA, the bravery and commitment of Rosa Parks to challenge racist segregation laws has marked her as a Hero for us now – she risked a great deal to stand up for her belief in justice for all, an objective we regard as a noble one. But the mainstream of white citizens may not have found this to be a noble goal at that time, given the cultural acceptance that white people mattered more than black. A similar argument can be made about the suffragettes, who risked their liberty, reputation, relationships and even their lives. Their goals may seem noble to us now. But then?

Noble intentions are one aspect of heroism, but the personal characteristics of the individual are also involved. Heroic figures embody the values and virtues that their society admires and respects. If society values military might, then skilled but entirely ruthless generals are heroic. It is possible to see how figures such as Elon Musk, Warren Buffet and even Donald Trump are viewed as heroic by some sections of society, in which taking risks in pursuit of business success is highly regarded. But these are not the characteristics that inspire me, and these ideals are not my personal values. If society cherishes the value of human life, then anyone who puts his or her life on the line to save another person is a Hero. If relieving suffering is a general goal, then health professionals who worked through the devastation of the Covid pandemic are certainly Heroes. For me, the recipe for a Hero seems to be bravery and self-sacrifice, together with a goal that is highly valued in society, and by me.

So, in conclusion, my Heroes are those who have courage in the face of serious threat, compassion for the suffering of others, and a willingness to put their own safety at risk to ensure the safety and wellbeing of another person or animal or group.

<u>Introduction</u>

When the author started this project, the accounts written were of men and women who had displayed heroism in the context of military combat. However, it is very clear that many individuals have made as great a contribution to benefit the nation as the warlords. The author therefore decided to extend the scope of this book to include those whose contribution to the nation's development came in the form of great achievements. While every person mentioned deserves acclaim, the author recognises that no-one is perfect and he hasn't sought to hide or disguise any faults or flaws displayed, even in the lives of these great people. The following brief accounts were written as the author's contribution to the Warwick Writers' Group where the material each of us has recently written is shared.

In carrying out the research needed to write this book, the author drew heavily on the excellent but very long and detailed accounts which can be accessed on the internet, particularly in the encyclopaedias, Britannica and Wikipedia. To avoid the accounts reading too much like a history book, very few dates have been included in the text. However, if the reader wishes to place the subject of an account into a historical context, lists have been included as appendices at the end of the book which give the dates of significant events in British history; the dates of the Roman Emperors, the reigns of Kings and Queens of Britain and the period in office of Prime Ministers. The dates of the lifespans of each individual described in this volume are included in order of date of birth in the index of this book. An ordered list has also been included of the names of those considered as great Britons by a poll carried out by the BBC. The author was surprised at some of the names listed which include at least one name which the author would categorise as a national villain!

The portraits included for each hero and achiever have been downloaded from the internet. The author has written to the source organisations of these pictures, Alamy, Art UK, Bridgewater Images, Discover Worcestershire, Flickr, Getty Images, History Hit, Media Storehouse, Red Bubble, The Courier and Wikimedia to ascertain any copyright issues which might have been infringed.

The scope of this book has been limited to those living up to and including World War II. Almost without exception, all these heroes and achievers are commemorated with magnificent statues, many of which are in London, but several exist in the towns and cities particularly associated with their lives. The author doesn't pretend that the coverage is exhaustive but he has attempted to include a representative sample of achievers over a range of important activities. The reader may well have other heroic individuals in mind whom they consider deserved inclusion in such a volume but a line had to be drawn somewhere.

The author is well aware that those who are the real national heroes are almost always anonymous. Some of their names may be inscribed on the Menin Gate in Ypres or on the wall of the National Memorial Arboretum near Alrewas, Staffordshire. However, as the years roll on, their identity as real people whose lives contributed to the life of society around them are known only to God. The senior officers whose lives are recounted in this book must be seen to represent these heroes who fought and died under them. Lest it be thought that these senior officers occupied locations of relative safety during battle, let it be noted that included in this volume are Nelson, Wolfe and Gordon who all died facing hostile action. At Waterloo, Wellington survived a canon ball which took the leg of his second in command, Lord Uxbridge, with whom he was conferring. The sang froid exchange between the two on this occasion went,

Uxbridge:-   *By God, Sir, I've lost my leg!*
Wellington:-   *By God, Sir, so you have!*

Among those whom I would describe as the anonymous real heroes are:-

the sailors who endured the harsh conditions of the Hanoverian navy to lose their lives as they destroyed the ships with which Napoleon would have invaded this country,

the soldiers sheltering in the World War I trenches, awaiting the order to go over the top where, in spite of the assurances of their senior officers that artillery bombardment had silenced the German fire power, were mowed down by a relentless hail of enemy bullets as they emerged from their trenches,

the fighter pilots in World War II who attacked Goering's aerial armada of bombers whose planes carried rear gunners aiming to shoot down the attacking fighter planes,
and
the bomber crews who flew over strategic targets in Germany, well defended by anti-aircraft artillery, to bomb and neutralise the enemy's ability to wage war.

The marching song of the Grenadier Guards emphasises the real heroism of the ordinary soldier in contrast to the famous names of heroes of antiquity.

> *Some talk of Alexander and some of Hercules,*
> *Of Hector and Lysander and such great names es as these,*
> *But of all the world's great heroes, there's none that can compare,*
> *With a tow row row row row row to the British Grenadiers.*

Queen Boadicea

Queen Boadicea (Boudica)

Boadicea's husband, Prasutagus, was king of the Iceni tribe and his kingdom was an autonomous unit within the Roman Empire where he ruled as an ally of Rome. However, on his death, Boadicea and her daughters were abominably treated by the Romans who had them flogged and stripped Boadicea of her power. Boadicea led the Iceni in revolt against Rome and sacked Colchester, the Roman capital of Britain, London and Verulamium (St. Albans). However, in the long term, Boadicea's Celts could not withstand the military might of the Roman army. Boadicea was defeated and is reputed to have ended her life by committing suicide.

St. Alban

St. Alban

St. Alban is regarded as the first British person to be martyred for his Christian faith. Traditionally, it is believed that he was beheaded at the Roman settlement of Verulamium which is now known by the saint's name as St. Alban's. A splendid Abbey has been built on the site of Alban's martyrdom and this has been raised to cathedral status. It is the second longest church in England, just five feet short of Winchester Cathedral.

The most detailed account of Alban's life and martyrdom is found in 'The Ecclesiastical History of the English People', a document written by the Venerable Bede. Little is known about Alban's background, his status or his religious affiliation, except that he was a Roman soldier living in Britain at a time when Christians were being persecuted during the reign of Caesar Septimius Severus.

Alban met up with a Christian priest, Amphibalus, who was fleeing persecution and Alban offered to shelter him in his house. Amphibalus stayed at Alban's house for several days. Alban was so impressed by this priest's bearing, his prayerfulness and his piety, that he became a Christian himself. Sadly, news of what Alban was doing leaked out and got back to the ears of the authorities who set out to arrest this Christian priest. When they arrived at Alban's house, they found Alban dressed in the priest's robes and claiming himself to be the priest. Alban was arrested and taken before a judge, giving Amphibalus a chance to escape.

The judge was performing sacrifices to pagan gods when Alban was brought into his presence. When he discovered that Alban was not the priest but was just impersonating him, he was so enraged that he ordered that Alban should suffer the same punishment that had been set for the priest. However, Alban was given the opportunity to escape this fate by renouncing his Christianity and conforming to the rites of the Roman religion. Alban refused to do this with a declaration that is still used in services carried out at St. Alban's Cathedral.

'I worship and adore the true and living God who has created all things'

This further enraged the judge who ordered that Alban should be scourged. When the judge realised that Alban's faith was not going to be shaken under torture, he ordered that he should be beheaded.

In my opinion, the story should end with a simple statement that Alban was taken out and executed. However, this period in history is regarded as the dark ages. Then, many who became Christian, expected that accounts of special stories like this should be associated with miracles. There was also the requirement by the church that before a person could be officially recognised by the church as a saint, they must have a proven miracle to their credit. Thus, the end of the story has been embellished with details to which I don't give much credence.

Alban was led to his place of execution which lay on the other side of the fast flowing River Ver. They couldn't use the bridge to get across because it was clogged with curious townsfolk who had assembled to witness the execution. Anxious to get his ordeal over quickly, Alban raised his eyes to heaven and the river dried up, enabling the execution party to get across without using the bridge. The astonished executioner threw down his sword and requested that he might be executed alongside Alban.

There were individuals in the party who could act as alternative executioners and the party moved on to the execution site on a hill whose slopes were covered in beautiful wildflowers. On reaching the summit of the hill, Alban complained of feeling thirsty and a spring opened up at his feet. The second executioner beheaded both Alban and the first executioner who had cast down his sword, requesting to share Alban's fate. No sooner had the executions been carried out than the eyes of the second executioner popped out of his head and Alban's head rolled down the hill, another spring issuing from the ground where the head came to rest. On hearing of these miracles, the judge ordered that no further persecution of Christians should take place and he himself honoured Alban's martyrdom.

Queen Bertha of Kent

Queen Bertha of Kent

When did Christianity first come to Britain? There is evidence that it was brought to Britain within the first generation of the birth of the church on the day of Pentecost. Legend has it that the missionary which established the first church in England was none other than Joseph of Arimathea, who had made available his own tomb to receive the body of Jesus after He was taken down from the cross. The site where Joseph established his church was at Glastonbury and again, legend has it the he planted his staff in the ground there which took root and grew into a thorn tree.

Christianity was alive in Britain during the time it was under Roman occupation. Alban, the first English martyr met his death at the hands of the Romans. Constantine, who was domiciled for a time in York, had a vision of the cross which inspired him to fight for Christianity under that sign when he became Emperor.

However, right into the Saxon era, Christianity in Britain was very much a minority religion, vying with the pagan faiths which held sway in the country at the time. Queen Bertha must be credited with giving the Christian faith recognised status in Saxon Britain. Most of the heroes featured in this book achieved that status by being great military leaders, being individuals of extreme artistic or intellectual ability, serving the country as wonderful philanthropists or having great acumen as politicians. Queen Bertha was unique in that the means by which she achieved greatness was by being a devout woman of prayer. The cynic might doubt this to be a means of achieving anything. However, as Tennyson asserted,

> ***More things are wrought by prayer than this world dreams of.***

and the answers Bertha received to her prayers speak for themselves.

Bertha was a Frankish princess, daughter of Charibert I and great-granddaughter of the more famous King of the Franks, Clovis I. She married King Ethelbert of Kent, but only on condition that she should be allowed to continue to practise her Christian faith. She came to England with her chaplain, Ludhard, and was given what had been formerly a Roman church, just outside Canterbury, for her to carry out her Christian worship. This church was in a ruinous state but Bertha had this restored as her private chapel and dedicated this little church to St Martin of Tours. St Martin's church is still in use today and is accepted as the oldest church in the English speaking world where Christian worship has taken place continuously since 580 A.D. Together with Canterbury Cathedral and St Augustine's Abbey, it constitutes what is now a UNESCO world heritage site.

Bertha's dearest wish was that her husband, Ethelbert, should convert to Christianity, and this became the burden of much of her prayers over the next seven years. The first step to Ethelbert's conversion was persuading him to be prepared to receive a mission to his kingdom from the Pope. Bertha was delighted to be able to contact Pope Gregory I, inviting him to send a mission to Kent. Thus, St Augustine arrived in Kent with his team of missionaries. Augustine was favourably received by Ethelbert who became a Christian as he received teaching from Augustine and his team. Augustine founded an abbey in Canterbury, on a site which Ethelbert had granted to him, which he dedicated to St Peter and St Paul. This became the base from which Christian missions were sent out throughout England to enable the Christian faith to become firmly established in this country.

The Pope wrote to Bertha, complimenting her, both on the firmness of her faith and her understanding of spiritual matters. She is commemorated in Canterbury with a statue and a Bertha trail has been set up, consisting of fourteen bronze plates, set into the pavement and running from St Martin's Church to the Buttermarket.

King Alfred the Great

King Alfred, the Great

When Alfred came to the throne, England was menaced by the Danes who had taken over the Saxon kingdom of Northumbria and threatened to take control of the rest of England. Alfred had to take refuge from the Danes in the Somerset marshes where he made plans to defeat the Danes. The story is told that when sheltering in a country cottage, the woman who owned the cottage, not knowing she had a royal guest, gave Alfred the task of watching over some cakes she was baking. Alfred was so engrossed in his planning that he neglected the cakes which got burnt. His plan involved raising an army in secret and then confronting the Danes which he did at the battle of Edington where the Danes suffered a defeat. In the peace treaty which followed, England was divided into two, Danelaw and Wessex, the dividing line following the Roman road now known as Watling Street (A5) which runs from London to Holyhead. Alfred took control of London which led to all Saxons, not under Danish controlled lands, accepting Alfred as King of England. In time, the hostility between the Danes and the Saxons subsided and a united kingdom of England emerged.

Alfred encouraged culture, made wise laws and took defensive measures which deterred any fresh hostilities from the Danes. He founded the English navy, building ships which were twice as large as those of the Vikings who would otherwise, have continued to menace English coastal settlements.

Hereward the Wake

Hereward, the Wake

Hereward was the son of a Saxon chieftain but was exiled by his father before the Norman conquest had taken place. It seems likely that he had been a troublesome young man. He returned to England three years after the William the Conqueror's invasion and found the country to be controlled by the Normans. Using the easily defended marshland of the Fen country in Cambridgeshire and Norfolk, he carried out a successful campaign of guerrilla warfare against the Normans. His best known assault on property controlled by the Normans is the storming and sacking of Peterborough Abbey.

St Thomas a Becket, Archbishop of Canterbury

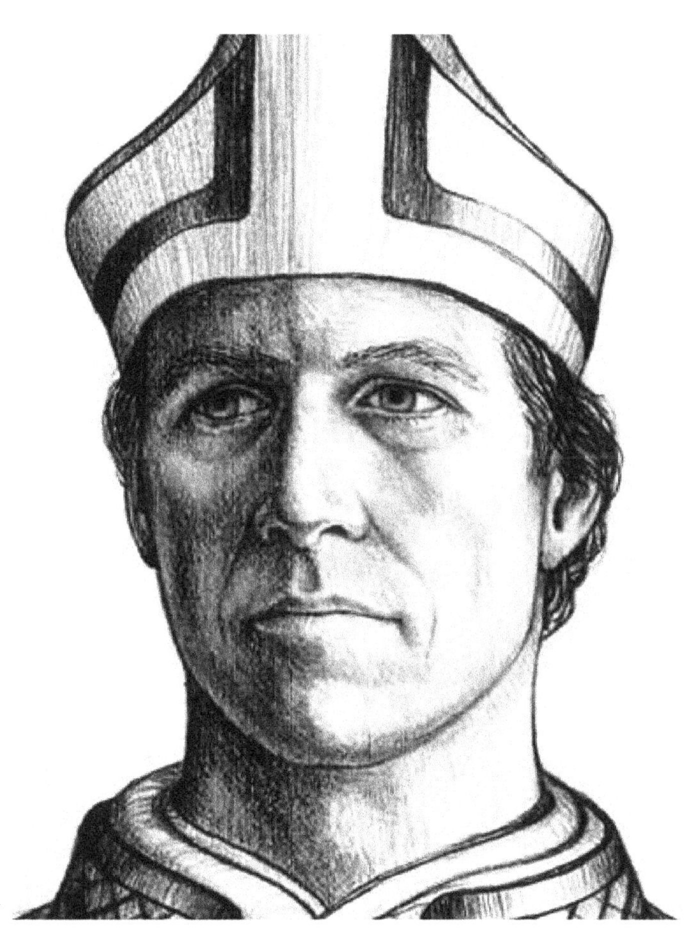

St. Thomas a Becket, Archbishop of Canterbury

All of us live under some form of authority, in most cases, more than one authority. Problems arise when there is an inconsistency or clash between the requirements of different forms of authority. In such cases, if we are wise, we will be guided by the higher authority's requirement. For example, a young person living with parents of a criminal mentality might be urged by such parents to commit a criminal act. However, this would be forbidden by the law which is an authority, higher than the young person's parents. They would therefore be advised to abide by the higher authority. What authority is there which is higher than a person's parents or nation. The highest authority is of course God, but where does this leave a person who doesn't believe in God. When we were created, God bestowed on us the gift of a conscience and most people should regard this as the highest form of authority under which they are living. Thus, the excuse by German war criminals who committed atrocities in the Nazi death camps, that they were only obeying orders, was not an acceptable defence in the Nurnberg trials of war criminals. Thomas a Becket was a historic personage who found himself caught between two conflicting authorities.

Thomas had a humble start to life. His parents, Gilbert and Matilda Becket, were Londoners. Gilbert was a small landowner. Thomas's career is evidence that even in the middle ages, young people of humble background but with ability could achieve advancement. Becket learnt much from a wealthy friend of his father, Richer de L'Aigle and he spent some time on Richer's estate in the South of England. His formal education was carried out at Merton Abbey and later, at a London grammar school, probably St. Paul's.

Thomas's first job was as a clerk at the business of one of his father's friends where his ability came to the attention of Theobald of Bec, the then Archbishop of Canterbury. Theobald took him into service and Thomas's career started to take off. Theobald entrusted him with important missions to Rome, and later appointed Thomas as Archdeacon of Canterbury. He became prebendary of both St. Paul's and Lincoln Cathedrals and held the office of Provost of Beverley. Theobald was so impressed with Thomas's efficiency that he recommended Thomas to King Henry II to fill the post of Lord Chancellor. The nearest modern equivalent would be Prime Minister. The Lord Chancellor probably acted in much the same capacity as a Grand Vizier in the court of an oriental potentate.

Becket became very much the trusted friend of the king. Henry's son, another Henry, was sent to live with Thomas who was being very effective in dealing with the barons and landowners and collecting from them the taxes due.

There was a certain amount of friction between King Henry and the church whose power Henry was seeking to limit. Thus, on the death of Theobald, Thomas was appointed Archbishop of Canterbury. He wasn't even a priest when his appointment was announced but became ordained the day before being consecrated as Archbishop. With his friend in charge of the church, the king expected a smooth passage in his attempt to limit the power and influence of the church. However, things did not turn out as the king had hoped. As Archbishop, Thomas regarded himself as no longer under the secular authority of the king but under the divine authority of God. He interpreted this to mean that he was required to obstruct any attempt to limit the church's power and authority. Thus King Henry and Thomas fell out.

Thomas resigned from the post of Lord Chancellor of England as he realised a conflict of loyalty would exist between this office and his new post. He opposed the king's attempts to make the clergy answerable to secular courts and attempted to recover and extend the rights pertaining to the Archbishopric of Canterbury.

The king attempted to persuade senior clergy to oppose Thomas in his stance or face dire political consequences. Henry introduced the Constitutions of Clarendon before an assembly of senior clergy. Its provisions sought to uphold the rights of the king in the way the church was governed, to reduce clerical independence and to weaken the ties of the church with Rome. He managed to persuade all the clergy to sign their assent to this document and all agreed to do so with the exception of Thomas. He was prepared to agree to the provisions but not to sign the document of assent.

Becket was summoned to Nottingham castle to face charges of contempt of royal authority and misuse of his position as Lord Chancellor. On being convicted of these charges, Becket stormed out of the castle and sought sanctuary in Europe where he received protection from King Louis VII of France. Thomas spent two years at the Cistercian Abbey of Pontigny but King Henry issued threats against the Cistercian order which had many houses in England. This forced Thomas to move from Pontigny to a different religious house in Sens. Thomas fought back by threatening to excommunicate King Henry.

While Pope Alexander III sympathised with Becket, he sought to resolve the problem which existed between Thomas and Henry with a diplomatic approach and sent Papal legates to England to act as arbitrators. Henry accepted a compromise which allowed Becket to return to England.

Soon after his return, the Archbishop of York, assisted by the bishops of London and Salisbury, crowned King Henry's son and heir apparent, the young Henry, as King. It wasn't unusual in those troubled times for the heir to the throne to be crowned before the death of his father to ensure a smooth transition of power, should anything untoward happen to the reigning king. However, the privilege of crowning a king of England was the prerogative of the Archbishop of Canterbury and Becket excommunicated the three bishops. When king Henry heard this, he had fit of pique. Different accounts exist of the actual words the king used but it is generally accepted that in effect, he declared,
> ***"Who will rid me of this turbulent priest?"***

Four of Henry's knights interpreted his invective as a royal command and made their way to Canterbury where they hid their weapons and armour under their cloaks beneath a tree outside the cathedral and made their way in to confront Becket. They demanded that he should go to Winchester to give an account of his actions but Becket refused. The knights went outside to retrieve their weapons but were observed by a monk who sought to bolt the cathedral doors to exclude the knights and in order to ensure the safety of those in the cathedral. Becket told the monk to unlock the doors, stating that it was not right for a house of prayer to be used as a fortress. He then proceeded down the aisle for the service of vespers. The knights, now fully armoured, rushed into the cathedral to attack Becket, wounding a monk who attempted to disrupt them on their way and crying,
> ***"Where is Thomas Becket, traitor to the King and Country?"***

On hearing the knights, Becket declared,
> ***"I'm no traitor and I'm ready to die."***

In the attack which followed, Becket tried vainly to defend himself but was overcome by the knights' superior force. The wounded monk stated that as he died, Becket declared,

"For the name of Jesus and the protection of the church, I am ready to embrace death."

On preparing Becket's body for burial, the monks discovered that under his clerical robes, Becket wore a hair shirt, a sign of penitence.

Over the next couple of years, the story of Becket's death spread far beyond England and he became venerated as a martyr. Two years after his death, Becket was canonised by Pope Alexander III. King Henry made public penance for the unwanted outcome of his invective against Becket in a pilgrimage to the site of his martyrdom in Canterbury Cathedral. This became the focus of pilgrimage for many years to come. As an act of reparation for the murder, Becket's sister, Mary, was appointed Abbess of Barking Abbey. King William the Lion of Scotland, who had known St. Thomas as a young man when at Henry II's court, ordered the building of Arbroath Abbey which he then dedicated to St. Thomas of Canterbury.

The four knights, realising that their action had far exceeded anything King Henry had intended, fled to Scotland and were excommunicated by the Pope. They journeyed to Rome to receive forgiveness from the Pope. This was granted on provision that they spent fourteen years on a crusade.

An order of chivalry and many churches, both in England and on the continent, have been dedicated to St. Thomas of Canterbury.

Robin Hood

Robin Hood

Robin Hood is a person who is the subject of legend and folklore without any firm historic evidence of his existence. Robin is depicted as a skilled archer and swordsman. He is said to be person of noble birth who returned from the crusades to find the country being badly ruled by the king's brother, John, in the absence of the king who was fighting in the crusades. Robin discovered that his property had been confiscated in his absence by the Sheriff of Nottingham and his life became a feud between himself and the Sheriff. He saw the injustices of the feudal system where the peasant classes were cruelly exploited by their feudal overlords and he set about robbing the rich to give to the poor. This noble work raised him to hero status but, as a robber, he was outlawed. He took refuge in Sherwood Forest and gathered around him a group of like-minded individuals (his merry men) which included men known as Little John, Friar Tuck and Will Scarlet. Wealthy travellers through Sherwood Forest, including the Bishop of Hereford, were robbed by Robin's men and their goods redistributed among the poor.

On the return of King Richard from the Crusades, he assessed what had gone wrong with the country under his brother John's rule and Robin Hood received a royal pardon.

King Richard,
the Lion Heart

King Richard the Lion Heart (Coeur de Lion)

Richard I is a controversial character. He was undoubtedly a brave warrior and an able military leader. He is lauded for espousing the crusades which had the noble objective of wresting Jerusalem from the control of Saladin, the leader of the occupying Islamic forces. His heroism was celebrated by the Victorians who erected an impressive equestrian statue to this king outside the Houses of Parliament. One of his main successes in the crusades was the capture of Cyprus which was an essential base for resourcing and maintaining the Christian armies fighting in the Holy Land. While in Cyprus, he married Berengaria, the eldest daughter of King Sancho VI of Navarre but she didn't came to England until after Richard's death.

From the time of the Norman conquest, the kings of England had used the arms of Normandy, which constituted two lions passant and regardant, as their heraldic badge of chivalry. Richard added a third lion to represent himself and this has since been a national symbol of England included in the royal standard and worn by English sports teams.

However, there is much about Richard which is discreditable. He rebelled against his father, Henry II. He established bad relationships with his erstwhile allies in the battles fought during the crusade, notably Philip, King of France and Leopold of Austria. On his return from the crusades, Richard took a route through territory controlled by Leopold and he was captured and imprisoned, For some time, his whereabouts were unknown in England but, when his location was discovered, the English raised a huge ransom to secure his release. During his reign, Richard spent less than six months in England. In spite of his absence, Richard was seen as a heroic figure by his subjects.

When he was not on crusade or in captivity, he lived in France in the territories he controlled as hereditary Duke of Normandy and Count of Anjou. When besieging the small castle of Châlus-Chabrol, he was hit in the shoulder by a crossbow bolt. The wound turned gangrenous and led to Richard's death. The castle was taken before Richard died and the archer who had fired the fatal shot was brought before Richard. The archer turned out to be no more than a boy and he expected to be executed but Richard said,
"Live on, and by my bounty behold the light of day".

The boy was freed and given a monetary reward by Richard.

Richard has been described as a bad son, a bad husband, and a bad king, but a gallant and splendid soldier. Although included in this anthology, he scarcely deserves to be recognised as a great English hero.

Earl Simon de Montfort

Simon de Montfort

Napoleon Bonaparte described Simon de Montfort as one of the greatest Englishmen. This accolade is surprising on two accounts. Simon worked against the tyranny exercised by autocratic rulers whereas Napoleon aspired to achieve such authority for himself. Secondly, Simon de Montfort was technically French and of the same nationality as Napoleon himself. However, when Simon de Montfort came to this country and made his mark, he earned the reputation of being more English than the English.

His father, Simon de Montfort, after whom Simon had been named, was a prominent French nobleman. Simon de Montfort senior led crusades, particularly the Albigensian Crusade and the Barons' Crusade, and was accompanied by his sons on these ventures. The Albigensian crusade was directed against a group known as the Cathars. Although the Cathars would describe themselves as Christian, they held fundamental beliefs which were heretical. They were not monotheistic and believed in two Gods, an evil god of the Old Testament and a good God of the New Testament. The evil god transmuted into the devil in New Testament times. The Pope declared the Cathars to be heretics and sponsored a crusade against them. During this crusade, Simon de Montfort senior, who can at best be described as a religious bigot, massacred the Cathars and provided an example of an action which is described as genocide.

Simon de Montfort senior was killed at the siege of Toulouse and his eldest son, Guy, was killed at the siege of Castelinaudary. The younger sons, Simon and Amaury faced a dilemma on how to divide their parent's inheritance between them as they had claim to important property in both England and France. Their mother had been Countess of Leicester. They decided that Amaury should succeed to the property in France while Simon should take control of the English part of the heritage. Simon made his way to England to oversee the de Montfort lands held here. He expected to be accepted as Earl of Leicester by virtue of his mother's title but this recognition did not come until some time later. However, he was warmly accepted by Henry III who favoured French speaking nobility at his court. Simon and Henry became firm friends. Simon married the king's sister, Eleanor, and became godfather to Henry's son, Prince Edward.

On finally acquiring the title, Earl of Leicester, Simon expelled the Jews from Leicester. This proved popular among the citizens of Leicester as the Jews were disliked for the practice of usury. This was something which Christians were forbidden to carry out at that time in history. The Jews lent money and became rich by charging high rates of interest. Simon was fiercely antisemitic and encouraged the massacre of Jews in many English cities including Winchester, Lincoln, Derby, Cambridge and Northampton.

Simon and Henry III fell out when the king discovered that Simon had borrowed a large sum of money from his wife's uncle, Thomas II of Savoy, and named Henry III as security for this loan without first having sought the king's permission. Facing the threat of being imprisoned in the Tower, Simon and Eleanor fled to France.

Simon eventually made peace with the king and returned to England but was disturbed by the way the king dealt with his barons, refusing to abide by the Provisions of Oxford, a document to which the king had earlier assented which allowed for a form of parliament to have some authority in the way national affairs were run. In despair, Simon returned to France but returned two years later at the invitation of the barons to lead a rebellion against the king to ensure that the 'Provisions of Oxford' were adhered to. Henry gave in and allowed Simon to take control of the Council. Prince Edward however was able to secure support from a significant number of barons who were opposed to Simon. They disrupted the parliament sitting in Oxford and hostilities ensued. The royalists were able to trap Simon and the reformist army in London. However, Simon led the reformist army out of London and gave battle to the king at Lewes, winning a spectacular victory and capturing King Henry and Prince Edward.

Simon used his victory to set up a parliament based on the 'Provisions of Oxford' but in a modified form. It was to consist of two chambers, one reserved for the nobility and the other, an elected chamber of representatives from towns which had become boroughs by virtual of a royal charter. This was the type of parliament from which our present Houses of Commons and Lords have evolved and this achievement is the one for which Simon deserves acclaim as a hero of the country. He had established an institution which has not only benefitted this nation to the present day but has been used as a model by which democratic nations have set up their own structures of government.

Henry III retained the title and authority of king but the control of national affairs was effectively carried out by Simon de Montfort. Prince Edward was imprisoned in Hereford but managed to escape. He rallied the support of the Welsh marcher lords and other barons who had become disaffected with Simon de Montfort, perhaps resentful of his rise to power. In particular, these included Gilbert de Clare, Earl of Gloucester, the most powerful baron in the land. He was Simon's ally at the Battle of Lewes, but had fallen out with Simon and his sons. He joined Prince Edward who attacked the forces of Simon de Montfort's son, another Simon, at Kenilworth and captured more of de Montfort's allies.

Simon de Montfort crossed the Severn, his army boosted by Welsh infantry provided by his ally, the Prince of Wales, Llywelyn ap Gryffudd, expecting to rendezvous with forces from Kenilworth under his son. When he saw an army approaching Evesham, flying de Montfort banners captured at Kenilworth, Simon initially thought that this army would increase the strength of his own force. However, he discovered that this army, which was larger than his own, was being led by Prince Edward. The Battle of Evesham ensued. De Montfort led his army in an uphill charge against Edward's army but his numerically inferior force could not prevail and de Montfort and his sons were killed in this battle.

De Montfort is specially remembered and revered for establishing the beginnings of the Parliamentary democracy enjoyed in Britain and in many other modern countries. A university and a concert hall in Leicester are named after him as are a bridge on a major highway and a school near Evesham.

Sir William Wallace

William Wallace

In identifying heroes and achievers who have made a spectacular impact on national life, I have been conscious that there might appear to be too much emphasis on English achievements. It is important that while we are still one nation, the credit due to the lands which make up Great Britain with a Celtic heritage must be recognised. Indeed, many of those included in this anthology were not born in England. Simon de Montfort was born in France, Henry V in Wales, the Duke of Wellington in Ireland and Florence Nightingale in Italy. David Livingstone was a Scot, as were the next two heroic characters I have included in this book, and the following one was Welsh.

From an obscure beginning, William Wallace came into prominence as a champion of his fellow Scots who had been subjugated to English rule under King Edward I, nicknamed, 'the Hammer of the Scots'. The Scots were being taxed by Edward I, forced to serve in his armies and imprisoned for infringing laws which he had imposed on the nation. One of William Wallace's first acts of defiance was to kill William Heselring, the English Sheriff of Lanarkshire.

William was joined by another Scottish hero, Andrew Murray. Scots clamoured to join their movement and the force they assembled defeated the English at Scone, Ancrum and Dundee. They cleared the English from Inverness and North-East Scotland, the Western Isles and much of the South of Scotland.

Seeing most of Scotland liberated from English rule, Edward sent an army to face Wallace and Murray at Stirling Bridge but this army was comprehensively defeated with the loss of over 5,000 men. Sadly, a few months after this, Andrew

Murray died from the wounds he had received at this battle. The Scots army moved south, harassing the retreating English army and entering the northern counties of England, intent on plunder. They laid waste to large swathes of countryside before Wallace turned north and his army returned to Scotland.

Wallace was knighted, awarded the title, 'Guardian of Scotland' and made commander of the Scottish army.

Smarting from the defeat at Stirling Bridge, Edward I marched north with a much stronger army. Wallace underestimated the strength of this army and was himself soundly defeated at the Battle of Falkirk.

Wallace escaped from the battlefield and went abroad to raise support for the Scottish cause. When he returned to Scotland, he found that King Robert the Bruce had agreed a truce with Edward I. Wallace thus found himself a fugitive with a price on his head. He was betrayed at Robroyston near Glasgow where he had taken refuge and was handed over to the English to be transported to London to be tried.

This may seem puzzling as so many leading Scots who had been defeated in battle against the English were just summarily executed. Why was Wallace treated differently? Those who had been executed after battles with the English would at sometime have signed an oath of loyalty to Edward. Reneging on this oath was a treasonable offence and merited the death sentence. On no occasion had William Wallace sworn allegiance to Edward I and in those days, fighting to preserve your rights and property was a perfectly acceptable thing to do. Even today, declaring war is not in itself regarded as a crime. However, the English were determined to exact revenge on Wallace.

Although he couldn't be accused of treason by breaking an oath of allegiance, he was accused of committing atrocities against civilians in time of war, sparing none on the basis of their age, sex, or status as a monk or a nun. This has aroused considerable interest among the legal profession as the first example of a prosecution being based on what would now be called, war crimes against international humanitarian law.

Whether or not this was true, the English were determined to get a conviction and Wallace was sentenced to death. The sentence was carried out at Smithfield by the brutal process of his being hung, drawn and quartered.

A plaque was unveiled as recently as 1956 on the wall of St. Bartholomew's Hospital in Smithfield near the site of Wallace's execution which states in Latin words which translate to :-

I tell you the truth. Freedom is what is best.
Son, never live your life like a slave!

King Robert the Bruce

King Robert I of Scotland   (Robert the Bruce)

The early part of Robert the Bruce's military career is complicated as it involves a three sided conflict between two Scottish families, the Comyns and the Bruces, and the English king, Edward I. The Scottish families each considered they had a claim to the throne of Scotland. King Edward I considered himself to be the overlord in Scottish affairs who therefore had a right to arbitrate over matters like deciding between claimants to the Scottish crown. The Comyns' claim lay through an elder niece of the Scottish king, William the Lion, while the Bruce's claim was through a younger niece. However, the Bruces were one generation closer to William the Lion than the Comyns.

Edward I decided in favour of the Comyn claimant, John Balliol. This was followed by a series of battles between all three forces involved in the matter as the belligerents reneged on oaths of allegiance and broke agreements. They frequently changed sides in a way which is difficult to follow on the basis of logic. Earlier, Robert the Bruce had joined William Wallace's revolt against the English. In the ensuing hostilities, William Wallace was captured and taken to London where he was brutally executed in the barbarous manner adopted in mediaeval times.

At a meeting arranged between the two Scottish claimants to the throne at Greyfriars Abbey in Dumfries, Robert the Bruce accused John Comyn of behaving treacherously and he killed him in the ensuing argument. This was regarded by the church as an act of murder and Robert was excommunicated by the Pope.

Although technically excommunicated by the church, Robert the Bruce was crowned king of Scotland by the Bishop of Glasgow who granted Robert absolution. It would appear that, by tradition, the Earls of Fife had the right to crown the kings of Scotland. Thus, the day after the coronation, Isabella, Countess of Buchan, arrived and claimed this right, so a second coronation was held in which Isabella acted on behalf of her brother, the current Earl of Fife. He couldn't perform the ceremony because, not only was he under age, but he was in English hands.

Robert both won and lost battles but started to become discouraged when he couldn't see himself gaining any significant advantage. Folklore tells the story of how Robert, while hiding in a cave, contemplated a spider attempting to build a web but kept failing in his attempts to construct a stable web. However, after many attempts, the spider did succeed in its objective, inspiring Robert with the attitude,

'if at first you don't succeed try, try and try again until you do.'

Over the next eight years, Robert destroyed the members and supporters of the Comyn family whom he saw as a threat to his kingship. He continued to harry the English but avoided confrontation in a major battle. He thus earned himself the reputation of being one of the greatest tacticians of all time in the matter of guerrilla warfare.

A point was reached in the conflict when possession of Stirling Castle, which was held by the English, was seen as crucial to the Scots achieving victory. The castle was besieged by the Scots. Edward I had died and was succeeded by his son, Edward II, who marched with a huge army to relieve the castle. In the skirmishing between the English and the Scots before the battle proper, Robert encountered the English knight, Sir Henry de Bohun, whom he defeated and killed in personal combat. This was a great morale booster for the Scots.

When Edward reached Bannockburn, located near the castle, he was surprised to be confronted by the Scots who were already battle ready before Edward himself had a chance to organise his own army into a fit state to give battle. Consequently, he suffered a crushing defeat. Edward II had to flee the battle and only narrowly escaped being killed in the fighting. However, he refused to renounce his claim to being overlord of Scotland. With the English army defeated, Stirling Castle was soon captured.

Robert the Bruce was now the undisputed ruler of Scotland. The victory was followed by the Scots raiding the northern parts of Lancashire and Yorkshire. Robert also turned his attention on Ireland, seeking to establish a Gaelic speaking alliance with the Irish against the English. This ambition was helped by the fact that Robert was descended from Irish royalty on his mother's side and was linked by marriage to the de Burgh family who were Earls of Ulster. Initially, the combined Scottish-Irish Gaelic force seemed unstoppable, inflicting a series of defeats on the English. However, as they moved south from Ulster, the force alienated the Irish population by pillaging to provide food for their troops. They were finally defeated by the English at the Battle of Fauchard and were driven from Ireland. The Irish Annals of the time describe this as one of the greatest things done by the English for the Irish as it put an end to the starvation that was being caused by the Scots' pillaging.

Towards the end of his reign, Robert achieved some diplomatic successes, the best known of which was the Declaration of Arbroath. Edward III signed the Treaty of Edinburgh-Northampton which recognised Scotland as an independent nation and Robert the Bruce as its king. This led to the Pope lifting the excommunication of Robert.

Towards the end of his life, Robert suffered from a skin disease which was referred to at the time as leprosy. This disease is not related to tropical leprosy and would be easily treatable today. However, it is believed that this disease undermined Robert's health and ultimately led to his death. Realising that his days were numbered, Robert made a pilgrimage to the shrine of St. Ninian. He remained for five days at this shrine before sailing back home. He convened a final council of prelates and trusted nobles who met by his bedside. During the meeting, he gave a large amount of silver to the representatives of religious houses present. He repented of the fact that he had been unable to go on a crusade and requested that his heart should be taken to the church of the Holy Sepulchre in Jerusalem before being returned to Scotland to be buried in Melrose Abbey. His body was interred in Dunfermline Abbey. Robert provided funds to enable his final wish to be fulfilled, that perpetual prayers and masses should be said for him at some of the prominent Scottish churches.

Owen Glendower

Owen Glendower

Owen was born into a prosperous Anglo-Welsh family. He was descended from the princes of all three Welsh provinces and his father was the hereditary Prince of Powis, one of these provinces. He was also a descendant of King Edward I.

Owen was fostered at the home of a lawyer who became a justice of the King's Bench. He was sent to London to study law at the Inns of Court and remained there for seven years. On his return to Wales, he married his foster parent's daughter, Margaret, and established himself as squire of the lands he had inherited from his ancestors.

Owen served in the armies of King Richard II and under John of Gaunt and his son, Henry Bolingbroke, who was later to become King Henry IV. His military service involved fighting on the Scottish border and helping to defeat a Franco-Spanish-Flemish invasion fleet off the Kent coast.

Owen's rebellion against the English would probably never have taken place but for the greed and treachery of Baron Grey de Ruthyn, an English landlord who owned property adjoining that of Owens's. Baron Grey seized some of Owen's land and Owen's letter to the English Parliament, appealing for redress, was ignored. Further, Baron Grey concealed from Owen, a royal command to levy troops for service on the Scottish border. Owen's failure to respond to this command, of which he had no knowledge, enabled Baron Grey to have Owen declared a traitor. Owen's situation was further complicated by the political upheaval taking place in England. Henry Bolingbroke deposed King Richard II, declaring himself to be King Henry IV. Owen and the Welsh were supporters of King Richard and a serious revolt broke out in the border city of Chester when one of King Richard's officials was publicly executed. Owen declared himself to be the Prince of Wales in the presence of three-hundred men who were largely family and inhabitants of North-East Wales. These became his first followers, and thus started his fifteen year revolt against the English.

As might be expected, the rebellion started with an assault on the property of his enemy, Lord Grey, by burning Ruthyn. Owen's men then took over Rhuddlan, Denbigh, Flint, Oswestry and Welshpool which were seen as English towns. Following this, the Welsh in the north and centre of Wales went over to Owen. Owen continued his battle against the English, largely by using guerrilla warfare tactics, rather than by confronting the enemy in open battle.

Owen's supporters, the Tudors, took over Conwy Castle but had to give this up to Henry Percy (Hotspur), son of the Duke of Northumberland, who had been sent by the King to quell the revolt. Hotspur then went on to defeat Glendower's men at the battle of Cader Idris. Owen secured two major victories against King Henry and effectively occupied all of North Wales. Owen's attempt to increase his force by recruiting troops from Scotland and Ireland failed, as King Henry was able to intercept and execute these reinforcements.

Henry sent a force under Sir Edmund Mortimer to fight Glendower but Mortimer was defeated at the Battle of Bryn Glas. Owen offered to release Mortimer for a large ransom but the King was not prepared to pay this, possibly because Mortimer's nephew had a better claim to the throne than himself. Mortimer was able to negotiate his release by declaring support for Owen and marrying one of his daughters.

When England's enemies had news of Owen Glendower's success, they began to give him support. He received naval support from Scotland and the French provided him with troops and supplies. Glendower was now joined by troops from Glamorgan and the Rhonda Valley. With his army thus augmented, Glendower went on to defeat an English army, which had been sent to invade Wales, at the Battle of Stalling Down in Glamorgan.

Glendower's success led to Welsh students being admitted to the universities of Oxford and Cambridge. Welsh labourers working on English farms and even archers from the English army, returned to Wales to support his rebellion. Glendower continued by taking Aberystwyth and Harlech Castles and ravaging the south, burning Cardiff Castle. He was able to repel a number of military expeditions into Wales and his self-proclaimed title of Prince of Wales was confirmed by a proclamation of his supporters. Glendower set up a parliament where he set out his plans for the future of Wales. This involved founding two new universities, one it the north and the other in the south. He also reintroduced traditional Welsh laws and establishing a national Welsh church.

Glendower negotiated an arrangement with Edmund Mortimer and Henry Percy which would take the fight into England itself, Glendower extending the border of Wales to beyond the Welsh marches, Percy taking over the north of England and Mortimer, the South.

The French defeated an English fleet in the channel and raided Guernsey, Jersey and Plymouth. The French went on to cause devastation, all along the channel coast, landing on the Isle of Wight and setting fire to Dartmouth. The French landed at Milford Haven and joined the Welsh forces. This army failed to capture Pembroke Castle but the combined Franco-Welsh force invaded England, crossing Herefordshire into Worcestershire. Ten miles from Worcester, they met an English army and the two forces took up battle positions about a mile apart. This possibly marks the zenith of Owen's rebellion.

After eight days during which no hostile action had been taken by either side, the French and Welsh retreated for no obvious reason. The French returned to France and their king, Charles VI, preoccupied with fighting the English in the Hundred Years War, discontinued his support for Owen Glendower.

Although Owen had achieved much success in the early days of the rebellion, he couldn't match the resources that the English were able to bring to the conflict. The much larger and better equipped English forces under Prince Henry gradually began to retake Wales, taking advantage of the fact that many Welsh castles had remained under English control. Prince Henry adopted a different strategy from his father, Henry IV. He set up an economic blockade which reduced Glendower's ability to trade and cut off his access to weapons. Prince Henry's forces were able to move to the west, capturing Aberystwyth and laying siege to Harlech Castle. When this castle fell, Owen's wife, Margaret, and two of his daughters were captured and sent to London where they were imprisoned in the Tower where they died in captivity. Owen was able to escape by disguising himself as an old man and slipping through English lines at night.

Glendower and a small band of followers were able to set up their headquarters in a remote part of Wales but were unable to launch any major offensive against the English. They continued by using guerrilla tactics and were able to carry out raids, not just within Wales, but across the border into England. He successfully ambushed an English force at Brecon and captured and ransomed a leading Welsh supporter of the English. This was the last time Glendower was seen alive by the English.

When Henry IV died and Prince Henry succeeded to the throne as Henry V, he adopted a more conciliatory approach to the Welsh. He offered royal pardons to all who had been involved in the rebellion, except to Owen himself for whose capture, a large reward was offered. Owen was never betrayed but the rebellion petered out and ended after Owen Glendower died. Owen had spent the last years of his life, disguised as a Franciscan friar and living with one of his daughters.

John Wycliffe

John Wycliffe

John Wycliffe was born near Richmond in Yorkshire. He was a very intellectual and highly intelligent man who really understood the fundamentals of the Christian faith and eloquently exposed the abuses which had crept into the mediaeval church of his day. While he was particularly critical of the Pope and the role he played in church life, there was only one church in his day and he never considered breaking away from the Roman Catholic Church. However, his writings influenced the reformers of the next generation, particularly John Hus, the Czech reformer. Thus, John Wycliffe has become known as 'the Morning Star of the Reformation'.

John received his school education near his home before moving on to Merton College, Oxford University. The two things which most influenced John during his early years at Oxford were a book written by Thomas Bradwardine, the then Archbishop of Canterbury, and the impact of the Black Death. The Archbishop's book,

'On the Cause of God against the Pelagians'

would have greatly influenced John's thoughts as it expounds St. Paul's doctrine of salvation by grace in contradistinction to the view of the Pelagians, that a place in heaven is earned by doing good works. The Black Death and its consequences left John with a pessimistic outlook on the future of humankind.

John was disturbed by the lack of education and general incompetence of the clergy holding office in English parishes and saw the Black Death, which had seen a disproportionate number of clergy lose their lives, as a grim recompense for their inadequacy. Sadly, the dead clergy were replaced by even less competent individuals who were able to buy the living of vacant benefices in English parishes. Buying a living was a good investment because it guaranteed a secure, lifelong, generous income and a position of prestige in society. The buying of livings was regarded by John as the sin of Simony. The sin of buying church preference is so named after Simon Magus, the sorcerer featuring in the New Testament who thought that he could purchase from St. Peter the ability to confer the power of the Holy Spirit on individuals which would give them miraculous powers. He was roundly rebuked by St. Peter.

Acts ch 8 v 20,21 *Peter answered, "May your money perish with you because you thought you could buy the gift of God with money. You have no part or share in this ministry because your heart is not right with God!"*

On graduation, John became Master of Balliol College and was awarded the living of the parish of Fillingham in Lincolnshire. Noting John's ability, Simon Islip, Archbishop of Canterbury, made John head of Canterbury Hall, an institution where young men trained for the priesthood. The following year, Simon Islip died and was succeeded by Simon Langham who had a monastic background. Langham replaced John with a monk and although John appealed to Rome against being sacked in this way, his appeal was unsuccessful. This event is typical of the antagonism which existed at that time between monks and secular clergy at Oxford.

John gave up his living at Fillingham to take over the parish of Ludgarshall which was not far from Oxford and this enabled him to maintain his connection with the University. In due course, John obtained his doctorate and was awarded the living of St. Mary's, Lutterworth, which was under the patronage of the crown. He retained this position for the rest of his life.

John was sent along with a bishop to Bruges to meet a papal representative. He was there to uphold national interests in the matter of disputes which had arisen between the king and Pope Gregory XI. On his return from Bruges, John thought profoundly about his role as a Christian minister who should be widely propagating the Christian gospel. He realised that his position as a professor at Oxford University didn't offer sufficient scope to pursue this objective. Apart from Simony which has already been mentioned, he could see that the church was far from being well run. John invariably resorted to the Bible for guidance in how affairs should be run. The way that Jesus conducted his mission was very different from what was happening in England. John thought about the instructions Jesus had given to those he sent out on missions, first the twelve apostles and then later, seventy-two other disciples.

Luke ch 10 v 3,4 *Go! I am sending you out like lambs among wolves. Do not take a bag or purse or sandals, and do not greet anyone on the road.*

What John saw in the English church did not match up to this model. Well paid priests were living in big houses, preaching poorly prepared sermons to congregations of scarcely literate peasants and having no interest in outreach.

John became very much involved in national politics when he issued a document
'On Civil Dominion'
in which he attacked the wealth of the church and called for the divestment of all church property. This provoked a reaction from the church hierarchy and the document was officially condemned by Pope Gregory XI. Wycliffe was summoned to appear before William Courtenay, Bishop of London. The meeting was acrimonious but little action could be taken against Wycliffe as he was supported by two very powerful nobles, John of Gaunt, Duke of Lancaster, and Henry Percy, the Earl Marshall. However, Wycliffe came under attack from clergy who felt threatened by his document.

Pope Gregory XI issued a Bull against Wycliffe, probably because Wycliffe had declared there was no legal requirement to pay taxes to Rome. Wycliffe was summoned to Lambeth palace to appear before a panel of bishops but again, Wycliffe had support in high places. The Queen Mother, Joan of Kent, forbade the bishops to pass sentence against Wycliffe. Wycliffe wrote a letter defending what were described as his less obnoxious doctrines and the bishops, who were divided on the issue, came to a compromise position which forbade Wycliffe to speak further on this matter.

Wycliffe then wrote another document in Latin and in English, worded in such a way that it would be understood by the laity, demanding that it should be a legal right for any excommunicated person to be able to appeal to the king against the excommunication. This was an important issue because in those days, the general understanding of the power of the Pope, who regarded himself as God's Vicar (substitute) on earth, was that excommunication by the Pope would disqualify a person from entering heaven. The issue went no further as Pope Gregory XI died before the matter got to Rome.

Wycliffe next attacked the doctrine of transubstantiation which claimed that as the bread and wine are consecrated during the Eucharist, they change form to become the actual body and blood of Jesus. This is manifestly untrue. Indeed, when Jesus inaugurated the Lord's supper and declared as he broke the bread and poured the wine, 'this is my body, broken for you' and 'this is my blood which is shed for you,' his body at that time had not been broken nor had his blood been shed. However, transubstantiation was still an integral part of the catholic church's teaching and so firmly held by the people of his day that Wycliffe lost a lot of support including that of important members of the aristocracy. Although many in important posts, like the Chancellor of Oxford University, declared Wycliffe's views heretical, Wycliffe asserted that no-one could change his views on the subject and he wrote a treatise on the matter in the plain English of the day to be understood by the common people. He submitted this, not to the Pope, but to the King.

The catholic church still teaches the doctrine of transubstantiation and within catholic churches, a presence light is mounted near the consecrated bread and wine, stored in an aumbry, to indicate that a real part of Jesus actually resides there. This invites acts of reverence like bowing or genuflecting before the aumbry but such acts are regarded by the reformed church as akin to idolatry. The protestant church follows Wycliffe's teaching and rejects transubstantiation but acknowledges that the consecrated bread and wine are special. The protestant view uses the term, consubstantiation, that is, the elements of communion remain just bread and wine but have the power to sanctify those who receive them during a service of Holy Communion if they partake, fully understanding what these elements represent.

Wycliffe's teaching was a contributory factor to the outbreak of the Peasant's Revolt in Kent. Wycliffe did not approve of the revolt but it led to the peasants executing one of Wycliffe's opponents, Simon Sudbury, Archbishop of Canterbury. Even though apparently safe in the impregnable stronghold of the Tower of London, the peasants were able to enter the Tower, unopposed and arrest the Archbishop sheltering there.

Wycliffe had long been critical of monasticism, which had become corrupt, and of the existing system of church government, which allowed the appointment of so many incompetent clergy to a large number of parishes. Wycliffe looked to scriptural precedents for guidance in how church affairs should be run. Jesus sending out seventy of his disciples on a mission was to Wycliffe's mind, far closer to the way the church should be operating. The church shouldn't allow parishes to be run by incompetent clergy, receiving a generous income and living in comfortable vicarages. Therefore, Wycliffe recruited young, able men who were prepared to face poverty as part of their vocation. Wycliffe trained them to preach the gospel and followed the Biblical precedent by sending them out in pairs. The Pope did not approve of this development and referred to these itinerant preachers as 'Lollards', which he intended as a term of disparagement. However, the Lollards took this epithet as a title of honour and their ministry had an impact right across England.

Wycliffe realised that clergy could get away with preaching false doctrine unchallenged, as too many people were illiterate and even those who could read were not proficient in Latin. Wycliffe therefore became one of the first men to translate the Bible into the everyday English which was commonly spoken at the time. He translated it from the available version in Latin known as the Vulgate. Thus, ordinary people would soon be in a position to challenge doctrines preached from their churches which were contrary to the teaching contained in the Bible.

Wycliffe spent his final years at his parish in Lutterworth. He continued his writings, many of which were critical of the unworthiness of so many of the clergy, the corrupt monks and the papacy. The Pope in office during Wycliffe's final years, Urban VI, had not turned out to be the reforming Pope that Wycliffe had hoped for. Wycliffe continued to assert the supremacy of Scripture as the authoritive rock on which the teaching of the church should be based. While celebrating Holy Communion at his church on Holy Innocents Day, 28th December, Wycliffe suffered a stroke and died a few days later.

The Council of Constance declared Wycliffe to be a heretic and commanded that his writings should be burned. The Council stated that his body should be exhumed from consecrated ground as, being a heretic, he had put himself outside the church. A few years later, the next Pope, Martin V, commanded that this order should be carried out. Wycliffe's body was dug up, burned and the ashes scattered in the River Swift which flows through Lutterworth.

Today, Wycliffe is revered by the Anglican church. An important institution named after Wycliffe is Wycliffe Hall, Oxford University. This is now a foremost theological College in the Church of England.

.

King Henry V

King Henry V

Henry V had a relatively short reign but his outstanding successes against the French during the 100 Years War have led to his being regarded as one of Britain's greatest military leaders. His reputation has been enhanced by Shakespeare in his play where Henry, as the eponymous hero, is portrayed in glowing terms. No doubt, this would have pleased the Tudors who had espoused the Lancastrian cause in the Wars of the Roses. As Prince of Wales, Henry had earned his spurs as he fought against Owen Glendower who led the Welsh in a revolt against the English, and against the powerful Percy family fighting from their duchy of Northumberland. Not all of Henry's time was spent in warfare. He studied at Queen's College, Oxford University, and took a special interest in literature and music. He was the first king to have had his education carried out in English and went on to promote the use of the English language in government.

Some in England doubted the legitimacy of Henry V's father, Henry Bolingbroke, who had taken the throne by deposing his cousin, Richard II. However, Henry V, was Prince of Wales and eldest son of King Henry IV, and his claim to the throne was not disputed.

Henry's great grandfather, Edward III considered that he had a legitimate claim to the French throne through his mother but this claim had been rejected and was a cause of what we now describe as the 100 years war. The war had been dormant during the reigns of the two kings who preceded Henry V but Henry re-entered the war in pursuit of this claim. He landed with his army in France and captured Harfleur. He then marched with his army towards Calais but this manoeuvre proved demanding and left his army exhausted and malnourished. He was met by a vastly superior French army at Agincourt to fight a battle which initially might have been regarded as no contest. However, the heavily armoured French knights became bogged down in ground which had become soft and muddy as a result of heavy rain the previous night and were picked of by the English archers who were very much the heroes in this battle. Skill with the bow and arrow had been recognised in England as of vital importance for its soldiers in time of war and many towns in England have streets called 'the Butts' which have developed on sites which had been archery training grounds in the middle ages.

Following his success at Agincourt, Henry was able to take over most of northern France. There was little opposition from the French whose nobility had been discouraged by the defeat at Agincourt and started to quarrel among themselves. The hostility was ended by a treaty signed between Henry V and Charles VI of France. By this Treaty of Troyes, Henry was recognised as successor to Charles VI who was elderly and was suffering from both mental and physical illness. Henry married Charles VI's daughter, Catherine of Valois, which strengthened the dynastic claim of Henry's descendants to the throne of France. Contrary to expectation, Henry predeceased Charles and his infant son succeeded him as king of England and France. As soon as he was old enough, Henry VI was crowned king of France in Paris (not Rheims Cathedral, the traditional coronation church for the French monarchs as this was still held by the Dauphin) However, under the kingship of a mere boy with no military expertise or experience, the English were unable to hold on to much of the territory which Henry V had taken and this fell back into French control.

Whereas Shakespeare's account of Henry V would paint him as an unblemished hero, there are events which occurred during these wars which are certainly not to Henry's credit. Henry was preoccupied in repelling the third wave of attack from the French. He was concerned that prisoners, captured during the battle of Agincourt, might turn against those holding them captive. He therefore ordered that the prisoners should be killed. During his siege of Rouen, the city was starving and found that it could no longer support the women and children. The garrison drove the women and children out of the city believing that Henry would allow them to pass through his lines. Henry refused to allow this and the women and children were left to starve in the ditches surrounding the town.

Queen Elizabeth I

Queen Elizabeth I

The reign of Elizabeth has been cited as one of the most illustrious in English history and therefore she deserves a place in our gallery of heroes. Although identified as next in line to the throne should Mary Tudor die childless, Elizabeth's accession to the throne was beset with risks and danger. The factions seeking to oust Mary Tudor, who had caused so much discontent in the land through her vigorous persecution of protestants, would leave protestant Elizabeth as the obvious contender to succeed Mary. Queen Mary was advised that her throne would never be secure while Elizabeth was alive and whenever a revolt against Mary's rule broke out, Elizabeth was always suspected of being complicit, even without any hard evidence being available. Thus, when Wyatt's rebellion took place, Elizabeth was imprisoned in the Tower in spite of her protests of being innocent of any involvement. The Lord Chancellor, Stephen Gardner, who was the catholic Bishop of Winchester, worked hard to have Elizabeth put on trial but Elizabeth's supporters in the government convinced Mary to spare her half-sister in the absence of any incriminating evidence. Elizabeth was transferred from the Tower to house arrest in Woodstock and on this journey, she was cheered by crowds all the way.

When Elizabeth ultimately became Queen, a bill was introduced to end the repressive measures exercised in the previous reign. Although receiving support in the House of Commons, the Catholic bishops in the House of Lords opposed the bill. However, many bishoprics, including that of Canterbury, were vacant at the time which enabled Elizabeth to appoint enough protestant bishops to get the bill through the House of Lords.

Elizabeth was an intelligent and pragmatic queen. She was the first English monarch to recognise that a king or queen ruled by popular consent. She was wise in her choice of advisers and established a positive relationship with parliament. Under such a queen, England was able to emerge from the mediaeval feudal system into the renaissance world. Her trust in God, honest advice and the love of her subjects were the key to her successful reign. Her reign has come to be regarded as a time when crown, church and parliament worked in constitutional balance.

Elizabeth never married and is often referred to as the Virgin Queen. It seems she suffered abuse as a child at the hands of her foster father, Thomas Parr. She expressed an intention of marrying her childhood sweetheart, Robert Dudley, but her chief adviser, William Cecil, expressed his disapproval of such a match. It was feared that had she married Dudley, the nobility would rise against her. During her reign, she would have been seen by foreign princes as a highly eligible woman and although courted by many senior royal figures from European countries, she firmly remained single. She is said to have stated that she would rather be a beggar woman and single than a queen and married.

In spite of setting her face against marriage, she had a number of special male favourites at court but her favour was not always wisely placed. In particular, she took a great liking to Robert Devereux, Earl of Essex. He was given a number of prestigious military commands but he failed miserably to secure the objectives for which these commands were created. When abroad with his armies in Europe or Ireland, he didn't communicate with the Queen who was unaware of what he was doing. In many cases, he was disobeying her direct orders. Towards the end of her reign, Essex tried to raise a rebellion in London with the objective of seizing the Queen and taking over the government. Like all his previous enterprises, this failed and Essex was arrested and executed. Elizabeth came to realise her misjudgement in bestowing so much favour on this unworthy man.

Elizabeth faced a threat to her throne from Mary Queen of Scots who had sought refuge in England after being driven out of Scotland. Although she had received sanctuary from her cousin, Mary became the focus of plots to replace Elizabeth with the catholic Mary. These plots were encouraged by the Pope and any persecution of Catholics which took place during Elizabeth's reign were not so much directed against them because they were catholic but because of their involvement in attempts to dethrone her. Elizabeth believed that faith was personal and Francis Bacon explained her attitude by stating that 'she did not want to make windows into men's hearts and secret thoughts'. It was with great reluctance that Elizabeth allowed the execution of Mary Queen of Scots when her spy master, Sir Francis Walsingham, provided conclusive evidence that Mary was involved in one of these plots.

The protestant Dutch faced persecution from the Spanish who were occupying the Netherlands and Elizabeth signed a treaty promising military support to the Dutch. This and the activities of British seafarers who robbed Spanish treasure ships returning to Spain with gold they had looted from the indigenous South and Central American people, led Philip II of Spain to decide to take the war to England. Sir Francis Drake, the foremost of daring English sea captains, destroyed the Spanish invasion fleet in a raid on Cadiz. He had earlier discovered that Spanish ships, moored on the Asian side of the Isthmus of Panama were unarmed, considering themselves safe from attack from the English. Sir Francis sailed round Cape Horn and attacked these Spanish ships, returning to England via the Indian Ocean, thus completing a circumnavigation of the earth.

Philip II built a new invasion fleet, the Armada, and sailed these up the Channel, intending the ships to anchor off Holland in preparation for conveying an army from the Spanish Netherlands under the Duke of Parma to invade England. Sir Francis Drake skilfully used British ships to harry the Armada, using fire ships to deflect the Armada from their intended destination of Holland. The Armada had to continue its voyage through the North Sea and very few Spanish ships actually succeeded in rounding the north of Britain to return home. At this time when invasion was threatened, Elizabeth in full armour addressed her army assembled at Tilbury and is quoted as declaring,

"I know I have the body of a weak and feeble woman but I have the heart and stomach of a king, and of a king of England too, and think foul scorn that Parma or Spain or any Prince of Europe should dare to invade the borders of my realm."

This image of Elizabeth can often lead her to be regarded as a warrior queen but apart from the wars against Spain and Ireland, she sought to secure objectives beneficial to Britain by diplomacy rather than war. She followed a largely defensive policy but was still able to raise the status of England abroad. This amazed the Pope who declared,

"She is only a woman, only a mistress of half an island and yet she makes herself feared by Spain, by France, by the Holy Roman Empire, by all!"

Her half-brother, Edward VI, had established diplomatic relations with the Tsardom of Russia and Elizabeth fostered this relationship by corresponding with the Tsar, Ivan the Terrible. The Tsar was disappointed that Elizabeth's focus was on commerce rather than forging a military alliance. An English merchant who had a prominent position in the Muscovy Company developing trade links with Russia, was appointed as Ambassador to Ivan's court.

Elizabeth encouraged the exploration of the American coast and Sir Walter Raleigh established a settlement he named Virginia in honour of the Virgin Queen. The territory covered was larger than the present day state of Virginia and extended to include what we now call the Carolinas and New England. This was the first English settlement in North America.

Elizabeth awarded a charter to the East India Company whose brief was to establish English trade with all the countries east of the Cape of Good Hope and west of the Straits of Magellan. This company went on to control half of the world's trade and took over substantial territory in India.

During the latter years of her reign, Elizabeth discovered that she could raise money by granting monopolies rather than by going to Parliament to raise taxes. This practice led to abuse and a delegation from the House of Commons petitioned the Queen. Elizabeth addressed this delegation in an oration which has come to be known as her 'Golden Speech'. She professed her ignorance of the abuses and she made promises to this delegation with her usual appeal to the emotions which won them over.

Her reign lasted until the beginning of the seventeenth century when her health started to fail and the death of special friends drove Elizabeth into prolonged states of melancholy. When her chief minister, Robert Cecil, told her she must take to her bed, she snapped,

" 'Must' is not a word to use to princes, little man"

She died in 1603 at Richmond Palace.

Sir Francis Drake

Sir Francis Drake

Sir Francis Drake is the most famous of a band of bold English seafarers who played a dominant role in naval battles fought against the Spanish in the reign of Elizabeth I.

He started his nautical career as an apprentice on a ship captained by a relative, William Hawkins. By the age of 18, he had completed his apprenticeship and obtained a position on a small barque engaged in trading along the south coast of England, the Netherlands and France. The owner of the barque was so impressed with Francis that he bequeathed the barque to him.

It would appear that Drake served under Sir John Hawkins who sought to break into the slave trade off the west coast of Africa which was dominated by the Spanish and Portuguese. Although just working as a common seaman, Drake would have received a small share of the profits from this trade and therefore bears some culpability.

Drake's first independent enterprise was to the Isthmus of Panama, known as part of the Spanish Main. He captured the town of Nombre Dios. This was the centre to which the treasure, which the Spanish had looted from Peru, was taken. From here, it was transported en route for its transit to Spain. Drake was unable to secure any of the treasure as the Spanish managed to retake the town. He therefore turned his attention to raiding Spanish treasure ships and mule trains bearing treasure from Peru to Nombre Dios. On this trip, Drake discovered the Pacific Ocean on the other side of the Isthmus of Panama where unarmed Spanish ships lay moored and he determined that one day, he would find a sea route to the Pacific Ocean and return.

When Drake returned to Plymouth with the treasure he had pirated from the Spanish, the government was unable to publicly acknowledge his success as a temporary truce had been signed with the Spanish but Drake was nonetheless welcomed home as a hero.

Drake served under the Earl of Essex in the war against the Irish but very little credit can be assigned to Drake during this episode of his career as several atrocities were committed. These included executing Irish prisoners from castles which had surrendered after being besieged.

A few years later, Drake sailed again for the Americas, determining to round South America via the Magellan straits and sail north along the coast of the nation we now call Chile. The voyage was not without difficulty and Drake lost ships due to stormy weather, even before he had left the English Channel. However, he ultimately entered the Pacific Ocean and sailed north, plundering Spanish settlements and capturing Spanish ships along the way. He continued north up the coast of North America, founding a colony he named New Albion, claiming this for Elizabeth I and her successors. He then sailed west, rounding the Cape of Good Hope and returning to England three years after setting sail with at least one of the ships, in which he had set sail from Plymouth, intact. This was the 'Pelican' which had been renamed on the voyage as 'the Golden Hind'. The ship was laden with looted Spanish treasure and the amount he gifted to the Queen exceeded her annual income. Drake was knighted by the Queen on the deck of the 'Golden Hind'. Elizabeth took care that the Spanish should remain unaware of Drake's exploits in South and Central America.

Following his knighthood, Drake became involved in politics. He served as MP for three West Country constituencies and became Mayor of Plymouth.

When war broke out with Spain, Drake was ordered to lead what has become known as 'the Great Expedition' to attack Spain and its American colonies. He set sail from Plymouth with a fleet of 21 ships and 1,800 soldiers under his command. He successfully attacked and destroyed Spanish towns and settlements both on the Spanish mainland and in the Americas. Drake rescued a number of Turks who were being used as slaves by the Spanish. He sailed on north to discover the colony of Roanoke which had been founded by Sir Walter Raleigh. He replenished this and returned to England with many of the original colonists, arriving at Portsmouth to a hero's welcome.

Drake was given a new commission to harass and destroy Spanish shipping, especially the ships which were being prepared as an armada to enable an invasion of England to take place. Drake discovered this Spanish fleet in Cadiz and attacked it, sinking thirty-nine Spanish ships, a feat which has been described as 'singeing the King of Spain's beard'. This delayed the launching of the Spanish Armada by a year. During this commission, Drake captured a huge amount of Spanish goods which realised a considerable sum for the treasury, Sir Francis retaining a significant amount for himself.

The following year, a rebuilt armada left Spain. The English were expecting this and were getting ready to repel the attack. A probably apocryphal tale is told of Drake's reaction to news that the armada had been sighted while he was playing bowls. Drake continued with his game, stating that there was time to finish his game and still beat the Spaniards. In fact, it is probable that Drake knew that he would have to wait for high tide before launching his ship. When the Armada arrived, it was pursued by the English ships. Drake managed to capture the ship which was carrying a huge amount of wealth to be used for paying the troops and financing the war. The Spanish Admiral moored his fleet in French waters believing that here, he would be safe from English attack. Drake ordered fire ships to be launched to sail into the Spanish fleet. This caused disarray among the Spanish ships. The captains had to raise their anchors and sail away from Calais to avoid catching fire. They were pursued by English ships which prevented the Spanish from landing on English soil. The remnants of the armada made its way around the north of Britain and limped back to Spain. They lost further ships on the journey to the storms they encountered off the coast of Ireland. In total, the armada lost sixty-three ships before reaching home.

Drake's role in subsequent attacks on the Spanish ships and cities were largely unsuccessful and reflect little credit on Drake. At the age of fifty-six, he died at sea of dysentery, a common tropical disease at that time. His remains were buried at sea.

William Shakespeare

William Shakespeare

Shakespeare is often acclaimed as the greatest writer of English and one of the world's most accomplished dramatists. He wrote thirty-nine plays, one-hundred and fifty-four sonnets and a few other longer pieces of verse. His plays have been translated into most of the world's widely spoken languages and are still performed more than those of any other playwright. He was born on St. George's Day, 23rd April, in Stratford-upon-Avon to John Shakespeare, who was a successful glove maker, and Mary Arden, who had an affluent family background. He died on the same date at the age of fifty two. On hearing of this coincidence, a child I knew expressed the hope that he had managed to open his birthday presents before he died! Shakespeare was educated at the King's School in Stratford. At the age of eighteen, he married Anne Hathaway who, at twenty-six, was eight years older than himself. The marriage was hastily arranged, the Chancellor of Worcester Cathedral allowing the banns to be read only once instead of the customary three times. Six months later, the couple had Susanna, the first of three children. Almost two years later, they had twins, Hamnet and Judith. Sadly, Hamnet died when he was only eleven but the cause of his death is unknown.

During his career, Shakespeare appears to have shared his time between London and Stratford. There is a story that he had to flee to London to avoid being prosecuted for deer poaching by the local rich landowner, Sir Thomas Lucy. There is a picture in Charlecote, the ancestral home of the Lucy family, of Shakespeare being brought before Sir Thomas to face this charge of poaching.

Shakespeare started his career in the theatre in a very humble way by minding the horses of wealthy patrons when they were attending a performance. He joined a group of players known as 'The Lord Chamberlain's Men' at a playhouse in Shoreditch known as 'The Theatre'. Not only did Shakespeare contribute to the work of this group as an actor but wrote many of the plays which they performed. Although there is no documentary evidence to prove it, it is believed, that Shakespeare starred as the principal actor in many of these plays. Queen Elizabeth was reigning at this time and it is suggested that some of his historical plays, particularly Richard III, were propaganda, containing an element of anti-Yorkist sentiment. This would curry favour with the Queen whose Tudor dynasty was the successor to the Lancastrian faction who fought the Wars of the Roses.

When James I came to the throne, the company was awarded a royal patent and they changed their name to 'The King's Men'. London theatres faced frequent closure to check the spread of bubonic plague which was often rampant in the city. The company built their own theatre, 'The Globe', on the South Bank where their success continued. The company also took over Blackfriars indoor theatre. As a major investor in this successful company, Shakespeare became quite a wealthy man. He was able to buy the second largest house in Stratford and contributed generously to the work of the local church. This house, 'The New Place', can still be visited in Stratford.

Shakespeare has had a number of detractors over the years, many of whom have suggested that these plays could only have been written by university educated playwrights like Christopher Marlowe, Francis Bacon, Thomas Nashe, and Robert Greene. However, there is no firm evidence to support this contention and it may be regarded as no more than intellectual snobbery. Robert Greene attacked Shakespeare with a particularly vitriolic piece of writing in which he ascribes the name, 'Upstart Crow' to Shakespeare. This name has been used as the title of a television programme which humorously parodied parts of Shakespeare's plays. It is almost certain that his last three plays, which include Henry VIII, were written in collaboration with others.

Shakespeare retired to Stratford, three years before his death. This was before the Globe Theatre caught fire and burned down during a performance of Henry VIII. The Vicar of Stratford suggested that Shakespeare's sudden, unexpected death may have been due to a fever he contracted after a heavy night's drinking in the company of fellow playwrights, Ben Johnson and Drayton. Shakespeare was survived by his wife and two daughters, the elder of whom married a physician, John Hall. Their house, Hall's Croft in Stratford, is open to visitors. Shakespeare was buried in Holy Trinity Church, Stratford. When the church was recently restored, care was taken not to disturb Shakespeare's tomb in view of a curse against any who disturbed his bones. This curse is included in the epitaph carved into the stone covering the grave. Many memorials exist to Shakespeare including one in Poets' Corner, Westminster Abbey and another in Southwark Cathedral, so near the Globe Theatre where many successful productions of Shakespeare's plays were performed.

Film versions exist of most of Shakespeare's plays. His work has inspired and influenced other authors and art forms. The works of Thomas Hardy, Charles Dickens and Herman Melville all have elements in which Shakespeare's influence can be seen. Thousands of pieces of music stem from Shakespeare's work including Felix Mendelssohn's 'Incidental Music for a Midsummer Night's Dream', Sergei Prokofiev's ballet, 'Romeo and Juliet' and Verdi's operas, 'Otello', 'Falstaff' and 'Macbeth'. The musical, West Side Story is the story of Romeo and Juliet, set in a modern environment. Many expressions which have crept into the English language like 'with bated breath' and 'a foregone conclusion' find their origin in Shakespeare's plays.

Although Shakespeare's plays are masterpieces of the English language, his plots are so clever, that they have been enjoyed in translation well beyond the confines of Britain.

Oliver Cromwell
Lord Protector

Oliver Cromwell, Lord Protector

Oliver Cromwell is remembered as a politician of considerable ability who led the forces of parliament against the despotic rule of King Charles 1. While Oliver is hailed for heroically implementing one of the most important steps in the process of establishing the way England would be governed, he is regarded by many as a controversial personality. His actions were not always consistent with his declared principles.

Cromwell was born in Huntingdon where he attended the grammar school and went on to study at Sidney Sussex College, Cambridge University. By religious conviction, he was a Puritan. He became an MP during a time when there was conflict between King and Parliament over the levying of taxes. This led to civil war breaking out between the forces of the King and those which supported Parliament. Initially, the war went in the King's favour as he had a well-trained and better equipped army. Cromwell recognised the need to improve the quality and training of the Parliamentary army and established what has become known as the 'New Model Army'. This became a powerful force and soon began to reverse the earlier defeats the parliamentarian forces had suffered at the hands of the King's army, ultimately winning the war.

After Charles I had been executed, Cromwell defeated the Scottish royalist armies, who had proclaimed Charles I's son as King Charles II, in battles at Dunbar and Worcester. He conducted a campaign against the Irish Catholics and this involved massacring the inhabitants of some Irish cities in what has been described as an act of ethnic cleansing. About 40% of the Irish population died as a result of these massacres!

At the end of the civil war, Cromwell found himself in a very powerful position as head of the army. He was offered the title of king but refused this accepting instead, the title of Lord Protector of the republic which had been set up. This became known as the Commonwealth. As Lord Protector, he had powers which exceeded that of the king he had deposed and he dissolved the parliament whose power he had fought to uphold. Under his leadership, many of the reforms were established which were very beneficial to the nation. He reorganized public finances, promoted the liberalization of commerce in order to ensure the prosperity of the merchant classes and established English naval supremacy. He took Jamaica from the Spanish and established England as leader of the European Protestant countries. However, mild persecution of Catholics took place in England during his tenure of power.

At his death, Oliver was succeeded by his son Richard. Although not without ability, Richard didn't have a power base in either the army or parliament. A period of chaos ensued until the monarchy with reduced power was restored under Charles II. The royalists exhumed Cromwell's corpse, beheaded it and hung the body in chains. His skull was burned at Tyburn.

Today, an impressive statue of Cromwell stands outside the Houses of Parliament.

John Bunyan

John Bunyan

John Bunyan was born in Elstow, Bedfordshire, to Thomas and Margaret Bunyan. Thomas was an itinerant tinker, a trade in great demand in those days, and John became apprenticed to his father. He continued to follow this trade for some years. However, not only did John follow his father's trade, but picked up his bad habit of using foul language. He swore like a tinker. The family were probably not as poor as may have appeared in an autobiographical work as John was educated at Bedford Grammar School.

Both of John's parents died when he was sixteen. The civil war had just broken out and John enlisted in the Parliamentarian Army. He records an incident in his army career which John attributed to divine grace. He was selected to be part of a party which was to embark on a hazardous mission. So keen was a fellow soldier to be involved in this action that he volunteered to go in John's place. During the ensuing action, this soldier was killed when he received a musket wound to the head.

John married a pious young woman. They had four children, two boys and two girls. Sadly, their eldest daughter was born blind. The newlywed couple had very few material goods, their most valuable possessions being two religious books which John's wife brought into their marriage. The impact of the teaching in these books, including the sermons he heard at his church, which had a strong puritan bias, must have had a profound effect on John. He began to take stock of his life and recognised that he was the leader of an unruly group who were involved in all sorts of vice and antisocial habits. While playing a game which was popular at the time called tip-cat on a Sunday afternoon, after having heard a sermon that morning preached against sabbath breaking, and this included playing games on Sunday, John heard an audible voice. The message he received from the sky was:-

This led to a time when Bunyan endured a period of intense, internal mental and spiritual conflict, even leading to his having irrational fears that should he enter a church, the church bell might fall on him and kill him.

While travelling his rounds as an itinerant tinker, he was passing through Bedford where he became engaged in conversation with a group of four women. He was so impressed with the spiritual content of their conversation that he decided he would attend their church. They met in St. John's Church in Bedford, but as a non-conformist group, they met in the afternoon. As John imbibed the teaching and ethos of this group, John felt urged to preach himself. With the support of this congregation, he started his preaching ministry and discovered that he had a great gift in this direction. He preached not only in church but to groups in the surrounding countryside. He eventually moved with his family to Bedford and published his first book, *'Gospel Truths Opened'*.

The religious tolerance which had allowed Bunyan to preach outside church came to an end when the monarchy was restored. The non-conformist group were no longer allowed to meet in St. John's Church. While preaching at a farm, thirteen miles from Bedford, John was arrested under the Religion Act. This Act made it illegal to preach, to a group of five or more people outside the family, other than within the parish church. The real reason for this arrest was not so much because John was preaching but from a fear that these religious gatherings could be a cover for plotting against the newly restored king.

Bunyan was brought to trial under the indictment that he had:-

"devilishly and perniciously abstained from coming to church to hear divine service and having held several unlawful meetings and conventicles, to the great disturbance and distraction of the good subjects of this kingdom"

He was sentenced to three months imprisonment with the threat of deportation if he continued to preach unlawfully. Bunyan refused to accept this condition and this resulted in his time of imprisonment being extended to twelve years. This inevitably led to a time of hardship for the family but they received support both from his fellow members of the non-conformist Bedford Meeting Group and other supporters. He was also able to earn a limited amount of money while in prison and sold some of the religious tracts he wrote. It appears that prison conditions weren't arduous although these varied, depending on the mood of the gaolers or the authorities. John had the company of other imprisoned nonconformist preachers and he had a Bible and a copy of Foxe's Book of Martyrs. He also had writing materials, enabling him to write the book, *'Grace*

Abounding' and he started to write his masterpiece, *'The Pilgrim's Progress'.* From time to time, he was even let out of prison to spend time with his wife and family and during this time, his daughter, Sarah, was born. His second child, Joseph, was born after he was released from prison. While in prison, he was appointed pastor of the nonconformist Bedford Group and was even allowed by the authorities to preach there! However, John was not unaware of the hardship his imprisonment was having on his wife and family and had misgivings about whether he was doing the right thing. He stated,

> *'"O, I saw in this condition I was a man who was pulling down his house upon the head of his Wife and Children; yet thought I, I must do it, I must do it,"*

The mood of religious toleration in the country improved and the King issued a declaration of indulgence which ended the laws which had been passed against the nonconformists. Thousands of nonconformists were released from prison and this included Bunyan and his fellow inmates in Bedford Gaol. Bunyan immediately obtained a licence which allowed him to preach.

When Bunyan's wife died, he was left with four young children, one of whom was blind. He soon remarried. His second wife, Elizabeth, was only eighteen years old, but in those days, this wasn't considered to be a young age to get married.

While continuing as pastor of the Bedford Meeting, he travelled on horseback all over Bedfordshire to take his preaching ministry well beyond Bedford Town. John became known as Bishop Bunyan. He also continued with his writing and completed his book, *'The Pilgrims Progress'*, an allegory of the Christian life in which the hero, Christian, encounters such pitfalls as the Slough of Despond, Doubting Castle and Giant Despair. Superstitious religion and Catholicism are described as the toothless giants, Pagan and Pope. *'The Pilgrim's Progress'* sold very well and became a very popular book in the Victorian era. In total, fifty eight of Bunyan's works were published, some of them posthumously by his wife. His next best known book after *'The Pilgrim's Progress'* is another allegorical work, *'The Holy War'* in which Bunyan uses military terms and jargon he picked up while serving in Cromwell's army. John Bunyan also wrote a hymn which has become much loved in spite of its archaic language and style.

He who would valiant be
'Gainst all disaster,
Let him in constancy,
Follow the master.
There's no discouragement
Shall make him once relent.
His first avowed intent

To be a pilgrim.

In allegorical style, the word *'pilgrim'* is used to represent a Christian. Many Christians have found this hymn to be a great source of encouragement when going through difficult times. Many famous authors claim to have been encouraged by Bunyan's writings including Nathaniel Hawthorne, Herman Melville, C. S. Lewis, Charles Dickens, Louisa May Alcott, George Bernard Shaw, William Thackeray, Enid Blyton, Charlotte Brontë, Mark Twain, and John Steinbeck.

When John Bunyan journeyed to London to visit a friend, he was caught in a storm on the way and developed a fever when he reached London. This led to his death, aged fifty nine. His wife died three years later. Although much of his life had been spent in relative poverty, especially the time he was in prison, his estate on death was worth £43. This may not sound a great deal but in modern terms it would be worth the equivalent of £5,200.

John Bunyan was very much a unique person in whom, the Holy Spirit was able to work in a special way.

Sir Christopher Wren

Sir Christopher Wren

While Christopher Wren is universally acclaimed as the architect of St. Paul's Cathedral, very few are aware of the versatility of this brilliant man who was not only a great architect but an astronomer, mathematician and physicist.

Christopher was born in East Knoyle, Wiltshire. His father was rector of the parish but later became Dean of Windsor. His mother, Mary, was the only child and therefore, sole heiress, of a wealthy landowner and this meant that Christopher could enjoy living in a family with an affluent background. Sadly, Mary died when Christopher was quite young. Several of his brothers and sisters had died within a year of their birth and Christopher himself was described as a sickly child. However, his health improved and he survived to reach the age of ninety. The family had to keep a low profile during the period we know as the Commonwealth because of their royalist sympathies and Christopher received his early education from a local clergyman. However, he was able to continue his education at Westminster School whose headmaster, Dr. Busby, was high principled and was prepared to treat sons of both impoverished royalists and puritans alike, regardless of which party held ascendancy at the time.

Christopher's education had made him proficient in Latin and mathematics as well as in drawing. Many of his drawings were so good that they were used to illustrate a book on anatomy. From Westminster School, Christopher went on to study at Wadham College, Oxford University. Here, he took an interest in scientific studies which led to Christopher and like-minded friends founding the Royal Society which has become the foremost scientific society in the nation. Christopher's breadth of knowledge and expertise facilitated discussion held among members of the Society.

Christopher was elected as a Fellow of All Souls College where he initiated a number of lines of scientific research. In particular, he was able to successfully inject fluid into the blood stream of dogs. This was the first time this had been achieved with a live animal and had an important implication for later lines of medical research. His next academic appointment was as Professor of Astronomy at Gresham College, London. Interestingly, this post required Christopher to give lectures each week in Latin and English. The year after the restoration of the monarchy, Christopher was elected Savilian Professor of Astronomy at Oxford University. He made contributions to a number of scientific fields beyond astronomy including mechanics, microscopy, surveying and meteorology.

Wren's contemporary scientists, Hooke and Halley, had ascertained that the planets followed elliptical orbits around the sun. Wren challenged them to provide a law of force which would explain this motion. Halley took this problem to Isaac Newton who was able to answer this question on the basis of his theory of gravitation. It would appear that answering this question prompted Newton to write his famous treatise, the Principia.

Wren showed an interest in restoring the old St. Paul's Cathedral which was badly falling into disrepair and went to Paris to study architecture. Soon after the Great Fire of London, Wren was appointed King's Surveyor of Works which meant he had an important part to play in the rebuilding of London. He is credited with the rebuilding of fifty-one churches but was assisted in this task by a number of other very able architects like Nicholas Hawkesmore. This work included his master-piece, St. Paul's Cathedral. The Great Fire of London had inflicted further damage on the old cathedral so that there was no point in just patching it up with Wren's ideas which would have required the melding of two very different styles of architecture, Gothic and Classical. These would have clashed. Instead, the old St. Paul's could be demolished to make way for a completely new cathedral designed by Christopher Wren in its entirety. Wren is also credited with designing in gothic style, the western towers of Westminster Abbey, providing the building with the profile which gives extra prominence to a remarkable church. These towers were added by Hawkesmore a few years after the death of Wren.

The income from the work in which he was now engaged led the thirty-seven year old Wren to consider that he could at last afford to get married and he married his childhood sweetheart, the thirty-three year old Faith Coghill. They had two children, Gilbert, who suffered from convulsions and died before he was two, and Christopher, who in due course was to succeed his father as an architect. Sadly, Faith died before she was forty. His mother-in-law, Lady Coghill, stepped in to look after Christopher junior.

Eighteen months later, Wren married again. His second wife, Jane Fitzwilliam, was the daughter of a prosperous London merchant. They had two children, a daughter, Jane, and a son, William. This marriage again was short, Jane dying of tuberculosis. Wren's two wives and deceased son were buried in the chancel of St. Martin-in-the-Fields. Although living to ninety, Christopher was married for less than ten of those years.

Christopher Wren's activities were not restricted to academia, science and architecture. He was active in public life. He narrowly failed to win a parliamentary seat in two by-elections, first for Cambridge University and then for Oxford University. However, he was successful at his third attempt and won the seat for Plympton Erle. He had four spells in Parliament. He twice won the seat at New Windsor but for an unknown reason, these elections were declared null and void. At a general election, he was returned unopposed for Weymouth and Melcombe Regis but did not contest the seat at the following general election.

Long after Christopher had retired from active work, he used to pay unofficial visits to St. Paul's Cathedral to inspect the progress being made in his greatest work. On one of these visits, when the cathedral was almost finished and Wren was over ninety, he caught a cold. A few days later, when he was apparently enjoying a nap, a servant found that he was unable to wake Christopher. He had died in his sleep. A memorial stone to Sir Christopher Wren has been inscribed onto black marble and installed in the floor under the centre of the dome. It includes the words,

'Lector, si monumentum requires, circumspice.'

This translates as, 'Reader, if you require a monument, look around you.'

While we tend to associate Wren's work with the churches he rebuilt in London, he was involved in many other architectural projects. His first enterprise on qualifying as an architect was designing a new chapel for Pembroke College, Cambridge University. He later designed a chapel for Emmanuel College, another Cambridge college. At Oxford, he designed the New Theatre and the Garden Quadrangle of Trinity College. He designed the Monument, a secular erection which is a great column surmounted by simulated flames, to commemorate the Great Fire of London. He designed the Royal Observatory, the Royal Hospital, Chelsea, home of the Chelsea pensioners, and he reconstructed the state room at Windsor Castle. He designed the Windsor Guildhall but the Council asked him to include more pillars as they weren't satisfied that the pillars around the periphery would support so large a ceiling. Sir Christopher was confident they would but he provided the extra columns as requested, leaving a small gap between the top of the columns and the ceiling. He also designed Greenwich

Hospital which has been declared a UNESCO world heritage site. Wren was involved in architectural projects at Kensington Palace and Hampton Court Palace. King Charles II hoped to spend many of his remaining years in Winchester and Sir Christopher was commissioned to design the King's House but the King died before it was completed.

Sir Christopher Wren has been commemorated by having his portrait included on the reverse of a £50 note.

Sir Isaac Newton

Sir Isaac Newton

As this is written for an audience of individuals among whom there will be, many without a scientific background, the following can give no more than a flavour of the vast achievements arising from the genius of Isaac Newton. Readers who have encountered the work of Newton, purely from their own studies of science and mathematics, may well find interesting the lesser known aspects of Newton's life as a theologian, a geographer, a politician, a reformer of English currency, a justice of the peace and a detective.

Sir Isaac Newton ranks with Albert Einstein as one of the two greatest theoretical physicists of all time. Arguably, Newton may also be regarded as the greatest mathematician who has ever lived. He was born prematurely near Grantham on Christmas Day to a recently widowed mother. The baby was so small that he could be fitted into a quart pot! His mother remarried a member of the clergy when Isaac was only three and he was left to be brought up by his maternal grandmother. Isaac intensely disliked his stepfather. He never forgave his mother for marrying him and deserting him as a small child. The intensity of his dislike can be appreciated from something Newton wrote at the age of nineteen as part of his confessional in which he confessed to threatening to burn the house of his mother and stepfather over their heads.

From the age of twelve, Newton was educated at the King's School, Grantham. On being widowed for a second time, Newton's mother withdrew him from school, hoping for him to take up farming as a career but Newton had no interest in farming. He was returned to school as a result of his mother being persuaded to do so by the school's headmaster. Here, he excelled academically and it appears that he was partly motivated to succeed in order to get revenge on the school bully.

On the recommendation of his uncle, Newton was awarded a place at Trinity College, Cambridge University where he lived initially as a substrar, that is a student who earned money by performing menial duties of a valeting nature. However, on being awarded a scholarship, his living expenses were covered until he was awarded his M.A. When the university closed temporarily as a precaution against the great plague which was rampant at the time, Newton continued his studies at home where he developed the branch of mathematics we call calculus, made discoveries in the field of optics and propounded his theories of mechanics and gravitation. The popular apocryphal story that Newton's exposition of his theory of gravitation arose from his being hit on the head by an apple falling from a tree, is an embellishment of Newton's own account. Seeing an apple falling from a tree, he mused on the phenomenon of falling objects. From his formulation of the laws of mechanics which includes the assertion that to every action, there is an equal and opposite reaction, he realised that just as the earth exerted a downward force on the apple which he called gravitation, so the apple would exert an equal and opposite force on the earth. He proposed that the force of gravitation between two bodies was proportional to the mass of each of those bodies and inversely proportional to the square of the distance between them. We now know these principles as the universal laws of gravitation. Using these laws, Newton was able to explain the elliptical orbits of the planets round the sun, which had been discovered by the astronomer, Kepler.

A problem to which Newton applied his laws of gravitation but which he was unable to completely solve was the determination of an analytical description of the moon's orbit around the earth. Although the moon orbits the earth in a roughly elliptical path in a way which is analogous to the planets orbiting the sun, the problem is complicated by the fact that the moon's orbit is also influenced by the gravitational pull of the sun. (The planets are sufficiently distant from each other that they only have a minor gravitational effect on the respective orbits of their neighbouring planets.) The problem of the moon's orbit is thus the three body problem for which a straightforward simple analytical solution has not thus far been determined. Newton complained to fellow astronomers that concentrating on this problem made his head ache so much that it kept him awake at night. Although pressed by his fellow astronomers to complete his analysis, he refused on the grounds of the insomnia that it was causing him and he decided to think no more about it.

When the university reopened, Newton returned to be elected as a Fellow of Trinity College. It was usually a requirement for Fellows to become ordained as Anglican priests but these archaic rules were no longer being enforced during this period of history which we know as the Restoration. Thus, Newton declined the suggestion that he should be ordained. Although Newton had signed his assent to the thirty nine articles, a document which represented accepted doctrine of the Church of England, Newton realised that although a Christian, his religious views were unorthodox and did not conform to mainstream Anglican teaching. His stand on this was important for he was later able to take up a professorship which had a definite requirement that the holder should not be holder of an ecclesiastic office which would detract from the time he would be able to devote to scientific work. It was necessary for King Charles II to grant permission for this post to be filled and he was able to support Newton's appointment in view of Newton's assertion that he need not be ordained.

The professorship to which Newton had been appointed included the requirement that he should lecture on geography. To support his lectures, Newton rewrote 'Geographia Generalis', the standard textbook on the subject. During the time he held this professorship, Newton was elected to become a Fellow of the Royal Society, an honour which is still coveted as the most prestigious award a British scientist can receive.

Not only had Newton invented calculus but his work was considered to have advanced every branch of mathematics then studied. Calculus was later independently invented by Leibnitz, a German mathematician. While there is no dispute in the priority of discovering calculus, Leibnitz used a more powerful notation to represent derivatives. Whereas Newton used the very simple $f'(x)$ and $f''(x)$ notation to represent the first and second derivatives of a function, Leibnitz used dy/dx and d^2y/dx^2 which proved a more powerful notation in the development of the subject. Out of loyalty to Newton, Cambridge used Newton's notation for some time but calculus at Cambridge fell behind its development in Europe until the university adopted Leibnitz's notation.

Other areas of mathematics for which Newton may be given credit are the generalised binomial theorem, Newton's identities, the classification of cubic plane curves and the theory of finite differences. He was the first to use fractional indices and employed coordinate geometry to derive solutions to Diophantine equations. Newton approximated partial sums of the harmonic series by logarithms. His work on infinite series was inspired by Simon Stevin's decimals.

Newton made a significant contribution to the science of optics. He showed that white light could be separated into colours, using a glass prism and then using another prism, the colours could be reformed as the original white light. He called the multicoloured image produced by a prism, a spectrum, and he referred to the process of light splitting into colours, as dispersion.

Dispersion causes a defect in which the image of an object, formed by lenses, is split into coloured images which are not completely superimposed in the same plane to faithfully represent the appearance of the original object.. This defect is known as chromatic aberration. Chromatic aberration is not a problem with images formed by curved mirrors and therefore, Newton considered that a telescope made using a mirror would be superior to one using lenses. Newton ground out a concave mirror whose perfection he tested using an interference phenomenon which we describe as Newton's rings and thus produced a high quality reflecting telescope. The principle behind this telescope has been used in the construction of the great reflecting telescopes used in important observatories around the world today.

Newton published a treatise on light (Opticks) in which he postulated that light consisted of tiny corpuscles, rejecting the idea that light was a wave phenomenon. He based this conclusion on the fact that light travels in straight lines and is not observed to be diffracted. In fact, light is diffracted but the diffraction is not immediately observable because the wavelength of light is so small. A later scientist, Huygens, insisted that light was a wave phenomenon and two scientists, Young and Fresnel, were able to prove that Huygens was right. However, quantum mechanics has since shown that as well as being a wave phenomenon, light also had a corpuscular nature as Newton had postulated. We refer to the light corpuscles as photons. In his treatise, Opticks, he was able to show how prisms could be used as beam expanders and this has been crucial to the development of narrow-linewidth tunable lasers.

A contribution which Newton made to the theory of heat transfer is known as Newton's Law of cooling. This states that the rate at which a hot body cools is proportional to how much its temperature exceeds that of its surroundings provided the body is in a forced draught. The codicil is necessary because if the body is not in a draught, the hot body would raise the temperature of its immediate environment as it cools, invalidating the condition required for the law to hold.

Newton's great publication which summarised so much of his scientific thought is known as the 'Principia'. This might never have been published but for the financial help and encouragement of the astronomer, Edmond Halley. In this work, he propounded, among other theoretical matters, the basic laws of mechanics, he provided an analytical determination of the speed of sound in air and he showed how his theory of gravitation accounted for the orbits of the planets. The 'Principia' led to Newton being universally recognised for the great mathematical scientist he was.

Newton served two terms as Member of Parliament for Cambridge University as a member of the Whig party. He was knighted by Queen Anne on a visit to Trinity

College and spent the later years of his life as master of the Royal Mint. It is likely that in view of his outstanding contribution to mathematics and science, he was rewarded with this post as a sinecure, that is, a well-paid, prestigious post which required little input or work from the holder. However, Newton did not see it in this light and took his duties very seriously. He re-coined the nation and discovered that one fifth of the returned old coins were counterfeit. Counterfeiting was a very serious crime but it had proved very difficult to detect and prosecute counterfeiters. To counter this problem, Newton himself played detective, going in disguise into bars, listening carefully to chatter and entering into conversations himself. He had himself appointed as a justice of the peace in the home counties and by cross examining witnesses, informers and suspects, was able to convict nearly thirty counterfeiters.

Newton's interests were not restricted to science. He was a theologian and wrote tracts dealing with the way the Bible may be interpreted literally and symbolically.

Newton was not a shrewd investor and along with many others, he invested heavily in the South Sea Company which suddenly went bust after a meteoric rise in the value of its shares. This event has come to be known as 'the South Sea Bubble'.

Astounding as his achievements were, Newton appears to have been a modest person. When applauded for some of his contributions to science, he stated,

"If I have seen further than others, it is by standing on the shoulders of giants."

Robert Hooke who carried out research on the elasticity of materials was a fellow scientist who was often in dispute with Newton. In his correspondence with Hooke, Newton used a variation of the much quoted aphorism by stating that,

"A dwarf standing on the shoulders of a giant sees the further of the two."

Hooke was known to be a very short man, but this statement made by Newton would put himself in the role of the dwarf. In a memoir, Newton wrote,

"I do not know what I may appear to the world, but to myself I seem to have been only like a boy playing on the sea-shore, and diverting myself in now and then finding a smoother pebble or a prettier shell than ordinary, whilst the great ocean of truth lays all undiscovered before me."

Another human aspect of Newton's personality is evidenced by something his niece said of him during a time she was recovering from smallpox. She described him as 'her very loving uncle'. Newton spent the last years of his life, living with his niece and her husband at Cranbury Park near Winchester. He died in his sleep and his funeral was attended by members of both the nobility and scientific community. Newton was the first scientist to be buried in Westminster Abbey. He was a bachelor and had no children but died intestate, having divested so much of his wealth among his relatives during his latter years.

The 'Systeme International de unites' (SI system) is a system of units universally used by scientists in quantifying scientific measurements. The unit of force used in this system is the 'Newton', so named in honour of his contribution to the science of mechanics.

John Churchill
Duke of Marlborough

John Churchill, Duke of Marlborough

John Churchill, Duke of Marlborough, is recognised as one of Britain's greatest generals but few are aware of just how far his strategy, tactical acumen and leadership place him above other great generals. He was truly, a military genius.

Marlborough's military career was chequered as he fell in and out of favour as his involvement in politics generated problems which were not always resolved in Marlborough's favour. At that time, there was the underlying threat of a Jacobite rebellion and parliament was developing into a two party system, Whig and Tory. Marlborough's relationship with royalty was not always harmonious.

As a member of a family of minor gentry, he became page to the Duke of York who later became King James II. On reaching adulthood, he played a leading role in the Battle of Sedgemoor, decisively defeating the army of the rebellious Duke of Monmouth. He was rewarded by King James with the title of Baron Churchill of Sandridge and promoted to the rank of major general.

In spite of providing the support which secured James' position as king, John Churchill became uneasy when James declared himself to be Catholic. He detested the way any identified as Monmouth's supporters were ruthlessly persecuted and savagely punished by Judge Jeffreys. Churchill had privately declared that should the king attempt to change the protestant tradition of the nation, he would instantly leave his service. When he saw some prominent political leaders renouncing their protestant faith to become Catholics and receive royal favour, and anticipating a succession of catholic kings after James, Churchill made it clear to the king that he was not prepared to renounce his faith as a protestant in order to remain in his service.

Churchill was among the group who invited William, Prince of Orange, to become king in place of James. When William of Orange landed and was joined by Churchill, James saw that he could no longer retain the military services of Churchill and fled with his son to France.

William had married King James' daughter, Mary. As part of their coronation honours as joint monarch's, Churchill was created, Earl Marlborough, and sworn in as part of the privy council. However, Marlborough retained contact with the deposed James, perhaps to keep his options open should the political scene change. Therefore, he was not fully trusted by William and Mary.

Marlborough's detractors have seen Marlborough's defection to William as a treacherous act and even King William was suspicious of Marlborough's motivation. It is difficult not to see Marlborough's defection as an act of ruthless ingratitude. However, other biographers have seen Marlborough's actions as arising from patriotic, moral and religious motives.

Britain joined a coalition of European nations which had united to thwart the ambitions of the French King, Louis XIV, who was threatening to dominate Europe. Marlborough remodelled the army and sailed to the low countries with 8,000 men under his command. Marlborough's main achievement during the 'Nine Years War' was at the Battle of Walcourt where Marlborough earned the praise of the allied commander as having displayed extraordinary military ability for such a young officer, beyond that of many experienced generals.

King William went to Ireland to deal with the threat posed by the former king, James, who was raising an army there. After defeating James at the Battle of the Boyne, William returned to England and gave Marlborough the commission to go to Ireland to disrupt the enemy supply chain. Marlborough achieved this by taking the ports of Kinsale and Cork. It is considered that this campaign showed Marlborough's grasp of the importance of disrupting the enemy's supply chain, tact in dealing with other senior army commanders, and in having meticulously planned logistics.

In spite of his success in Ireland, William did not grant the ambitious earl the honours he expected and Marlborough used his influence in parliament and the army to arouse discontent at the king's preference for foreign military commanders. Marlborough's influence was so great that it is said that William, a man not normally prone to fear, actually feared Marlborough. Queen Mary was so incensed with Marlborough that she ordered her sister, Anne, to dismiss Marlborough's wife, Sarah, from her service. Anne, the heir to the throne, refused. Marlborough himself was dismissed from all the civil and military posts he held. Acting on slender evidence that Marlborough and a number of others had written a letter, apparently advocating the restoration of James II, Mary had Marlborough arrested and confined to the Tower. During this time, Marlborough's youngest son, Charles, died. Due to lack of evidence that this crime had been committed, Marlborough was released after five weeks confinement.

Shortly after this, Mary died and there was a degree of reconciliation between William III and Marlborough, although Marlborough was known to complain of the king's coolness towards him. Marlborough was restored to his civil and military posts and became governor to the son of Anne, the next in line to the throne. When William had to return to Holland, Marlborough was a member of the council left to run the country.

An important aspect of British foreign policy was the maintenance of a balance of power among the European nations. The two most influential powers were France and Austria. France was ruled by the Bourbon dynasty and Austria by the Hapsburgs. The Hapsburg king of Spain, Charles II, died childless, having bequeathed his title to Louis XIV's grandson, who became Philip V of Spain. This bequest was made on condition that Philip would renounce his claim to the French throne. Philip refused to do this, leading to the prospect that France, united with Spain, would become unduly powerful in Europe. This situation led to what is known as the War of the Spanish succession and led to European powers including Britain, forming a Grand Alliance against France.

The Grand Alliance nominated Archduke Charles, son of the Hapsburg Holy Roman Emperor, as king of Spain in place of Philip. Shortly after this, King William III died. In many ways, he would have been in ideal person to lead the Grand Alliance. He was succeeded by his sister-in-law, Anne, who bestowed on Marlborough the honours, including the Order of the Garter, which he had felt the previous reign had denied him. He was also appointed Captain General of British armed forces both at home and abroad.

Britain declared war on France and Marlborough was given command of the allied forces. Marlborough outmanoeuvred the French general, Marshal Boufflers, and captured Venlo, Roemond, Liege and Stevenswert. Following this success, the Queen promoted Marlborough to Duke.

Further tragedy struck the family when Marlborough's eldest son died of smallpox. Marlborough and his wife had been at their son's side. In spite of his grief, Marlborough returned to the continent where his tact and reputation as a great general enabled him to hold together the discordant elements of the Grand Alliance.

Then followed a campaign which sealed Marlborough's reputation as one of the greatest military commanders ever. He dealt a crushing blow to the French at the Battle of Blenheim, in which Marlborough's skill in the timing of forced marches, cunning tactics and strategy, logistics, planning and wise use of his outnumbered fighting men, enabled this victory to be achieved. France's ally, Bavaria, was knocked out of the war and the subsequent capture of Landau, Trier and Trarbach ended Louis XIV's hopes of an early end to the war. In the light of this great victory, the Queen awarded Marlborough the manor of Woodstock and promised that a great palace would be built for him. Sadly for Marlborough, the special relationship between the Queen and her erstwhile favourite, Marlborough's wife Sarah, began to cool. No longer the timid adolescent who was happy to be dominated by her forthright and beautiful friend, Anne became disenchanted with the arrogance and tactlessness of Sarah Churchill and the once warm relationship foundered as Sarah fell out of favour with the Queen.

The months following Blenheim proved frustrating for Marlborough as he faced a lack of cooperation from his Dutch ally and the French gained a number of successes on the battlefield. The Battle of Ramillies which ensued was probably Marlborough's most successful action. Marlborough adjusted his plans and marched into French territory where Louis XIV was anxious to engage Marlborough in battle to avenge Blenheim. For the loss of only 5,000 men, killed or wounded, he inflicted far greater casualties on the French who lost over three times Marlborough's casualties. Following this victory, a series of towns fell easily to Marlborough's advancing troops.

Through diplomacy, Marlborough managed to thwart attempts of France to draw King Charles XII of Sweden into the war but squabbling and dissent among his allies caused Marlborough to experience much anxiety. The French began to have successes in the war, in particular in driving Marlborough's very able co-commander, Prince Eugene of Savoy, from Toulon. Bruges and Ghent defected to the French.

Prince Eugene of Savoy was able to re-join Marlborough and Marlborough sought to regain the initiative against the French by leading a forced march to the river Scheldt which he crossed at Oudenaarde. Meanwhile, the French under Marshal Vendome and the Duke of Burgundy had crossed the river, further north with the intention of besieging the town. Marlborough moved to engage the French and, assisted by the fact that there was dissension between the two French commanders, won a decisive victory. This left the French completely demoralised. Strategic advantage was restored to the allies and Prince Eugene was left to besiege Lille which fell to him later in the year. The allied forces retook Bruges and Ghent, and soon, the French were completely expelled from the Low Countries.

Marlborough defeated the French Marshal, Villars, to take the town of Tournai and turned his attention to taking Mons. Desperate to prevent this, Villars was ordered save the city and he marched on the village of Malplaquet. Two days later, Marlborough engaged the French in battle. His two flanks, commanded respectively by the Prince of Orange and Prince Eugene, suffered disastrously in their assaults on the French but Villars had to weaken his centre to support his flanks enabling Marlborough to break through and secure victory. Although victorious, the allied losses were severe, much greater than those of the French whom they had defeated. Marlborough considered that this was the best French defence he had encountered during the war. On his return to England, Marlborough's political enemies used the dire casualty figures sustained in the Battle of Malplaquet to sully Marlborough's reputation.

Peace talks with France failed and although not directly involved in these talks, Marlborough was unfairly blamed for this failure by his detractors in England, claiming that Marlborough considered continuation of the war was in his interests.

Marlborough returned to England but found the political landscape unfavourable. The Tories had won the election and his wife Sarah had irrevocably fallen out with Queen Anne. His own health was beginning to fail but he returned to Europe to fight his final and one of his best campaigns. Marlborough and the French under Marshal Villars confronted each other in battle formation. The allies feared that through distractions he was facing at home, Marlborough would lead the army to experience casualties on a scale they had suffered at Malplaquet. However, Marlborough conducted an incredible military manoeuvre in which he organised a secret night march through what may have appeared impregnable enemy lines without losing a man, to besiege the fortress of Bouchain. Villars discovered himself completely outmanoeuvred and was unable to prevent the surrender of Bouchain. The success of this campaign has few equals in military history.

However, anxious to get a peace treaty signed and needing to remove any obstacle which would allow the war to continue, the government recalled Marlborough home and a charge of corruption was levelled against him. Anne dismissed Marlborough as head of the army and he was replaced by the Duke of Ormonde who returned to the continent with orders from the government forbidding him to commit British troops against the French. This order ruined Prince Eugene of Savoy's campaign in Flanders. The war was finally ended with the Treaty of Untrecht.

With problems mounting at home on many fronts, Marlborough returned to Europe where he was rapturously welcomed by the populace of the allied nations for the great and successful general he had been. He became reconciled with the Queen and returned home where he was restored to his former offices. He continued in favour when Anne was succeeded by George I who ushered in the House of Hanover. Although remote from the hostilities, Marlborough was able to direct the strategy which defeated the Jacobite rebellion from London.

Marlborough suffered a couple of paralytic strokes but made a fairly good recovery and he remained mentally sharp. He was able to move into the east wing of the partially completed Blenheim Palace with his wife, Sarah.

Marlborough's detractors would point out that Marlborough was ruthless in achieving his ambitions, and his success in gaining wealth gave him a reputation for avarice. However, the recognition of Marlborough as one of the best, if not the greatest commander in British military history, is shared by many historians and notably, by the Duke of Wellington. Marlborough had courage and common sense. He had the quick wits which enabled him to recognise his opponents' weaknesses and take advantage of battlefield situations. His tact enabled him to tolerate the capricious whims of politicians, both at home and among his European allies.

John Wesley

John Wesley

John Wesley was an Anglican cleric who led a great religious revival which, in turn, led to the foundation of the Methodist church.

John was one of nineteen children born in the family of Samuel Wesley, the Anglican rector of Epworth, and his wife, Susannah, who herself had come from a large family of twenty-five children. Only nine of John's brothers and sisters survived into adulthood. John had a traumatic experience when he was five years old. The rectory where the family was sleeping caught fire. John's parents were aroused by shouts of fire from outside and managed to shepherd all the children out of the house except for John who was stranded in an upstairs room looking out of the window. The whole house was threatening to be engulfed in flames and the burning roof about to collapse. He was rescued by two parishioners, one standing on the other's shoulders, and just able to lift John out. John later used a quote from the prophet Zechariah to describe himself as 'a brand snatched from the fire'.

Zechariah ch 3 v 2 *Is not this man a burning stick snatched from the fire?*

The Wesleys' family life was organised along very formal religious lines and great store was set by education. John's parents taught all their children to read and expected them to become proficient in Latin and Greek. They were also encouraged to learn by heart significant passages of the Bible. To ensure that they were up to date with their studies, Susannah examined each child before their midday meal and before they turned in for the night. When he was eleven, John was sent to the Charterhouse School in London where his education continued to embrace a firm religious tradition.

On leaving school. John went on to Oxford University. In due course, he became ordained and was unanimously elected a Fellow of Lincoln College. The main subjects in which he lectured were Greek, philosophy and the New Testament. On completing his master's degree, his father requested John to assist his ministry and John returned home where he became curate of the daughter church of his father's parish at Wroot.

John continued to follow an extremely devout and religious life, believing that this would lead to his salvation He denied himself many things so that he could be generous in his alms giving.

At the request of the Rector of Lincoln College, John returned to Oxford, a necessary condition for continuing his fellowship. His younger brother Charles had just matriculated at Oxford and like his older brother, he was intensely concerned with the importance of living a devout Christian life. He and like-minded friends had formed a society which was devoted to these objectives. John identified himself with this society. The members met regularly for worship and prayer, fasted on Wednesdays and Fridays and visited gaols to minister to the prisoners, in some cases, helping to pay off the debts of those who were in prison as debtors.

The spiritual state of Oxford University at that time was at a very low ebb, and the students began to ridicule the society, giving it the name, 'the Holy Club' which was meant as a term of derision. Wesley welcomed the fact that some at Oxford were derisive of his group as he felt this was a form of persecution which Christians should expect and hence, authenticated the group as being truly genuine in the way they practised their faith. An anonymous pamphlet described the group as 'the Oxford Methodists' but instead of taking this as the intended term of derision, Wesley turned the tables on his detractors by declaring that they had chosen to compliment the group by describing them with this title. Hence, the term 'Methodist' became established as a label for Wesley's movement.

After a period of fifteen years, Wesley was invited by James Oglethorpe, an enterprising American colonist, to take up a ministry at Savannah, a settlement he had established in Georgia. It was on the voyage out there that John and Charles came in contact with a group from the Moravian Church. John was particularly impressed with their piety and faith. On an occasion when they encountered a particularly fierce storm during which the mast broke and the ship appeared to be in danger of foundering, most of those on board showed signs of panic. However, the Moravians had calmly sung hymns and resorted to prayer. The deeply personal faith of the Moravian Christians affected John and was reflected in the way Methodism developed under his leadership.

The Wesley brothers' ministry in Savannah was not remarkable in comparison with their later achievements. However, while in America, Wesley published his first hymn book, 'A Collection of Psalms and Hymns'.

Although moderately successful among the European settlers, John and Charles failed to have any spiritual impact on the native American population. I feel that this was largely due to the fact that their ministry lacked the fire which later characterised their preaching. This change in the power of their ministries came about as a result of the influence of the members of the Moravian Church whom the Wesleys had met on their way to America. While impressed with the Wesleys devotion and piety, they feared that the Wesleys were attempting to earn their salvation by their lifestyle and good works, rather than by grace, that is, through the divine, unmerited favour of God. This fear was confirmed when Charles Wesley was taken very ill and it was feared that he might die. The Moravians visited Charles and during their conversation, asked him on what basis did he feel he had an assurance of going to heaven. He asserted that his confidence was based on the quality of the life he had led, an answer which left the Moravians very perturbed.

The Moravians discussed the spiritual state of the Wesleys.

"The Wesleys are living by the Pelagian heresy. Yes. they have clearly given their lives to Christ but without claiming the salvation He came to bring which offers the gift of eternal life."

"If a gift is not claimed, it is forfeit."

"The Wesleys are rather like two people living on the edge of the estate of a bountiful Lord. The houses on the edge of the estate are of poor quality and the available food is not good to eat, but this bountiful Lord has built new beautiful homes near his palace which he has invited any of those in the poor houses, to come and live in as a gift from himself. To any who move into these houses, he will supply good quality food, free of charge. Although there is no obligation to do so, for these come as free gifts, many who move into these houses choose to work for the Lord in gratitude for what he has done. The Wesleys are like two people who decide to work for the Lord without taking up the offer of the gift of a good house and high quality food, not realising that their current situation is not really satisfactory."

"Although they have been told that these houses come as a gift, it's as if they don't really believe this and think that by working for the Lord, they will in due course, have earned enough credit to be able to claim one of these houses. They

just don't realise that one of these houses is already available to them as a gift from the Lord."

"How can we enable the Wesleys to accept the free gift of salvation without destroying what is already good about their ministry?"

"We must earnestly pray for them!"

The Moravians are nothing if not great people of prayer. On one occasion when the world was going through a particularly troubled time, they organised a year long prayer meeting. During this, there were members of the Moravian church, praying at the church on a rota basis, 24/7, for a whole year. The improvement in the world situation over that year was attributed by the church to the power of this prayer vigil. Thus, John and Charles Wesley themselves became the focus of their Moravian friends prayers. The burden of the prayer was that the Wesleys would cease to rely on the idea that salvation is earned through good works and come to realise that salvation comes by the grace of God. Their prayers were dramatically answered.

The Wesley brothers returned to England, depressed by how limited had been the effect of their ministry in Savannah, in contrast to the dramatic response they had seen to the preaching of their Moravian friends. They thought a lot about their faith and received counselling from a Moravian minister, Peter Boehler, who was in England at that time, prior to his joining his fellow Moravians in America. John Wesley attended a meeting of the Moravians at their chapel in Aldersgate and during this meeting, as he listened to a reading of Luther's preface to St. Paul's letter to the church in Rome, John felt himself strangely moved. He realised how mistaken he had been in thinking that he needed to earn salvation by his own good works. God is no man's debtor. John came to a full realisation of something which had been missing from his ministry, that knowing that mankind could not achieve salvation by their own efforts, God had provided another way. He had come to earth in the person of Jesus, to illustrate to the world while in human form as Jesus, the wonderful nature of God and He had died on the cross to pay the price Himself for John's own shortcomings and sins. John described how his heart felt strangely warmed as he came to realise at that point that he did trust in Christ alone for salvation. He had a deep assurance that Christ alone had saved him from the consequences of his sins which would otherwise have led to his eternal spiritual death. From that time, John's preaching had the power and fire it had previously lacked.

John's brother, Charles, had a similar experience, and expressed this experience in a hymn which is very popular in churches today.

And can it be that I should gain
An interest in the Saviour's blood!
Died he for me who caused his pain!
For me who him to death pursued?
Amazing love! How can it be,
That Thou, my God, should'st die for me?

Long my imprisoned spirit lay,
Fast bound in sin and nature's night;
Thine eye diffused a quickening ray;
I woke, the dungeon flamed with light;
My chains fell off, my heart was free,
I rose, went forth, and followed Thee.

One might say that the Holy Spirit had entered into John's and Charles' very beings in a special way to produce this enlightening of attitude and associated empowerment.

Others have had similar experiences and perhaps it is worth noting some striking Biblical examples.

On the day of Pentecost, Jesus' disciples, huddled together in their secret room, fearful of discovery and arrest, experienced the Holy Spirit coming upon them in a spectacular way. They could immediately go out on to the streets and preach with power and conviction and win thousands of converts in a day.

Saul of Tarsus, like the Wesleys, was very concerned with earning his way into heaven. He believed that this could be achieved by obeying every scruple of the Jewish law. His experience on the Damascus Road was equivalent to John Wesley's experience in the Aldersgate chapel. The Holy Spirit was able to enter Saul and as St. Paul, he became the greatest missionary of all time, preaching a doctrine, not of good works, but unmerited divine grace. As St. Paul had to spend some time getting trained before he could launch himself into the ministry God had appointed for him, so John Wesley spent time learning from his Moravian mentors.

John Wesley went to the Moravian headquarters in Germany where he spent some time, observing their practices and learning from them. On his return to England, he continued to spend time with the Moravians, imbibing their ethos. He did not have his own church in which he could preach and found that he was not welcomed to preach at other churches in London because the ministers at these churches realised that Wesley's preaching had a power that they lacked. An Oxford friend of the Wesleys, George Whitfield, whose preaching was perhaps even more powerful than that of the Wesleys, had the same problem as John in not being welcomed to preach in London churches.

George Whitfield moved to Bristol where the city was in a state of some uproar as a result of the massive social changes which had come in the wake of the Industrial Revolution. The people were ready to receive the Christian teaching that George Whitfield brought them and he attracted enthusiastic crowds to hear him preach. Much of George's preaching was carried out in the open air and he invited John to do the same. This was contrary to what John had felt was the right and reverend way to preach God's word but he decided that he should follow George's example. Wesley was amazed by the response to his open air preaching. For fifty years, he continued this style of ministry, travelling on horseback all over the country. He preached in the churches that would receive him but for the most part, his oratory was conducted in fields, halls, cottages and chapels. Without any preconceived plan, he formed Methodist Societies in places where his ministry had been enthusiastically received.

As Wesley became increasingly successful, he began to experience persecution from established Anglican clergy and magistrates. Wesley flouted their man-made regulations regarding who was allowed to preach within parish boundaries. Local priests had regarded as these their exclusive domain. He was attacked by Anglican clergy in their sermons and in print and on occasions, they led mobs to physically attack Wesley and those who were receiving his ministry. However, Wesley remained undeterred and he and his followers continued to work among the poor and the needy.

Wesley sought out men who were not ordained into the Church of England as he himself was, but had the gift of preaching, to become lay preachers. He established chapels in places where Methodism had taken root. These Methodist congregations were not without problems as some of the members proved very disorderly. In chapels where this problem was being experienced, Wesley wrote and signed by his own hand, tickets which would allow admission into services of those who were deemed orderly and well behaved and these tickets were renewed every three months. Thus, the disorderly element dropped out of Methodism without creating further disturbance.

Wesley undertook to visit quarterly each of the new Methodist societies that had been created but as the growth of the movement continued, Wesley could not keep up with this pressure and so he drew up a set of rules for the United Methodist Societies which formed the basis of modern Methodism.

As numbers increased, it was necessary to establish a means to keep Methodism coherent and doctrinally sound. John set up a conference consisting of himself and Charles, four ordained ministers and four lay ministers. These conferences were regularly convened and 'the Conference' became the ruling body of Methodism.

A key feature of Wesley's faith was his insistence on the divine authority of the teaching contained in the Bible. Although he was well read, he described himself as 'a man of one book', so important was the centrality of Scripture to his faith.

A fundamental theological issue created a time when the relationship between Wesley and Whitfield became strained. Two basic facets of reformation Christianity were propounded by the theologians, John Calvin and Jacobus Arminius. Calvinism asserts that the people who become Christian have been foreordained to do so by God. Arminianism holds that God wishes everyone to become Christian, but the choice is left for the individual to make for himself. Becoming a Christian is a matter of the way one uses one's will to do so, rather than a matter of predestination. Whitfield embraced Calvinism while Wesley held to the teaching of Arminius. This caused a time of alienation between the two leading figures of Methodism but they quickly became reconciled. It is not known for certain which of them was first to use in print their phrase, 'agree to disagree'. When George Whitfield was later asked if he expected to see John Wesley in heaven, he replied,
"I fear not for he will be so close to the eternal throne and we will be at such a distance, that we will barely be able to get sight of him."

The apparently contradictory nature of Calvinism and Arminianism has long been debated. How can such contradictory views be reconciled? This is one of many Christian paradoxes. If Arminius was standing inside St. Paul's Cathedral, under the dome, and Calvin, flying in a helicopter above the dome, and they were comparing what they saw, Arminius would claim that the dome was concave while Calvin might insist the he saw the dome as a convex structure. They would both be right! In reality, many who have used their free will to make the conscious decision to become Christian, on coming to faith, have felt that this is what God had intended for them, all along.

An analogy which illustrates how human free will and God's predestination are not mutually exclusive is provided by the example of a grandmaster chess player playing against a player, more lowly ranked than himself. At the beginning of the match, the grandmaster asked his opponent,
 'on which square do you want your king to be when I deliver checkmate?'
The weaker player thought to himself that this was very arrogant and that even if he lost the match, he would make sure that his king was not on the specified

square. The weaker player pointed to a random square and the match began. It soon became apparent that not only was the grandmaster going to win but that the weaker player's king was being driven towards the square where the grandmaster had declared he would deliver checkmate. The weaker player did all that he could to avoid this, at times, purposely making bad moves if he thought that this would keep his king away from the fatal square. However, checkmate was ultimately delivered with the king on the specified square. The weaker player had complete freedom of choice within the rules of the game to move his pieces where he wished. However, ultimately, the grandmaster was in control and ended the match in the way he had predicted. So too with us in life. We have freedom of choice, but God is ultimately in control of our preordained destiny.

Wesley vehemently opposed slavery and was mentor to William Wilberforce, the politician who managed to get the slave trade abolished. A young African American was so impressed by Wesley's abolitionist message that he converted to Christianity and founded the African Methodist Episcopal Church which ran very much in the Methodist tradition.

Wesley encouraged women to become teachers of the faith and as he discovered women who potentially had the gift to preach, he allowed them, not just to teach, but to preach as well. In line with an ancient practice found in Scripture, Methodist women, including those who preach, are encouraged to wear a hat or some other suitable head covering when in church.

Wesley was a vegetarian and later in life, he abstained from drinking wine for health reasons. He strongly warned against alcohol abuse, telling some that although wine may sparkle in the cup, in reality, it is poison and I beg you to throw it away. Methodists became leaders in the 19th century teetotal and temperance movements, and abstention from drink has become a rule of life for modern Methodists.

John Wesley loved music and was particularly moved by a performance of Handel's Messiah which he heard while attending a performance at Bristol Cathedral.

Wesley favoured celibacy but in later life, he married Mary Vazeille, a well-to-do widow with four children. However, the marriage was not happy and Mary left John. She felt unable to compete with the demands on John's time and devotion which were imposed by the ever growing Methodist movement.

Wesley remained strong and energetic with good eyesight, right up to the age of eighty-six but noticed a serious deterioration in his health on reaching the age of eighty-seven. Wesley's achievements during his active life were immense. He travelled widely on horseback to supervise the ever growing Methodist movement. It is estimated the total distance he travelled was 250,000 miles. He preached three times a day, a total of about 40,000 sermons. He launched Methodist churches and commissioned many who would preach in them. He gave very special support to orphanages and schools. He died a poor man because he was so generous in his charitable giving. He gave away £30,000 which may not sound much in modern terms due to inflation but in reality, it would be the equivalent of many millions.

As Wesley lay dying at the age of eighty-seven, he was surrounded by his friends. He grasped their hands and said repeatedly,

"Farewell, farewell. The best of all is God is with us."

He was buried at his chapel on City Road, London.

Lancelot (Capability) Brown

Lancelot (Capability) Brown

Lancelot Brown was a very prominent landscape gardener. His parents were in service at Kirkharle Hall in Northumberland, his father, the land agent, and his mother, a chambermaid. He attended the local school until he was sixteen. On leaving school, he worked as head gardener's apprentice at Kirkharle Hall. On completing his apprenticeship, he moved south to Oxfordshire where he received his first landscaping commission to create a new lake in the park of Kiddington Hall. His nickname, 'Capability' derives, not from his being a very capable person which he undoubtedly was, but because he would inform would be clients that their property had the 'capability' of being improved.

Lancelot obtained a post with Lord Cobham to work at Stowe Gardens in Buckinghamshire. Here, his line manager was William Kent who was England's foremost landscape gardener at the time. He was soon appointed head gardener and undertook the ambitious creation of a grassland and woodland feature which is known as the Grecian Valley. Lord Cobham allowed Lancelot to undertake freelance work and he soon became well known by the landed gentry as a very capable landscape gardener. One of his early freelance projects was the landscaping of land on the banks of the Avon around Warwick Castle.

Lancelot was a fast worker, surveying areas which he was commissioned to landscape on horseback and rapidly developing a vision in his mind of what needed to be done. As his clientele increased, he was soon earning the equivalent in modern currency of one million pounds a year. As his reputation grew, he was appointed to a very prestigious post as King George III's master gardener at Hampton Court Palace.

Now, quite a wealthy man, Lancelot bought an estate for himself at Fenstanton in Huntingdonshire. As a prominent resident in this area, he was appointed High Sheriff of Cambridgeshire and Huntingdonshire but as he so often worked well away from home, he had to delegate many of the duties of this office to his son, Lancelot junior. It is estimated that he was responsible for landscaping more than one-hundred-and-seventy estates around the nation's great houses and the vistas he created remain to be enjoyed today. Among the better known of his landscapes are those around Blenheim Palace, Warwick Castle, Harewood House, Belvoir Castle, Highclere Castle, Appledurcombe House and Milton Abbey. He also planned the layout of Milton Abbas Village near Milton Abbey. Parts of Kew Gardens owe the way they are laid out to Lancelot Brown. In order that his clients shouldn't have to wait decades for any trees he might plant to mature, he was able to transplant fully grown trees into sites where he had planned woodland among his landscapes. He would arrange for huge hollows to be dugout which, being fed from small watercourses, would soon contribute to his landscape as large lakes. His creations were gardenless landscapes which swept away any formally laid gardens which may have existed before Lancelot's transformation had taken place.

Lancelot's estate planning was not restricted to creating scenic parkland. He was involved in smaller urban projects like landscaping the college gardens along 'the Backs' in Cambridge. He also designed smaller formal flower gardens in stately homes but taking care that these didn't interfere with the overall view of the major landscape he was creating. However, unlike his majestic parklands, these small, more formal gardens have been swept away with new developments which have since taken place over the years. Lancelot didn't restrict himself to horticulture but also involved himself in architecture. It was important to him that the stately home, around which his landscapes were laid out, should blend in with the finished product. He therefore designed architectural features into these properties which would give the finished product, house and landscape, an integrated appearance which would appeal to an artist, seeking a vision which he would enjoy putting to canvass. Lancelot's first project which involved remodelling a country house was at Croome Court in Worcestershire.

His style was to create undulating grassland, extending from the house and punctuated with tastefully located clumps of trees and interrupted by a picturesque lake. It is interesting that Lancelot should describe his landscape to others in grammatical terms. Explaining his design to a client, he said,

"I make a comma, and there" pointing to another spot, "where a more decided turn is proper, I make a colon; at another part, where an interruption is desirable to break the view, a parenthesis; now a full stop, and then I begin another subject".

The natural appearance of Lancelot's landscapes delighted his clients but he was not without detractors. One satirist wrote that he hoped to die before Brown so that he could see heaven before it was 'improved'.

In his diversion into making changes to the design of stately homes to fit in with his vision of the overall impact of the appearance of house and landscape, Lancelot was helped by the master builder, Henry Holland. His son, another Henry, was also involved in these projects and in time, became a great collaborator of Brown. In due course, Henry Holland junior became Lancelot's son-in-law when he married his eldest daughter, Bridget.

Two of Lancelot's sons went to Eton, the elder, Lancelot junior, becoming M.P. for Huntingdon and the younger, John, joining the Royal Navy and rising to the rank of admiral.

Lancelot continued to work and travel until he suddenly collapsed and died on the doorstep of Henry and Bridget's house in London after spending a night out at the home of Lord Coventry.

Lancelot has been commemorated by the issue of a stamps illustrating his landscapes. Also, the fountain at the centre of the cloister of Westminster Abbey was dedicated to Lancelot 'Capability' Brown.

General James Wolfe

General James Wolfe

James Wolfe was born in Westerham, Kent. His family had significant military and political connections. He was destined for a military career and entered his father's regiment when he was thirteen years old. He reached the rank of major by the age of eighteen and became a lieutenant colonel when he was twenty three.

As a young officer, he saw extensive service in the War of Austrian Succession in Europe and was involved in the suppression of the Jacobite rebellion at the battle of Culloden. He refused an order to kill a Highland officer, captured at the end of the battle.

Wolfe first saw action at the Battle of Dettingen. The British army was under the command of King George II. This was the last time a British army has been under the direct command of the King. The British army had moved eastwards against a very large French army. This manoeuvre was a mistake as it left the British army trapped against the River Main and surrounded by enemy forces. However, instead of capitulating, King George launched an attack against the French near the village of Dettingen. This was a fierce encounter with large casualties on both sides. Wolfe's horse was shot from under him. The French were driven through the village which was then occupied by the British. King George failed to mount an effective pursuit of the French but the victory secured the independence of Hanover. James Wolfe's gallantry during this battle had been observed by the King's brother, the Duke of Cumberland. Wolfe was left devastated when his brother, a fellow officer, died of consumption later that year.

Wolfe's regiment was left to garrison Ghent and he missed being involved in the Battle of Fontenoy which resulted in an allied defeat. When Wolfe's regiment was recalled from Ghent to reinforce the Duke of Cumberland's army, Ghent was attacked and taken over by the French. A major French objective was to capture Maastricht which would open up the way to taking over the whole of Holland. Cumberland's army engaged the French under Marshall Saxe at the Battle of Lauffield. This was a very large battle and Wolfe was badly wounded. The French secured a narrow victory but both sides remained battle ready. However, hostilities ceased following an armistice and the war ended with the Treaty of Aix-la-Chapelle.

Wolfe made good use of the next eight years of peace, keeping his mind active by studying Latin and Mathematics. He kept himself physically active by energetically improving his swordsmanship. He toured Ireland and visited France where he was entertained by a former colleague in arms, the Earl of Albemarle, who was British ambassador. As Britain's relationship with France deteriorated again, he was urgently recalled. What became known as the Seven Years War was declared and fighting between the British and the French erupted in North America.

Wolfe was promoted to colonel and his regiment was posted to Canterbury in anticipation of a French invasion into Kent. Wolfe thought this unlikely but he kept his men fully trained up. During this time, Wolfe suffered a deterioration in health and it was feared that he may have been suffering from consumption, the disease which had carried off his brother. However, Wolfe was still fit enough to be involved in active service.

It was realised that an offensive was needed against mainland France to relieve the pressure being experienced in northern Europe by Britain's German allies. Therefore, an amphibious raid was planned against the French seaport, Rochefort, on the Atlantic coast. During this expedition, Wolfe served under Sir John Mordaunt as Quartermaster General. Wolfe was sent ashore to scout enemy terrain and returned with the assertion that in his opinion, he could capture the town with five hundred men. Mordaunt refused to give Wolfe permission and the expedition returned without achieving anything. Mordaunt was court-marshalled for refusing to attack but acquitted. Wolfe however had learnt lessons in amphibious warfare and as one of the few officers who had acquitted themselves well during this affair, he came to the notice of William Pitt, the Elder. He decided to promote Wolfe over the heads of more senior officers to the rank of Brigadier General.

William Pitt decided that the French were much more vulnerable in North America than Europe and sent a force under Major General Amhurst to take Louisville in Nova Scotia at the mouth of the St. Lawrence River. Wolfe served under Amhurst as a Brigade General. Capture of Louisville was considered essential in order to realise the main objective of capturing Quebec. Wolfe distinguished himself well in this battle in the way he prepared for the assault and his aggressive advance on the city which soon capitulated. The onset of winter prevented the further incursion of the British forces into Canada that year and Wolfe returned home. His role in the capture of Louisburg brought Wolfe into the attention of, not just the Prime Minister, but the British public.

William Pitt decided to appoint Wolfe to lead the assault on Quebec and promoted him to the rank of Major General. The British tactics of attacking the French on several fronts with relatively small armies meant thar Wolfe had only a small force under his control. However, knowing that only a limited amount of time was available before the next winter would make hostilities impossible, he launched one of the most daring campaigns in British military history. The French general, the Marquis of Montcalm considered that one side of the city of Quebec was safe from attack because it was protected by a two hundred metre high cliff, the Heights of Abraham, which any attacking force would have to mount before attacking the city. He therefore organised his defence around the other sides of the city.

Wolfe made his way to Quebec with only four-thousand-four-hundred men in small boats. He had just two small cannons. Early in the morning, he led his troops up this cliff which the French had considered insurmountable, assembling them on the Plains of Abraham. The French defence here was very weak and the battle lasted only fifteen minutes. However, as Wolfe advanced with his army, following the retreating French troops, he was shot, being wounded in the arm, the shoulder and fatally, in the chest. As Wolfe's fainting form was supported by those around him, they declared to him,
"See how they run".
"Who runs?" he asked.
"The enemy, sir," they told him. "They're giving way everywhere."
"Then tell Colonel River to cut off their retreat from the bridge. God be
        praised, I die contented."
With that, General James Wolfe breathed his last.

The fall of Quebec enabled the rest of French speaking Canada to be taken the following year. Wolfe's body was returned to England and he was buried in the family vault at St. Alfege's Church in Greenwich, alongside his father who had died earlier that year.

What more can be said of James Wolfe? Although his health was not good, he was active and restless. One of his generals stated that in battle, Wolfe seemed to be everywhere. He earnt the respect of his soldiers by marching into battle, bearing the same arms as his infantry, a musket, cartridge case and bayonet. Few other officers did this.

Wolfe was a cultured man. Before the Battle of the Plains of Abraham, he recited Gray's Elegy to his officers. This contains the line,

'The paths of glory lead but to the grave.'

He declared to his officers that he would rather have written that poem than win a victory in the forthcoming battle.

At an earlier time in Wolfe's career, someone at court suggested that Brigadier Wolfe was mad. King George II retorted,

"Mad is he? Then I wish he would bite some of my other generals!"

Wolfe never married but was betrothed to Kathleen Lowther. He carried her portrait in a locket. Wolfe had a premonition of his death at the Battle of the Plains of Abraham and gave this locket to a lieutenant in his army to return to his fiancée. This command was dutifully obeyed.

Thomas Gainsborough

Thomas Gainsborough

Thomas Gainsborough was born in Sudbury, Suffolk. He was the youngest son of his father, a weaver, and his mother, the sister of a local clergyman. He spent his early days in a house in Sudbury which has now been renamed, Gainsborough House, and is now a museum dedicated to Thomas's life and work.

As a ten year old, Thomas displayed his talent for painting both portraits and landscapes. He moved from Sudbury into London to study art and became associated with the artist, William Hogarth, whose pictures were very much an unfavourable comment on the social climate of the time.

He married Margaret Butt, the illegitimate daughter of the Duke of Bedford. The Duke had conferred a modest annuity on his daughter and in the early days, the family had to rely very much on this as Thomas's paintings weren't selling well. Thomas and Margaret had two daughters, Molly and Peggy. The family moved to Ipswich where Thomas earned his living by painting portraits of the local merchants and squires, but these were by no means wealthy men and Thomas earned just about enough to get by.

Thomas and his family moved to Bath and this greatly benefitted his career as he received commissions to paint the portraits of some of the really wealthy gentry living there. He sent some of his work to the Society of Art (now the Royal Society of Art) to be exhibited in London. Thomas also submitted work to the Royal Academy to be displayed in their annual exhibition. His work was appreciated and he was invited to become a member of the Royal Academy. While the pictures on display enhanced Thomas's reputation, he didn't have an easy relationship with the Royal Academy and after a few years, he ceased to submit his paintings to be exhibited by the Academy.

As his reputation grew, Thomas faced increasing demand to paint portraits of the wealthy gentry and their wives. Although securing him a good income, Gainsborough was not entirely happy with the situation in which he found himself as the pressures on his time to meet the demands of his clients left Thomas no time to devote to his first love, landscape painting. Neither was he enamoured by his clients and wrote in very disparaging terms of them to a friend. He referred to them as 'damn gentlemen' and realised that they made dangerous enemies. He stated that they acted as if they were rewarding him with their company whereas Thomas considered that he was only enticed to share their company by the money they paid him He stated that

'the only thing about gentry worth looking at was their purse but that their hearts were in the wrong place so it was difficult to get sight of it!'

After a few years, Gainsborough was wealthy enough to move back to London and live in Schonberg House, a prestigious residence in Pall Mall. He studied new techniques to improve his art and experimented with a device known as a 'Showbox' which enabled him to compose landscapes he was trying to paint by backlighting them on to a ground glass screen. He again exhibited his portraits in the Royal Academy including those of celebrities like the Duke and Duchess of Cumberland. Thomas now fouind that he could combine two aspects of his work, portrait painting, by which he earned his income, and landscape painting, which he could work in as backdrops to his portraits. He was able to skillfully combine these in a way that the landscape reflected the mood of his sitter, such as melancholy. He displayed some of these pictures in exhibitions he put on in his own home, Schonberg House.

Among Gainsborough's sitters were Johann Christian Bach, son of the composer, Johann Sebastian Bach, King Geroge III and Queen Charlotte, and many other royal personages. On the death of the main painter of royalty, who had the strange sounding jobtitle of Principal Painter in Ordinary, the King awarded the post, not to Thomas Gainsborough, but to his rival, Joshua Reynolds. This was a strange choice as Gainsborough was, and remained, the King's favourite painter.

Thomas Gainsborough was the most successful painter in two spheres. He founded the eighteenth century landscape school with Richard Wilson and shared acclaim as the greatest British portrait painter with Joshua Reynolds,.

One can form a wonderful impression of what Thomas was like as a man from comments made by his contemporaries. The essayist, William Jackson, described him as one who was seen by his closest friends as a person who was sincere and honest and always alive to every feeling of honour and generosity. Henry Bate

Dudley, who was famous for the way he composed letters, said of letters written by Gainsborough, that they offered the world as much beauty and originality as did his paintings. The art historian, Michael Rosenthal, described Gainsborough as the most proficient and at the same time, the most experimental artist of his time. The famous artist, John Constable, said that looking at Gainsborough's paintings brought tears to his eyes and he didn't know where they came from. Thomas was noted for the speed at which he painted and he worked more from his observation of nature, both human and the natural world, than by the formal following of academic rules.

Gainsborough's paintings became popular from the mid nineteenth century. Their value rose rapidly when the Rothschild family started collecting them and one of his pictures sold for six-and-a-half-million pounds.

Thomas Gainsborough died of cancer at the age of sixty-one. He is buried in the churchyard of St. Anne's Church, Kew. Later, his wife and nephew, Gainsborough Dupont, his only known assistant, were interred with him.

Captain James Cook

Captain James Cook

Jams Cook was a navigator and explorer whose wide ranging journeys and explorations changed the detailed knowledge of the map of the world more than the explorations of any other person.

James' father was the foreman of a farm in Yorkshire. His employer was impressed with James' enquiring mind and paid for his schooling until he was twelve. In his early teens, James worked on his father's farm but for a time he had a brief apprenticeship at a general store near Whitby which brought him into contact with ships and the sea. At the age of eighteen, he was apprenticed to a well-known ship owner in Whitby. This work gave him considerable experience in all aspects of shipping and he assiduously studied mathematics and navigation. Much of his time at sea on collier barques was spent in the dangerous waters of the North Sea, giving him the confidence to sail the seas anywhere in the world. While James could have carved out a lucrative career for himself in commercial shipping, he volunteered to serve in the Royal Navy which promised a more adventurous life. His natural ability to command brought him the attention of his superiors and by the age of twenty-nine, he was in command of the HMS Pembroke.

This was a challenging time for the navy as Britain was involved in the Seven Years War against France. James saw action in the Bay of Biscay and was given command of a captured French warship. He was involved in the siege of Louisbourg, Ile Royale in Nova Scotia and the amphibious assault on Quebec, led by General Wolfe. James' charting of the course of the St. Lawrence River was a crucial contribution to the success of this engagement. In the winter months while not at sea, he mastered surveying and was able to map the coast of

Newfoundland. He observed an eclipse of the Sun and sent an important account of his observations to the Royal Society.

The Royal Society and the Admiralty worked together to organise three scientific expeditions to the Pacific Ocean. James Cook was appointed to be leader of these expeditions. His ship was the HMS Endeavour, a small but sturdy converted coal barque. A main objective of one of these voyages was to conduct the scientists on board to Tahiti where they might establish an observatory and observe the transit of Venus across the sun. It was also expected that he might locate Terra Australis which was conjectured to exist but which hadn't been actually discovered. His further objectives were to discover new lands which he was to map and, where appropriate, claim them for the British crown, especially if these might be suitable for establishing military bases.

During these expeditions, he discovered New Zealand and spent six months charting the whole of the coast of this country. He then crossed the Tasman Sea where he surveyed the south-east coast of Australia and navigated the Great Barrier Reef. He charted Tonga and Easter Island, discovered New Caledonia in the Pacific Ocean and discovered the South Sandwich Islands and South Georgia in the Atlantic Ocean. Although he sailed just beyond the Antarctic Circle, this was not sufficiently far south for him to discover Terra Australis (Antarctica). He failed to discover either a North-West or a North-East passage which would be suitable for sailing vessels to sail past the north of Canada. James Cook also mapped the coastlines of several European islands. Cook's voyages of discovery involved him circumnavigating the earth three times which included journeying both from east to west and west to east.

On his voyages, Captain Cook insisted on his sailors being fed a good diet and they escaped succumbing to scurvy. They remained healthy until stopping at Jakarta for provisions where many of the crew contracted dysentery and fever. Thirty of them died. He wrote a scientific paper on the diet he used for sailors on his ship to avoid scurvy for which he was awarded a prestigious medal by the Royal Society.

On a return visit to Tahiti, the natives stole one of Captain Cook's cutters. He didn't resort to the most tactful means of recovering this vessel but with a troop of sailors and marines, arrested their chief. His party was followed by a huge crowd of Polynesians, urged on by the chief's wife. When Cook's party turned to defend themselves against a hail of stones and rocks thrown by the islanders, they fired back, killing some of them. A serious skirmish broke out. Captain Cook and some marines and sailors were killed with just a few of the arresting party making it safely back to their ship, the HMS Resolution. A few days later, the ship fired cannons and muskets at a crowd of Hawaiians on the shore, killing thirty of them before sailing for home.

Apart from the hostilities experienced at Tahiti with its tragic conclusion, Captain James Cook could claim to have changed the map of the world by peaceful means more than anyone else in history.

Viscount Horatio Nelson

Viscount Horatio Nelson

Nelson came into prominence as a very able naval officer in the French Revolutionary and Napoleonic wars. His valour as a fighting man, always entering the thick of the fray, resulted in his sustaining very serious injuries fairly early in his career. He was blinded in one eye in one encounter. After sustaining an injury to his right arm in another, he had to have this amputated. He was subject to the brutal surgery without anaesthetic provided for injured sailors, regardless of their rank. During his career at sea, Nelson succumbed to many serious diseases including malaria, dysentery and possibly, yellow fever. Further, Nelson was prone to seasickness. Most of us would want to leave the navy after such experiences but not Nelson. He delighted in being in action and during periods of unemployment when at home on shore leave, he would be pushing the admiralty to provide him with a new command.

Nelson came from a moderately wealthy family. He was the sixth of eleven children. His father was a Norfolk vicar and Nelson was the nephew of Robert Walpole, the first man to fill the office of Prime Minister. He joined the navy at a young age and, through the influence of a relative who was a senior naval officer, he rose rapidly through the ranks. He gained experience through serving under several illustrious naval commanders before securing a command of his own. The skill and enterprise with which he conducted his ship brought Nelson to the attention of his seniors as a particularly able naval officer.

Nelson was sent to Madras where one of his early commands involved supporting the East India Company by escorting convoys transporting the goods which were essential to their trade. His first experience of battle when in command came when he had to drive off enemy shipping attacking a convoy which was transporting a considerable quantity of the Company's money to Bombay.

While serving in the Indian Ocean, Nelson contracted a serious bout of malaria. Nelson returned to England where he took his lieutenant's exams. On being commissioned lieutenant, he was sent to the Caribbean. While on that side of the Atlantic, the American War of Independence broke out. While Nelson, along with other British naval commanders, fought several successful actions at sea, the crucial battles were fought on land and Britain lost its American colonies as America gained its independence.

Nelson was appointed as Master and Commander of another battleship but before he could take commend, he fell seriously ill with dysentery and suspected yellow fever. Nelson was discharged and returned home to recover. Once he had almost completely recovered, Nelson agitated for the command of another ship and was given command of a Royal Navy frigate.

While in the Caribbean, Nelson had befriended many plantation owners and had absorbed their philosophy on slavery. He married Fanny, a wealthy slave owner and was therefore at variance with Wilberforce and the abolitionists whom he regarded as hypocrites. However, Nelson's behaviour towards situations of slavery which he encountered were enlightened and not in line with his declared political beliefs. Any West Indian slave who escaped to a Royal Navy ship, including Nelson's, was signed on as a member of the crew, received full pay and was discharged as a free man at the end of their service. He secured the release of 24 slaves being held in a Portuguese galley and supported the proposal that West Indian slaves should be released and replaced by paid Chinese workers. He rescued a black Haitian general and his servant from the French and recommended that he should be taken into service on a British ship until he could be discharged, knowing full well that this general's mission was to end slavery. The Nelson family had a black servant called Price whom Nelson publicly acknowledged to be as a good a man as ever lived.

When a peace was concluded between Britain and France, Nelson was for some time underemployed. He was on half pay as a reserve officer. In spite of petitioning senior naval officers of his acquaintance, there were too few ships in service in the peacetime navy for a command to be made available for Nelson. Nelson spent much of this time, trying to find employment for former members of his now redundant crews. However, when France annexed the Spanish Netherlands (Belgium) which was regarded as a neutral buffer state, war with France resumed. Nelson was recalled to duty and given command of the Agamemnon, a 64 gun battleship.

Nelson proceeded to be involved in a number of successful naval actions, the most notable being the Battle off Cape St. Vincent. Nelson played a prominent part in this victory although, when he saw the opportunity, he had disobeyed orders to achieve this success. He was involved in further successful action around Cadiz, engaging and capturing a number of hostile warships. However, Nelson was not always successful and did encounter reverses in fortune. The attack on Santa Cruz de Tenerife was a failure, and in this battle, Nelson was hit in the right arm by a musket ball. The injury was so severe that the arm had to be amputated and Nelson returned to England to recuperate.

Nelson was fearful that the fleet wouldn't want the services of a one-armed admiral. However, new danger was afoot as Napoleon was waging war on Britain's allies on the continent. Nelson was recalled to service and embarked on the Vanguard, the flagship of the fleet he was to command. Nelson's objective was to locate and destroy the French fleet. Nelson's fleet sailed to Toulon but taking advantage of bad weather which was causing some disarray among the British ships, Napoleon moved his ships to the eastern Mediterranean. Nelson pursued him to Egypt, expecting him to have made for Alexandria but Napoleon had anchored his fleet in Aboukir Bay which lay at a different part of the Nile estuary. When Nelson discovered the location of the French fleet, the ensuing naval battle had an element of surprise for the French. As their ships were moored fairly close to land, they expected to be attacked just from the sea side of their fleet. However, Nelson managed to sail some of his ships between the French fleet and the land. Nelson attacked the French fleet from both landward and seaward sides and although the French fleet outgunned the British, it was totally destroyed in the ensuing encounter which we know as the Battle of the Nile. Napoleon had to leave his army stranded in Egypt and managed to evade British ships as he crossed the Mediterranean, back to France. During this battle, Nelson had been struck on the forehead and a flap of skin fell over his good eye leaving Nelson to believe he was blinded. He was taken below decks to be seen by the surgeon who realised that not too much damage had been done. He replaced and bandaged the flap of skin and Nelson was able to return on deck to continue to supervise the battle.

On his return from the Nile, Nelson called in to Naples where he received a rapturous welcome from Ferdinand IV, King of Naples. Here, he was entertained by a British diplomat and special envoy to Naples, Sir William Hamilton and his wife Emma. Nelson became infatuated with Emma and the couple embarked on an extra-marital affair. I have always been puzzled by Sir William's apparent acquiescence to this relationship but it does seem that Sir William was in failing health. Meanwhile, in England, it was debated what honour should be bestowed on Nelson in view of his spectacular victory. Many considered he should have been created a viscount, but in the event, he received the title, Baron Nelson of the Nile.

King Ferdinand's wife, Maria Carolina, advocated an aggressive policy towards the French. A few years earlier, her sister, Marie Antoinette, had been beheaded during the French Revolution. The Neapolitans, helped by a naval blockade provided by Nelson, had initial success, retaking Rome from the French. However, with the arrival of reinforcements, the French retook Rome and attacked and entered Naples.

Nelson arranged for the evacuation of the royal family and the Hamiltons from Naples to the safety of Palermo and continued to blockade the city. Meanwhile, a popular counter revolutionary force under Cardinal Ruffo was able to come to the relief of Naples. However, to end the bloodshed and looting by the ill-disciplined Neapolitan forces, Ruffo agreed to end hostilities and arrange safe conduct for the French to return to France. Nelson was angry that this truce had been arranged without reference to himself, and contrary to the agreement which Ruffo had made with the French, had a large number of them executed before allowing the rest to return home.

For a time, Nelson was the senior naval officer in the Mediterranean while his otherwise senior, Admiral Lord Keith, was sent to carry out duties on the Atlantic. On Lord Keith's return to Mediterranean duties, Nelson, who was now living openly with Lady Hamilton, started to annoy Lord Keith through insubordination, on one occasion returning to Palermo without being given leave to do so but cited poor health for needing to do this. When the admiralty received a negative report from Lord Keith, Nelson was recalled to England, being told his health was more likely to improve in his home country than on the Mediterranean.

Nelson and the Hamiltons returned to England by land following a circuitous route which took in many major cities including Vienna and Prague. The party finally reached England, disembarking at Great Yarmouth where Nelson was accorded a hero's welcome and was awarded the freedom of the borough. On arrival in London, he attended court as a special guest and banquets were held in his honour.

It was at this time, Nelson's wife, Fanny, met Emma Hamilton. Unlike Sir William Hamilton, Fanny was not prepared to tolerate her husband's philandering and the couple became divorced.

The strategy being adopted by the British in the war against Napoleon was a blockade of ports controlled by the French. Several Baltic nations, the Russian, Prussians, Danish and Swedish, although opposed to Napoleon, objected to the British, operating in a way that interfered with their trade, and formed a neutral armed alliance to oppose this.

Nelson joined a fleet under Admiral Sir Hyde Parker to deal with this problem. The combined fleet sailed from Great Yarmouth for Copenhagen where Admiral Parker just intended to blockade the Baltic but Nelson persuaded him to allow him to launch a pre-emptive strike against the Danish fleet. Admiral Parker granted Nelson reinforcements to do this. He was to wait in reserve to engage the Swedish and Russian fleets, should they arrive to support the Danish. He arranged to signal Nelson to return to the main fleet, should the battle be perceived to be going badly for Nelson. Initially the battle did start to go badly for the British and Admiral Parker hoisted the prearranged signal. When Nelson's flag officer reported this to Nelson, Nelson told the officer he should have been watching for the Danish commodore hoisting a signal signifying his surrender. He then explained to his flag officer that as he only had one eye, he had a right to be blind sometimes. He raised his telescope to his blind eye and looked towards Admiral Parker's ship, reporting to his flag officer, 'I see no signal'. The battle continued and both fleets suffered severe damage. In the end, Nelson prevailed and he went ashore at Copenhagen to negotiate a truce which was accepted by the other nations of the armed neutrality. On his return to Britain, Nelson was rewarded by being elevated to the rank of viscount, an honour Nelson had long coveted.

In view of a fear that Napoleon was preparing a fleet for use in an invasion of Britain, Nelson's next commission was to patrol the English Channel. Apart from a failed attack on Boulogne, Nelson saw little action during this period. The Peace of Amiens was signed between Britain and France and with failing health, Nelson retired to England where he stayed with the Hamiltons. He regularly spoke in the House of Lords where he supported the government of Addington. During this time, Nelson and the Hamiltons toured around much of England and Wales, visiting many towns and sites of significant beauty or interest. During this tour, Nelson was feted as a great hero in every place he visited. Lady Hamilton purchased Merton Place, a country estate in Surrey, and Nelson lived there with the Hamiltons until William's death.

War broke out with the French again and Nelson was recalled into service. He was given the powerful battleship, the HMS Victory, to be his flagship and ordered to take command of the British ships in the Mediterranean, currently anchored at Malta. He was to blockade Toulon where the French fleet was anchored. The French fleet managed to elude Nelson and Nelson gave pursuit, believing they had sailed to the eastern Mediterranean. However, the French managed to pass through the Straits of Gibraltar into the Atlantic. They fought a battle with a British fleet off Cape Finisterre but only suffered minor losses and returned to Toulon. Nelson returned to England feeling disappointed that he had failed to bring the French fleet to battle but in England, he continued to receive a rapturous welcome from the crowds.

News came to London that the French and Spanish fleets had combined and were anchored near Cadiz. Nelson went to London to discuss with the war cabinet, the action which needed to be taken. While waiting to meet the cabinet, Nelson found himself in a waiting room in the company of Major General Sir Arthur Wellesley who was later to become the Duke of Wellington. He was waiting to be debriefed on his operations in India. Wellington's report of what is the only meeting known to have taken place between these two famous military commanders is interesting. Wellington described Nelson's account of what he had been doing as so vain, self-centred and boastful that Wellington initially felt quite disgusted. Nelson had no idea who he was talking to. Nelson left the room and when he was informed of Wellington's identity, he immediately returned and continued the conversation. This time, Wellington described the conversation as one of the most interesting and informative discussions he had ever had. The topics ranged over the war, the state of the colonies and the world situation.

Having reported to the war cabinet and hearing their instructions, Nelson returned to Merton to put his affairs in order and then made his way to Portsmouth. He was cheered by crowds as he made his way to the Victory and sailed to the Spanish coast where he took over command from Vice Admiral Collingwood. He met with the captains of the ships in his fleet to explain his plan of battle. The enemy were moored near Cape Trafalgar. He correctly expected the enemy to be lined up in typical battle formation and Nelson's plan was to adapt a tactic which had been successfully used by the British navy before. He would sail with two columns of ships, respectively under his and Collingwood's command, into the centre of the enemy line, breaking their fleet into two halves. After saying a prayer, the fleet sailed towards the enemy, the British having twenty seven ships to the thirty three ships in the combined French and Spanish fleets. Nelson had hoisted the well known signal,

'England expects every man will do his duty'.

The fleets soon became within firing range and as lead ship, Victory initially suffered considerable damage, men falling to cannon fire around Nelson and his captain, Hardy, as they walked on deck giving orders. Hardy advised Nelson to change into a less conspicuous uniform as he was wearing his military honours which made him an obvious target. Nelson refused, declaring that it was good for the morale of the men to have their admiral amongst them, dressed in a way which showed he was a successful naval commander. As the battle proceeded, Hardy was suddenly aware that Nelson was not by his side and turned to see Nelson, kneeling on the deck and then falling on to his side. He declared to Hardy that his back had been shot through and he had not long to live. The shot had come from a musket fired from a range of about fifty feet, fired by a French marksman mounted on the mast of an enemy ship. He was carried below decks where he was made as comfortable as possible. He was kept informed of the progress of the battle and left instructions about the ordering of his affairs when the fleet returned home, making special mention that Emma Hamilton should be given good care. On being given news that the battle was good as won, Nelson prayed 'thank God I have done my duty'. He said to his captain, 'Kiss me Hardy'. His last words were 'God and my Country'. and then he died at the age of forty seven, three hours after he had been struck by the musket bullet.

Nelson's body was preserved in a cask of brandy mixed with camphor and myrrh and the seriously damaged Victory was towed back to England. His body was laid in state in the painted hall of Greenwich Hospital and the crush of people queueing to pay their respects almost overwhelmed the officials who were supervising the event.

On hearing the news of the victory at Trafalgar and of Nelson's death, King George III declared in tears,

'We have lost more than we have gained. The country's splendid and decisive victory has been dearly purchased'.

Nelson's funeral was conducted at St. Paul's Cathedral and his remains were mounted in a sarcophagus, which had originally been carved for Cardinal Wolsey but never used, and lowered into the Cathedral crypt.

Nelson's success as a leader, partly lay in his ability to be aware of the needs of his men so that his relationship with them was based more on love than authority. He was confident in his own ability and was able to make good decisions in battle as he was shrewd in assessing his enemy's weaknesses.

 On the debit side, Nelson was a vain person, desiring to be noticed by both his superiors and the public and was easily flattered. He was subject to insecurities and experienced violent mood swings.

In 1966, a memorial to Nelson in Dublin was blown up by Irish republicans, declaring that Dublin was no place to commemorate a one-eyed English adulterer.

Arthur Wellesley
Duke of Wellington

Arthur Wellesley, Duke of Wellington

In common with Simon de Montfort, another individual who has been included in our survey of English heroes but who was not originally English, technically, neither was Arthur Wellesley. Simon de Montfort was born in France and Wellesley, in Dublin, Ireland. He was the fifth son of the Earl of Mornington and came to England at a young age. He spent part of his education at Eton College, being one of that school's many alumni who in due course, became Prime Minister. He wasn't specially well suited for life at Eton and was sent to a military academy in France. His widowed mother described him in disparaging words as,

'*food for powder and nothing more*'.

At the age of eighteen, he was commissioned in the army but became addicted to gambling and fell into debt. Thus, he was rejected when he proposed to Catherine Pakenham. He managed to quit his gambling and concentrate on his army career. He purchased the commission of lieutenant colonel and saw service in Flanders. This was a useful time for him as he was able to learn from his commanders, but more from their blunders than their successes. On completion of this tour of duty, he sought civilian employment but was unsuccessful. He therefore remained in the army and was posted to India. He won battles against the forces of Indian maharajahs and was able to negotiate a successful peace. In India, he demonstrated admirable qualities required of a military commander, good decision making, common sense, attention to detail and ensuring the security of supply lines. He demonstrated care for the wellbeing of his soldiers and maintained good relationships with the civilian population. Napoleon showed how out of touch he was with Wellesley's qualities when he wrote him off as a 'Sepoy General'. However, his ability was recognised in England and on his return from India, he was awarded a knighthood.

Sir Arthur Wellesley had a very strong sense of duty. He married Catherine who had been an earlier sweetheart of his but she did not prove to be specially successful as a wife or a society hostess. Sir Arthur entered parliament when he saw there was a need to protect the reputation of his brother, Richard, from the attacks of influential detractors. Richard had been viceroy of India. The government sent Sir Arthur to Ireland to be their chief secretary for Irish affairs. His next assignment was in Europe where he defeated a small Danish army and was then sent to Portugal to support them in their revolt against Napoleon. Sir Arthur won a victory against Napoleon's forces by defeating the French General Junot at Vimeiro. Sir Arthur had planned to pursue the French army but was prevented from doing so by senior officers who arrived in Portugal from England. Instead, they signed a treaty which enabled Junot to repatriate, a move which was unpopular in Britain. This led to the senior officers, including Wellesley, facing a court martial but Wellesley was acquitted.

Wellesley persuaded the government to let him return to the Iberian peninsula, warning them that Portugal was still in danger of being overrun by the French. His arrival in Lisbon caught the French marshal on the ground, Soult, by surprise and he was able to capture Oporto and drive the French back into Spain. Wellesley had the foresight to see the need for a defensive line across the Lisbon peninsula and he secretly constructed the impregnable Lines of Torres Vedras. A French army seeking to reinvade Portugal was again caught out by surprise when they encountered these lines and retreated back into Spain. I think that Wellesley had hoped that the French might have attempted to storm these defences and suffered severe casualties in a failed attempt to breach the line.

Although his combined Anglo-Spanish army was smaller than the French armies occupying Spain, Wellington entered Spain to conduct a campaign known as the Peninsula War. Although suffering some reverses, he was largely successful in his battles against larger French armies. Had all the French armies in Spain come together, they would have so outnumbered Wellesley's forces that they would have conclusively beaten him. However, in such circumstances, Wellesley would not have given battle and in any case, the French were unable to combine their forces. Although allies of France at the time of the battle of Trafalgar, the French had succeeded in alienating the Spanish. The Spanish were outraged when Napoleon deposed their king and put his own brother, Joseph, on the Spanish throne and the French did not buy their food from the Spanish but just took whatever they wanted from the grudging Spanish. Thus, they had great difficulty in keeping their individual armies fed and they just could not have acquired enough food to supply their combined armies if located in just one place. Wellesley on the other hand insisted that the British government should provide him with the funds to purchase anything he needed from the Spanish who were only too pleased to support him.

Wellesley's success in winning battles against the French and successively driving them out of their strongholds led to his being awarded a peerage, initially as a Viscount but this was followed by promotion through the various ranks of peerage until he was finally created the Duke of Wellington. There were a couple of occasions when Wellington had found his progress hampered by his troops being uncharacteristically ill disciplined. They sacked property and resorted to plunder after capturing cities and enemy equipment when they should have been available to continue their army's advance. This led Wellington on one occasion to describe his troops as the scum of the earth. However, he ultimately drove the French from Spain, crossed the Pyrenees and entered Toulouse four days after Napoleon had abdicated. The length of the lines of communication between Napoleon, who was primarily occupied by his campaign in eastern Europe, and Spain prevented his being able to significantly influence the conduct of his armies in Spain. They were involved in what Napoleon regarded as no more than a sideshow.

With the abdication of Napoleon, the French monarchy was restored under the Bourbon king, Louis XVIII, and Wellington was appointed ambassador to his court. He represented the Foreign Secretary at the Congress of Vienna, convened to settle European affairs after the Napoleonic wars but this congress was short lived as Napoleon escaped from Elba, where he had been exiled, to raise another army with the objective of reasserting his domination of Europe.

He marched north to confront the British army under Wellington. To start with, the battle was fairly evenly fought. At a point, later in the battle, Napoleon had to leave the field for a time, due to his health which was now beginning to fail, leaving Marshal Ney in charge of the French army. Wellington commanded some of his infantry regiments to retreat over a hill to a position on the other side, out of sight of the French. Here they reformed their defensive squares. Marshal Ney, believing he was observing a wholesale retreat of the British army, ordered his cavalry to charge after them, only for them to be mown down by fire from the British squares as they reached the other side of the hill. This was a decisive tactic in the battle but it was not yet quite won. The victory came when the British army was joined by the Prussian army under Blucher who had made a forced march to follow the sound of the gunfire. While Wellington may have underplayed the importance of the Prussians in finally securing victory, there is no doubt that he deserves the credit for defeating Napoleon. However, nations are very nationalistic in the way they write up history and German history books credit Blucher with the victory at Waterloo.

Weeping for the vast number of men on both sides who had fallen in the battle, Wellington declared,

Wellington's wish was granted. Wellington became Commander in Chief of occupied France. He opposed the imposition of punitive reparations on the French people and organised loans which enabled French finances to be restored to a sound footing. His wise moves earned the gratitude of the delegates of the congress which was reconvened to settle European affairs after Napoleon had finally been removed. He returned to England, having been awarded the most senior military rank in the armies of six European nations. The British rewarded Wellington with a gift of half a million pounds and a stately home at Stratfield Saye in Hampshire. His London home, Apsley House, used to have the unique address, No.1, London. This is now owned by English Heritage who have set up a Wellington Museum there but his family retain an apartment at this house. King Ferdinand of Spain granted the Duke a large estate near Granada which the family still own.

Wellington joined the cabinet of the Earl of Liverpool as Master General of Ordinance but exempted himself from being a party politician who would automatically oppose any legislation of the Whig government which subsequently came into power. When the Tories were returned to power under Canning, Wellington found it difficult to work under Canning who worked as a subtle political mover and was specially disappointed when Canning extricated Britain from its European commitments. Wellington's attempts to establish cooperation and unity among his erstwhile European allies would now fail and Wellington reproached himself for not having been able to achieve this cooperation when a delegate at the Congress of Vienna. However, Wellington was respected abroad as being a particularly honest man.

Wellington turned his attention to the Irish problem, recognising that violence in Ireland would only end if Catholic emancipation was established, allowing Catholics to sit in parliament, representing Irish constituencies. However, Canning mismanaged Catholic emancipation leading to a mass exodus from the government of Wellington and other cabinet ministers.

When Canning died, Viscount Goderich became prime minister but he relinquished the post after five months and the King summoned Wellington to form a government. On becoming Prime Minister, Wellington sought to reunite the Tory party, forming a cabinet which excluded the ultra right wing members of the party. He succeeded in establishing a number of important reforms including Catholic Emancipation. This move had a melodramatic twist as it resulted in a duel being fought between Wellington and an ultra Tory, the Earl of Winchelsea.

In 1848, revolutions took place in almost every country in Europe. These coincidences were probably coordinated. But for Wellington's wise handling of the Chartist movement, there could well have been revolution in this country too.

Wellington failed to see the importance of Parliamentary reform which would result in pocket boroughs with small populations no longer being able to have representation in parliament at the expense of emerging major cities like Birmingham. His government was defeated by a combination of reformers and vengeful ultra Tories and Wellington resigned his premiership.

A difficulty faced by the next government in getting the Reform Act passed lay in the intransigence of the House of Lords who would resolutely oppose this bill. The only solution would be for the king to appoint enough Whig peers to get the legislation through. Recognising the future danger that this would represent for the future makeup of the House of Lords, Wellington persuaded his fellow Tory peers to leave the chamber and abstain from voting on this bill. Thus, the Reform Act became law, resulting in a more democratic makeup of the House of Commons. While Wellington led the Tory peers, he continued to lead then away from fatal clashes with the House of Commons.

When the Whig government was dismissed by Willian IV, Wellington was again invited to become Prime Minister, but the sixty-five year old duke refused, insisting that Robert Peel should become Prime Minister. This demonstrates a realistic reticence which is rare in politicians. Wellington served as Foreign Secretary in Peel's government.

Wellington died of a stroke while in Walmer Castle, his residence as Lord Warden of the Cinque Ports. Other characteristics of this remarkable man, which are overshadowed by his considerable military and political achievements, were his great love of children, his somewhat eccentric dress sense and his mastery of repartee. To a blackmailer, he retorted, 'publish and be damned' and of those who were prone to flatter him, he stated, 'I am but a man'. The posthumous description of him as 'the Iron Duke' is unmerited as Wellington was neither cold nor hard-hearted.

While Wellington is chiefly remembered for his military genius, it shouldn't be forgotten that he also was that rare person, a completely honest and incorrupt politician.

Elizabeth Fry

Elizabth Fry

Elizabeth was born into a wealthy banking family and married a banker. Her mother was related to the founder of Barclay's Bank and her husband had connections to the chocolate manufacturer, W.S.Fry. Like her contemporary, the Earl of Shaftesbury, Elizabeth had the attitude we would describe as 'noblesse oblige'. Being aware of her privileged status as a member of a very wealthy family, she considered that she had a duty to use this privilege to serve those less fortunate than herself.

Elizabeth was a Quaker and was considerably influenced by some of the preachers at her church. At the suggestion of a friend, she visited Newgate Prison and immediately saw that the conditions of the prisoners, especially the women inmates, were so atrocious that this was an area in which she could focus her reforming zeal. She returned the following day with food and clothing for those prisoners whom she deemed to be in special need.

Newgate prison was badly overcrowded. Men and women were not segregated. Some of the women were incarcerated with their children in small cells where they did their own washing and cooking and they had to sleep on straw. Not all the prisoners had even been put on trial. For many. Newgate Prison was the last stopping place before being deported to Australia in ships where the conditions were deplorable.

Elizabeth found that she couldn't immediately involve herself in working for prison reform as her husband had lost a lot of money in bad investments and the family were on the verge on insolvency. However, with the help of her brother, Elizabeth's family became restored to prosperity, releasing Elizabeth to embark on getting necessary reforms carried out in prisons.

She founded the Association for the Reformation of the Female Prisoners in Newgate. This association provided materials which could be used in prison to train the female prisoners in skills, particularly in forms of needlework, which would enable them to earn a living on their release, While the work of this association was initially focused on Newgate Prison, it led to the creation of the British Ladies' Society for Promoting the Reformation of Female Prisoners whose scope covered the whole nation. She raised funds which enabled the establishment of a prison school for any children who had been incarcerated with their mothers. Elizabeth worked to change the ethos of prisons, from being run under a regime of harsh punishment for offenders, to a recognition that prisons had a responsibility to work towards the rehabilitation of those who were their responsibility while in prison.

Elizabeth became the first woman to be called upon to give evidence to select committees of the Houses of Parliament. Her representation led to the passing of the Gaols Act. This act led to male and female prisoners being housed in separate accommodation but was otherwise ineffective as no provisions were made to ensure its requirements were adhered to. Elizabeth was able to draw the attention of a select committee of the House of Lords to this problem. She pointed out that far from being rehabilitation establishments, prisons were just schools for crime. Elizabeth's representations led to the Prisons Act which brought all prisons under central control and prisons became subject to inspection.

It was not uncommon for death sentences to be pronounced for relatively trivial crimes. Elizabeth fought to get such sentences commuted to transportation but she detested the process of transportation and only advocated this as the lesser of two evils. Women being transported were ferried through London to the docks in open carts where they were subject to abuse and insults from passers-by. Conditions on the transportation ships were little better than those which existed in slave ships. Knowing what lay ahead, women prisoners destined for transportation used to riot on the day before this sentence was to be carried out.

Elizabeth persuaded the prison governor to arrange for prisoners to be transported in closed carriages and she and other members of the British Ladies' Society for Promoting the Reformation of Female Prisoners would accompany these unfortunate women on this journey from prison to the docks. Elizabeth didn't leave these women as soon as they reached the docks but went on board to persuade the captain of the transportation ship to ensure that the women, who in many cases were accompanied by children, should get an adequate share of food and water on the long journey. She and other members of the Ladies' Society provided the women with the materials and sewing tools which would enable them to make things on this journey which they could sell to raise money on reaching their destination. Elizabeth not only fought to improve the conditions on the transportation ships but lobbied to get improvements made in the conditions which existed in the Australian factories where many of these women would end up working, She visited over one hundred prison ships and saw some twelve thousand convicts. Her activity in this direction saw the establishment of a movement to end transportation but transportation was not ended until twenty years after her death. Elizabeth was still visiting transportation ships until two years before she died.

Elizabeth's work came to the attention of royalty. Queen Victoria was a great admirer of Elizabeth Fry and granted her several audiences. When she came to the throne, she contributed generously to her work. During a state visit to Britain, King Frederick William IV of Prussia became highly impressed with her work when he accompanied Elizabeth on a visit to Newgate Prison. Having met the reforming Czar, Alexander I, on his visit to London, she was invited by him to visit Russia to see what improvements could be made in Russian prisons. She was also invited to France to do similar work and was able to overcome the language barrier which existed as she visited French prisons.

Robert Peel, the Prime Minister who established the London police force, was also very impressed with Elizabeth. He promoted a number of Acts in Parliament which furthered the causes for which Elizabeth was working.

After seeing the body of a young boy who had died from hypothermia after spending the night in the open in London, Elizabeth established a night shelter in London for the homeless and opened a soup kitchen.

On a visit to Brighton, she discovered the plight of many poor families living in that town and established the Brighton District Visiting Society whose members visited those living in impoverished conditions to provide what support they could. This society was successful in its work and soon became duplicated in other towns and cities in the country.

Elizabeth opened a school for nurses in Guy's Hospital which came to the attention of Florence Nightingale. Impressed with the quality of nurses who graduated from this school, she took a team of them with her to work in the hospital at Scutari, which had been established to treat the soldiers wounded in the Crimean War.

Elizabeth died of a stroke in Ramsgate and she was buried in the Friends' Burial Ground in Barking. Out of respect for Elizabeth, the Ramsgate Coastguard flew their flag at half-mast, a tribute normally reserved for royalty. Over a thousand people stood in silence by this flag at the time Elizabeth's burial took place in

Barking. Elizabeth has been commemorated by her picture appearing on the reverse of a £5 note where she is depicted, reading to prisoners in Newgate Prison..

Michael Faraday

Michael Faraday

Michael Faraday is so different from many of the other individuals who have been included in this pageant of British heroes. Many of them have been very able military commanders but who owed their success to the preparedness of those they led to sacrifice their lives in the service of the country for whom they were fighting. By contrast, Michael Faraday was very much a man of peace. He is a pre-eminent example of a poor boy made good. His family were far from well off and moved to London from Westmorland, where his father had been an apprentice to the village blacksmith, in the hope of being able to take advantage of the better employment prospects in the capital. Michael's parents were profound Christians and Michael, the third of four children, espoused this faith throughout his life. This faith was the source of some of the key decisions he made in the ordering of his life and affairs.

Faraday married Sarah Barnard, a girl he met at his church where Faraday served as a deacon and later, an elder. Faraday had a strong sense of the unity of God and nature which was apparent in the way he conducted his research.

The formal education Michael received was limited but he was well able to educate himself. Had he had training in trigonometry, he would have taken the theoretical aspect of his researches to greater depth but this was left to James Clerk Maxwell who was able to build on Faraday's research and formulate the laws of electromagnetic phenomena. James Clerk Maxwell acknowledged that although not having the tool of trigonometry at his disposal, the way Faraday was able to represent the way electromagnetic phenomena manifested themselves in empty space, was itself evidence of a fine mathematical mind.

Michael was the ultimate experimental scientist. He made remarkable discoveries in both physics and chemistry, establishing the concepts of electric and magnetic fields and explaining the phenomenon of electromagnetic induction. He discovered the laws of electrolysis, isolated benzene, a basic substance in the development of organic chemistry and invented a laboratory heating tool which was later developed to become what we know as the Bunsen burner. He established the terms, anode, cathode, electrode and ion as the vocabulary of those working in the fields of batteries, electronics and electrolysis. His invention of the electric generator and its close relative, the electric motor, revolutionised life as we now know it. The electric generator enabled the vast quantities of electricity, which we take for granted in our homes, hospitals, industry and transport, to be produced and propagated. The generator is effectively a coil which, when rotated in a magnetic field, can produce alternating or direct current electricity.

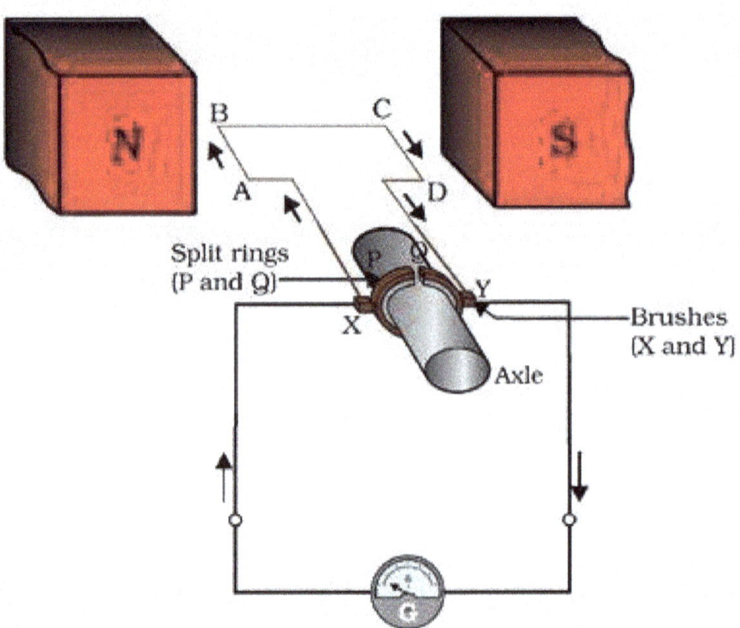

The electric motor is essentially the same thing, a coil in a magnetic field which rotates when an alternating current is passed through it. Where would the world be today without these devices? Faraday's persistence as a scientist is remarkable in view of the fact that many simple components which we take for granted as readily available off the shelf like copper wire, electric terminals, simple batteries, devices to measure current and voltage, had to be made from scratch by Faraday.

The career route by which Faraday was able to become an experimental scientist is interesting. He started work as an apprentice in a firm of bookbinders. Faraday was an avid reader and this job gave him access to the reading material which he used to self-educate himself. He established friendships with members of the City Philosophical Society with whom he held discussions and attended lectures. The principal scientist of the day was Sir Humphrey Davey who had discovered sodium and potassium and invented the miners' safety lamp which gave miners an early warning, should the methane level in a mine start to reach a dangerous level. Faraday attended a series of lectures by Sir Humphrey and neatly wrote up these lectures, binding the notes into a three hundred page book which he presented to Sir Humphrey. Duly impressed, Humphrey Davey took on Faraday as a laboratory assistant at his base, the Royal Institution.

Evidence of the danger faced in those days by pioneer researchers into chemistry is provided by a couple of accidents which Davey and Faraday experienced at the Royal Institution. Davy had damaged his eyesight as a result of an accident with nitrogen trichloride. Faraday was entrusted with preparing samples of this very unstable substance and both Faraday and Davey were injured when one of these samples exploded!

The results of Faraday's research were widely publicised and he was elected, not only to the Royal Society in this country, but to similar philosophical societies abroad, notably in the United States, France and the Netherlands. Oxford University awarded Faraday an honorary doctor's degree. However, seeking honours and rewards was contrary to Faraday's religious principles. He twice refused to become President of the Royal Society and turned down a knighthood which was offered in recognition of his services to science. He preferred to remain as just Mr. Faraday. Prince Albert arranged for him to be given a grace and favour residence near Hampton Court. The government sought Faraday's advice on producing weapons for use in the Crimean War but Faraday refused to be involved with this on ethical grounds.

When assistant to Humphrey Davey, Faraday discovered some new chemical compounds, conducted the first experiments on the diffusion of gases, succeeded in liquefying a number of gases and investigated the alloys of steel. He produced several new types of optical glass, one of which was able to rotate the plane of polarisation of light when placed in a magnetic field. He also discovered diamagnetism. He was the first scientist to report on metallic nanoparticles and can thus be considered as the pioneer of nanoscience.

Faraday is best known for his work on electricity and magnetism. Faraday's boss, Sir Humphrey Davey and another member of the Royal Society, William Wollaston, tried to construct an electric motor. They discussed the project with

Michael Faraday who went on to successfully construct two forms of electric motor. In so doing, Faraday established the foundation of modern electromagnetic technology. In his excitement, Faraday immediately published his results but without acknowledging the contribution of the earlier work by Davey and Wollaston. This led to a serious falling out and Faraday was assigned to other fields of research. Could this have partly been chagrin on Sir Humphrey's part at being eclipsed as the great scientist he was by his junior assistant? Michael did suffer a brief nervous breakdown but it is not clear whether this falling out was its cause.

Changing the field of his work delayed the big results which would stem from Faraday's research for several years but after the death of Davey, Faraday discovered the secrets of electromagnetic induction and was able to build the first electric generator and constructed the device we now know as the transformer. He went on to invent the electric dynamo from which have been developed modern power generators and motors. Contrary to the scientific opinion of his day, Faraday realised that although electricity could be generated in a number of ways, there was only one type of electricity.

Subsequent development and understanding of electricity and magnetism was considerably helped by the way Faraday was able to represent the regions around electric currents and magnets where their effect could be experienced. We call these regions electric and magnetic fields. Faraday realised that although it cannot be seen or felt, space was a definite entity with physical properties. How does one magnet or electric charge recognise the vicinity of another magnet or electric charge, which they will either attract or repel, unless something is happening in the space between them? Space is elastic, behaving in some ways like a huge lump of rubber which if distorted, attempts to resume its original form. For example, gravity can be seen to come into operation if space is recognised to resemble a huge stretched elastic sheet. If a heavy weight is placed on that sheet, it will sag, producing a hollow around the weight. If another weight is placed nearby, it will slide into the hollow created by the original weight. This is gravitational attraction. Faraday realised that electric charges and current distorted space in a different way, creating invisible tubes, known as tubes of force or flux, around the current or charge. These constitute what is known as an electric or magnetic field. A magnet placed in the field created by an electric current will align itself with the magnetic tubes of force in its vicinity and an isolated particle bearing an electric charge (e.g. an electron) will move along the electric tubes of force which stretch between two oppositely charged bodies. In such a field, positive charges will move from positively to negatively charged bodies and negative charges will move in the opposite direction along these tubes of force. By convention, the tubes direction is defined as the direction a positive charge will travel. The strength of the field may be represented by the closeness with which the tubes of force are packed and this is referred to as flux density. Tubes of force, although invisible, behave as if they are repelling each other and at the same time, trying to become shorter like a piece of stretched elastic.

If a piece of wire which is part of a complete circuit of wire, is moved through a magnetic field, such as would exist between the poles of a horseshoe magnet, a current is induced in the wire. If a piece of wire is held in such a magnetic field and a current is passed through it, it will experience a force which will endeavour to move the wire at right angles to the field. The directions of motion in each case can be determined by what are known as the left and right hand rules. The English language and traffic convention help us to remember them. It is possible to hold the thumb and first two fingers so that the three digits are mutually at right angles to each other.

If the **First** finger of the left hand is held in the direction of the **F**ield and
     the se**C**ond finger held in the direction of the **C**urrent,
      the thu**M**b will point in the direction the current carrying wire will
        Move.

This is the motor effect.

If the **First** finger of the right hand is placed in the direction of the **F**ield and
     the thu**M**b is pointed in the direction of a wire is constrained to **M**ove
      across the field,
     the se**C**ond finger will point in the direction the **C**urrent, is induced
      to flow.

This is the generator effect.

But how do we remember which hand to use when applying these rules? In this country, cars (**motors**) drive in the left.

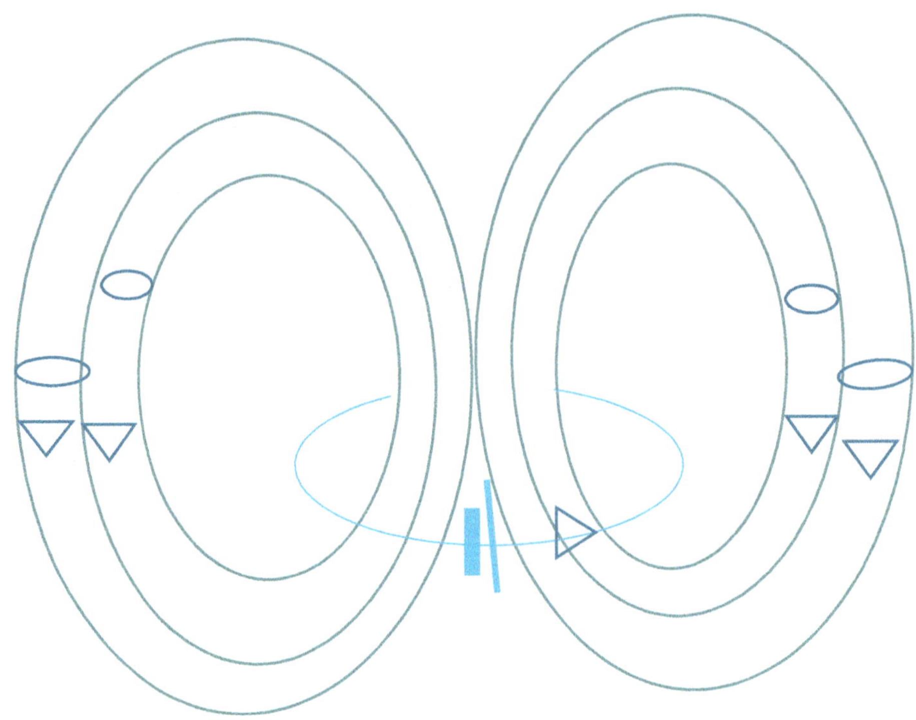

Magnetic tubes of force (magnetic flux)
generated by a current flowing in a loop.

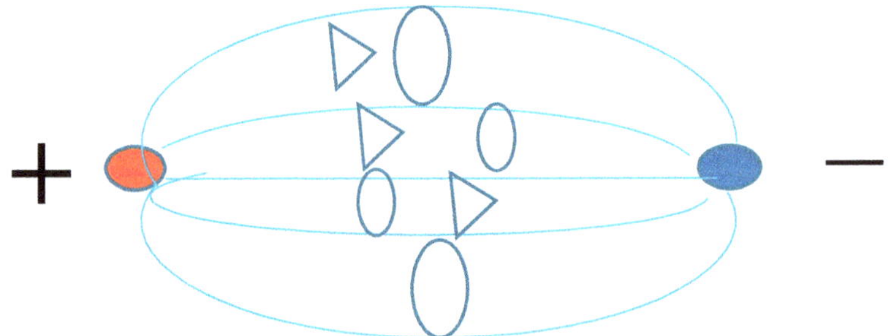

Electric tubes of force (electric flux) created
between two oppositely charged bodies.

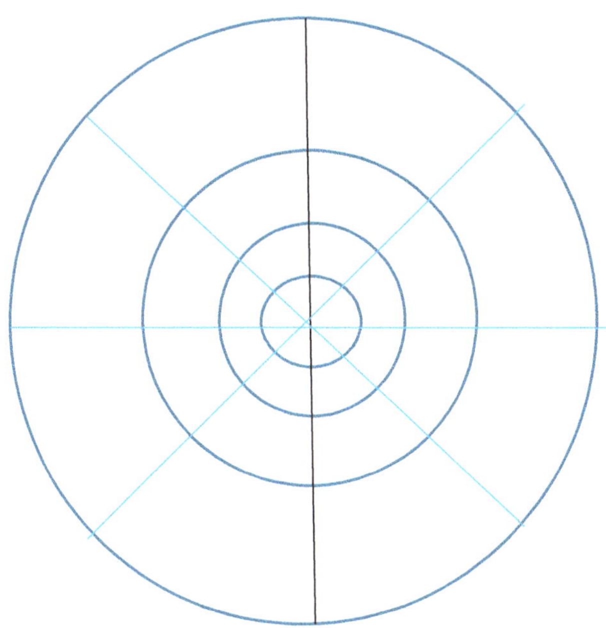

Tubes of force are closely packed so they won't normally have a circular cross section.
The diagram shows a section through a field.
The more closely packed the tubes of force (flux), the stronger the field.
Hence, in the diagram, the field is strongest at the centre.

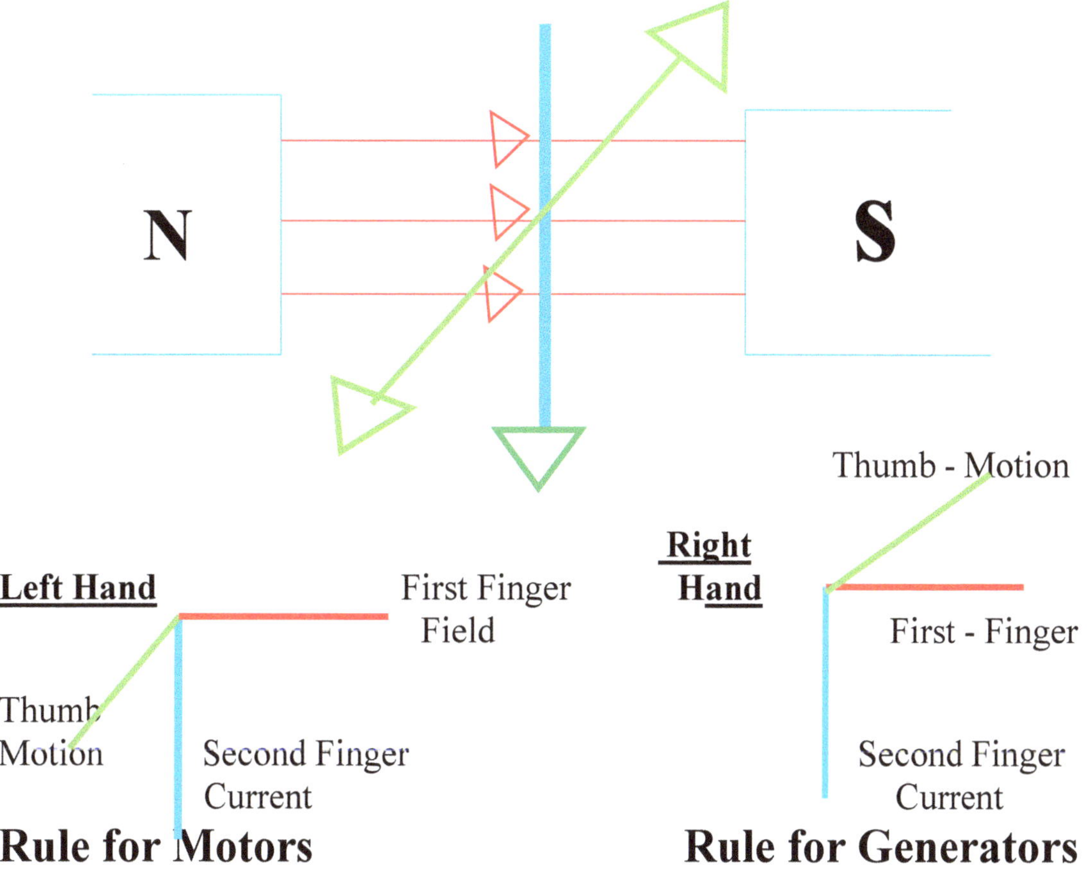

Faraday carried out very important research projects with far reaching effects, both for the government and private enterprise. He was instrumental in the preparation of the high quality optical glass which Chance Brothers needed for the lighthouses which they were involved in constructing. He carried out a meticulous forensic investigation into a mine explosion which killed ninety-five miners. He showed that the explosion was linked to coal dust and could have been prevented by better ventilation. Owners of coal mines failed to recognise the risks that Faraday had exposed and sixty years later, another colliery disaster occurred which had resulted from the dangers that Faraday had warned against. He was actively involved in the construction of lighthouses and carried out investigations into the electric lighting to be used in these buildings. He also investigated means of preventing the corrosion of hulls of ships.

Faraday could also be identified as an environmental scientist, investigating air pollution and its causes, industrial pollution at Swansea and the disgusting condition of Thames river water. He was involved in planning the 1851 Great Exhibition in the Crystal Palace, then located in Hyde Park, and in judging exhibits. The National Gallery sought his advice on cleaning and protecting the artwork on display. Being a gifted communicator, his views on education were sought. The lectures he instituted for school children at his headquarters, the Royal Institution, are still being delivered today over the Christmas break. Faraday's lectures were a delight to attend as he made use of exciting visual aids. One area of national life of which he was very critical was the public fascination with the occult.

Roads, buildings, parks and schools in London are named after Faraday. Outside London, Faraday's name is commemorated in buildings where technology is studied at many universities. Many streets in countries outside the United Kingdom are named after Faraday. Even the United Kingdom station in Antarctica bears his name. The SI unit (Systeme Internationale des Unites) of capacitence, the Farad, also derives its name from Faraday.

Faraday has been commemorated in the design of both postage stamps and bank notes, the £20 note depicting him delivering a lecture at the Royal Institution. The Faraday Institute for Science and Religion was created to enable the relationship between science and religion to be better understood and this study would have been dear to Faraday's heart as he saw his faith as integral to his scientific research.

In a BBC survey conducted to discover whom the public considered to be the greatest 100 Britons (*see appendix*), Faraday was ranked at twenty-two, a much lower ranking than I consider he deserves. I think our former prime minister, Margaret Thatcher would share my appreciation of this great scientist. Whatever one may think of her politics, I consider that she should be commended for borrowing a bust of Michael Faraday from the Royal Institution and having it displayed in a place of honour in 10, Downing Street during her occupancy.

Anthony Ashley-Cooper
Earl of Shaftesbury

Anthony Ashley-Cooper, Earl of Shaftesbury

Lord Ashley, as he was known, was a prodigious social reformer, He was very much an example of Noblesse Oblige. Observing the immense social problems of his day, he recognised that having been born into a position of nobility and influence, it was incumbent on him to use these advantages to better the lot of many in the society in which he lived. He richly deserves the appellation, 'the Poor Man's Earl'.

He fought poverty and exploitation on many fronts but even someone of his position in society had difficulty in getting the legislation needed to improve things through parliament. In our day and age, it would seem blindingly obvious, that these laws should be in the statute book but then, he encountered opposition. He was a supporter of the Zionist movement, involved in the work of the YMCA and was an active member of the evangelical movement of the Church of England. However, these activities are peripheral to his main work of social reform.

After attending a primary school which appears to have been absolutely horrendous, Ashley was educated at Harrow and Christ Church, Oxford University, where he gained a first class honours degree in classics.

It has been difficult to find a portrait of Ashley to illustrate this account, in which a man with such great love for his fellow men looks pleasant and benign. Perhaps the way he appears in portraits is due to his early home life which seems to have been particularly loveless. Ashley was denied any parental love or affection. This was not uncommon among the English aristocracy, even when circumstances compelled them to pay some sort of attention to their children. To Ashley, his parents were formal and frightening. In adult life, Ashley disliked his father and referred to his mother as a 'she devil'.

Fortunately, Ashley did not grow up devoid of receiving affection as this was provided by his sisters and the family housekeeper, Maria Millis. Maria read the Bible to him and taught him to pray. The reality of the love which Maria showed towards Ashley, borne from her profound Christianity, made an indelible mark on Ashley which he took into his later life.

As a committed teenage Christian, Ashley had two experiences while at Harrow School which were to have a profound effect on the way he directed his later life.

First, he was very disturbed to witness the irreverence exhibited at a pauper's funeral where the coffin was carried by drunken pall bearers.

Secondly, in the school grounds was an unsavoury, mosquito ridden duck pond which Ashley considered could be a source of disease and should be filled in. He chose a very unusual way of bringing this to the school authorities' attention. He described this pond in a poem he had written in Latin as a school exercise. This had the desired effect. The pond was promptly filled in but it had another effect. It greatly increased Ashley's self-confidence and showed he had the skill to promote decisive action in the face of indifference. This skill was an invaluable asset to Lord Ashley in his later career as a parliamentarian.

The conditions existing in lunatic Asylums

Lord Ashley's first campaign was to improve the dreadful and inhumane conditions which existed in what were then known as lunatic asylums. He became M.P. for Woodstock and out of loyalty to his friend, the Duke of Wellington, he refused to join Canning's government. He was however, very quickly elected to a number of parliamentary committees including, using the terminology of the day, the select committee on pauper lunatics. One of the madhouses he visited was the White House in Bethnal Green where he discovered that the inmates were left chained from Saturday afternoon till Monday morning. They were then washed down with freezing cold water and their bedding cleared of accumulated excrement. One towel was provided for 160 inmates! They were then provided with a meal in which the meat was so hard that a dog couldn't eat it.

Ashley's committee recommended that a Board of Commissioners should be appointed by the Home Secretary, possessing extensive powers of inspection, licensing and control. Having delivered his maiden speech in the House in support of this bill, Ashley was appointed as one of these commissioners. Ashley sponsored two acts for the better care and treatment of lunatics. However, Ashley realised that, although improvements had been made, much more needed to be done. A select committee was appointed to investigate the possibility that sane persons were being confined to lunatic asylums. Ashley reported that in his experiences, very few sane people had been so confined but he supported all the recommendations of the committee. Although lesser known than some of his other achievements in the field of social welfare, Ashley's effort in improving the conditions of the insane was one of his most important pieces of work,

Child Labour

Ashley was aware that children were working excessive hours in the Lancashire and Yorkshire cotton and woollen mills. He introduced what has become known as the Ten Hours Act. The provisions of this required that :-

Children working in these industries should be at least nine years old.
No person under the age of eighteen was to work more than ten hours a
    day or eight on a Saturday.
Inspectors were appointed to ensure that these children attended school.
No-one under twenty five was to work nights.

This bill was amended by the Whig government to ensure that no children under eighteen should work for more than nine hours a day.

A member of Parliament from Lancashire declared that if there was one man in England devoted to the interests of factory people, it was Lord Ashley. They could always rely on him as a ready, steadfast and willing friend.

Mines and collieries.

Ashley introduced the Mines and Collieries Act which outlawed the employment of women and children underground in coal mines. His speech in parliament was so well delivered that the Prince Consort wrote to Ashley commending him on this venture. Even one of Ashley's most intransigent political opponents came over to Ashley at the end of his speech to tell him, "You know how opposed I have been to your views, but I don't think I have ever been put into such a frame of mind in the whole course of my life as I have been by your speech."

Climbing boys

Ashley strongly supported efforts to prevent boys being employed as chimney sweeps. These children were often illegitimate and were sold by their parents to unscrupulous employers. These boys' eyes and throats were filled with soot, they had lacerated skin, were in danger of suffocation, and cancer of the scrotum was an occupational hazard.

Although a bill outlawing the employment of boy chimney sweeps was passed, it was only enforced in London. Other acts which Ashley attempted to get passed proved to be ineffectual. Ashley finally persuaded Parliament to pass the Chimney Sweepers Act. This ensured that firms employing chimney sweeps had to be licensed and they could not employ children. This law was enforced by the police and finally ended the employment of boys as chimney sweeps.

Education Reform

In those days, education for the poorer classes was very haphazard but a group of volunteers had set up a charity known as the Ragged School Union. This established schools staffed by volunteers to educate poor children and was a charity very dear to Ashley's heart. Ashley became president of the Ragged School Union and stated,

"If the Ragged School system were to fail, I should not die in the course of nature, I should die of a broken heart."

Housing Reform

Landlords were exploiting poor people by renting very substandard accommodation for as much as the tenants could possibly afford to pay. Two Lodging Houses Acts were passed at Ashley's insistence to combat the need for people to be forced to live in unhealthy dwellings. These required that lodging houses should be registered and that no property should be rented out for living accommodation until it had been inspected by the local authority. The local authorities were given powers to enforce the regular cleaning and whitewashing of property and there was a requirement to report any case of infection or fever to the Poor Law medical officer. Local authorities were given the power to purchase and manage existing rented property or to build new properties for renting out which local boards of health were required to inspect. These properties may be thought of as early examples of council houses. Charles Dickens, who was well aware of the conditions in which poor people had been living, described these measures as the best acts of parliament ever to come into law.

Religious Activity

Ashley was an evangelical Christian. For some time, he was president of the Evangelical Alliance and was also president of the British and Foreign Bible Society which sought to translate the Bible into as many languages as possible. Of all societies, he described the British and Foreign Bible Society as the one nearest his heart. He disapproved of the ritualism carried out in Roman Catholic churches and some High Anglican churches but he supported catholic emancipation.

The situation in the Middle East where large tracts were sparsely inhabited was very different to what exists today. Ashley was the first major politician to propose resettling the Jews in Palestine which he saw as a land without a people and the Jews as a people without a land, He would be horrified to see what is happening in Palestine today. He became president of the London Society for the Promotion of Christianity among the Jews.

Measures taken to limit the use of drugs

Ashley became first president of the Society for the Prevention of the Opium Trade. This society had been founded by Quaker businessmen who lobbied to get the opium trade abolished. The work of this society led to the creation of the Royal Commission on opium which was set up to investigate the opium trade and its effects.

....

The nation was greatly saddened by the death of Ashley, Lord Shaftesbury at the age of eighty-four. The streets from Grosvenor Square to Westminster Abbey were lined with poor people who thronged the streets to see the passage of his coffin. Although his funeral was carried out in the Abbey, he was buried by his request at St. Giles. One biographer said of Ashley, that "No man has in fact ever done more to lessen the extent of human misery or to add to the sum total of human happiness". In a sermon preached just a few days after the funeral, Charles Spurgeon, London's greatest preacher at that time, stated,

"In the Earl of Shaftesbury, we have, in my judgment, lost the best man of the age. He lived for the oppressed; he lived for London; he lived for the nation; he lived still more for God."

Ashley is commemorated in Piccadilly Circus by a beautiful fountain but sadly most people don't realise its significance and simply refer to it as the statue of Eros. In fact, the statue doesn't represent Eros, the Greek God of love, but this is not a serious misconception as it is fitting that such a man of love should be commemorated by a symbol of love. In reality, the statue represents Anteros, the Angel of Christian Charity, which is again, a fitting symbol for such a man of love.

Isambard Kingdom Brunel

Isambard Kingdom Brunel

Isambard Kingdom Brunel must be regarded as one of the greatest engineers ever. His expertise extended over the areas of civil engineering, railways, shipbuilding and pioneering the prefabrication of important community buildings like hospitals. He was a very influential figure in the industrial revolution which was to transform this country. Brunel was a pioneer of modern engineering and as such, he was prepared to get his hands dirty and take personal risks in the projects he masterminded, experiencing a number of very serious accidents in the course of his career.

Isambard was born in Portsmouth to a French father, Sir Marc Isambard Brunel, and an English mother, Sophia Kingdom. Hence his name which combined the identities of both parents. He had two elder sisters. When he was just two years old, the family moved to London. The family were not rich and had constant money worries.

Isambard's early education was carried out by his father, a competent engineer, who found his son to be an apt student. From the age of four, he was taught the fundamentals of observation techniques which he could translate into drawings. By the age of eight, he had mastered Euclidian Geometry and the basic principles of engineering. By this time, he could speak fluent French. He demonstrated a great aptitude for mathematics and mechanics, and enjoyed making drawings of buildings, identifying what he saw as design faults in them. At the age of fourteen, Isambard's father, who himself had received a good education in France, arranged for Isambard to continue his education at prestigious French institutions including Lycee Henri IV in Paris. As a foreigner, he was unable to enrol at the Ecole Polytechnique so completed his education under the tutelage of a prominent horologist who had nothing but praise for Isambard's ability. Isambard then returned to England but found that his father, Marc Brunel, had accumulated considerable debts and was in prison. Marc Brunel made it known that he had received an offer from the Czar of Russia to clear his debts if he would go and work there. The government. recognising Marc's ability, arranged to pay off his debts if he would remain in England.

Tunnels

Marc became the chief engineer of the Thames Tunnel Company and Isambard worked under his father to build a tunnel under the Thames. The earth under the Thames at the point where the tunnel was being constructed was waterlogged soil and loose gravel, and thus, the construction of the tunnel was a very dangerous task. Marc Brunel had designed an ingenious tunnelling shield to protect the workers from cave-ins but accidents did occur resulting in the tunnel flooding and killing workers. Isambard himself was badly injured and narrowly escaped death as a result of one of these incidents. Work on the tunnel had to be stopped for a few years and it took six months for Isambard to recover from his injuries. Ultimately, the tunnel was completed and is now part of the London Underground system.

Bridges

A competition was held for civil engineers to submit designs for the Clifton Suspension Bridge, spanning the River Avon at Bristol. Isambard spent his time as he recuperated from the Thames tunnel accident in designing such a bridge. The competition was judged by Thomas Telford who had also submitted his own design. Brunel's four designs were rejected in favour of Telford's but the general public objected, requiring a new competition to be held. Brunel won this and the Clifton Suspension Bridge was constructed to Brunel's design. A number of factor's delayed the completion of the bridge and it was not completed until five years after the death of Brunel. At the time of completion, the bridge had the longest span of any in the world.

Further important bridges were designed by Brunel including the Royal Albert Bridge, spanning the Tamar and providing a rail link between Devon and Cornwall, the Somerset Bridge near Bridgewater and the Windsor and the Maidenhead Railway Bridges, built in Berkshire over the Thames. The Tamar Bridge wasn't completed until the year after Brunel's death. The Maidenhead Railway Bridge was the widest and flattest bridge in the world and is still part of the main-line. It now carries trains which are ten times heavier than the locomotives used in the time of Brunel.

A very unique set of bridges, constructed by Brunel, are known as the Three Bridges, London. They allow the Grand Union Canal, Windmill Lane and the Great Western Railway to cross over each other.

Railways

Brunel was appointed chief engineer of the Great Western Railway. His vision for the Great Western Railway was for it to be a line where you could purchase a ticket in London which would take you all the way to New York by rail and ferry. Brunel personally surveyed the whole route to be taken by the Great Western Railway from London to Bristol. He was also visionary in his decision to lay tracks with a seven foot width which was much larger the accepted standard gauge of four feet eight inches, used on all other British railways at the time. Brunel had calculated that railways of seven foot gauge would allow trains to run at higher speeds, give greater comfort to passengers and increase the capacity of the railway to carry goods as larger trucks could be used. Brunel considered the standard gauge was just a left over from the very early days of railways when George Stephenson pioneered the first passenger railway. However, a decision was taken after Brunel's death that all British railways should conform to the standard gauge.

Brunel selected twenty year old Daniel Gooch to be Superintendent of Locomotive Engines and they decided to build at a railway factory located near Swindon. Early engines, built to Brunel's specification, were not satisfactory but they finally produced the 'North Star' which was an excellent locomotive. The decision to locate his railway works at Swindon required housing for those who would work there. Brunel responded to this need by building what has become known today as the 'Railway Village'. The houses were provided with an appropriate infrastructure of shops, hospitals, churches and schools.

The construction of the Great Western Railway involved Brunel in many design, construction and building ventures. He built the Box Tunnel which was the longest tunnel in the world at that time and its opening completed the line from London to Bristol. Brunel designed Paddington Station as well as the smaller stations of Mortimer, Charlbury, Bridgend and Culham. His train sheds at Frome and Kingswear still survive. A quite different enterprise, undertaken by Brunel but connected with the railway, was the design of the Royal Hotel in Bath. located opposite the railway station.

Brunel was not afraid to experiment with innovations and he attempted to exploit an atmospheric (vacuum) traction technique which could move trains at great speeds but this technology proved fraught with difficulties and was abandoned.

Transatlantic Shipping

Part of Brunel's vision when building the Great Western Railway had been for it to have been an integral part of a transport system involving both railway and shipping which would enable a passenger to travel from London to New York on a single ticket. He therefore offered his services, free of charge, to the Great

Western Steamship Company which was working towards making a transatlantic passenger service possible. Technical challenges had to be met to construct a steamship capable of such long journeys. It was not considered possible for a steamship to be able to hold sufficient quantities of fuel and fresh water to enable a journey of such a distance to be achieved. Technical advances had enabled boilers to be constructed which could run on salt water without needing to be regularly cleaned out. Thus, without the need to carry vast quantities of fresh water, extra space would be available for fuel. Brunel worked out that the capacity of a ship to carry cargo went up as the cube of its linear dimension whereas, the resistance presented by the water through which a ship was sailing only went up as the square of its linear dimension. Thus, proportionately, a larger ship would experience less resistance than a smaller ship. Brunel calculated that if a large enough ship could be built, it could carry enough fuel to enable an Atlantic crossing to be made.

Brunel was entrusted with the design of such a ship and this was constructed as the 'Great Western', which was motivated by steam powered paddle wheels and also, carried four masts to harness wind power. It was built of wood but strongly reinforced with iron components. At 72 m, the 'Great Western' was the longest ship ever built. On its maiden voyage across the Atlantic, it carried seven passengers, over 600 Mgm (tons) of coal and a cargo. Brunel missed out on travelling on this maiden voyage as he had been injured in a fire which occurred on the ship when returning from London after fitting out. The crossing took just over fifteen days and arrived with one third of its coal supply unused, showing that Brunel had been correct in his calculations, having included a comfortable safety margin. This journey had proved the commercial viability of crossing the Atlantic by steamship and over the next eight years, the 'Great Western' made sixty four crossings between Bristol and New York. It was the first ship to hold the Blue Riband, having made the westbound crossing in fifteen days, thirteen hours and the eastbound crossing in just over fifteen days, twelve hours.

With the commercial success of the 'Great Western', Brunel's genius was in demand to create yet more great ships. His next ship, the 'Great Britain', was over as third as long again as the 'Great Western'. The many modifications in its design from earlier ships has led it to be recognised as the first modern ship to be built, constructed of metal rather than wood, powered by an engine rather than sail or oars and propeller driven rather than by paddles. Three years after its launching, it ran aground off the coast of Ireland. It was successfully salvaged and for a time, was used around Australia. The fully restored ship still exists as a museum piece in Bristol.

The third great ship designed by Brunel was the 'Great Eastern', a vessel even larger and more advanced than its predecessors. It was luxuriously furnished as a passenger liner, capable of transporting over four thousand passengers, and was expected to run non-stop between England and Australia. It had a huge capacity for carrying fuel as at the time, it was not realised that Australia had coal deposits of its own. Although the concepts built into Brunel's ships were well ahead of their time, the 'Great Eastern' was a failure in that the purpose for which it had been built was not realised. The reason was economic rather than due to any shortcomings of the 'Great Eastern' itself. The building of the ship had exceeded its budget and the public were not ready to embark in great numbers on trans-oceanic voyages. However, the 'Great Eastern did achieve success in a totally different application It proved the ideal ship for laying the first enduring transatlantic telegraph cable, enabling telecommunication between North America and Europe.

Prefabricated Buildings
Working with fellow engineer, William Eassie, who was involved in the launching of the 'Great Eastern', Brunel designed prefabricated huts which were used in the Australian gold rush and by the British and French armies in Crimea. He designed the prefabricated units which could be built into the wards of a hospital, complete with the features necessary for good hygiene; - ventilation drainage, sanitation and temperature control. These units were built into the Renkioi Hospital near the hospital at Scutari where Florence Nightingale had started her work, caring for those wounded in the Crimean War. Patients were transferred from the Scutari Hospital to the Renkioi Hospital where the death rate among patients dropped by ninety percent. Florence Nightingale was delighted with this improvement and referred to the prefabricated buildings as 'those magnificent huts'. Hospitals today are still being built from prefabricated units.

Personal Life
Brunel married Elizabeth Horsley, the daughter of the composer, William Horsley, and they set up home in Duke Street, Westminster. He enjoyed being involved in his children's fun and games but unfortunately, while attempting to perform a conjuring trick for his children, he swallowed a sovereign. This proved very difficult to remove. Forceps couldn't grasp it and even a machine Brunel designed himself couldn't get it out. Brunel's father suggested that he should be strapped to a board, turned upside down and shaken. This did ultimately succeed in shaking the coin loose. He travelled to Teignmouth in Devon to recuperate. Brunel liked the area so much that he bought an estate and commissioned an architect to build a manor house for him. Sadly, Bruncl, who was a heavy smoker and suffered from Bright's Disease, died of a stroke and never saw his house and its associated gardens completed.

Brunel was elected a Fellow of the Royal Society. Since his death, he has been recognised for his achievements in so many ways with streets, shopping malls, car parks and schools being named after him. Brunel University near London is also named after him. The Royal Mint struck £2 coins to celebrate his two-hundredth anniversary. His inclusion of hospitals and clinics in places where his employees worked provided a basis on which Aneurin Bevan was able to create the National Health Service.

David Livingstone

David Livingstone

While David Livingstone is chiefly remembered as a missionary explorer who spent much of his life in what was known as darkest Africa, his life and work brought benefits well beyond the native populations to whom he ministered in Africa. He was a scientific investigator and explorer. He had enlightened views on the British Empire, seeing it, not as domains, subject to the British crown, but as an area which would benefit from the commercial and educational advantages that could be shared through the agency of an expanding empire. He crusaded for the abolition of slavery. As a doctor, he was able to minister to both the physical as well as the spiritual needs of those among whom he worked.

He was preoccupied with discovering the source of the Nile because he thought that such a discovery was so important, that success in making this discovery would give him the fame and status which would increase his influence as he sought to get slavery abolished.

David was born into the family of cotton millworkers as the second of seven children. They lived in a cotton workers' tenement building on the banks of the Clyde. When only ten years old, David, along with his brother, worked twelve hour days, tying together any threads on the spinning machines which had become broken. This work was necessary to support David's impoverished family but it developed in David the characteristics of persistence, endurance and an empathy for all who spend their life in labour.

David's father was an active Christian and David received part of his education at the Sunday School run by his father. In spite of his long working hours, David was able to attend Blantyre village school along with other mill children. He also self-educated himself by extensive reading. David had a deep interest in science and on occasions when he was able to get into the countryside, he spent his time searching out animal, plant and geological specimens from the local limestone quarries. This interest led David to investigate the relationship between science and religion.

At the age of twenty-one, David picked up a pamphlet which encouraged young people to volunteer as missionaries in China. The pamphlet suggested that it would be specially useful if applicants could also be qualified doctors. Livingstone came to an agreement with the mill owners that he could continue to work for them on a part time basis (Easter until October) enabling him to be self -supporting while at university. He enrolled at Anderson University, Glasgow, where he studied medicine and chemistry. He also attended theology lectures delivered by an anti-slavery activist.

He applied to the London Missionary Society and was accepted as a probationer. He attended further study at Ongar College in Essex which included Greek, Latin, Hebrew and theology. The London Missionary Society then sent David to Charing Cross Hospital Medical School where he studied medical practice, midwifery and botany. He finally became a fully qualified doctor and an ordained minister of the Congregational Church. One of David's tutors had assessed him as a little short of brilliant but despite a heaviness of manner, he had good common sense, quiet vigour, good temper and substantial character

Although David had initially responded to a vocation to become a missionary in China, the London Missionary Society had misgivings about sending missionaries there as the Opium War was being fought. Other destinations like the West Indies were suggested However, largely as a result of meeting the African missionary, Robert Moffat, it was decided that David would be the ideal person to work, not at an established mission station, but to go into the un-evangelised areas of Africa. This suggestion was confirmed in Livingstone's mind when he attended a meeting at Exeter Hall where the speaker explained that the slave trade would be ended if African chiefs did not need to sell slaves in order to trade but could enter into legitimate trading arrangements, promoted by missionaries This would be augmented by preaching the gospel and introducing school education.

Livingstone sailed for Africa in the company of the Rosses, a married missionary couple He made good use of the time afforded by this long voyage, studying Dutch and the Tswana language. He also received a good grounding in navigation from the ship's captain. On landing in South Africa, David and the Rosses made their way across country to Robert Moffat's missionary station at Kuruman but arrived before Robert Moffat had returned from Britain. David spent some time, getting acclimatised to the Tswana culture. He made a long trek with an artisan missionary, Roger Edwards, to a remote area called Mabotsa where Edwards obtained permission from the London Missionary Society to set up a mission station. David involved himself in the physical work required to build and set up this station.

When the Moffats arrived back in Africa, David went to meet them by the Vaal River and travelled back with them to the mission station in Kuruman. The journey took about eighteen days. During this journey, David was not only able to spend a lot of time learning from Robert but also met Mary, his daughter, who had been born and brought up in Africa.

One of the activities in which David was involved when back at Mabotsa was defending the villagers and their herds from attacks by lions. On one such occasion, Livingstone got a clear shot at a lion but the shot didn't kill the lion who sprang at David while he was reloading, pinning him to the ground and breaking his arm. Two other members of the mission came to David's aid but were themselves attacked and injured by the wounded lion before it dropped down dead. Livingstone set his broken arm himself and the bone mended strongly although not perfectly set. He was able to use his arm to lift heavy weights and shoot but the arm was a source of pain to David for the rest of his life. He was never able to lift his arm above his shoulder. During his recovery, he was tended by Mary Moffat. They became engaged and got married the following year.

As a result of irreconcilable differenced which arose between himself and fellow missionary, Roger Edwards, David decided to move further into the interior and established a mission station at Kolobend. David had little success in converting the natives here but after two years of patient persuasion, he converted their chief, Sechele. Sechele was far more successful than David in winning converts from his tribe. One is reminded of the example of the American evangelist, Eliezer Ham, who felt he had failed in his mission to a farming community as he had only won one convert. However, that convert was Billy Graham, the most successful evangelist of the twentieth century. Although Sechele had won many converts, his own Christian faith was not strong and he frequently lapsed into his native culture where many things contrary to Christian teaching, including polygamy, were practiced.

Livingstone moved on, setting up further mission stations. In the company of the explorer, William Cotton Oswell, he crossed the Kalahari desert and discovered the great lake, Ngami. He had heard of a river which could potentially be a highway to the sea and moved on to the discover the headwaters of the Zambezi. In recognition of his discoveries, Livingstone was awarded a medal by the National Geographical Society. Livingstone sent his wife back to England and continued with his exploration. He followed the Zambesi to the centre of Africa where he received considerable help from the local chief, Sekelefu. With bearers and translators, provided by Sekelefu, Livingstone made his way west to the Atlantic coast but realised that the route he had travelled over difficult terrain would not be a suitable trade route. He therefore retraced his steps back to the Zambesi and followed this river eastwards to the Indian Ocean. This journey enabled him to map most of the course of the Zambezi and he became the first European to see the waterfall which the natives called 'the Smoke that Thunders'. Livingstone renamed this feature to become known today as the Victoria Falls. Livingstone became famous as the first European to cross the centre of Africa from west to east.

As result of observing the appalling acts enacted by slave traders, Livingstone's primary objective became the elimination of slavery. He considered that a key to achieving this objective would be the setting up of a trade route along the Zambezi to the centre of Africa controlled by a company which subscribed to Christian ethics. He took as his motto, 'Christianity, Commerce and Civilisation' which is inscribed on his statue by the Victoria Falls. He hoped that trade carried out following these principles would be an alternative the African chiefs would turn to instead of selling their people as slaves.

Livingstone returned to England where he made good use of his time. He was honoured by the National Geographical Society. He wrote up his journal describing his missionary travels. This book became a best-selling travelogue and included field science and exceptionally sympathetic descriptions of the African natives. He proposed that further missions should be sent out and trading stations established along the Zambezi. These trading initiatives should operate on ethical lines which he expected to contribute to the end of the slave trade.

Livingstone received enthusiastic support and encouragement and proposed returning to Africa to set up more trade routes into the interior but the London Missionary Society was not prepared to finance a venture which was not primarily concerned with missionary work. However, Livingstone was now a celebrity in great demand as a public speaker and he did receive support from the Central Government. He was appointed Her Majesty's Consul with a roving commission to explore and establish trade via routes extending from the east coast to the centre of Africa.

What follows could be regarded as a major failing on Livingstone's part as he put his goals ahead of the wellbeing of those who travelled with him. During his previous time in Arica, Livingstone had suffered thirty bouts of malaria but he made light of this and overstated the quality of the land they would encounter. He travelled through a marshy region with totally inadequate supplies of quinine. His wife and other missionaries including their children died of malaria.

Livingstone envisaged continuing his exploration as a solo explorer, supported by a team of native porters. However, the Foreign Office had more ambitious plans and sponsored a much larger expedition up the Zambezi with a prefabricated boat which could explore Lake Nyasa and be dismantled when encountering impassable rapids, to be carried past the rapids and reassembled further up the river to where it flowed smoothly. Apart from the scientists on the expedition being able to collect large quantities of botanical, ecological and geological material which was returned to the United Kingdom institutions for research, the expedition was otherwise a failure and the government ordered its recall. Many consider that the failure was partly due to Livingstone proving to be an unsafe leader.

Thus, Livingstone had great difficulty in raising funds for further expeditions but he was able to return to Africa, this time entering the continent from Zanzibar. His objective was to discover the source of the Nile. In reality, there is no one source of the Nile as it is fed by many tributaries. The two main tributaries are known as the Blue and the White Niles which converge at Khartoum. The Blue Nile rises in the hills of Ethiopia while the White Nile rises in central Africa. The Victorian explorer, John Speke, is credited with discovering a source of the Nile in Uganda where a stream bubbles into existence somewhere between Lake Victoria and Lake Tanganyika. Livingstone had doubts as to whether this was the true source and carried out his exploration further to the south and west. His expedition was beset with difficulties, many of his porters deserting the expedition, returning to Zanzibar with the false information that Livingstone had died. A large amount of the provisions carried by the expedition was stolen.

Livingstone did however make further discoveries and became the first European to reach Lake Bangweulu from which flowed the Lualaba River. He conjectured that this was the source of the Nile but came to realise that these were the headwaters of another great African river, the Congo.

Livingstone made further discoveries, notably Lake Ngami and Lake Malawi and the courses of many rivers that fed the Zambezi but then began to get extremely ill, suffering a number of very serious complaints, including pneumonia, cholera and tropical ulcers on his feet. He was horrified to witness the massacre of four-hundred Africans by Arab slave traders at a market on the banks of Lualaba river, and this left him too disheartened to continue his exploration. He returned to Ujiji, an Arab settlement of the eastern shores of Lake Tanganyika, suffering from ill health throughout this journey.

Livingstone had completely lost contact with the outside world for six years. The New York Herald sent the explorer, Henry Morton Stanley, to find Livingstone which he succeeded in doing at the Arab settlement of Ujiji. The words exchanged between these two men at such a momentous meeting are so formal as to be humorous. To Stanley's greeting of

"Dr. Livingstone I presume?"

Livingstone replied,

"Yes, I feel thankful that I am here to welcome you."

Livingstone died at the age of sixty from malaria and dysentery. His heart was buried in Africa but his body was carried by an expedition, led by two of his faithful porters, to an eastern coastal town, Bagamoyo, a distance of over 1,000 miles. The journey took sixty-three days. From there, his remains were returned to London by ship and he lay in state ay the headquarters of the Royal Geographical Society before his interment at Westminster Abbey.

Livingstone was loved by the Africans he encountered because of the courtesy and respect he showed them and he earned the unending loyalty of his porters. His vision of colonisation was far removed from Cecil Rhodes' ambitions to create an empire. To Livingstone, colonisation meant the settlement of European Christians in the places he had explored in Africa to promote trade and to continue propagating the gospel. Thus, Africans have revered Livingstone's name but detested that of Rhodes and whereas names based on Cecil Rhodes' name have been eradicated and changed for modern African names, places named after Livingstone still bear that name.

Livingstone wrote that if his disclosures regarding the evils of the slave trade should result in its suppression, he would regard that as a greater achievement than the discovery of all the sources of the River Nile.

Livingstone influenced political thought, not just in Africa, but in Britain. He was part of the evangelical and nonconformist movement which changed the national mindset from a belief that the British had a divine right to rule lesser races to the modern ethical approach adopted in the matter of foreign policy.

Florence Nightingale

Florence Nightingale

The name, Florence Nightingale, conjures up the image of a nurse, wandering at night through the wards of Scutari Hospital, comforting soldiers wounded in the Crimean War, carrying a lamp to illuminate her way. She is frequently described by the epithet, 'The Lady with the Lamp'.

> *Lo! in that house of misery*
> *A lady with a lamp I see*
> *Pass through the glimmering gloom,*
> *And flit from room to room.*

 Fortunately, this is the description left for posterity. It is a modification of an earlier name she had been given by soldiers in the Scutari hospital. They had seen her attack a padlock with a hammer to retrieve medicines locked away in a cupboard, earning her the title, 'The Lady with the Hammer'!

While she is rightly commended for her work at Scutari, her contribution to life go far beyond her service in that army field hospital. Florence was a prodigious writer and a mathematician of considerable ability. She developed representations of statistical data to emphasise the importance of her case when she was petitioning for action to be taken. These representations were far a more effective presentation than a mere page of figures, e.g. A pie chart, indicating that an entity only represents 2% of a population or 1,786 out of 89,317, has a much greater impact than the mere statement of the fact.

Florence was born to a wealthy and well connected family who at the time, were living in a villa in Tuscany. She was named after the city of her birth in Italy as had been her elder sister, Frances Parthenope. While, as an intelligent and educated woman, Florence could see that there was so much wrong with the position woman occupied in society and supported the women's suffrage movement, even she held some misconceptions which were the accepted belief of her day. She considered that generally, men were more capable than women. She preferred the friendship of powerful men, claiming that men had done much more to help her achieve her goals than any woman had. She described herself as a man of action or as a man of business. She had observed with distaste the over feminisation of women in the passive and lethargic lifestyle to which her mother and older sister had degenerated. Women of Nightingale's class didn't attend universities. They weren't encouraged to follow careers. Their purpose in life was to marry well and raise a family. However, Florence's father had an enlightened outlook and he personally saw to Florence's education, teaching her Latin and Greek, writing, history, philosophy and Italian, and, an unusual subject for a woman to follow at that time, mathematics.

Florence had an inner conviction that her life should be spent in the service of others and realised that she had a divine vocation to become a nurse. Although this decision aroused her mother to great anger, Florence persisted and took steps to educate herself in the art and science of nursing, even ending a nine year courtship as she considered marriage would interfere with her decision to devote her life to nursing.

While her detractors may have portrayed Florence as stubborn, opinionated and forthright, she had to be all of these to get things done. In reality, her contemporaries described her as attractive, slender and graceful. She was very charming and her smile was radiant.

She established a lifelong friendship with Sidney Herbert who became Secretary of State for War and was able to call upon his support during the time she was working as a nurse in the Crimea as well as being able to offer Sidney useful advice herself.

In her early years, Florence was a great traveller and her description of the antiquities she visited during her visit to Egypt marked her out as a very talented writer. On visiting Germany, she was profoundly influenced by a Lutheran church at Kaisersweerth-am-Rhein. Florence regarded the care she observed being shown to the sick and destitute by the pastor and deaconesses of this community to be a turning point in her life. She received four months medical training at the Kaisersweerth Institute. On her return to England, she was appointed to the post of superintendent at Institute for the Care of Sick Gentlewomen.

When the Crimean war broke out, reports were received in England of the appalling conditions in the military hospital in Scutari where the wounded soldiers were sent for treatment. Scutari was about three hundred miles from the main British camp at Balaklava on the Turkish side of the Black Sea. Florence volunteered to serve in a nursing capacity at this hospital and, with the support of Sidney Herbert, she was sent out to this hospital with a group of thirty eight volunteer nurses. Her aunt, Mai, and fifteen catholic nuns were among these volunteers.

On her arrival at Scutari, Florence discovered that the medical staff were overworked, hygiene conditions were poor, there were inadequate medical supplies and medicines, facilities for food preparation were missing, and many soldiers were dying from infected wounds. To make matters worse, officials, who should have been seeing that adequate facilities were available, seemed to be totally indifferent. Florence communicated with the government via a letter she sent to the Times and this achieved a positive response. Isambard Kingdom Brunel was commissioned to build a prefabricated hospital which could be shipped to the Dardanelles. Thus, the building, which became known as the Renkioi Hospital, was constructed in Turkey and an efficient manager appointed. The government sent out a sanitary commission to flush out the sewers and improve ventilation. The death rate fell to one percent of that being experienced at Scutari. A significant contribution to this reduction in the mortality rate was the way Florence implemented improvements in hospital hygiene. Even such common-sense measures as handwashing had previously been neglected. During her first winter at Scutari, the number of soldiers which died from infectious diseases had been ten times the number who died from battle wounds. Florence herself became critically ill but was nursed back to health by her head nurse, Eliza Roberts.

Florence's experience in the Crimea gave her first-hand evidence of how medical care could be improved in Britain. She had access to those in high places and she exploited this to ensure that the right things actually happened. On her return, she campaigned to have sanitary conditions and ventilation improved in British hospitals. Indeed, she went beyond just campaigning for these improvements to be implemented in hospitals. She was aware that illnesses experienced by ordinary working class people were largely due to the insanitary conditions in which they lived. She petitioned for basic sanitation to be universally incorporated into people's homes. She lobbied the minister responsible for public health to strengthen the bill requiring all owners of existing property to pay to be connected to main drainage. Historians now believe that this move was crucial in extending life expectancy by twenty years within a very short period of time.

During a public meeting to recognise Florence's work during the Crimean war, the Nightingale fund was established to raise money for the training of nurses, From the £45,000 at her disposal from this fund, Florence established a school for nurses at St Thomas's Hospital which has evolved to become the Florence Nightingale Faculty of Nursing and Midwifery of King's College, London University. The first nursing graduates from Florence's school began work at the Liverpool Workhouse Infirmary. The introduction of trained nurses into the British workhouse system is regarded as a very significant contribution which Florence made to the betterment of the poorest classes in the country.

Florence advocated autonomous leadership of nurses and established a system where nurses came under the authority of senior nurses known as Matrons.

Florence wrote a book, 'Notes on Nursing', which was primarily intended as a guide for those caring for sick patients in their own homes but it became the basis of the curriculum, not only at the school Florence had established, but in other institutions set up to train nurses. The fact that those entering the nursing profession were being professionally trained raised the public perception from regarding nurses as ignorant and uneducated people to that of being competent, well trained persons, fulfilling an important role in society. The previously low regard in which nurses were held was heightened by the way Dicken's caricatured nurses in his novels.

Florence's work and books inspired the nurses working in the American Civil War and she was approached by the American government for advice on organising field medical care in war zones. Her ideas inspired the setting up of the United States Sanitary Commission. Florence mentored Linda Richards who was able to return to America as a nurse with sufficient training to establish high quality nursing schools. Linda went on to pioneer the education of nurses in both America and in Japan.

Florence was a prodigious writer. The fact that she was a profoundly religious woman comes through in her writings. She had connections with the Unitarian Church, and although unorthodox in some of her beliefs, she remained a committed member of the Church of England. However, she was critical of some of its practices and she openly stated that she often found secular hospitals were better run than those with a religious foundation. She was influenced by the Wesleyan movement and considered that genuine religion should manifest itself in active care and love for others. She wrote a religious book, 'Suggestions for Thought', in which she explored her own unorthodox religious views. Florence believed that pagan and eastern religions also contained much genuine revelation and believed that the ideal health practitioner should be inspired by a religious as well as professional motive. Florence wrote a book, 'Cassandra', which protested against the over feminisation of women, leading them to live a life of thoughtless indolence. The title, Cassandra, arose from her fear that her ideas would be ignored as were Cassandra's. Cassandra was a Trojan princess and priestess who served in the Temple of Apollo. Apollo gave her the gift of prophecy but when she rejected his advances, he added the curse that no-one would believe her prophetic warnings.

Florence made a detailed study of the sanitary conditions in rural India where she was the leading figure in introducing improvements in the medical care and public health services of India. After ten years of sanitary reform, she was able to report that the mortality rate among soldiers in India had dropped from nearly seventy per thousand to less than twenty. Every year on International Nurses Day, the President of India honours deserving members of the nursing profession with the National Florence Nightingale award.

As well as being honoured for her work by the Red Cross and St. John's Ambulance, Florence became the first woman to receive the Order of Merit and she received the Freedom of the City of London. Her birthday, 12th May is celebrated as International Awareness Day.

Although, in later life, Florence was affected by an extreme form of brucellosis, she continued to work. From her bed she carried out pioneering work on hospital planning which was propagated not only in England but across the world. She died peacefully in her sleep at the age of ninety at her home, 10, South Street, Mayfair

Posthumously, the Florence Nightingale Declaration campaign has been supported by nurses throughout the world through the Nightingale Initiative for Global Health. The United Nations General Assembly set aside 2010, the centenary of Florence's death as the International Year of the Nurse, and 2011 to 2020, the bicentenary of Florence's birth, as the United Nations Decade for a Healthy World.

The Nightingale Pledge is a modified version of the Hippocratic oath which nurses make in America on graduating at the end of their training.

Many hospitals throughout the world have been named after Florence Nightingale. During the Covid epidemic, the temporary hospitals, set up to cope with the increase of patients arising as a result of the epidemic, were named Nightingale Hospitals.

Statues commemorating Florence Nightingale have been set up in many public places in cities as have stained glass windows in churches. Her image appeared on postage stamps and on the reverse of a £10 banknote issued by the Bank of England.

General Charles Gordon

General Charles Gordon

Charles Gordon was born in Kent to a family with a great military tradition. His father was a general and he and his brothers all became the fifth generation of career soldiers. Charles' father's military service meant that he himself was never able to settle in one place for long. However, Charles received his education in a settled environment at Taunton School from where he went on to train as an officer at Woolwich Military Academy.

As an army officer cadet, Charles Gordon was known for his high spirits and his combative nature. He was prepared to break rules if he considered them to be unfair or stupid, a quality which did not endear him to his superiors, and led to their delaying Gordon's graduation for two years.

Gordon chose to be commissioned into the Royal Engineers. This was an elite regiment who were involved in reconnaissance work, leading parties tasked with storming obstacles and undertaking the hazardous function of being the rear guard when the army was in retreat. Gordon had chosen the Royal Engineers because this regiment offered scope for his particular capacity for map making and designing fortifications. He was a charismatic leader whose men were eager to follow but he was distrusted by his superiors because of his tendency to disobey orders which he considered to be stupid.

One of Gordon's first jobs was to construct the fortifications of Milford Haven. Here he came under the influence of a devout Christian couple and warmly embraced their faith but he refused to become uniquely attached to any particular Christian denomination. However, Gordon's Christian faith resulted in his life and personality shining through to reveal a rare man of principle and integrity as he encountered many situations in which he had to deal with totally corrupt and greedy officials in high places.

When the Crimean War broke out, Gordon volunteered to fight there and was given the dangerous job of mapping out the defences of the Russian stronghold of Sevastopol He frequently had to move to positions where he came under Russian fire and was wounded by a Russian sniper. He spent thirty-four consecutive days in the trenches around Sevastopol, facing particular danger during the assault on the fort at Redan, and he became covered on blood and mud as he had to take cover many times from enemy fire. He earned a great reputation from the British high command who used to say,

'If you want to know what the Russians are doing, send for Charlie Gordon,'

During this war, Gordon became addicted to Turkish cigarettes and smoking was described as his most conspicuous vice. At the end of the war, Gordon was part of the international commission tasked with establishing the new border between the Russian and Ottoman Empires.

With this task completed, Gordon was recalled to Britain and posted to Chatham barracks. He found life so boring here that he implored the authorities to send him somewhere where the British were involved in military action. He was sent to China where the British were involved in the Opium War but this ended just as Gordon arrived. However, another conflict was underway.

The Taiping rebellion was taking place against the Chinese government. The Taipings were led by Hong Xiuguan who proclaimed himself to be the younger brother of Jesus Christ, and were committing appalling atrocities against the Chinese peasants. The scale of this rebellion can be appreciated from an estimate of the number of casualties sustained as one hundred million. As the Taipings approached Shanghai where a large number of European and American expatriates were living, a militia of mercenaries of mainly Europeans and Asians was raised under the command of an American, Frederick Ward, and the British General, Staveley. Gordon was attached to this force as an engineer officer. The initial objective of this militia was to clear the Taipings from a thirty-mile radius of Shanghai.

In one of the battles to achieve this, Ward was killed and replaced by Burgevine, another American, Burgevine was an unpleasant character. He was alcoholic, greedy and racist and the Chinese governor of the province asked General Staveley to replace him with someone who was good-tempered and honest. Staveley had no hesitation in selecting Gordon who had so impressed him with his attitude and bearing that he was described as a blessing from heaven. Although

Staveley held Gordon in high regard, he did acknowledge that he found him difficult to get along with.

The militia of which Gordon took command was described as the 'Ever Victorious Army' but it is unlikely that they could have lived up to this name except for the leadership of Gordon. The only criticism that the Chinese authorities had of Gordon was the cost of keeping his army in the field, but this was due to Gordon insisting on paying his men promptly and in full. The situation was rather different in the Chinese army whose corrupt leaders withheld money from their soldiers to make themselves rich. They instructed their men that they should make up for any shortfall in pay by taking plunder from any settlement they overcame in battle.

One of Gordon's first actions as leader of this army was to relieve Changsu, a town, forty miles north west of Shanghai, which was under siege by the Taipings. The ease with which Gordon secured this objective won the respect of his troops. He made a point of treating prisoners of war well. The knowledge of this made it much easier for Gordon to achieve the surrender of his opponents and many Taipings deserted to join Gordon's 'Ever Victorious Army'.

Gordon's success was largely due to the tactics he used. He manoeuvred his troops to outflank his opponents or sometimes, to cut off their retreat. He deplored the tactics used by the imperial Chinese army, also opposing the Taipings, which invariably went for a frontal attack. This led to huge casualties on both sides. Unlike the previous commanders of the 'Ever Victorious Army' who had regarded the canals as an obstacle to advancing their troops, Gordon saw the canals as a feature which could be exploited. He armoured a paddle steamer, the Hyson, and sailed this up a canal to both surprise and outflank the Taiping forces. The enemy panicked and fled in disarray. He was able to bombard the defences of the city of Quinsan, occupied by the Taiping, with the Hyson's gun, making it an easy objective for his forces to take. The Chinese peasantry, who had been oppressed for years by the Taiping, emerged to cut down the fleeing Taipings.

Gordon felt uncomfortable in commanding an army consisting of mercenaries who fought only for pay but he ensured that they were paid regularly and Gordon was justified in taking stern disciplinary action against any of his troops who resorted to looting, plunder and mistreating civilians. To remove the temptation to loot, he didn't allow his men to enter some of the towns where they had defeated the Taiping.

Burgevine, the incompetent and obnoxious American officer whom Gordon had replaced as commander of the 'Ever Victorious Army', raised his own army of mercenaries and joined the Taiping. His army was surrounded and defeated by Gordon but Burgevine deserted his own men and escaped, only to be soon captured by Gordon's forces. It must have given Gordon great pleasure to send Burgevine to the American consul in Shanghai with a letter requesting that he should be expelled from China.

Gordon led his forces from the front armed with little more than his swagger stick. He earned the respect of friend and foe alike. The fact that Gordon seemed to be immune from enemy bullets, even when in the most hazardous of situations, earned him the reputation of having supernatural powers. Gordon, who treated prisoners of war fairly and humanely, was greatly angered when the Chinese Imperial army entered a town he had taken and executed the prisoners of war. Not only did Gordon consider that this had besmirched his honour, it was a stupid thing to do. Knowing that they would be fairly treated, the Taiping would have readily surrendered but in the light of the atrocity committed by the Imperial army, they were prepared to fight to the death.

The 'Ever Victorious Army' did not take part in the final action of the war, the capture of Nanking, as the 'Imps', Gordon's term for the imperial army, demanded this honour for themselves. During this war, Gordon's 'Ever Victorious Army' had won thirty-three successive battles but at the considerable cost of nearly half its officers and nearly a quarter of its men.

Gordon refused any financial reward for his success in this war, stating that he was satisfied with knowing that as a result of his action, over one-hundred-thousand lives had been spared. However, he did accept a number of decorations including the 'Imperial Yellow Jacket', the highest honour available under the Chinese Imperial system. He was rewarded in Britain by being appointed a Companion of the Order of the Bath. The reputation of his success in China often led to his being nicknamed, 'Chinese Gordon'.

On his return to Britain, Gordon was appointed British representative on the international commission charged with maintaining navigation on the Danube. Gordon found this work rather boring but on meeting up with an old friend, Romolo Gessi, in Bucharest, he was able to find to find many other distractions to interest himself and his friend during their off-duty time. During a time when they were in Bulgaria, a couple brought to their attention the fact that their seventeen year old daughter had been taken into the harem of an Ottoman Pasha. They sought the aid of Gordon and Gessi to get their daughter released. Gordon and Gessi were able to arrange to interview the girl and when they discovered that she wanted to return home, they informed the Pasha that if the girl was not immediately released, they would have the situation publicised in the British and Italian press. This threat proved sufficient to secure the girl's release.

On being sent to inspect the British war graves in Crimea, Gordon had a chance meeting with the Egyptian Prime Minister, Raghib Pasha, as he passed through Constantinople. The Suez Canal had just been completed and Raghib admired anything European. He recognised what an asset Gordon would be to the Egyptian administration and negotiated with the British government to secure Gordon's service under the Ottoman Khedive, Ismail Pasha. When Ismail met Gordon, he was surprised and very impressed to find that such a person was not at all materialistic and was unconcerned with securing financial remuneration.

Although technically part of the Ottoman Empire, in reality, Egypt was an independent state. The Khedive was nominally a Moslem but enjoyed European wine and had an ambition to Westernise, not just Egypt, but the adjoining states like Sudan to the south. The British soldier, Sir Sidney Baker, was sent with an expedition along the White Nile to Khartoum with the objective of annexing this region into an Egyptian empire. Baker only succeeded in setting up a few trading posts along the banks of the Nile. The Khedive decided to replace Baker with Gordon as governor of what was known as the Equatoria Province. Baker had been paid a salary of £10,000 (the equivalent of about one million in current values) When Gordon was offered this post, he declined Baker's salary, stating that £2,000 would be sufficient for himself.

Once in Khartoum, Gordon worked hard to end the slave trading which was rife but found his attempts thwarted by an institutionally corrupt Ottoman bureaucracy. Gordon established a good relationship with the people of Equatoria who were appreciative of his efforts to stamp out the slave trade. These people traditionally worshipped the spirit gods of nature and were a fertile ground for the work of Christian missionaries in the area. Gordon gave encouragement and support to these missionaries and saw it as his way of contributing to God's work in Equatoria.

Gordon's forces intercepted slave convoys, releasing the slaves and arresting the slavers. It was difficult to make provision for thousands of released slaves, far from their homes, and corrupt Egyptian officials sold many of them back into slavery. Gordon came into conflict with the Egyptian governor of Khartoum over his opposition to Gordon's efforts to end the slave trade. This lead to Gordon informing the Khedive that he no longer wished to work in Equatoria.

Gordon returned to London where he was approached by Sir William Mackinnon, a wealthy Scottish ship owner, and Leopold II, King of Belgium, to help them as they formed a trading company to take over much of central Africa. Their aim was to improve the lot of the native Africans. Gordon accepted their assurance that their objectives were philanthropic. This work would require Gordon to return to Egypt and resume his former office. As Gordon had promised the

Khedive that he would return, Gordon made good his promise and went back to Egypt where he was appointed Governor General of the entire Sudan. Gordon appointed European officials to replace the corrupt Egyptian ones but these new officials proved no lees corrupt than the ones they had replaced and far from supporting Gordon's efforts to suppress the slave trade, they turned a blind eye to it.

A financial crisis occurred when Egypt became bankrupt and hardly able to service its debts. A group of financial commissioners, led by Evelyn Baring, travelled to Cairo to take control of Egypt's finances. Gordon travelled north to meet this team with the suggestion that the interest payments required of Egypt might be suspended until the economy improved. However, Baring, whom Gordon found to be pretentious and patronising, was not prepared to consider the merits of Gordon's proposal. With Egypt bankrupt, Gordon could barely pay his officials let alone proceed with the necessary reforms he had in mind.

Meanwhile, Gordon's attempt to eliminate the slave trade met with opposition from the richest of the slave traders, Rahama Zobeir, who was known as the king of the slave traders. However, Gordon's subordinate, Gessi Pasha, fought with great success and defeated the slave traders in a couple of key battles. Gessi finally captured Zobeir with two-hundred-and-fifty of his men and had them executed. Gordon sacked the corrupt Governor of Equatoria and replaced him with Dr. Emin Pasha, a man who had won Gordon's respect as capable and incorrupt. However, with corruption elsewhere in the system, and lack of finance, making it impossible for him to carry out the necessary reforms, Gordon returned to Cairo to resign his governorship. He felt that he had failed and had a minor nervous breakdown.

On his return home, Gordon enjoyed a career break. He rented a flat in London and spent a fortnight visiting Ireland. He was appalled at the poverty he discovered and labelled this a scandal. He considered ending this to be as morally important as ending the slave trade. Gordon urged the government to buy land owned by the Anglo-Irish elite and give it to the Irish tenant farmers. He pointed out that this would end the need for the Irish to seek independence. When he returned to London, Gordon spent his time socialising with his family and a few friends which included Lord Tennyson and Florence Nightingale.

Gordon visited the Holy Land and used this experience to deepen his own faith and explore Biblical sites. He suggested an alternative site for the crucifixion than the traditionally accepted location where stands the Church of the Holy Sepulchre. Those of us who have visited the Holy Land can appreciate that 'Gordon's Calvary' has features which support his assertion, the caves in rock formation giving the hill an uncanny resemblance to a skull. This ties in with the Biblical name, Golgotha. 'the Place of the Skull'.

King Leopold II asked Gordon to take control of the Congo Free State but on his return home, the government had a more urgent assignment for Gordon. A revolt had arisen in the Sudan led by a charismatic figure who described himself as the Mahdi. As it was the beginning of a new Islamic century, the Mahdi considered that he was fulfilling the Islamic tradition that at such a time, a figure like himself would emerge to destroy the enemies of Islam. He declared a 'jihad' against the Egyptian state where much discontent was brewing as a result of the heavy taxation being imposed by Baring to pay off Egypt's debts. The Mahdi defeated a small demoralised Egyptian army sent to oppose him and seemed able to take over everything in his path. However, Khartoum did seem capable of resisting the Mahdi's forces but the English Prime Minister, Gladstone, didn't consider Khartoum was worth the expense of protecting.

William Stead, the editor of the Pall Mall Gazette, a popular newspaper of the time, arranged to interview Gordon. Initially, Gordon was only interested in talking about the Congo Free State but after a lot of prompting from Stead, he was prepared to open up about Khartoum. He was very critical of Gladstone's policy. When Stead published his version of the interview, there was an outcry and the general public clamoured for Gordon to be sent to Khartoum.

Gladstone had won the recent general election which he considered gave him a mandate for withdrawing British forces from parts of the world where trouble appeared to be brewing. However, not all his cabinet shared this attitude. A leader of this faction was the Adjutant General, Sir Garnet Wolseley. Wolseley met with Gordon to discuss the situation in the Sudan and Gordon came away with the impression that his presence was needed there. In view of public opinion, Gladstone agreed that Gordon should be sent to Khartoum to advise on the best way of protecting the lives of any British living in Khartoum. While Gladstone believed that Gordon would be sent to Khartoum in a purely advisory capacity, he was unwell when Gordon was met by a subcommittee of the cabinet to define the role he was expected to fulfil. Gordon was given the impression that he was being sent there in an executive rather than a purely advisory capacity.

Gordon had to inform King Leopold II that in view of the instructions he had received from his own government, he would be unable to take up the post Leopold had offered him in the Congo which greatly displeased Leopold.

Gordon proceeded to Khartoum with a brief that he should organise the evacuation of British nationals from Khartoum but on reaching Egypt, the Khedive appointed him Governor General of Khartoum and ordered him to set up a government in the Sudan. Gordon interpreted this as meaning that he was to use his initiative and adopt an active role in running the affairs of the province.

When Gordon arrived back in Khartoum, he took stock of the situation. As the city stood at the confluence of the White and Blue Niles, much of the city was surrounded by large rivers. He had eight thousand soldiers under his command, all armed with Remington rifles and a huge stock of ammunition. Gordon felt confident that he could defend the city against the Mahdi and considered that this was his duty in view of the fact he had been created Governor General. He organised the evacuation of about two-thousand-five-hundred people into the safety of Egypt as the government had required him to do but disobeyed their orders by remaining in Khartoum to defend thy city.

Gordon started to become mentally unstable and did a number of foolish things, including entering into communication with the Mahdi with demands that the Mahdi, who regarded himself as the successor to Mohammed, would obviously reject. Gordon was publicly critical of Gladstone's policy in dealing with the threat posed by the Mahdi. Some of those in London who had been most enthusiastic about sending Gordon to Khartoum began to have reservations about the wisdom of this decision. However, British public opinion firmly supported Gordon and it was clear that there was a general feeling that the government should send a force to support him. Initially, the government, angered by what they saw as Gordon's insubordination in remaining in Khartoum after supervising the evacuation, were not prepared to do this. They felt that Gordon deserved whatever fate was coming to him.

Entries in Gordon's diary indicate that he thought of himself as a champion of Christianity, fighting against the Mahdi, but as the Egyptians were largely Moslem, he refrained from describing the conflict as a religious war. It almost appears that Gordon had a death wish, hoping to die, fighting for Khartoum.

Gordon energetically organised the defence of Khartoum making good use of steamers which he armoured and which maintained contact with the outside world as they sailed up and down the Nile. He was disparaging about the Arab, Egyptian and Turkish troops under his command whom he considered to be badly trained and mutinous but he had every respect for the black soldiers from South Sudan who had formerly been slaves. They were prepared to fight to the death rather than face slavery which would have been their fate had they come under the control of the Mahdi.

Gordon's problems increased as the siege became more intense and it was difficult for the steamers to get in and out of Khartoum. Gordon maintained morale by regularly organising successful raids on the besieging troops and having a military band perform free concerts in the central plaza. Although the Mahdi's forces had destroyed telegraph lines out of Khartoum, Gordon installed his own telecommunications system within the city so that he could keep in touch with troops defending the city walls, from the governor's palace, He gave the enemy a false impression about the number of troops defending the city by putting up wooden dummies dressed in uniform along the city walls.

Responding to public opinion but against Gladstone's wishes, the government at last agreed to send a relief force to Khartoum under Field Marshal Sir Garnet Wolseley. The preparation of this force was unnecessarily slow and, once it had reached Egypt, it made very sluggish progress along the Nile,

Meanwhile, the situation in Khartoum was getting worse and the people were suffering starvation. Gordon told the civilians that they were free to leave the city and even join the Mahdi's army if they wished. About half the population left the city. Gordon received a letter from the Mahdi offering him safe passage out of the city but Gordon declared that he would stay and, if necessary, fall with the town.

Knowing that a relief force was approaching, the Mahdi met with his generals to discuss what action should be taken. The Nile was low at that time of the year and this had opened up a section where the city was badly defended. The Mahdi decided that now was the time that he must storm the city or retreat. His men swarmed across the shallow stretch of the Nile, into the city, killing all of the remaining seven-thousand defenders. There is no reliable eyewitness account of how Gordon died but it is believed that dressed in his best uniform, he stood at the top of the governor's palace steps, firing at the insurgents with his revolver until he himself was cut down. Following the death of Gordon, an estimated ten thousand civilians in the city were killed by the soldiers who had entered the city until the Mahdi ordered the massacre to cease. Two days later the relief force arrived at Khartoum.

The failure to rescue Gordon was a major blow to Gladstone's popularity and the acronym by which he had become known, GOM (Grand Old Man) became inverted to MOG (Murderer Of Gordon). Queen Victoria herself was angry with Gladstone and her disapproving communication with her Prime Minister found its way into the press. Field Marshal Wolseley was annoyed at being recalled home after the death of Gordon, as he had been given to understand that part of the objective of his expedition was to re-conquer the Sudan, and he wrote to Queen Victoria describing Gladstone in disparaging terms as 'the tradesman who has become a politician'

After Khartoum, the Mahdi was able to set up his own Islamic state. Its regime was very harsh, slavery was restored, and it is estimated that over a ten year period, this regime caused the death of nearly eight million people.

While this account has concentrated on the career of Gordon as a soldier, his philanthropy should also be remembered. After the death of his father, Gordon became very involved in social work, particularly in ensuring that the homeless poor boys, who used to beg in the streets of Gravesend, should be properly fed. He made great efforts to find them homes and jobs, even allowing them to lodge in his own home. He became a trustee of the local 'Ragged Schools' committee. The 'Ragged Schools' were a network of privately-funded schools attended by children whose parents were too poor to afford the school fees which were necessary at that time. This enabled these children to receive an education.

A number of memorials have been erected to commemorate Gordon. Gordon's tomb lies in St. Paul's Cathedral. A statue of Gordon used to stand in Trafalgar Square between the two fountains but this has been removed to the Victoria Embankment and is located in front of the Ministry of Defence building. Gordon's regiment, the Royal Engineers, commissioned a statue of General Gordon riding a camel to be installed outside the Royal School of Military Engineering in Chatham. A copy of this statue was recast and erected in front of the palace in Khartoum but this was removed in 1958 when the Sudan became independent.

Mary Slessor

Mary Slessor

Mary was the second of seven children, born into a very poor family in Aberdeen. The family moved to Dundee to find work but the only place where they could afford to live was in a slum area. Mary's father was a shoemaker but due to his alcoholism, he was unable to continue with this trade and had to take a job as a labourer in a mill. Her mother was a skilled weaver and she also arranged to work at the mill. At the age of eleven, Mary became a 'half-timer', spending half her time working at the mill and the other half, attending the school provided by the mill. By the age of fourteen, Mary had become a skilled jute worker, working from six in the morning until six in the evening with only an hour for meal breaks. Mary's father and brothers died from pneumonia leaving just Mary, her mother and two sisters.

Mary's mother was a devout Presbyterian who avidly read 'the Missionary Record', a monthly magazine published by the church. Mary too became interested in missionary work and when a mission opened near her church, Mary joined this at the age of twenty-seven. On hearing of the death of David Livingstone, Mary decided that she would like to follow in his footsteps. She was accepted by the Foreign Mission Board of the United Presbyterian Church for training at their college in Edinburgh. On completion of this, she set sail for the mission field in Nigeria, accompanied by her cousin, Michael, who was also a missionary. The boat's cargo was hundreds of barrels of whiskey. This was ironic in view of the way Mary's father had been affected by alcohol. Could the power of God, working through Mary, be more effective than the power of the Devil, working through the demon, drink?

For three years, Mary worked at the mission station in Calabar, an area inhabited by the Elik people who were deeply steeped in the superstitions of their pagan religion. Although now domiciled abroad, she assigned a large proportion of her salary to support her mother and sisters in Scotland. This required Mary to adopt economies which she achieved by eating the same food as the natives. Her hopes of going deeper into the Calabar region had to be put on hold as Mary contracted Malaria and had to return to Scotland to recover.

Fully recovered, Mary returned to Nigeria just over a year later and was now able to move to a mission station, three miles deeper into Calabar territory. Here, Mary was confronted with issues arising from the native culture. A western style education was not available and the people were thus, largely illiterate. Human sacrifice took place and Mary had to intervene to prevent the servants of a deceased village elder being sacrificed to accompany their lord into the next world where they could continue to serve him. The people also had a strange superstition about twins who were regarded as bringers of bad luck. Any twins born were left out to starve or be eaten by animals. Mary saved hundreds of twins abandoned in the bush from this fate. She was also able to stop the practice of determining the guilt of suspects by requiring them to drink poison.

The reason that Mary had such an influence on the people among who she worked was the easy way in which she had mastered their language and inspired unreserved friendship with these people. This impressed representatives from the mission headquarters who had gone out to inspect the work being done in Nigeria.

After three years, Mary had to return to Scotland again to recover from another health issue. As she recovered, she was able to use her time, travelling round Scotland and speaking at many churches of her experiences in Nigeria.

Mary returned to Nigeria for a third term as a missionary but was greatly saddened on receiving news of the death of her mother and sister. Although they were not with her in Nigeria, their death left Mary with an overwhelming sense of loneliness as the regular correspondence she shared with her mother had given them a sense of their being near one another. However, Mary also felt a new sense of freedom to undertake more dangerous work as there would be no-one who would worry unduly about her safety.

Mary was the driving force in establishing the Hope Waddell Training Institute in Calabar which provided education and vocational training for the Elik people. She moved further inland into the region populated by the Igbo tribe. Here, she had to battle against the same pagan practices she had eliminated from the Elik tribe. She adopted children she found abandoned and arranged for other missionaries to seek out twins which had been left to die and bring them to the safety of mission stations. This led to many mission stations becoming alive with babies.

In situations where Mary was a lone worker, she often came into conflict with those in authority, earning herself the reputation of being an eccentric. However, her presence worked to stimulate trade, establish educational opportunities and introduce social changes. Her diplomacy enabled disputes to be settled and all the time, her prime work was that of an evangelist. Her work was followed with interest in the U.K. and she became known as the White Queen of Okoyong, the settlement where she was living. In due course, she became Vice Consul of Okoyong where she presided over trials held in the native courts. Her work was recognised in Britain where she was bestowed with the Order of St. John.

Mary's health began to fail as she was afflicted with recurrent fevers, the legacy of the malaria she had contracted during her first tour of missionary duty in Nigeria. While staying at a remote outstation, she suffered a particularly severe return of this fever and died.

Mary's work cannot be overrated. She was more than a missionary, fulfilling many roles as she served God in Africa. Of course, she preached but she served the people among whom she worked in many other ways. She was both a nurse and a nanny, a gifted linguist and teacher, and also, a skilled negotiator who managed to dissuade tribes from going to war with one another

Her body was transported back to Duke Town where she was given the colonial equivalent of a state funeral. Government officials attended in uniform and flags were flown at half-mast. The Governor General, Sir Frederick Lugard, telegraphed a message of consolation from Lagos and published an appreciative eulogy in a government gazette.

In West Africa, Mary is still referred to as Queen of Okoyong. While Mary is widely commemorated in Nigeria and Ghana with monuments and buildings named after her, she is also remembered in many ways in the U.K. A bust of Mary Slessor is to be found in Hall of Heroes in the National Wallace Monument in Stirling. Schools, streets and churches have been named after her. Mary is honoured on a £10 note issued by the Clydesdale Bank and she has even had an asteroid named after her.

Sir Edward Elgar

Sir Edward Elgar

Britain has lagged behind the rest of Europe in producing great classical composers. While a very large number of British classical composers are listed on the internet, very few have become recognised as sufficiently great that their names have become household words. Thomas Tallis, Henry Purcell, Hubert Parry, Ralph Vaughn Williams, Arthur Sullivan and Benjamin Britain are among the best of British composers but their work doesn't quite reach the heights of some of the great continental composers. However, in Edward Elgar, we find a composer whose work matches in splendour that of the great German and Austrian composers. In view of the fact that Elgar is arguably the greatest of British composers, it is surprising how long it took him to gain recognition in this country for his work. The recognition ultimately came and for this, Elgar must owe a debt of gratitude to his wife for her support and effort on his behalf.

Edward was born in Worcester. He was the fourth of seven children. His mother, Ann, was a catholic and Edward was baptised and brought up a catholic. His father, William, was a violinist of professional standard and was also, organist of Worcester's Roman Catholic cathedral. William's main source of income was his shop where he sold sheet music and musical instruments. He also worked as a piano tuner.

Edward received piano and violin lessons from the age of eight and when he was ten, he composed music for a play which he and his brothers and sisters had devised. Forty years later, Edward decided to rearrange these compositions of his youth and found that only a few changes were needed. Apart from his violin and piano lessons from local teachers, Edward was largely, a self-taught musician. He borrowed books on the theory of music from the cathedral music library and worked through organ playing instruction manuals. He started to learn German in the hope of being able to study music at the Leipzig Conservatory but his father couldn't afford to send him there. Thus, on leaving school, he became a clerk at a solicitor's office. He didn't particularly enjoy this work but found an outlet for his musical capability by giving an occasional public violin or organ recital.

He left the solicitor's office to embark on a full time music career, giving violin and piano lessons, accompanying singers on the piano, performing violin recitals, composing and arranging music, and occasionally, conducting orchestras. He also helped out at his father's shop. The distinguished violinist, Adolf Pollitzer, considered that Elgar had the talent to become a virtuoso violinist but having gone to London to hear performances of famous violinists, Elgar himself decided that he was not quite up to the standard required.

At the age of twenty-two, Elgar took up the post of conductor to the band of the Worcestershire County Lunatic Asylum. This may seem a strange occupation for an ambitious musician but the experience gained here gave Elgar a real feel for the tone and capability of the instruments in the band. These included the woodwinds; clarinet, flute and piccolo; the brass instruments; cornet and euphonium; and of course, the strings; violin, viola, cello and double bass. He also became professor of violin at the Worcester College for the blind sons of gentlemen.

Elgar's brother, Frank, ran a wind quintet and Edward regularly played the oboe in this. His compositional skills were in demand for this group for whom he arranged the music of great classical composers.

Elgar was employed as a violinist in a prominent Birmingham orchestra for whom he performed in every concert for seven years. When the orchestra played one of Elgar's own pieces, the 'Serenade Mauresque', the first of his compositions to be performed by a professional orchestra, Edward was invited to conduct. However, he insisted on playing in his usual place among the violinists. The applause at the end of the performance was rapturous and Elgar, violin in hand, had to join the conductor on the rostrum to receive the appreciation of this perceptive audience.

Elgar made frequent visits to London in an attempt to obtain recognition and get some of his work published but without success These visits left Edward virtually penniless and very discouraged as he had expended considerable energy in his attempts to make his mark in London. He sadly confided with a friend that he had come to recognise that his failure was due to lack of talent!

Elgar attempted to further his musical career by visiting Europe, attending concerts in Leipzig and Paris, and meeting some of the great European composers. He became engaged to Helen Weaver, a student at the Leipzig Conservatoire, but the engagement was broken off after a year causing Edward considerable distress. However, he was never without attractive women admirers with whom he formed close friendships. Of these, Caroline Alice Roberts, one of his pupils and daughter of Major-General Sir Henry Roberts, became his wife when Elgar was in his early thirties. Caroline Alice was eight years older than Edward. The Roberts family were horrified at their daughter, marrying an unknown musician who was a catholic and worked in a shop, and Alice was disinherited. Edward and Alice were married at the Brompton Oratory and Alice worked relentlessly to get Edward the recognition she knew he deserved.

Alice was fully aware of her husband's genius and she persuaded him to move to London to be near the centre of the music establishment in the city. Here, they had their only child who was named Carice, based on a combination of the syllables in her mother's two Christian names. In London, Elgar took every opportunity of hearing new music, in particular, by attending concerts at Crystal Palace where he was able to learn orchestration techniques by listening to the music of composers such as Berlioz and Wagner. Two publishers published some of Elgar's violin pieces and organ voluntaries. However, one opportunity was cruelly snatched from him when the Royal Opera house cancelled at the very last moment, a time that had been set aside for their orchestra to run through some of his work. This was because another composer who was better known than Elgar at the time, Sir Arthur Sullivan, had arrived unexpectedly to rehearse some of his own music. When Sullivan discovered some time later what had happened, he was absolutely horrified.

With no employment opportunities opening up in London, Elgar was obliged to return to his native Worcestershire and he settled with his wife and daughter in his wife's hometown of Great Malvern. The Worcester Festival Committee invited him to compose a work for the Three Choirs Festival and Elgar composed 'Froissart', conducting the first performance of this in Worcester Cathedral. He continued to make his living by teaching music, conducting local music ensembles and composing music for festivals in the Midlands but he only just about earned enough to live on and was beginning to come depressed. He was encouraged out of his depression by his friend and publisher, August Jaeger, who assured him that recognition would come.

Sure enough, his 'Enigma Variations' were premiered in London by an orchestra conducted by an eminent German conductor, Hans Richter. This major work received wide acclaim and established Elgar's reputation as a really gifted composer, not only in England, but in Germany and Italy. On the death of Sir Arthur Sullivan at the turn of the twentieth century, Elgar took on his mantle as Britain's pre-eminent composer.

Elgar's next composition, Cardinal Newman's poem, the Dream of Gerontius, set to music, was written for the Birmingham Triennial Music Festival'. This wasn't immediately received with enthusiasm in this country. One reason for this was that the choir which sang the premiere of this work wasn't very good. However, the main reason arose from the Roman Catholic theology of the poem in which Gerontius spends time in purgatory. This was contrary to the doctrinal stance of the Protestant churches. However, the wonderful quality of the actual music was appreciated in spite of the indifferent performance of the premiere. The work received rapturous acclaim when performed in Germany. Because of the theological problem, the Dean of Gloucester would not allow it to be performed in his cathedral and the text of the lyrics had to be modified before the Dean of Worcester would sanction its performance in Worcester Cathedral

The five 'Pomp and Circumstance Marches' are among the best known of Elgar's compositions and the first of these is the only piece of music which has received a double encore at the promenade concerts performed at the Royal Albert Hall. At the suggestion of the contralto, Clara Butt, Elgar asked the poet, Benson, to put words to this music and the result we now know as 'Land of Hope and Glory'. It is believed that Elgar would have preferred less jingoistic words but the music is generally held to be a firm favourite, almost a National Anthem. Indeed, at sporting events like the Commonwealth Games where the home countries compete as separate nations, it has been used as the English National Anthem. It is sung annually at the last night of the proms and in America, it is sung at High School and University graduations.

A three day music festival to celebrate Elgar's work was held at the Covent Garden Opera House. The King and Queen attended the first night and returned again for the second night's performances. The music on the final night consisted mainly a selection of Elgar's orchestral pieces and was conducted by Elgar himself.

More honours were to follow. He was knighted at Buckingham Palace and appointed Professor of Music at Birmingham University. He made a number of visits to the United States and was awarded a doctorate by Yale University.

His first symphony was a national and international triumph. It was performed all over the world, in New York as well as at most of the capital cities of Europe. In one year, it was performed over one-hundred times. His violin concerto which was commissioned by the great violinist virtuoso, Fritz Kreisler, was almost as great a triumph. Its premiere was performed by Kreisler and the London Symphony Orchestra under the baton of Elgar himself. Elgar went on to compose many other great pieces of music, but none quite received the acclaim of his first symphony and the violin concerto.

Elgar was among those honoured at the coronation of George V. He received the Order of Merit which is very special as it is restricted to only twenty-four holders at a time.

When the 1st World War broke out, Elgar was horrified at the carnage but saw it as his patriotic duty to support the war effort. 'Land of Hope and Glory' was already a popular song at this time but he composed a number of other patriotic pieces of music. Rudyard Kipling's verses which he set to music proved very popular. He joined the army volunteer reserve and signed up as a special constable in the police force.

Elgar's health deteriorated towards the end of the war and Alice arranged for them to move to the country. They rented a house in Sussex and as Elgar recovered in health, he started to compose again, producing four major new works which were all well received. The chamber music he wrote was premiered at the Wigmore Hall and received rapturous reviews in the press.

Elgar's work went out of fashion in the post war years but his admirers, including the young musicians, Yehudi Menuhin, John Barbirolli and Malcolm Sargent, continued to present his works. A performance of his second symphony was conducted by Adrian Boult when he was young and virtually unknown. This performance was commended in the press for bringing the grandeur and nobility of the piece to a wider public. Alice Elgar herself wrote of the enthusiasm with which her husband's work was received at a concert of his compositions given at the Queen's Hall. Alice died soon after this concert at the age of seventy-two from lung cancer. Edward moved back to Worcestershire and settled in the village of Kempsey.

Without the support and encouragement of his wife and with no great demand for his work, Elgar composed very little during his widowhood but he wrote some music for the 1924 British Empire Exhibition. Soon after this, he was appointed Master of the King's Music. Elgar was now able to indulge in some of his hobbies which included experimenting as an amateur chemist in a laboratory he had built in his garden, going to the races and following football. He supported a Midland team, Wolverhampton Warriors. In his younger days, he had enjoyed cycling but now, his preference was for being chauffeur driven and making excursions to the countryside. He went on a cruise to Brazil which took him up the Amazon to Manaus where he enjoyed a concert at the impressive opera house, the Teatro Amizonas.

He has been described as the first composer to take advantage of the gramophone which had recently been invented. Fred Gaisberg of HMV arranged sessions at

Abbey Road to record many of Elgar's works including the Enigma Variations, his symphonies and concertos.

During an operation late in 1933, it was discovered that Elgar had inoperable colon cancer and he died the following year at the age of seventy-six. Elgar was buried next to his wife in the churchyard of St. Wulstan's Roman Catholic Church in Little Malvern.

Elgar has been honoured by having many roads named after him. He is represented by a number of statues in prominent cities and was made a Freeman of the City of Worcester. Elgar was awarded honorary degrees from many universities and received honours from a number of European nations. He has been depicted on one of the issues of the twenty pound note.

Baron Robert Baden-Powell

Baron Robert Baden-Powell

Lord Baden Powell was an army officer who is chiefly remembered for being founder of the Boy Scout movement. He was the son of the Reverend Professor Baden Powell, who taught Geometry at Oxford University, and his third wife, Henrietta Smyth, daughter of an admiral. He was born in Paddington and was the fifth surviving child of his father's third marriage. He had four older half-siblings. Three elder siblings had died in infancy before Robert was born so there was a seven year age gap between Robert and his next oldest brother. Robert's father died when he was three but his mother was determined that this shouldn't prevent her children from making a success of life.

When he was very young, Robert enjoyed playing with dolls. He was ambidextrous and could paint well with either hand. He learnt to play the piano and the violin, and he enjoyed acting. Robert won a scholarship to Charterhouse, a prestigious public school. His holidays were adventurous and often involved canoeing or sailing expeditions with his brother. The woods near his school were out of bounds but this didn't prevent Robert and his brothers playing in them. The games often involved stalking one another while at the same time, avoiding being detected by teachers, so this might be regarded as Robert's introduction to scouting.

On leaving school. he was commissioned into a cavalry regiment and served tours of duty in India and South Africa. He developed his scouting skills among the Zulus of Natal province and was mentioned in despatches. Robert's activity impressed his superiors leading to promotion and a posting as aide-de-camp to the Commander-in-Chief and Governor of Malta. Working for the Ministry of Defence as an intelligence officer, he frequently travelled, disguised as a butterfly collector, and he incorporated plans of military installations he reconnoitred into his drawings of butterfly wings.

Baden Powell returned to Africa and saw action in the second Matabele War in which he was involved in the relief of Bulawayo where many employees of the British South Africa Company were besieged. He commanded reconnaissance expeditions behind enemy lines and many of the ideas he incorporated into the Boy Scouting movement were conceived here. An American scout, Frederick Burnham, introduced him to the Stetson hat and the neckerchief which later became incorporated into the Boy Scout uniform.

After serving in Rhodesia, Baden Powell was posted to the Gold Coast (Ghana) where he fought in the Fourth Ashanti War. At the age of forty, he was promoted to the rank of Colonel and thus became the youngest colonel in the British army. He was given command of the 5th Dragoon Guards who were serving in India.

Baden Powell returned to Africa just before the second Boer War and was instructed to maintain a mounted mobile force on the boundary of the land occupied by the Boers. Baden Powell didn't interpret his orders in quite the way his superiors had intended but prepared Mafeking to withstand an extended siege, amassing considerable stores into the city. The town was besieged by a Boer army of eight-thousand men but the city was able to hold out. They succeeded in this, partly due to many deceptions devised by Baden Powell, like establishing minefields which appeared real to the Boers but which were really fake. Baden Powell himself carried out reconnaissance activities and discovered that the Boers had not removed the railway. He therefore sent an armoured train, manned by riflemen, into the heart of the Boer encampment where they inflicted heavy casualties before the train returned to Mafeking. A contingent of boys, which became known as the Mafeking Cadet Corps, was formed in which boys took over many jobs carried out by men, so freeing them to fight. Baden Powell was sufficiently impressed with the courage and bearing of these boys that he included their example when he later formed the Boy Scout movement and published a handbook for this movement. The siege of Mafeking aroused considerable interest among the British public because the Prime Minister's son, Lord Edward Cecil, was also among the besieged. The Boers lacked the artillery they needed to break the siege. Ultimately, the siege was raised after two hundred and seventeen days. This news was met with great rejoicing at home where Baden Powell had become a national hero.

On the other hand, the British high command in South Africa were critical of Baden Powell's activity. In view of the limited armaments available to the Boers, they felt that Baden Powell had the resources to lift the siege himself. He could then have established mounted patrols to maintain a British presence along the border of land controlled by the Boers and gather intelligence as they patrolled. This was the primary purpose for which Baden Powell had been sent to that part of the theatre of war. However, Baden Powell returned to England amid great popular acclaim. He was promoted to the rank of lieutenant-general and invited by the king to Balmoral where he was invested as Companion of the Order of the Bath.

Baden Powell was given the task of organising the South African Constabulary, a colonial police force, but he was only able to carry out this work for a period of seven months as he encountered a period of ill health and had to return home.

On his return to Britain, he was appointed Inspector General of Cavalry and he organised this force into a very efficient scouting branch of the army, well ahead of anything in the service of continental armies. He realised that this was the main use that cavalry should be used for in World War I as cavalry could no longer be an effective force against the modern machine guns, available at the time. However, his superior officers, Kitchener and French, disagreed with him and large numbers of horses were sent to support the army in Europe where they were fairly ineffective. The largest commodity exported from Britain to Flanders during the war was horse fodder!

The other important post to which Baden Powel was appointed was to head the Northumbrian Division of the newly formed Territorial Army. This was originally based at Richmond Castle but Baden Powell moved its headquarters to Catterick Garrison which is still the main army base in the north of England.

Before the outbreak of World War I, Baden Powell began the formation of what has become the Boy Scout movement. A significant event, which might be regarded as the official launch of this movement, was a camp held on Brownsea Island at the head of the Solent. The book. 'Aids to Scouting', which he had written on his return from South Africa, primarily as a military training manual, was being adopted for its ideas by many involved in youth work. Soon after the launch of the Boy Scout movement, he wrote 'Scouting for Boys' which became the fourth best selling book of the twentieth century. Scouting groups for both boys and girls were springing up spontaneously all over the country. The movement soon spread internationally. At a rally held at Crystal Palace, Baden Powell was met by both boy and girl scouts. He decided that a sister movement for girls under a different name should be established and the Girl Guides was formed under the leadership of Baden Powell's sister, Agnes.

Between the wars, a number of international scout camps were held called jamborees, which were attended by scouts from all over the world. At the third jamboree, Baden Powell was presented with a powerful Rolls Royce car and a caravan. The Baden Powells used these to tour round Europe. Under his dedicated leadership, the scout movement grew rapidly and just before the outbreak of World War II, there were 3.3 million scouts in thirty-two countries.

Robert Baden Powell married Olave St. Clair Soames two years before the outbreak of World War I. They shared the same birthday but she was thirty-two years younger than Robert. Their engagement caused a press sensation and to avoid media intrusion, they married in a private ceremony. Olave's sister, Auriol, died shortly after the end of World War I. Olave and Robert adopted her three daughters and brought them up as part of their own family. In due course, Olave became Chief Guide. She outlived Robert by thirty-five years.

The age at which a person could become a scout was eleven so Baden Powell started a junior version for boys between seven and eleven known as Wolf Cubs. These are now referred to as cub scouts. He used Rudyard Kipling's 'Jungle Book' to provide a background narrative for the cubs and their leaders are named after characters from this book, Akela, Bagheera, Baloo, etc. The cover of the 'Jungle Book' had designed into it, an Indian symbol of good luck, the swastika. The swastika was incorporated into the scouting medal of merit but this symbolism had to be quickly dispensed with as it became the emblem of Nazi Germany. Hitler banned the scout movement from Germany as its ideals were so contrary to those of his own youth movement to which it was seen as a serious competitor. Baden Powell's name was included in Hitler's 'Black Book', a secret list of those who were to be detained, following his planned conquest of England.

The contents of the 'Black Book' were not made public until the end of the war. Baden Powell died early in the war and was unaware of its existence or the fact that his name was included. He was perhaps politically naïve and had right wing leanings due to his distrust of communism. Before the war, he had met with Mussolini whom he described as a short, stout and genial person. He read 'Mein Kampf' and considered it contained some good ideas on education, health and organisation, although Baden Powell recognised that Hitler did not practice these so-called 'good ideas' himself. It should be mentioned that, much to the concern of the politically aware people in America who had the unexpurgated copy to read, the only version of 'Mein Kampf' available for British readers was an edited version with most of the extreme material and antisemitic sections removed.

Baden Powell retired from scouting on the occasion of the fifth world jamboree. The joint birthday of Robert and Olave Baden Powell is still marked as 'Founder's Day' by the scouts and 'World Thinking Day' by the guides. In his final letter to the scouts, Baden Powell urged them not to seek happiness by becoming rich or having a successful career but rather, by growing into the sort of person who can be of service to his fellow men. He urged them to try and leave the world a better place than when they entered it. He encouraged them to always 'Be Prepared'. This became the boy scout motto, often abbreviated to BP, the initials of his surname. He urged them that, even when they became an adult, they should keep the second scout promise which they had made when enrolling into the scout movement,

'I will do my best to help others, whatever it costs me'.

As mentioned above, Robert Baden-Powell died soon after the outbreak of World War II and is buried in St. Peter's Cemetery in Nyeri, Kenya. When Olave died, many years later, her ashes were taken to Kenya and interred beside Robert. This grave has been declared a national monument by the Kenyan government.

Emmeline Panhurst

Emmeline Pankhurst

Emmeline Pankhurst's name immediately comes to mind when one recalls the personalities associated with the campaign to secure women's right to vote. She was certainly the most militant of the suffragettes but the jury is out on the issue of whether or not she was the most influential figure in achieving suffrage for women. Some of those working along more peaceful routes to achieve this end may, in the long term, have been more influential as they avoided intensely antagonising those in power. However, it is those who gain publicity by taking violent and spectacular action who get noticed and no-one could fail to take notice of Emmeline Pankhurst. There is no doubt that Emmeline's contribution to the women's suffrage movement was extremely important to its success.

While there is no doubt that Emmeline was a sincere and courageous woman, she remains a controversial personality. She was disruptive and created dissent among those who shared her objectives but were not prepared to follow Emmeline's route to achieve those ends. The disunity she crated extended to members of her own family. During the course of her career, she appeared to take stands and change political adherence in ways which appeared inconsistent with her earlier persuasions.

Emily (the name she preferred to be known by rather than Emmeline) was born in Manchester to a politically active family on 15th July. She claimed her birth certificate was wrong, that she was born a day earlier, French Bastille day, and this is why she felt an affinity with the women among the French revolutionaries who stormed the Bastille. She claimed that Thomas Carlyle's history of the French Revolution inspired her throughout her life.

Emily's mother, Sophie, came from the Isle of Man where the Tynwald (Manx legislature or parliament) allowed women to vote but the Isle of Man does not have members sitting in the English Parliament.

Robert Goulden, Emily's father, had a progressive outlook. He befriended Americans who were active in the abolition of slavery and supported the concept of female suffrage. Although progressive in so many matters, the Gouldens were very much in tune with the culture of their time and although taking trouble to ensure their sons had a good education, they considered that their daughters priority should be making a good marriage and becoming a respectable home maker. However, Robert evidently recognised the fire in Emily, and on one occasion when she was feigning to be asleep, she heard her father mutter,

'What a shame she wasn't born a lad!'

When she was fourteen, Emily insisted on attending a meeting with her mother where Lydia Becker, the editor of a magazine, 'Women's Suffrage Journal', was speaking on women's voting rights. Emily left the meeting, deciding that what she had heard made her a convinced suffragist.

When she was twenty, Emily met and married Richard Pankhurst, a lawyer who supported the suffrage movement. Richard was forty-four. Emily suggested that they should flout convention and dispense with getting legally married but Richard pointed out that in so doing, she would be barred from taking a prominent part in political life. Later in life, Emily was very disapproving when her daughter, Sylvia, chose to live with a partner without going through a formal marriage ceremony. The Pankhursts had five children, Frank, Christabel, Sylvia, Adela and Henry, and hired a butler so that Emily would have the time to remain involved in political activities. Frank died in infancy from diphtheria and Henry died at the age of twenty-one from a spinal infection.

Richard left the Liberal party as his views became more aligned with socialist thinking but was unsuccessful when he stood for parliament. The Pankhursts moved to London and made their home a centre where left wing intellectuals could meet and discuss their ideas.

Emily aligned herself with the National Society for Women's Suffrage (NSWS), a nationwide group, committed to the cause of women's suffrage. However, this society split when its members could not agree on a new set of rules and Emily joined the breakaway group, the Parliament Street Society (PSS). Emily was again disaffected when this group became principally concerned with enfranchising single women as it was felt that married women had voting rights through their husbands. She therefore formed another group, based on her home in Russell Square, the Women's Franchise League, (WFL). This group was regarded as being quite radical, advocating women's rights beyond that of suffrage but in matters of divorce and inheritance, and made alliances with socialist organisations. They ridiculed the Spinster Suffrage party and sought a more militant approach against social inequality. As the group became more extreme, many members left and the group folded within a year.

Richard's shop in London was not successful and the Pankhursts moved to Manchester where Emily found herself actively involved in political organisations. It was during this phase of her life that Emily was recognised to be much more than just Richard's wife and one biographer described this development as Emily, emerging from Richard's shadow. She became active in the Women's Liberal Federation which was closely aligned with the Liberal party but was disappointed in the groups moderate approach to important issues. At this time, she became friends with Keir Hardy, a founder member of the Labour movement, and joined the Independent Labour Party (ILP) which Keir Hardy had helped to create. Emily was excited by the range of social injustices which this party was pledged to rectify. As an activist in this party, Emily found herself distributing food to the poor through the 'Committee for the Relief of the Unemployed'.

Emily was appalled at the conditions she discovered in the Manchester workhouse and worked vigorously to get these improved. Emily faced legal problems when she and two men violated a court order against ILP meetings. Unlike the two men, Emily escaped imprisonment which I think she would have welcomed as a sign of martyrdom to the cause of justice. It is likely that the fact she was a woman was a reason for her escaping imprisonment.

Richard developed a gastric ulcer which was probably caused by the stress of the political activity involved in his unsuccessful campaign to secure a seat in parliament. He appeared to have made a recovery and Elizabeth took her eldest daughter, Christabel, on a visit to a friend in Switzerland. However, while she was away, Richard suffered a relapse and wrote to Emily, urging her to return. It was during her return journey that Emily learnt of Richard's death through reading a headline in a newspaper.

The death of Richard left Emily in debt. She moved to a smaller house and obtained the post of Registrar of Deaths and Marriages in Chorlton. This work increased her awareness of the differences in men's and women's rights, particularly in the matter of illegitimacy. This further reinforced her conviction that women needed the right to vote before their conditions could be improved.

She declared that the position of women in society is so deplorable that we need to break the law in order to draw people's attention to the righteousness of our aspirations. She saw that years of well-meaning moderate speeches in parliament, by members who were sympathetic to women's suffrage, were not enabling any progress to be made in her cause. Therefore, with a group of like-minded colleagues, she founded the Women's Social and Political Union (WSPU). Membership was open only to women who were fully focused on achieving female suffrage. The WSPU eschewed any other organisation which, although sympathetic to their cause, was not fully committed to achieving the vote for women. Emily declared that 'Deeds not Words' should be the motto for the group. She stated that it was their duty to break the law to draw people's attention to why we do it.

The early militancy of the group was non-violent They made speeches, distributed leaflets and even met as a mirror parliament in Caxton Hall. They assembled outside parliament when a bill granting women's suffrage was being debated but when it got filibustered out, the group became so noisy that the police had to force them to move away from parliament. They regrouped and continued their noisy protest, demanding passage of the bill. Emily was pleased that the WSPU was now beginning to be recognised as an influential political force.

Emily was arrested for the first time when she tried to enter parliament to deliver a petition to Asquith, the prime minister. She was charged with obstruction and sentenced to six weeks in prison. She complained bitterly about the inhumane conditions she encountered in prison. Emily declared to the court that:-

> ***'The suffragists were not here because they were law breakers.***
> ***We are here in our efforts to become law.'***

Emily saw that getting herself put in prison was a way to publicise the suffragist movement and she struck a policeman to ensure that she would be put in prison again. She was imprisoned seven times before women gained the vote.

Even though many liberal M.Ps. supported women's suffrage, the Liberal party came into conflict with the WSPU because granting women suffrage was not treated as a priority. One of those who was targeted by the WSPU was Winston Churchill and his opponent declared that Winston had lost his seat because of the opposition of those he had laughed at. The Labour party also came into conflict with the WSPU until they made women's suffrage their priority. Emily criticised the political parties for putting party loyalty ahead of women's suffrage.

Emily feared that if the WSPU became too democratic, it would lose its militancy and she changed the party's constitution so that its decision making would be controlled by a relatively small committee. Emily and her daughter, Christabel, were elected to this committee. This development alienated some influential members of the WSPU and they left to found a rival organisation, the Women's Freedom League (WFL). Emily accepted that the WSPU was now autocratic but insisted that this was necessary for them to effectively function as a women's suffrage army in the field.

In 1908, half a million activists gathered for a rally in Hyde Park and this was followed by those present splitting into seven groups and peacefully marching through several areas of London. Angered by Asquith's indifference to this peaceful demonstration, the activists resorted to more violent measures, breaking windows, making inflammatory speeches in Parliament Square and even hurling rocks at 10, Downing Street. When two WSPU members were sentenced to two months imprisonment for their part in these activities, Emily reminded the court that over the centuries, men had adopted similar tactics to win legal and civil rights.

WSPU members who were imprisoned resorted to hunger strikes to publicise their cause. Attempts to force feed them were brutal and brought condemnation from both the WSPU and the medical profession.

Emily's tactics were not approved by more moderate suffragists who had combined into an organisation called the National Union for Women's Suffrage Societies (NUWSS). They argued that WSPU were carrying what were no more than publicity stunts which were hindering the passage of suffrage legislation through parliament. They refused to join a women's suffrage march when their demands that the WSPU should cease to publicise itself by damaging property were not met.

Emily sold her home and travelled widely abroad giving speeches. In America, these speeches had a mixed reception, not everyone being prepared to condone property destruction as a means of furthering the suffragists' aims. A Daily Mail journalist labelled Emily's branch of the suffragist movement as 'suffragettes' which he intended to be derogatory but Emily and her supporters were pleased to use this term to differentiate themselves from their more placid counterparts. This name, rather than suffragist, has come to be used to refer to those women who fought to secure the vote.

After selling her house and adopting an itinerant lifestyle as she embarked on a series of speaking engagements, Emily felt energised by the support and inspiration she could give to those who were sympathetic to her cause. Her children were now adult and could therefore live independently but Emily missed being unable to see so much of her children. On the verge of her leaving the country to embark on a speaking tour of America, her son, Henry, developed a spinal infection and became paralysed. Emily was hesitant to leave the country with Henry being so ill but the tour promised to be lucrative and she needed the money for Henry's treatment. The tour was successful, and on her return, she was able to spend time by Henry's bedside. He died a short time later and was buried next to his brother, Frank, in Highgate Cemetery. Emily had been booked to speak in Manchester on a date which closely followed the death of Henry, Emily addressed a crowd of five-thousand and members of the Liberal party who had come to heckle her remained silent.

After the Liberals suffered bad losses in the 1910 election, the Independent Labour Party (ILP) and a prominent journalist organised a conciliation committee. This included Emily's militant suffragettes, who temporarily suspended their militant activities, more moderate suffragists and fifty four MP's. There was a strong possibility that a bill going through parliament could become law, allowing certain women the vote. When this bill failed, Emily returned to the strident militancy with bombings and breaking windows which had disaffected the more moderate suffragists. Emily led a march of four-hundred women to Parliament Square and was allowed to enter parliament to present a petition but the prime minister, Asquith, refused to meet her. The Home Secretary, Winston Churchill, directed an aggressive police response to disperse the women gathered in Parliament Square. A few days later, Emily's sister, Mary Jane, who had attended the march, was arrested and sentenced to a month's imprisonment. Mary died at the home of her brother, Herbert, on Christmas Day, two days after her release from prison.

The WSPU suspended militant action while further conciliation bills were debated in parliament but resorted to window smashing and damaging property when the bills failed to get passed. Emily was arrested, tried at the Old Bailey, convicted of conspiracy to cause property damage and sent to Holloway Prison where she staged a hunger strike. When prison officials attempted to enter her cell to force feed her, Emily brandished a clay jug as a weapon and declared that if anyone entered her cell, she would defend herself. Emily was spared further attempts to force feed her. On release, she continued in her militancy, causing damage to property. She was frequently arrested and imprisoned where she went on hunger strike. Emily was now suffering ill health and was released before completing her sentence as the government feared a backlash, should she die in prison. This led to the Asquith government passing the 'Cat and Mouse' act which allowed the early release of suffragettes, on hunger strike and suffering ill health, to avoid the outcry which would arise should suffragette mortality occur while they were in prison.

Emily continued to get arrested and attempted to evade arrest by wearing disguises. She formed an all-female bodyguard who had ju jitsu training and violent scuffles occurred whenever the police tried to arrest Emily.

Over the next years, suffragette violence escalated with arson attacks on public buildings, burning slogans into golf courses and one suffragette hurled an axe at the carriage in which Asquith was travelling. The suffragette, Emily Davidson, threw herself in front of the King's horse at the Derby and was killed by this action. Over fifty thousand people attended her funeral.

There then followed a phase in which Emily and her daughters found themselves at odds with the way the movement should develop. Christabel was recognised by her sisters as their mother's favourite but they claim they felt no resentment about this. Christabel remained loyal to her mother to the end but Sylvia felt the movement was doing itself harm by continuing with actions which she felt were needlessly destructive. When Sylvia started to take independent political action, speaking at a trade union backed organisation, the East London Federation of Suffragettes, (ELFS), Emily feared that Sylvia was about to establish a rival suffragette organisation. She demanded that the word 'Suffragette' should be removed from the name of this organisation. Sylvia refused. The relationship between the sisters, Sylvia and Christabel, became strained. In a book she had written, 'The Suffrage Movement', Sylvia described Christabel as an unreasonable figure. She also considered that her mother's autocratic attitude was harmful to the interest of the suffrage movement. Thus, Sylvia found herself expelled from the WSPU. The third sister Adele was a very insecure figure. She was unemployed and a worry to her mother. Emily therefore paid for Adele to settle in Australia and she never saw her again.

With the outbreak of war in 1914, Emily realised that the threat from Germany was the priority which had to be countered before her own political ambitions and vigorously supported the war effort, putting the same degree of effort into her support as she had for championing women's suffrage. Christabel declared that suffragettes could not be pacifist at any price. She encouraged women to follow the example of French women and volunteer for jobs which had previously been thought of as men's work but which were difficult to staff with so many men being away in the war. This was the beginning of a process by which a sharp demarcation between what were regarded as men's and women's work started to disappear. WSPU members in prison were granted an amnesty and released. Sylvia and Adele estranged themselves further from Christabel and her mother by declaring themselves to be pacifist.

As a Poor Law Guardian, Emily had witnessed first-hand the hardships suffered by disadvantaged children. Thus, a particular concern for Emily was the plight of babies, born out of wedlock, to men serving on the front and she established an adoption home at Campden Hill. Emily herself adopted four children who came to live with her at her home in Holland Park. When challenged as to how, at the age of fifty-seven with no secure income, she was able to do this, she replied that she wondered that she had not taken on forty children.

She toured America, trying to persuade America to support Britain and Canada by entering the war. When, after two years, America did enter the war, she went to America again to encourage the American suffragettes who were still actively militant, to temporarily drop their militancy to support their nation in the more pressing aim of defeating Germany.

When the Bolsheviks emerged as the most influential political force in Russia, Emily was disturbed that they were advocating making peace with Germany. Emily saw this as a German victory and went to Russia to persuade the Russians to continue the war. She met with the Russian Prime Minister, Alexander Kerensky, but the meeting was difficult and unproductive. Kerensky told Emily that she could not understand the class based politics which was driving Russia, and that English women had nothing to teach the women of Russia. Emily left Russia, feeling disenchanted with left wing politics and began to distance herself from the Independent Labour Party with which she had been previously allied. When Emily returned from Russia, she was delighted to see that women's suffrage was well on the way with the Representation of the People Act. This removed the need for men to have a property qualification to vote and allowed women over thirty to vote. This age limitation was brought in, as so many men had been lost in the war and the number of women qualified to vote would otherwise outweigh the number of men. A bill was also passed which allowed women to sit in the House of Commons.

The WSPU decided to change its name to the 'Women's Party'. Although many tried to persuade Emily to stand for parliament, she insisted that Christabel would be a better candidate than herself. Emily announced that Christabel would fight for a seat in the forthcoming General Election. Complex negotiations took place before a suitable seat could be identified. In the end, Christabel became a candidate for Smethwick. The Conservative candidate was persuaded by his leader, Bonar Law, to stand down and Christabel, standing as a Woman's Party candidate, found herself in a straight contest with the Labour candidate. She narrowly lost the election by less than a thousand votes. One biographer described this defeat as the biggest disappointment of Emily's life. The Woman's Party fought no further elections and soon disbanded.

While maintaining a focus on women's empowerment after the war, Emily started to promote the British Empire whose tremendous wealth she saw as being the means of removing poverty and destroying ignorance.

As a result of her many trips to North America, Emily became particularly enamoured of the Canadian way of life in which she saw a greater equality among the sexes than in any other place she had visited. She therefore applied for and obtained the status of a British subject with the right of Canadian domicile. She moved to Toronto with her four adopted children. Here, she became active with the Canadian National Council for Combating Venereal Diseases (CNCCVD). She considered that attitudes to V.D. represented what she saw as a sexual double standard, operating in a way which was harmful to women. During a tour of Bathurst, the mayor showed her a home for fallen women. Emily asked him, 'Where is your home for fallen men?' Emily found the long Canadian winters to be stressful and after three years, returned to England.

Emily's daughter, Sylvia, chose to live with a man without going through a formal marriage, claiming that this was the most sensible option for liberated women. This contravention of a social norm, which Emily now valued greatly, upset Emily. Things became worse when Sylvia gave birth to a child, removing the chance of any reconciliation between mother and daughter.

Emily joined the Conservative party. As a former radical and supporter of the Independent Labour Party, her move from left to right may seem strange. She explained that her wartime experiences caused her to become disillusioned with left wing politics. The things she had learnt during her time in America had also contributed to this change in outlook. Some consider that she saw this move as a means of promoting women's place in society. The Conservatives had deployed themselves well during the war and now had a substantial majority in parliament. Emily stood as conservative candidate for Whitechapel. However, she never actually fought the election. The years of touring, lectures, imprisonment and hunger strikes had taken their toll. She died in 1928 at the age of sixty-nine.

Emily's funeral service was filled with her fellow workers and campaigners, particularly members of the WSPU. The press likened her funeral to an army mourning the death of a great general. The New York Herald Tribune_called her:-

> *"The most remarkable political and social agitator of the early*
> *part of the twentieth century and the supreme protagonist*
> *of the campaign for the electoral enfranchisement of women."*

Earl David Lloyd George

Earl David Lloyd George

David George was born of Welsh parents in Manchester but his father, William, died from pneumonia when David was only just over one year old and his mother, Elizabeth, moved back to her native Wales. She lived with her brother, Richard Lloyd, who was a shoemaker, a lay minister and prominent member of the Liberal party. Richard had a great influence on David and David adopted his uncle's surname to become David Lloyd George. David's cultural background was very Welsh and Welsh was his first language. He was agnostic rather than strongly evangelical in his faith but he remained a regular chapel goer all his life and appreciated good preaching.

David qualified as a solicitor and became very active in campaigning for his uncle's Liberal party during a general election campaign. David's practice flourished and he went into partnership with his brother. He married Margaret Owen who came from a well-to-do farming family.

David came into national prominence as a result of a case in which the nonconformists found themselves at odds with the Anglican church. According to an act of parliament, the Burial Laws Amendment Act, nonconformists had the same right as Anglicans to be buried in parish cemeteries. This act was being ignored by Anglican clergy who forbade the burial of a Baptist in the parish cemetery. On Lloyd George's advice, the Baptists broke open the gate which had been locked against them and carried out the burial. They were sued for trespass by the Vicar but the jury's verdict went against the Vicar. However, the judge mis-recorded the jury's verdict and declared in favour of the Vicar. Lloyd George realised that pressure had been put on the judge to do so. He therefore appealed to the Divisional Court of the Queen's Bench in London where the judge upheld the appeal. This case raised Lloyd George's reputation in Wales and led to his being adopted as the Liberal candidate for the Borough of Caernarvon for the forthcoming election. In due course, Lloyd George came to serve the County of Caernarvonshire as an Alderman, a Justice of the Peace and Deputy Lieutenant. He became M.P. for Caernarvon by narrowly defeating the conservative candidate and remained member for this constituency for fifty five years. Life was difficult for him during the early years that he was an M.P. as members were not paid at that time. He therefore carried on his work as a solicitor in Wales and opened an office in London with a partner, Arthur Rhys Roberts.

Lloyd George was keenly aware that Wales had its own national aspirations which were ignored by central government. One of his first acts in parliament was to form a group of Welsh Liberal M.Ps. who would seek the disestablishment of the Church of England in Wales, reform temperance laws and set up a devolved government in Wales to legislate for affairs which were particularly Welsh rather than national in nature. Thus, historians have referred to Lloyd George as:-

'the first architect of Welsh devolution and its most famous advocate'.

Although Lloyd George saw himself as very much a Welshman, he saw the best future for Wales would be as a self-governing unit within a federal United Kingdom. He was very much involved in the establishment of a number of Welsh institutions like the National Library of Wales, the National Museum of Wales and the University of Wales.

Lloyd George was not opposed to the British Empire but was critical of many of its aspects, particularly in territories which disregarded the freedom of the individual. He was very much opposed to the Boer War. The expense of this war was depriving the country of the cash needed to carry out much needed reforms at home. He considered that the British generals were mismanaging the war, allowing unnecessary hardship in the concentration camps they had set up and not taking adequate care of sick and wounded soldiers. His chief attack was directed against the Chamberlain family whom he accused of profiteering through the war. This attitude brought Lloyd George no popularity and after making an inflammatory speech in Birmingham, he had to be escorted out of the meeting, disguised as a policeman, to protect him from the angry crowd.

However, Lloyd George had built up a considerable body of support through his opposition to the Boer War and this was further strengthened by his opposition to an Education Act which discriminated against nonconformists but favoured schools controlled by the Church of England and the Catholics. This opposition had a unifying effect on the Liberals which had previously been divided in its attitude to the Boer War and at the election, the Liberals held every seat in Wales except for Merthyr Tydfil which was held by Labour. In the new parliament, Lloyd George was appointed President of the Board of Trade. As a cabinet minister, he was very much involved in passing an Act to repeal the existing Education Act. However, this failed to become law as a result of opposition in the House of Lords. The nonconformists were bitterly disappointed at the government's failure to honour one of its election pledges and Liberal support fell away.

Lloyd George acted in an advisory capacity to negotiators who were seeking to set up part of Palestine as a homeland for displaced Jews but this failed as a result of the refusal of the Turkish government to grant the charter which would allow this to happen.

As President of the Board of Trade, Lloyd George enacted legislation which affected merchant shipping, the Port of London and the railways. The owners of railways refused to recognise the railway unions but Lloyd George was able to avert a rail strike by persuading railway companies to negotiate with the elected representatives of the railway workers.

Following the death of the Prime Minister, there was a cabinet reshuffle and Lloyd George became Chancellor of the Exchequer. A pledge the Liberals had made during the election campaign was to reduce spending on armaments. Lloyd George attempted to reduce the proposed number of new battleships to be constructed from six to four but was thwarted by the conservatives who managed to get public support for constructing eight rather than only six new battleships. In view of public clamour, Lloyd George was defeated in cabinet and the estimates for building eight new battleships were approved.

While in office, Lloyd George came under pressure from the women's suffrage movement for although he had expressed lip service to the idea of female suffrage, this had not been matched by any strong support for the movement in parliament.

In what became known as the People's Budget, Lloyd George imposed heavy taxes on the wealthy, including a rise in income tax, the introduction of supertax and a significant increase in death duties. He also taxed the unearned income which arose from the increase in value of land owned. Taxes were also raised on alcohol and tobacco. This would raise money for welfare reforms as well as the building of the new battleships. The budget was strongly opposed by the Conservative party and the House of Lords but was ultimately passed. A new law, the Parliament Act, was introduced to reduce the power of the House of Lords, denying it the right to block finance bills and reducing its power to delay legislation for more than four years.

The outbreak of World War I, a month after the assassination of Archduke Ferdinand had triggered this, came as a surprise to Lloyd George. He was against going to war with Germany and the cabinet, with many pacifist members, was divided. The crucial factor which united the cabinet in being prepared to declare war on Germany was the German demand that it should be allowed to march its troops across Belgian land. This was naturally opposed by Belgium. Lloyd George was able to unify the cabinet in deciding that the country had to go to war on the basis of the Liberal party principle, that small nations had rights which needed to be upheld. As Chancellor of the Exchequer, Lloyd George raised money for the war by increasing super tax, income tax and excise duty on alcohol.

The outbreak of war led to Lloyd George being appointed Minister of Munitions, a new department. Big changes were needed as the country appeared to be in danger of running out of shells and Lloyd George earned considerable acclaim for the bold action he took. He took responsibility for arms production away from the generals and streamlined the cumbersome bureaucracy of the War Office. He resolved labour problems, improved the supply system and considerably increased the output of the armaments needed.

Lloyd George saw that conscription was necessary and saw the need to support our allies fighting Germany by sending them armaments. He advocated raising a Welsh division and required that nonconformist chaplains should be recognised by the army. He got little cooperation in his efforts from General Robertson, the Chief of the Imperial General Staff, and Lord Kitchener, the Secretary of State for War.

Lord Kitchener was killed when the ship which was taking him on a mission to Russia was sunk and Lloyd George succeeded him as Secretary of State for War. He was very critical of General Haig whom he blamed for the fact that the British forces were incurring great losses for very little gain. His relationship with General Robertson didn't improve and the Gallipoli campaign was a disaster. Lloyd George suspected that Robertson was allowing information to be leaked which was critical of Lloyd George's involvement in handling military matters. This led to Lloyd George being attacked in the press for interfering as a civilian in military matters which were beyond his competence.

The Prime Minister, Asquith, was proving to be a weak, vacillating wartime leader and it was clear to senior officials that he shouldn't continue in office. Asquith resigned and Lloyd George succeeded him as Prime Minister. He came into office with the nation demanding that he should take firm control of the way the war was being conducted.

Woodrow Wilson, the President of America which hadn't entered the war at that point, pressed for a negotiated peace but Lloyd George insisted that the war should continue until Germany was defeated.

One of Lloyd George's war aims was the destruction of the Ottoman Empire and he let General Robertson know that he wanted a major victory in the Middle East, preferably the capture of Jerusalem. Lloyd George was impressed with the performance of the French General, Nivelle, who had successfully counter attacked the Germans at Verdun and had expressed his confidence that he could break through German lines in forty-eight hours. He therefore arranged for General Haig to work under Nivelle in an all out attack against the Germans. This suggestion wasn't popular with Robertson and Haig but a compromise was agreed and the action went ahead. The British attacked first and achieved a victory at Arras although experiencing greater casualties than the Germans who had withdrawn to the shorter defensive position of the Hindenburg Line. The French then attacked the Aisne River and won some important strategic objectives but failed in their main objective of breaking through the German line. The losses experienced in this action pushed the French army to the point of mutiny. Whereas Haig had gained prestige after his victory, the overall failure to achieve the main objective lost Lloyd George credibility and the relationship between himself and the 'Brasshats' was further poisoned.

Meanwhile, the Germans resumed unrestricted submarine warfare which was seriously damaging British shipping. Lloyd George took the merchant fleet under government control and established a Ministry of Shipping. It was considered that the best way to protect British shipping was to have them sail in convoys, protected by warships. Admiral Jellicoe wasn't in favour of this idea, stating that the place of warships was with the Grand Fleet. He had fought at sea in the Battle of Jutland, the only major naval battle of the war. The British had lost more ships and men than the Germans but succeeded in driving the German fleet back into the Baltic, achieving their aim of preventing German naval access to the British coast. It was therefore a battle in which both sides claimed victory. Admiral Beatty was appointed as the new commander of the Grand Fleet. He was in favour of convoys and this reduced the loss of British merchant shipping.

Three American merchant ships were sunk by German submarines. Up until this point, the United States had been neutral but this act brought the Americans into the war. By the end of the war, the German submarine fleet had been defeated.

With the fall of the Czar, Russia withdrew from the war. Lloyd George welcomed the fact that the war would now be seen as a contest between a liberal democracy and an autocracy. He accepted the Russian government's proposal that the Czar and his family should be given refuge in Britain but the royal family objected, fearing that the arrival of the Czar in Britain could provoke a civil war against the monarchy. Thus, the Czar and his family remained in Russia where they were ultimately murdered by the Bolsheviks.

Lloyd George set up a War Policy Committee to regulate the future conduct of the war. General Haig had suggested that a Flanders campaign had a good chance of clearing the Germans from the Belgian coast from which German submarines were still operating. The War Policy Committee reluctantly agreed to this. The Flanders Campaign had limited success at Ypres but did not break the Germans as had been hoped. Ypres was followed by the Battles of the Somme and Passchendaele which took place in very poor weather conditions. These were long drawn out battles in which both sides experienced enormous casualties.

Lloyd George appointed Allenby to be the new commander of the British forces in Egypt, telling him that his objective was to capture Jerusalem by Christmas. Allenby succeeded in realising this objective. This led to Lloyd George's government playing a pivotal role in setting up a Jewish state in Palestine. Under the Balfour declaration, Palestine was to be divided into a Jewish region and an Arab region.

Now that Russia was out of the war, the Germans moved their forces from the eastern to the western front, launching a major offensive against the British and the French. The allies fell back forty miles in a state of confusion. Lloyd George introduced conscription, raising half-a-million men who were sent to the front. America was now in the war and Lloyd George urged Woodrow Wilson to send reinforcements as a matter of some urgency. The Americans moved ten-thousand fresh troops a day into the battle zone. The problem that they arrived ahead of their armaments was overcome by making British and French munitions available to them. The German offensive ran out of steam, they had no further reserves and were rapidly losing men. They lost their will to fight. Thus, the war ended with an allied victory on 11th November 1918.

Meanwhile, towards the end of the war, another disaster was overtaking the world. This was known as the Spanish flu epidemic because the first reported cases occurred in Spain but it was an airborne infection which spread throughout the world. It was particularly spread by soldiers returning home from the trenches. Because the war was still raging, the details of this disease's impact were withheld from the British public to avoid undermining morale. A quarter of a million people died in this country. Lloyd George also contracted the disease as did President Woodrow Wilson but they both survived.

As the war ended, Lloyd George's reputation rose to new heights and he led a coalition of Conservatives and Liberals who supported him to a landslide victory in the election held that year. He fought the election on a policy of making this country a fit place for heroes to live and the need to claim reparations from Germany to recover the expense of the war. The official opposition were the independent liberals led by Asquith.

Lloyd George represented Britain at the Paris Peace Conference, convened to settle affairs at the end of the war. He clashed with the other main representatives, President Wilson, Georges Clemenceau, prime minister of France, and Vittorio Orlando, the Italian prime minister, who were demanding reparations from Germany which Lloyd George realised would totally destroy the German economy for years to come. While acknowledging that reparations were called for, Lloyd George was unwilling to go as far as his allies were demanding. Lloyd George described his experience of the conference as sitting between Jesus Christ (Woodrow Wilson) and Napoleon Bonaparte (Georges Clemenceau). Lloyd George was a brilliant negotiator and Britain's interests were well served by this conference, securing mandates for Middle Eastern territories, which had been part of the Ottoman Empire, and taking over confiscated German colonies in Africa and the south Pacific, thus extending what was already a very large overseas empire.

Now that the nation was at peace, Lloyd George could proceed with important social reforms.

The Workmen's Compensation (Silicosis) Act made provision for compensation to be paid to workers who had experienced health problems as a result of working with rock which contained at least 80% silica.

The Education Act raised the school leaving age to fourteen and made provision for further part-time education for those who had left school.

The Blind Persons Act provided support for those unable to work by virtue of being blind and assistance for blind people who were only able to do low paid jobs.

The Housing and Town Planning Act provided subsidies for local authorities to build houses and established the principle that housing was a social service.

The Land Settlement (Facilities) Act encouraged local authorities to provide land, to be used for farming in rural areas and to be used for allotments in urban areas.

The Rent Act was introduced to protect working classes from being charged exorbitant rents but this act did not work as well as had been hoped for.

A series of acts greatly improved the rights of women. The Representation of the People's Act extended male suffrage and gave to vote to women who were over thirty. The Parliament Qualification of Women Act gave women the right to sit in Parliament, and the Sex Disqualification (Removal) Act provided that a person should not be disqualified from holding any public function or office by virtue of their sex or marriage.

The Unemployment Insurance Act extended unemployment insurance from the categories which were already covered, to virtually the whole of the working population.

The Agriculture Act ensured that farm labourers should receive a minimum wage, the state guaranteed the price of farm produce and tenant farmers were given greater security of tenure.

The Employment of Women, Young Persons and Children's Act prohibited the employment of young people below a certain age from working in transport, shipping, engineering, construction, factories and mines.

Lloyd George's government set up a Ministry for Health which led to major improvements in public health and wellbeing. The National Health Insurance Act increased health benefits and extended the eligibility to receive pensions to many more people.

The Easter Uprising in Dublin which had taken place under Asquith's premiership had been suppressed but it had left in its wake, an increase in Irish Republicanism. This was heightened by Lloyd George's disastrous attempt to impose conscription in Ireland during the war. Thus, although Lloyd George had won the post-war election with a landslide victory, the Irish constituencies were dominated by members from Sinn Fein. These immediately declared Irish independence. Lloyd George presided over the Government of Ireland Act which led to the Anglo Irish Treaty giving recognition to the Irish Free State. However, the parliament of six counties in Ulster used a provision in the Treaty which enabled them to opt out of being part of the Irish Free State and the Irish Boundary Commission was set up to establish a boundary between the six counties of Northern Ireland, which had opted to remain as part of the United Kingdom, and the rest of Ireland.

A number of issues occurred which undermined Lloyd George's popularity, especially with some of the conservatives in his coalition. They were neither happy with the setting up of the Irish Free State nor with the moves which were being made to grant independence to India. However, the final straw came with the cash for patronage scandal. It appeared that Lloyd George had sold peerages and knighthoods for cash. More than one hundred hereditary peers had been created. While nothing illegal had been done, this was an abuse of the honours system. Stanley Baldwin, the President of the Board of Trade, persuaded the conservatives within the coalition to end their membership of the coalition and fight the forthcoming election as an independent party. Lloyd George resigned.

Over the next decade, Lloyd George remained a prominent politician but predictions that he would return to power were never fulfilled.

Lloyd George became part of the Liberal shadow cabinet in opposition under the leadership of Asquith. The shadow cabinet unequivocally supported the way Baldwin, the then Prime Minister, handled the General Strike but Lloyd George clearly had misgivings about this and his relationship with Asquith was strained. Just before the meeting of the National Liberal Federation, Asquith suffered a stroke and resigned and Lloyd George became leader of the Liberal party. However, the parliamentary Labour party was now in ascendancy at the expense of the Liberal party and Lloyd George found himself leading a party which was supporting a minority Labour government. As the longest serving member of parliament, Lloyd George became Father of the House, an honorary position which carried no power.

In the thirties, Lloyd George showed an uncharacteristic lack of political judgement in his attitude towards Germany whom he considered had been treated unfairly in the provisions of the Treaty of Paris. He travelled to Germany where he met Hitler, describing him as the greatest living German and the 'George Washington' of Germany. He was convinced that German rearmament was for its own defence stating that the Germans have made up their minds never to quarrel with us again. However, by 1937, he became aware of the menace posed by a re-armed Germany and opposed Neville Chamberlain's appeasement policies. German invasion of Poland led to the outbreak of World War II.

Lloyd George continued to make speeches in the House of Commons but these were of a pessimistic nature and led Churchill to compare him to Philippe Petain who had become a Nazi puppet. Although his health and his voice were failing, he continued to attend Castle Street Baptist Chapel. He was created an earl in the New Year's honours list but he didn't live long enough to take his seat in the House of Lords. He died of cancer just before the end of the war at the age of eighty-two.

Lloyd George was a controversial personality. He is acclaimed as the man who won the war, but he distrusted his own commanders. He was an ardent Zionist but expressed many antisemitic opinions. He had championed workers' rights but later, alienated the working class, resulting in the swelling of the ranks of the Labour movement. Many liberals blamed him for wrecking the Liberal party through his disputes with Asquith. He also had a reputation for being a womaniser but justified this by saying that although he had weaknesses, it is only insipid, wishy, washy fellows who have no weaknesses.

However, Lloyd George is hailed as being one of our greatest Prime Ministers, a great leader in time of war and founder of what has become the welfare state.

Captain Robert Scott
of the Antarctic

Capain Robert Falcon Scott

Captain Scott was an officer in the Royal Navy who led two important expeditions to the South Pole, the 'Discovery Expedition', 1901 - 04, and the 'Terra Nova Expedition', 1910 - 13. His selection to lead these expeditions came about as a result of a chance meeting with Sir Clements Markham of the National Geographical Society. A role Sir Clements played in the NGS was to identify individuals who might be suitable to be involved on expeditions carried out on behalf of the NGS.

Scott was the third of six children born into a relatively affluent family with a tradition of its members serving in the Royal Navy. Scott passed the necessary entrance exam and entered the navy as a thirteen year old cadet. He passed out near the top of his class as a midshipman and one of his first voyages took him to St. Kitts in the West Indies where he first met Sir Clements who was impressed with the way Scott's cutter had won that morning's race across the bay. Sir Clement was further impressed with Scott's intelligence, enthusiasm and charm and kept him in mind as a potential leader of a future NGS expedition.

Scott's career in the navy progressed well with his gaining mainly first class certificates in the exams he took to become a lieutenant and then a torpedo officer. He was then about to enter a financially challenging period in his life. His father sold his business and invested unwisely, leaving his family in a poor financial state. When Scott's father died, not long after losing most of his money, his mother and two unmarried sisters were largely dependent on Robert and his younger brother, Archie, for financial support. Archie himself died a short time later, leaving the burden of supporting his family entirely on Robert's shoulders. Robert was naturally on the lookout for means of increasing his income beyond his basic pay as a naval officer. As a result of another chance encounter with Sir Clements Markham who was now president of the National Geographical Society, Scott was appointed to lead an expedition to the South Pole, even though he had no previous polar experience.

King Edward VII took a great interest in this expedition and honoured Scott, its leader, by making him a member of the Royal Victorian Order. Scott set sail on the ship, 'Discovery'. The team on this 'Discovery Expedition' had very little experience in Arctic or Antarctic waters. They also had hardly any training on the equipment they would need, and they found themselves on a steep learning curve with a number of mishaps on the way. They obviously had basic equipment like sledges, tents and skis and took dogs with them. The dogs quickly succumbed to disease but not before Scott had been impressed with their performance. He overcame his moral qualms and slaughtered dogs to provide the dog food which would increase the range of the surviving dogs.

On one of the expeditions, when making an early excursion into ice travel, they became trapped in a blizzard. When the weather finally settled to make the return journey possible, they lost one member who slipped over a precipice. The expedition also suffered from an outbreak of scurvy.

A march, undertaken by Scott, Ernest Shackleton and Edward Wilson, reached a latitude of 88°S which was only about 500 miles from the South Pole. However, on the return from this march, Ernest Shackleton suffered a physical breakdown and had to be invalided home. The following year, Scott set out on an expedition in a westerly direction. The experience gained the previous year proved valuable and this journey was fruitful. He discovered the Polar Plateau and gathered a number of important biological, zoological and geological specimens.

Some difficulty was experienced in arranging the return journey. The 'Discovery' had been trapped in the ice and it took the efforts of two relief ships and the use of explosives to free the ship. The relationship among those on board the 'Discovery' were strained as it was largely crewed by merchant seaman who didn't take easily to the Royal Navy formalities upon which Scott insisted. On the return of the 'Discovery' to the UK, Scott was hailed as a hero and had a number of honours bestowed on him. He was promoted to the rank of captain and was invited to Balmoral by King Edward VII who raised his status in the Royal Victorian Order to that of Commander.

The next few years in Captain Scott's life were very busy. He resumed his full-time navy career, becoming flag captain to to Rear-Admiral Sir George Egerton on HMS Victorious. He spent time in writing up a record of the expedition and found himself in great demand as a public speaker and as a guest at important receptions. Scott started moving in very exalted circles, meeting King Louis Philippe, Prince Royal of Portugal and Prince Heinrich of Prussia.

During the time he moved in high Edwardian society, Scott met the sculptress, Kathleen Bruce. They were obviously attracted but the courtship was stormy as Kathleen had other suitors and Scott's advances were not helped by the fact that he had to spend a large amount of time at sea. However, they finally married. Their only son, Peter, became a founder of the World Wildlife Fund.

As Scott was preparing for his next expedition to the Antarctic, he discovered that Shackleton was also preparing a polar expedition on which he hoped to actually reach the South Pole. This led to strained relations between the two men. Scott took exception to an article in which the names of himself and Shackleton were coupled together as if they shared joint leadership of the 'Discovery Expedition' whereas in reality, Scott was the undisputed expedition leader. He claimed that the area around the Ross Sea was designated as his territory of exploration and that if Shackleton was set on exploring the Antarctic, he should find a mooring for his boat, well away from McMurdo Sound and to the east of the meridian 170°W. Shackleton initially agreed to this stipulation but in the event, he couldn't find a suitable mooring away from the designated area so he set up his headquarters at Cape Royds. As this was close to the old Discovery base, Shackleton's action met with disapproval from the British polar establishment.

Shackleton returned from the Antarctic, having narrowly failed in his attempt to reach the south pole. Scott was released by the navy on half-pay to lead the next polar expedition from a converted whaler named the 'Terra Nova'. While the National Geographical Society had hoped that this expedition would be primarily for scientific research with reaching the South Pole as only a secondary objective, they didn't have full control of this expedition. Scott himself had the ambition to be the first person to reach the South Pole.

In his planning for the expedition, Scott realised that they would be unlikely to reach the pole relying solely on man drawn sledges and decided that motorised vehicles should be used. At that time, no such vehicles designed to be used in polar conditions were available and an engineer was appointed to design suitable vehicles. He came up with a design in which the vehicles would have tracks to improve their traction in the snow. Scott decided that dogs and horses would also be needed and sent Cecil Meares, a dog expert, to obtain suitable dogs from Siberia. He was also instructed to purchase some Manchurian ponies. Although a dog expert, Cecil Meares knew little about horses and the ponies he acquired were of poor quality and not up to the task they were required to perform.

The 'Terra Nova' set sail from Cardiff but without Scott who was still fund-raising for the expedition. Scott joined the ship later in South Africa. In due course, he arrived in Melbourne, Australia, on his way to the polar regions. Here, Scott received a telegram from the Norwegian explorer, Amundsen, indicating that he too was embarking on a polar expedition, indicating to Scott that there would be a race to the South Pole.

Serious problems then began to arise for the ill-fated 'Terra Nova' expedition. The 'Terra Nova' almost sank in a storm and then became trapped in sea ice just south of New Zealand, delaying progress for twenty days. This was a longer delay than that normally experienced by other ships whose progress had been hampered by sea ice. When they finally reached Antarctica, a mishap occurred during unloading and one of the motor sledges broke through the ice and sank.

The plan to set up a supply base at 80°S could not be realised because the weather deteriorated and the weak, un-acclimatised ponies slowed down the movement of supplies. In the event, the supply base had to be set up thirty-five miles north of the hoped for location. Laurence Oates, in charge of the ponies, advised Scott to shoot the ponies for food and proceed without them. Scott refused to follow this advice in spite of Oates telling him that he would come to regret this decision. In the event, four of the ponies were lost, either dying from cold or having to be shot. On their return to the supply ship, six more ponies were lost, three of them drowning when they fell through the ice.

News reached Scott that Amundsen had arrived with a huge team of cold adapted dogs and set up his base at the Bay of Whales, some two-hundred miles to the east and eighty-nine miles closer to the pole than the 'Terra Nova'.

Scott selected the team of five, including himself, Wilson, Bowers, Oates and Evans, who were to travel with him to the south pole He left instructions that Meares, a senior member of the base party, should set out from the 'One Ton Base' camp to journey to latitude 82°S with a strong team of dogs on about 1st March with the objective of meeting Scott as he returned from the pole. Had this command been followed, there is a good chance that Scott and most of his team would have returned alive.

The main polar party set out on 1st November, using ponies, motor sledges and dogs, leaving supplies at bases along the way for the use of the party which would finally set out from the pole on their return journey. The groups in the main polar party travelled at different rates and the party steadily reduced as groups were sent back to the 'Terra Nova' base, once they had made their contribution to setting up the supply bases.

Scott and his four associates set out for the pole, finally reaching their destination on 17th January, only to discover with extreme disappointment that Amundsen had beaten them to the pole. In the tent that Amundsen had left at the pole was a letter dated 18th December.

The disheartened party set out on the return trek of eight-hundred miles back to the 'Terra Nova' but encountered problems on the way. The weather deteriorated but the party still managed to cover the polar plateau stage of the journey, a distance of three-hundred miles, by 7th February. The next hundred miles involved descending the Beardmore Glacier. During this stage, the condition of Evans, one of the party, deteriorated very badly. He had some bad falls, the last of which was to the foot of the glacier where he died.

The party still had another four-hundred miles to travel across the Ross Ice Shelf as the weather again started to deteriorate and surprisingly, the deposits which had been left to supply the party on the return journey, proved to contain less provisions than expected. Thus, the party continued, suffering hunger and exhaustion. They reached the point where they had hoped to meet up with the dog teams on 27th February, three days earlier than expected, but the dog teams hadn't been sent. Unexpectedly, the temperature dipped to -40° C.

As they continued their journey, Captain Oates suffered very badly from frost bite and was unable to contribute to the workload or to pulling the sledges. He could only stagger along next to a member of the party who was dragging a sledge. He felt increasingly aware that he was delaying the party's progress northwards. When they next made camp, Oates made the remark which is often quoted,

"I am just going outside and may be some time."

Oates left the tent, never to be seen again.

After walking another twenty miles, the three remaining members of the team made their final camp on 19th March. They were only twelve miles short of the One Ton Depot but the blizzard outside, which lasted for many days, was so severe that they could make no further progress. The three men wrote their final letters to friends and loved ones. Included in Scott's note which he intended for the general public were the words,

"Had we lived, I should have had a tale to tell of the hardihood, endurance, and courage of my companions which would have stirred the heart of every Englishman."

Sir Winston Churchill

Sir Winston Churchill

Winston Churchill's leadership during World War II has led to his being regarded as one of our greatest Prime Ministers. While he may be thought of as a staunch Tory who rose steadily through the political ranks until the outbreak of the war led to his premiership, his life and political career is much more complex than this. In the course of his career, he served in the army, he won and lost parliamentary seats, held several ministerial posts and was prepared to change his party allegiance on matters of principle.

He was born in Blenheim Palace, the ancestral home of John Churchill, the first Duke of Marlborough, from whom Winston was descended. His father, Lord Randolph Churchill, was a prominent Tory politician who at one stage in his career, appeared destined to become Prime Minister himself. His mother, Jennie, was a celebrated American beauty.

Winston's early education was at a boarding school in Ascot where his academic performance and behaviour were poor. He was transferred to Brunswick School in Hove where both his behaviour and academic performance considerably improved and he passed the entrance exam to Harrow, a major public school. His father wanted Winston to follow a career in the army and on his third attempt, he secured a place at the Royal Military College, Sandhurst.

He was commissioned into the Queen's Own Hussars regiment and posted to Aldershot, the headquarters of the British army, but Winston was anxious to see action. He used his mother's influence to get transferred to a war zone. He was posted to India and joined expeditions to Hyderabad and the North West Frontier. He embarked on a course of self-education and began to read widely. He got his mother to send him books on history, philosophy and science and in particular, he asked her to send the political almanac, 'The Annual Register', to enable him to learn about politics. He went through an anti-Christian phase, declaring himself an agnostic but on further thought, he decided that Protestantism was preferable to Roman Catholicism as it was much more rational.

Winston declared himself a Liberal but wouldn't join the Liberal Party as he opposed their policy of Home Rule for Ireland. Thus, he aligned himself with the Tory Democratic Wing of the Conservative Party. He supported the idea that children were best educated in non-denominational schools and opposed the movement for women suffrage.

Winston volunteered to join the force fighting Islamic rebels in north-west India but was accepted on condition that his role would be more as a journalist rather than a fighter. This launched Winston's writing activity. His writing was initially reporting for a newspaper but during his life he wrote extensively on political matters, biographies and history. He wrote one novel, Savrola, which was a fictional Ruritanian romance. Winston found that writing was an antidote to the recurring bouts of depression which afflicted him during his life and which he called his 'Black Dog'.

He managed to get himself attached to Lord Kitchener's army where he served both as a subaltern and a reporter for the Morning Post. Kitchener was fighting an Islamic uprising in the Sudan and Winston played an important role in the Battle of Omdurman. He rode ahead of the main army, who were setting up a defensive position, to discover the location and speed of movement of the advancing Islamic army. His role was to relay this information back to the army awaiting the assault. At the end of this battle, he was critical of Kitchener's unmerciful treatment of wounded Islamic soldiers and determined to leave the army to pursue a career in politics. Resigning his commission involved Winston returning to India where he spent his leisure time playing polo, the only sport in which he showed any interest.

On his return to Britain, Churchill became actively involved in the affairs of the Conservative party where he impressed its leaders with his public speaking. He was selected to be Conservative candidate for a by-election at Oldham but Winston narrowly lost to the Liberal candidate.

In anticipation of the outbreak of the Boer War, the Morning Post, which employed Winston as a journalist, sent him to South Africa to report on events there. He travelled to the conflict zone near Ladysmith which was being besieged by the Boers. The train in which he was travelling was derailed by Boer shelling and although he was a civilian at that time, Winston was taken as a prisoner of war. He escaped from the P.O.W. camp and made his way to the safety of Portuguese East Africa. He returned to South Africa and joined the army which was still fighting to relieve Ladysmith and to take Pretoria. He was among the first soldiers to enter each of these as the British army succeeded in their objectives. Winston generally admired the Boers and treated anti Boer sentiment as prejudice and not an attitude which could be justified. On achieving victory, he urged the government to be magnanimous towards the Boers. His despatches to the Morning Post were read with great interest by the British public.

On Winston's return to Britain, he stood again for the Oldham parliamentary seat, winning it this time to become an M.P. at the age of twenty-five. He wrote a book about his experiences in the Boer War and this became the basis of lecture tours he made in Britain, America and Canada. This work was a financial necessity for Winston as, at that time, members of parliament were not paid. The following year, he gave these lectures in Paris, Madrid and Gibraltar.

While in parliament, Winston drifted to the left. He was openly critical of many of the government's policies and felt more at home with Asquith's Liberal party. He was at odds with Conservative party in his support for free entry into this country for asylum seekers. Churchill, as a free trader, voted against the government on its protectionist legislation. This annoyed the Prime Minister, Arthur Balfour, who arranged for the Oldham Conservative party to deselect Winston in the forthcoming election. Churchill therefore joined the Liberal Party.

The Liberals won the General Election with a massive landslide, Churchill winning the seat for Manchester North West. He was given a junior ministerial post as Under Secretary of State for the Colonial Office. He had the task of settling South Africa after the upheaval of the Boer War. This involved ensuring equality was established between the British and the Boers. He drafted a constitution for the state of Transvaal and oversaw the formation of a government for the Orange River Colony. He was very concerned about the relationship between the Europeans and the black African population, expressing disgust at the brutal way the Europeans had treated the Africans after a rebellion launched by the Zulus in Natal.

Over the next few years, up until the outbreak of World War II, Churchill experienced a roller coaster of a political career, winning and losing parliamentary seats, occupying various ministerial posts and, for a time, being in parliament without a ministerial office. As an M.P., his party allegiances changed and he fought his elections as a Liberal, as an Independent, as a Constitutionalist and as a Conservative. He served under a number of famous Prime Ministers, Asquith, Lloyd George, Baldwin and Chamberlain. The following accounts show the dates of elections Churchill fought and the years in which he was appointed to ministerial office. A list of Prime Ministers and their years of office is included in the Appendix to this book, should the reader wish to ascertain who were Prime Ministers during Churchill's parliamentary career.

In 1906, Churchill won the Manchester North West seat but in 1908, he narrowly lost this seat. Later that year, he comfortably won the seat for Dundee. He was re-elected to this seat in 1910 but lost it after twelve years in 1922. In 1924, he stood as an Independent in the Westminster Abbey byelection but lost. In the same year, he stood as a Constitutionalist at Epping. He won this seat and retained it in 1929.

During these years, he held a number of ministerial posts at both junior and senior level. In 1906 when he was a Liberal M.P., he became Under Secretary of State for the Colonial Office. In 1908, he was appointed President of the Board of Trade. At the age if thirty-three, he became the youngest person to hold Cabinet office for fifty years. During this year, he married Clementine Hozier at St. Margaret's, the church located just outside the Houses of Parliament. This happy marriage was important to Winston's career. He was probably not an easy man to live with but Clementine's faithfulness and affection provided Winston with a happy and stable background.

In 1910 he became Home Secretary and the following year; he was appointed First Lord of the Admiralty. In 1915, he requested the Prime Minister, Asquith, that he should be made Governor General of British East Africa. He resigned from government when this request was refused. During World I, he became Minister of Munitions in 1917 under Lloyd George. Two years later, he held the joint offices of Secretary of State for War and Secretary of State for Air. In 1921, Winston became Secretary of State for the Colonies. Three years later, he became Chancellor of the Exchequer.

As a government minister, Churchill was responsible for shaping a number of important policies.

He dealt wisely with the often fraught labour relations problems which frequently arose. Winston had to arbitrate in an industrial dispute between ship workers and their employers. Having settled this and in so doing, gaining a reputation as a conciliator, he set up a Standing Court of Arbitration to deal with future similar disputes.

Churchill introduced the Mines Eight Hours Bill which protected miners from being required to work shifts of longer than eight hours. He promoted the Trade Boards Bill which created trade boards which could prosecute employers who were considered to be unfairly exploiting their work force. He established the right for workers to have meal breaks and the principle of a minimum wage for workers. Under Churchill, labour exchanges, whose role was to assist the unemployed to find work, were set up throughout the country. He also promoted an unemployment insurance scheme.

In order to finance these reforms, taxes had to be raised and this met with stiff opposition from the House of Lords whose Conservative members would have to shoulder the burden of these taxes. They vetoed the budget. The government therefore called a General Election and the mood of the country was clearly demonstrated by the Liberals winning a convincing victory. Churchill was in favour of replacing the House of Lords with a different type of second chamber but in the end, the power of the House of Lords was curbed by his Parliament Act which restricted the Lord's power to obstruct legislation introduced in the House of Commons.

As Home Secretary, Churchill implemented acts which reformed the existing penal system. A distinction was drawn between criminal and political crimes, relaxing the penalties for those convicted of political crimes. Conditions in prisons were made less harsh, with a requirement that access to prison libraries should be available to prisoners and that prisons had the responsibility of providing a limited amount of entertainment for prisoners. The rules for solitary confinement were relaxed, automatic imprisonment for those defaulting on fines was abolished and people between the ages of sixteen and twenty-one would only be imprisoned if they had committed very serious crimes. Forty-three cases came before Churchill requiring him to authorise carrying out a death sentence. He commuted half of these.

Winston supported women's suffrage but would only back a bill granting votes to women if he was convinced that this was something the electorate really wanted and suggested a referendum. The Prime Minister refused to sanction this, leaving many women mistakenly believing that Churchill was opposed to women's suffrage. One suffragette attacked Churchill with a whip for which she received a six week prison sentence.

Striking miners in Tonypandy rioted against their poor working conditions and the Chief Constable of Glamorgan urged Churchill to send troops to deal with the rioters. When Churchill discovered that troops were already on their way there, he wouldn't allow them to proceed beyond Swindon, fearing unnecessary bloodshed. Instead, he sent two-hundred-and-seventy London police, not equipped with firearms, to end the disturbance. However, the riots continued so Churchill offered the services of a government arbitrator to settle the dispute. Both sides accepted this suggestion and the riots ended. Privately, Churchill considered that both the mine owners and the strikers had been unreasonable but the right wing press accused Churchill of being too soft on the rioters. The trades union movement regarded him as being too heavy handed and Churchill earned the long term suspicion of the Labour movement. This was ameliorated the following year when he had passed the Coal Mines Bill which imposed stricter safety standards in mines. In the same year, he introduced the Shops Bill to improve the working conditions of those employed in shops but this displeased many shop owners and was only passed after considerable modification.

As Home Secretary, Churchill became involved in a very unpleasant business which has become known as the Sydney Street siege. Three burglars of Latvian nationality had killed police officers in the course of their crimes and were now holed up in a house in Sydney Street, located in East London. The police had surrounded the house but were reluctant to go in in view of the fact that these desperate criminals were armed and prepared to kill. The house caught fire but it's not clear what caused the fire. The fire brigade arrived but Churchill was not prepared to risk more lives being lost and ordered the firemen not to enter the house until the fire had been brought under control and it seemed safe to do so. When the fire had been put out, the police did go in to find two of the burglars dead. Churchill faced some criticism for the way he had handled this emergency but claimed that he considered himself justified in managing things so that no further British lives were lost.

In 1911, Asquith appointed Churchill 1st Lord of the Admiralty, a post which Churchill filled with energy and determination. He visited naval establishments to build up morale and encouraged the building of more ships to match the rapidly growing German navy, threatening to resign if an order for four new battleships was cancelled. He realised the importance aircraft would play in any future war and ordered the construction of a hundred sea planes. To ensure that adequate fuel would be available for the navy, he convinced the government to buy a 50% share in the Anglo Persian Oil Company. His invitation to the Germans to engage in mutual de-escalation of their navies was refused.

On the outbreak of war in 1914, Churchill arranged for the navy to transport one-hundred-and-twenty-thousand troops to the continent. The arrival of the marines in Ostend caused the Germans to relocate their troops Although he was unable to relieve Antwerp, he asserted that the support he had given to the city enabled it to hold out long enough for the allies to secure Calais and Dunkirk. He had the navy blockade the German North Sea ports and sent submarines to the Baltic Sea to support the Russian war effort. He made Admiralty funds available to ensure that battle worthy tanks could be developed and manufactured.

British involvement in the Middle East theatre of war led Churchill to consider that attacking Turkey, would take pressure off Russia. He arranged to bombard

Turkish ports and land a force of British, Australian and New Zealand troops at Gallipoli. This assault failed and Churchill came in for a lot of criticism from the Conservatives who would only agree to join a coalition government if Churchill was relieved of his post at the Admiralty. Churchill resigned from the government but remained as an M.P. Although Churchill continued to attract criticism from the pro-Conservative press for the failure of the Gallipoli campaign, the Dardanelles Commission, convened to look into this military reverse, found that no blame could be attached to Churchill personally for this failure.

Churchill re-engaged in active military service, serving as a lieutenant colonel in the Royal Scots Fusiliers where they faced the Germans along the Belgian front. When his regiment lost its identity as a result of the regimental mergers which were taking place, he resigned his commission and returned to parliament.

When Asquith resigned and was replaced by Lloyd George, Churchill returned to Government as Minister of Munitions. He ended a strike by munitions workers along the Clyde by negotiation and managed to increase the output of this factory. When a second strike occurred, he ended this by threatening to conscript the strikers into the army.

In 1918, Churchill voted in support of the Representation of the People Act which gave some women the right to vote.

In the new government which came into power at the end of the war, Churchill retained his position in Government as Minister of State for War. In this office he had the responsibility for organizing the demobilization of the army but he kept a small contingent of conscripts to become part of the British Army on the Rhine (B.A.O.R.). He was one of the few ministers who opposed imposing harsh reparations on Germany to pay the expenses incurred by the allies during the course of the war. Churchill was very critical of Lenin's Communist Party which had come into power at the end of the Russian civil war.

On becoming Secretary of State for the Colonies, Churchill was involved in negotiations with Sinn Fein to formulate an Anglo-Irish Treaty. He was involved in the installation of Faisal as King of Iraq and Abdullah as King of Jordan. As a Zionist, he was in favour of Jewish immigration into Palestine but set limits on this in view of Arab objections which had led to rioting.

After a time out of government, Churchill became Chancellor of the Exchequer. In his budgets, he reduced the state pension age from seventy to sixty-five, provided pensions for widows, and reduced income tax. These measures were paid for by a reduction in military expenditure and taxes on luxury items.

During the General Strike, Churchill edited the gazette which presented anti-strike propaganda. He acted as an intermediary between striking miners and their employers. Churchill advocated the introduction of a legally binding minimum wage for workers.

When Labour won the 1929 General election, Churchill found himself out of office again and he became prone to the depression he described as 'Black Dog'. He also earned a reputation of being a heavy drinker although it is generally believed that reports on his drinking habits were exaggerated. He offset his depression by immersing himself in writing a biography of his ancestor, the Duke of Marlborough. Churchill went to the continent to visit some of the sites of Marlborough's battles. While there, he met a friend of Hitler who was then rising into prominence. This friend offered to arrange for him to meet Hitler but Hitler was not prepared to meet Churchill, considering that spending time with minor British politician would be time wasted.

As an opponent of Indian independence, Churchill was a fierce critic of Mahatma Ghandi whom he regarded as seditious. Although supported by many conservatives, his views on this enraged members of the Liberal and Labour parties. In the House of Commons, he opposed a bill which would give Dominion Status to India but when the House divided, only forty-three M.Ps. voted with Churchill.

Churchill's financial state became critical after suffering heavy losses in the Wall Street crash and he toured America to earn money by giving lectures which he hoped would go some way to restoring his finances. While in America, he was knocked down by a car in Fifth Avenue, New York, and suffered a serious head injury. He went to Nassau in the Bahamas to convalesce but continued to remain depressed about his financial and political future.

During a time he spent on the continent, Churchill contracted paralyphoid, a fever of the same severity as typhoid. He had to recuperate in a sanitorium in Salzburg. On return to his home at Chartwell, he had a recurrence of this paralyphoid and spent a month in a London nursing home before recovering.

Churchill was alarmed when Hitler came into power and Germany started to rearm. He was an outspoken critic of this evil regime and in the House of Commons, he expressed dismay that the government had reduced its spending on the air force. This meant that Britain would soon be overtaken by Germany in arms production. He could speak with authority on this as he had up to date information on the state of German armaments from data which had been clandestinely collected by two civil servants. He was critical of other fascist regimes in Europe. He opposed Mussolini's invasion of Ethiopia and considered that Franco was aligning himself too closely with Hitler and Mussolini.

In 1935, Baldwin won the General Election. Although retaining his seat with a large majority, Churchill was left out of government. The following year, King Edward VIII abdicated in view of national opposition to his wish to marry Wallis Simpson, an American divorcee. Churchill supported Edward VIII through this crisis and considered that his abdication was premature and unnecessary. However, he declared his loyalty to the next king who succeeded Edward, George VI.

Baldwin was succeeded as Prime Minister by Neville Chamberlain. During this time, Germany was displaying aggressive tendencies, aimed at its territorial expansion into Europe. Churchill called for a defence pact with the threatened countries of Europe, claiming that this was the only way to curb German aggression. Germany invaded Czechoslovakia, occupying the Sudetenland on the pretext that they had a right to do this as most of the inhabitants of the Sudetenland spoke German. Churchill was appalled by the lack of action against this on the government's part and spoke against this passive pacificism in the House of Commons. When Chamberlain signed the Munich Agreement which accepted Germany's right to annex the Sudetenland, Churchill described this act of appeasement as a total and unmitigated defeat. He spoke in the Commons, calling for the creation of a government of national unity to deal with the international crisis which was unfolding. Churchill gained great popularity through making this speech. Britain declared war on Germany when Germany invaded Poland.

On the day that war was declared on Germany, Chamberlain appointed Churchill, 1st Lord of the Admiralty. The outbreak of war increased the need to unite the country by setting up a coalition government but the Labour party, although being prepared to serve under a Conservative prime minister, were not prepared to serve under Chamberlain in the light of his failed policy of appeasement. This left only two possible candidates, Winston Churchill and Lord Halifax. Lord Halifax felt that he couldn't run a wartime government effectively from the House of Lords and thus, Churchill was asked to form a government. Churchill later wrote that he felt a profound sense of relief at being appointed Prime Minister as he felt that his whole life up to this point had been a preparation for holding this office.

Churchill was very encouraged by the British success at the Battle of the River Plate and warmly welcomed home the crews of the victorious battle ships. He commanded the captain of a British destroyer to board a German supply ship in Norwegian waters to release nearly three-hundred merchant seamen who had been captured by the Germans.

With the retreat of the British expeditionary force from Dunkirk, Lord Halifax pressed for seeking a peace treaty with Germany, but Churchill was strongly against this and with the support of the Labour members of his divided cabinet, Churchill's will prevailed.

Much of Churchill's success during the war arose from his brilliant oratory and this, despite suffering a speech impediment which made it difficult for him to properly pronounce 's'. Churchill worked on this problem and effectively overcame it although often his 's' was pronounced more like a 'z'.

In a great speech, he told the country that he had nothing to offer but
'blood, sweat and tears'
but he declared,
'We must achieve victory for without victory, there will be no survival'.

After the evacuation of the army from Dunkirk, a success which had exceeded all expectations, he made his famous

'we shall fight on the beaches but will never surrender'

speech in which he described the Dunkirk evacuation as a

'miracle of deliverance'.

The war entered its most dangerous phase when the Luftwaffe initiated a concentrated bombing assault on Britain. Had Germany secured air superiority, there was every probability that this would set up a situation where the Germans could successfully invade Britain. However, the Royal Air Force with its superior fighter planes were able to see off the Germans and Churchill paid tribute to their bravery in which he declared:-

'in the field of human conflict, never was so much owed by so many to so few'

Britain had increased its output and Churchill's morale was high, feeling that now, Britain could resist any attempt at invasion. However, he felt that without American involvement in the war, complete victory would be difficult to achieve.

Meanwhile, Churchill ordered the Western Desert Campaign in North Africa in response to Mussolini declaring war in support of Hitler and the occupation of North Africa by the Italians. This campaign went well while the British were just fighting the Italians but things became more difficult when Mussolini requested help from Hitler. Hitler sent his brilliant general, Rommel, leader of the Afrika Korps, to North Africa. This put the British on the defensive. General Goff was sent to Africa to command the British troops but he was killed when his plane was shot down. He was replaced by General Montgomery who proved an inspiration to the British troops who were able to defeat Rommel at the Battle of El Alamein.

Churchill had a good relationship with the American President, Franklin Roosevelt, and was able to receive supplies of food and munitions, via the North Atlantic, from America, which was not yet in the war. By making British naval bases in the Caribbean, Bermuda and Newfoundland available to the Americans, he was able to redeploy naval resources from these bases for operations elsewhere.

Churchill was aware, through intercepted German communications which were decoded at Bletchley Park, that Hitler intended to invade Russia. He tried to warn Joseph Stalin through his ambassador, Stafford Cripps, but Stalin didn't believe him as he distrusted Churchill who had often expressed anti-communist sentiments. However, when this invasion started, Churchill declared his support for Russia, stating:-

***'had Hitler invaded Hell, I would have at least made
a favourable reference to the Devil.'***

America entered the war after the Japanese attack on Pearl Harbour. Churchill went to America where he met Roosevelt to discuss the conduct of the war at the Arcadia Conference. This had the important outcome that the Americans would prioritise victory in Europe over defeating Japan. Churchill addressed a meeting of the U.S. Congress but that night he suffered a heart attack. To avoid public alarm, his physician described this with the euphemism, 'a coronary deficiency'. Churchill was prescribed several weeks bed rest to recover but he declared he didn't need this rest and immediately travelled to Ottawa to address the Canadian parliament. In his speech there, he made a reference to a prediction that the French had made at the beginning of the war, that Britain would have its neck wrung like a chicken. Churchill's response was

'some chicken, some neck'.

Meanwhile, things were going badly for the British in the Far East. The Japanese had invaded Burma and Malaya and the British garrison in Singapore had capitulated. Churchill described this as

'the worst disaster and largest capitulation in British military history'.

The Japanese occupation of Burma, restricted food imports from that country to India and flooding, crop disease and adverse weather conditions affected the harvest in India, leading to starvation. India requested grain shipments from Britain. Even though Britain itself had to conserve food supplies, Churchill ordered that large quantities of food should be sent to India. However, with only limited shipping being available in time of war, this aid was insufficient and a severe famine was experienced in Bengal in which nearly three million people died. Churchill was criticized for not responding to this emergency with greater urgency.

Although there were concerns for his health, Churchill made a deviation in his route to Russia when on his way to Moscow to meet with Stalin, so that he could visit the British troops in North Africa and raise their morale. In spite of their political differences, Churchill and Stalin got on well. Stalin was desperate for the Allies to open up a second front in Europe. Churchill could do no more than assure him that preparations for this were underway but was unable to commit himself to a date.

The tide of war began to shift with Montgomery's victory in North Africa and the Russian defeat of the Germans at Stalingrad. Commenting on the impact of these victories, Churchill stated,

***'This is not the end. It is not even the beginning of the end,
but it is, perhaps, the end of the beginning'.***

Churchill had to be away from Britain for a month to attend important meetings and conferences in North Africa. On his return, he addressed the House of Commons but went down with pneumonia the following day. Recovery required a month's bedrest but at the end of the month, he was back in action. During that year, Churchill attended a number of important conferences with his allies in Washington, Quebec, Cairo and Tehran. During these conferences, he had discussions with General de Gaulle, the leader of the Free French, and Chiang Kai Shek, the leader of the Chinese. The conference at Tehran was the most important of these as it was the first of a trio of conferences involving the big three, Churchill, Roosevelt and Stalin.

When in Tunis, Churchill became seriously ill with atrial fibrillation (arrhythmia) and had to remain in Tunisia until after Christmas, under the care of a specialist team who were drafted in to ensure his recovery. During 1943, Churchill had been out of the country for two-hundred and three days.

During the big three discussions in Tehran, Churchill had been committed to opening up a second front in Western Europe. Discussion with his American allies came to the conclusion that invasion across the Channel wasn't possible so Churchill suggested that having defeated Rommel's Afrika Korps, the front could be set up by invading Italy via Sicily from North Africa. This invasion was put into operation but advancing through Italy proved more difficult than anticipated and having fully occupied Italy, the army was confronted with the natural barrier represented by the Alps. It was decided therefore that an invasion across the

Channel would have to be undertaken. Thus, Churchill became enthusiastically involved in planning this invasion which was given the codename, 'Operation Overlord'. By this time, Britain had overwhelming air superiority over Germany and Churchill saw the potential of the Mulberry harbours which could be floated across the Channel to facilitate supplying the troops operating in a bridgehead created by troops landing in Normandy.

Churchill wanted to be actively involved in the Normandy landings but those around him realised that this would be unwise. The King also wanted to be involved and Churchill realised that this would create problems. Churchill therefore agreed that he wouldn't insist on landing with the invading troops provided the King was prepared to remain in Britain as well. The landings eventually took place. In the first few days of the invasion, eight-thousands lives were lost but this was considerably less than the twenty-thousand casualties that Churchill had feared would be incurred. Churchill was able to go to Normandy a few days after the allies had established their bridgehead and he visited Montgomery who had set up his headquarters five miles inland. On the day that Churchill returned to Britain, Germany launched its V1 flying bombs which caused considerable destruction in Britain, especially in London where the main casualties of this indiscriminate bombing were civilian.

As the war was drawing to a close, Churchill, Roosevelt and Stalin met in Yalta to debate the way that Europe would come under allied control at the end of the war. The Russians were well advanced across Europe by this time and thus could claim sovereignty over many Eastern European countries including Poland. Churchill was not in favour of this but as Roosevelt was not in good health at this conference, he was not able to give Churchill the support needed to effectively make his case. The formation of the post-war United Nations Organisation also came under discussion at this conference. There was general agreement on this.

In the latter stages of the war, a massive air raid was carried out on Dresden in which there were huge civilian casualties. It is now known that about twenty-five-thousand were killed which is less than the number initially feared to be dead. Churchill came under criticism for allowing this air raid which did little to advance military objectives but caused terror among civilians. Churchill decreed that future bombing raids should have clear military objectives in view.

On 7ᵗʰ May 1945, the allies accepted the German surrender and the next day was celebrated as Victory in Europe Day (V.E. Day). Churchill appeared with the King and Queen on the balcony of Buckingham Palace and later, gave a victory speech to the crowd gathered in Whitehall. He urged Ernest Bevin to join him to share the applause but Bevin refused saying to Churchill, "No, this is your day."

Churchill broadcast to the nation that evening, asserting that victory over Japan would soon follow this European victory.

Later in the month, the French attempted to put down a nationalist uprising in Syria. Churchill's instruction to General de Gaulle to desist was ignored creating a crisis in the Levant. In the end, British troops from Jordan had to be mobilised to restore order. The outnumbered French troops had to return to their base and de Gaulle was left feeling humiliated. Churchill allegedly told a colleague that he considered de Gaulle to be a great danger to peace and to Great Britain.

Churchill, accompanied by Attlee and Bevin, attended the Potsdam conference, convened to settle post war affairs. The conference went badly for Churchill who didn't perform well. Churchill's contribution was later described as appalling. He was unprepared and verbose. He upset the Chinese, exasperated the Americans and allowed himself to be led by Stalin whom he should have been opposing.

At the end of the war, the Labour ministers refused to continue in the cabinet under Churchill and a general election was held. In speeches made during the war, Churchill had shown himself unready to carry out the reforms that would be needed after the war but the Labour party were perceived as being more ready and able to carry these out. Churchill made some serious gaffes during the election campaign, resorting to party politics instead of dealing with the pressing issues facing the country. He tried to denigrate the Labour party by claiming they would introduce a form of gestapo. Attlee was easily able deny this claim in an election speech he broadcast in reply to Churchill's allegations. In delivering this eloquent speech, Attlee built up considerable prestige for himself. In Churchill's constituency of Woodford, he was only opposed by a single independent candidate but his majority was much less than he had expected. Because of the time required to collect the votes from nationals posted overseas, the result of the election was not officially known for several days after polling but it was clear that Labour would win. Lunching with his family in Downing Street before the result was officially declared, Churchill was very glum. Clementine tried to brighten his mood by pointing out that election defeat might be a blessing in disguise to which Churchill replied,

"At this moment, it appears very effectively disguised."

In the event, Labour secured a landslide victory.

Churchill now found himself as Leader of the Opposition. Post war Europe had been divided in a way which was not to Churchill's liking. In a speech delivered in America, he declared,

"From Stettin on the Baltic to Trieste on the Adriatic, an Iron Curtain has descended across the continent."

In this speech, he called for a 'special relationship' to be established between the United States and the Commonwealth within the framework of the United Nations charter.

In the 1951 General Election, the Conservatives returned to office with a narrow majority. Churchill was Prime Minister once again. A special concern for his administration was the building of sufficient houses. Their manifesto made a commitment to build three-hundred-thousand houses in a year. This target was achieved. Churchill was not in good health when he came into office and experienced a number of minor strokes. This was of great concern to King George VI who considered asking him to stand down in favour of Anthony Eden, but the King himself was not in good health and died before approaching Churchill on this matter. His successor, Queen Elizabeth II, requested Churchill that he should become a Knight of the Garter, the highest order of British chivalry. He accepted this offer and was knighted as Sir Winston Churchill. The Queen had wanted to create Churchill, Duke of London, but he refused this in view of his son, Randolph, not wishing to inherit this hereditary title.

Churchill considered that Britain's importance as a world power depended on the continued existence of the Empire. He reluctantly agreed to accept Nasser as ruler of Egypt after his successful coup and agreed to remove British troops from their base by the Suez Canal. Britain agreed to terminate its role in governing Anglo-Egyptian Sudan in return for Nasser abandoning Egyptian claims to the region. In Malaya, a crisis had erupted as communist guerrilla forces started an uprising but this was eventually put down by Commonwealth troops. An uprising in Kenya by the Mau Mau was similarly supressed but Churchill was a moderating influence on the way these rebellions were dealt with. He considered that adopting ruthless action would be contrary to British values and would generate adverse international opinion.

Soon after the coronation, Churchill suffered a serious stroke but this was kept secret while he recovered at Chartwell. Anthony Eden himself was unwell and unable to take over office but Churchill had recovered by the end of the year. Shortly after this, he retired to be succeeded by Anthony Eden who himself had recovered from his serious illness. Churchill remained an M.P. but seldom attended the House in his latter years. In 1963, President John F. Kennedy, with the support of Congress, made Churchill an honorary citizen of the United States. Sadly, Churchill was unable to travel to America and attend the ceremony where this honour would have been conferred. He became one of only eight people to receive this honour.

In 1965, Churchill suffered his final stroke and died shortly after. In common with the Duke of Wellington and William Gladstone, Churchill was given a state funeral, an honour which is rare for non-royals. His body lay in state in Westminster Hall for three days and was then conveyed to St. Paul's Cathedral for his funeral. His coffin was conducted by boat to Waterloo Station and thence by train, to be buried at St. Martin's Church cemetery in Bladon, Oxfordshire, which is not far from Blenheim Palace, his birthplace.

What else can be said of Churchill?

He had a ready wit and his repartee was brilliant. He wasn't a person with whom to trade insults in an argument. During a heated discussion with Bessie Braddock, the formidable Labour M.P. for Liverpool exchange, she accused Churchill of being drunk. He retorted,

> ***"Drunk I may be but in the morning, I'll be sober.***
> ***You are ugly and in the morning you'll still be ugly".***

He exasperated Lady Astor in an argument and she declared to Churchill that if she was his wife, she would put poison in his tea. Churchill replied that if he was her husband, he'd drink it! On receiving a rejection for one of the articles he had written as a journalist because he had ended a sentence with a preposition, he wrote in reply that he considered this to be:-

> ***"mere pedantry, up with which I will not put."***

When in a debate, an opposition speaker accused Churchill of trying to make him look a perfect fool, Churchill retorted that no-one is perfect.

Churchill was a prolific writer and was awarded the Nobel Prize for literature in recognition of his biographical and historical writings. He was a gifted amateur artist, completing hundreds of paintings, many of which are on display in what was his home at Chartwell. One of his hobbies was bricklaying and he built walls and small buildings in his garden as Chartwell. As a Liberal, he joined the Amalgamated Union of Building Trade Workers but he was expelled from this when he joined the Conservative party. He was very fond of animals and had many pets, mainly cats, but also dogs, lambs, bantams, pigs, goats and even fox cubs. He is quoted as saying that:-

> ***"Dogs look up to you, cats look down on you. Give me a pig!***
> ***He looks you in the eye and treats you as an equal".***

For all his accomplishments, Churchill is chiefly celebrated as a great leader in time of war. Although exhilarated by war Churchill, was never indifferent to the suffering it caused.

Baron Hugh Dowding

Baron Hugh Dowding

During the Battle of Britain, Air Chief Marshal Hugh Dowding commanded R.A.F. Fighter Command which played a crucial role in degrading the Luftwaffe so that Hitler's plans for invading Britain could not take place. However, at the time, Dowding, was hardly given credit for this as he had come into conflict with other senior air force officers and politicians. These had a totally different concept of how the air force should be organised and concentrate its resources to those of Dowding. Dowding lacked the tact and diplomacy which might have served him well in his arguments with those with whom he had to contend in promoting his views on the organisation of the air force.

Hugh Dowding was born in Moffat, Dumfriesshire, where he went to St. Ninian's Preparatory School. He went on to receive his secondary education at Winchester College. On completing school, he trained at the Royal Military Academy, Woolwich, from which he was commissioned into the Royal Artillery as a second lieutenant. He served with the Royal Artillery in Gibraltar, Hong Kong, Ceylon and India. On his return to the U.K., he attended the Army Staff College, Sandhurst, and on completion of his course, was promoted to captain.

Dowding became interested in aviation and attended, first the Vickers School of Flying, and then, the Central Flying School, where he was awarded his Wings. He transferred to the Royal Flying Corps but clashed with General Hugh Trenchard on the issue of pilots' welfare. Dowding considered that it was important that pilots should be allowed an adequate rest period to recuperate between sorties.

The Royal Flying Corps was a regiment in the army before becoming detached to form the Royal Air Force. In this newly formed arm of the services, Dowding operated as a pilot in Number 7 Squadron. He went on to become commanding officer of Number 16 Squadron and was involved in the Battle of the Somme.

On being recalled to Britain, he went through various stages of promotion, lieutenant colonel, colonel and then brigadier general becoming commander of Southern Group Command. When the war ended, he was given the first of a number of honours bestowed on him in his career, becoming Companion of the Order of St. Michael and St. George (C.O.M.G.). Later, he was appointed Knight Commander of the Order of the Bath (K.C.O.B.) and later still, as Knight Grand Cross of the Royal Victorian Order (K.C.R.V.O.). As he continued his service in the Royal Air Force, Dowding became a group captain and then air commodore and undertook the role of chief staff officer at Inland Area H.Q., Uxbridge. His next promotion was to the rank of air vice marshal and finally he became air chief marshal.

In the inter-war years, the air force was dominated by Hugh Trenchard who passionately believed that future wars would be won by bombing strategic enemy targets and tended to promote those who shared his views on bombing. Dowding on the other hand was more interested in the deployment of fighter aircraft.

At this time, a period of rapid advances in the design of aircraft was taking place. Although without scientific or technical training, Dowding showed himself apt at grasping the essential features of innovations being introduced into aircraft design. He was appointed commanding officer of the newly created Fighter Command. In this role, he oversaw an arrangement known as the 'Dowding System' by which early warning would be given of an aerial attack. This used the Royal Observer Corps to compensate for any shortcomings of the existing radar surveillance which was then in its infancy. An example of this was the reporting on the altitude of incoming aircraft detected by radar. The whole system was linked by cables which had been buried as a safeguard against bombing and operated from its headquarters at R.A.F., Bentley Priory, a country house just outside London. The system later became known as Ground Controlled Interception (G.C.I.).

Dowding predicted that in the event of war, he would need a large reserve of trained pilots and it was planned to set up a pilot training school in Canada. However, this was vetoed by the Canadian Prime Minister, Mackenzie King. Ultimately, Mackenzie King agreed to the setting up of the British Commonwealth Air Training Plan a year before the outbreak of war. In view of the fact that it took a year to train a pilot and another to prepare them for squadron flying in a war situation, this was far too late for Dowding. To build up the sort of reserve he needed to combat the Germans, whose pilots had already experienced flying in hostile conditions in the Spanish Civil War, Dowding would need a large pool of well-trained pilots. In the event, Dowding had to recruit his pilots from the Auxiliary Air Force, the R.A.F. Volunteer Reserve and the University Air Squadrons.

Dowding was fortunate that two excellent fighter planes had been developed, the Spitfire and the Hurricane, and he quickly brought these into service. He had to fight a battle with the authorities to get these planes fitted with bullet proof wind shields. He countered the argument that this would be too expensive by stating that if New York gangsters can equip their cars with such shields, there was no reason why this protection shouldn't be available to the R.A.F.

In 1939, Dowding was due to retire but in view of the inevitability of war breaking out, he was persuaded to stay on. How fortunate that Dowding remained in charge of Fighter Command at the beginning of the war. He had a better grasp of the strategy needed to provide an air defence to Britain than other senior air force officers at the time and was strong enough to oppose pressure from politicians, right up to the highest level. He resisted repeated requests from Churchill to send squadrons of aircraft to aid allied troops in the battle for France. Dowding knew that he couldn't fulfil his prime responsibility of defending Britain from air attack by squandering his very limited supply of planes and pilots in a futile enterprise. Had Germany gained air superiority, they would have exploited this in launching an invasion of Britain. Dowding was supported in his attitude by Sir Cyril Newall, the Chief of Air Staff, and Dowding's immediate superior.

The cabinet approved sending four squadrons to France. When Churchill later asked for six more squadrons, the cabinet refused to endorse this, realising that Dowding's argument that with the current rate of aircraft losses in France, the country would be without fighter aircraft in a fortnight. Churchill nursed a grudge against Dowding for being thwarted in this way and in his book, 'Their Finest Hour', he scarcely gave Dowding the credit he deserved for victory in the Battle of Britain. When France collapsed, Dowding worked closely with Air Vice Marshall Keith Park in organising fighter support to enable the British army to be evacuated from Dunkirk.

The beginning of the Battle of Britain started with what the Germans called the 'Channel Battle' where Luftwaffe planes limited their attack to shipping in the English Channel. Dowding sent planes located in airfields near the coast to intercept the German planes but knew this was risky. The British planes would face the disadvantage that the German planes leaving France had already reached optimum height for their operation and the British planes would be still climbing as they encountered the Germans. A lot of shipping was lost and Dowding suffered serious loss of his aircraft and pilots. Many pilots who bailed out after being shot down, landed unharmed in the sea but as their planes weren't equipped with dinghies and there was no coordinated sea rescue, they were still lost. Dowding was unwilling to commit any more aircraft to the 'Channel Battle'. Many of the ships lost were colliers and Dowding urged that coal should be transported from Wales by train rather than by sea.

While Dowding's abrasive manner led to his being disliked by the civil servants with whom he had to deal, he had an influential supporter in the press baron, Lord Beaverbrook. Lord Beaverbrook also didn't get on well with the civil service. His son was serving in Fighter Command and Beaverbrook considered that Dowding, with his care for the lives of his pilots, was the leader who was most likely to keep his son alive.

Throughout the Battle of Britain, Dowding coordinated his resources well. Within the integrated defence system he had created for Fighter Command, he marshalled resources behind the scenes to ensure replacement of aircraft and aircrew while maintaining a significant fighter reserve. He gave his subordinate commanders a free hand in the way they managed the detail of the battle.

British aircraft production accelerated at an amazing rate but the main problem Dowding faced was the loss of pilots. It took several months for pilots to be trained to a level where they could be effective in combat. Eighty per cent of Dowding's pilots were British but the force was augmented by pilots from the Commonwealth, Poland, Czechoslovakia, France and Belgium.

Dowding discovered from a system known as 'Ultra Intelligence' that the Germans were aiming to gain control of the skies with a massive air raid scheduled for 13th August. This they had designated 'Eagle Day'. Dowding was thus prepared for this onslaught and able to deploy his squadrons to meet this assault. In the battle, the R.A.F. lost fourteen planes in combat and another sixteen were destroyed on the ground before they could take off, but the enemy losses were seventy five planes. This was catastrophic for them and what had been called 'Eagle Day' became referred to by the Luftwaffe as 'The Black Thursday'.

In observing this battle, Dowden noted that the German planes were no match for his spitfires and hurricanes and were most effective when operating near the coast. This was because coastal regions were within the range that the supporting German fighter planes could fly before needing to return to France to be refuelled. Without the distraction of having to deal with the German fighters, the German bombers were easy to shoot down. Dowding decided that he needed to move his coastal aircraft to bases further inland.

Again, Dowding was warned by the 'Ultra Intelligence' system of another vast air raid by the Germans, targeting London and scheduled for 15th September. R.A.F. squadrons were organised to attack the Germans, both as they approached and as they left London. This involved rapid refuelling but resulted in the Germans failing to achieve any of their primary objectives and losing fifty of the four-hundred bombers they had sent over.

One of the great advantages that the British fighter pilots had in these battles lay in the fact that Dowding had ordered his squadrons to be rotated so that pilots returning from a sortie could be rested before taking to the air again. Thus, when they returned to the air, they were relatively refreshed compared to the German pilots who had not had rest breaks organised into their routine. The failure of the Luftwaffe to gain control of the skies resulted in the German plans to invade Britain being put off indefinitely.

Dowding realised that their failure of daytime raiding would result in the Germans concentrating on launching air raids in the night when his fighter planes would be ineffective. The switching of German bombing raids from the day to night-time was indeed the way the war in the air developed. Dowding discovered that the Germans were aided in directing their planes at night by a radio guidance system which they called 'dogleg' but which the British named 'headache'. Dowding ordered that the electronic jamming of this German radio guidance system should be made a priority.

Dowding was retired after the Battle of Britain. It would appear that Dowding's brilliance in the way he deployed Fighter Command was not appreciated at that time. It is only later that we have become aware that he conducted his resources in a way no-one else at the time would have done and that he is the one who deserves the credit for winning the Battle of Britain. Dowding was criticised by fellow senior air force officers for not following their favoured strategy which is known as the 'Big Wing' approach, that is, in the event of a Luftwaffe attack, all our available fighters should assemble into one huge squadron before moving in to fight the German planes. This approach would have been disastrous. It would take a long time to assemble such a squadron during which time, the Luftwaffe would have been unhindered, doing immense damage by bombing. However successful a 'Big Wing' assault on the Luftwaffe may have been, at some point, all the planes would have had to return to base to refuel, leaving them grounded, vulnerable and exposed to attack from a second wave of German bombers with no fighter planes available in the air to see them off. Dowding himself had lost many aircraft on the ground which had been unable to take off before the German bombers arrived to destroy them. Thus, Dowding always kept enough fighter planes in reserve to avoid this happening.

The 'Big Wing' approach to aerial warfare is reminiscent of the attitude of the World War I admiral, Jellicoe. He was reluctant to release warships to do the essential job of escorting Atlantic convoys and protect them from U-boat attack. Jellico considered that all the warships should remain in the 'Grand Fleet'.

Dowding was also criticised by senior air force officers for his failure to use his fighter planes to prevent German night-time bombing raids. This was unfair criticism as fighter planes could only operate at night if equipped with the advanced airborne radar not available to Dowding. Dowding's admirers say that not only would he have used this when available but he would have accelerated the development of this technology.

On leaving Fighter Command, Dowding was sent to the United States where his job was to procure any new types of aircraft which would further the war effort. However, Dowding was not popular in America because he was prepared to be outspoken in presenting his viewpoints.

Although his abrasive manner did not endear him to his superiors or the air ministry who resented the fact that he was able to prove them wrong in many instances, Dowding was, nonetheless, a humble and sincere man. He held the airmen under his command in great affection and referred to them as his 'dear fighter boys' and as his 'chicks'. His lack of humour led to his men nicknaming him 'Stuffy' but they appreciated that he genuinely cared for his men and did as much as possible to maintain their safety in the dangerous challenges they would face in aerial combat.

In later life, Dowding became increasingly bitter that the R.A.F. had not given him the recognition that he felt he deserved, passing him over for promotion to Marshall of the Royal Air Force. However, someone in an elevated position nationally must have fully appreciated Dowding's contribution to winning the war. It has already been mentioned that he was awarded with the orders of O.M.G., K.C.O.B. and K.G.C.R.V.O. He was also made a peer of the realm as Baron Dowding of Bentley Priory.

Dowding had unusual religious beliefs. He rejected Christianity in favour of spiritualism and wrote books on the subject. He claimed that he met dead R.A.F. boys in his sleep. Dowding believed that fairies were essential to the growth of healthy plant life. He was vegetarian and an anti-vivisectionist. In his honour, the National Anti-vivisection Society founded the Lord Dowding Fund to sponsor humane methods of using animals in research. The welfare of animals was a matter very dear to Dowding's heart and he made speeches in the House of Lords, calling for legislation to ensure the humane killing of animals in abattoirs.

Dowding laid the foundation stone of St. Georges Chapel which commemorates fallen airmen in what was R.A.F., Biggin Hill. He died at his home in Tunbridge Wells and his ashes were interred below the Battle of Britain Memorial Window in the Royal Air Force Chapel in Westminster Abbey.

Sir Arthur Harris

Sir Arthur Harris

Arthur Harris was born in Cheltenham, Gloucestershire. As Arthur's father's career as a government engineer required him to spend much of his time in India, Arthur did not grow up with a solid family background. He was looked after during his early years within the family of a Kent rector of whom Arthur retained fond memories. His elder brothers went to the prestigious public schools of Sherborne and Eton. With little money left to spend on the education of their third child, Arthur went to the lesser known All Hallows School in Devon. A former pupil of this school, who had become a famous actor, used to give to pupils of All Hallows School, tickets to plays in which he was performing. Arthur received such a ticket and was impressed by the story of the play in which the lead character found that he could advance better in Rhodesia where a person was judged more by their talents and ability than by their class. At the age of seventeen, before he had completed his secondary education, Arthur informed his father that he wished to emigrate to Rhodesia. Although this was not in line with his father's hopes for Arthur's career, he paid for Arthur to move to Rhodesia.

In Rhodesia, Arthur undertook various types of work including mining, coach driving and farming. The owner of one of the farms on which Arthur worked was impressed with Arthur's ability and trustworthiness and appointed him farm manager over a period when he had to return to England. Having gained experience in farm management, Arthur intended to set up as an independent farmer when the owner of his farm returned. However, on the outbreak of the first World War, Arthur considered it his patriotic duty to enlist in the army. He applied to join the 1st Rhodesian regiment but the only vacancies were as a machine gunner or a bugler. Having learnt to play the bugle at school, Arthur was appointed aa a bugler. He fought against the Germans in South West Africa where he first encountered the use of bombing in warfare.

When the South West Africa campaign ended, the 1st Rhodesia Regiment was disbanded. Arthur's immediate intention was to return to farming but he and his army colleagues realised that the real war was being fought in Europe and they travelled to Britain to join the British army. Arthur failed to find a position in the artillery or cavalry regiments but joined the Royal Flying Corps in which he was appointed a probationary 2nd lieutenant. He learned to fly and served with distinction on the western front, becoming a flight commander and ultimately commanding officer of 45 squadron. He flew a type of plane known as the Sopwith Camel and shot down five enemy aircraft, earning himself the Air Force Cross. He ended the war with the rank of major.

Following the end of the war, Harris decided to remain in the Royal Air Force, the new service arm into which the Royal Flying Corps had evolved. He made this decision instead of returning to Rhodesia as he and his first wife, Barbara, had just had their first baby. He was appointed Station Commander of R.A.F. Rigby and commander of the R.A.F. Flying Training School. Harris served a number of overseas postings, including spells in India, Mesopotamia and Persia. His squadron was equipped with fighter planes but were required to carry out bombing raids. They were able to accomplish this by carrying out major modifications to their aircraft.

On Arthur's return to the U.K., he was posted to command a heavy bomber squadron. In collaboration with Sir John Salmond who was Chief of Air Staff, he developed the training which would equip bomber pilots to carry out raids at night time.

He spent some time at the Army Staff College in Camberley but discovered that as a technocrat, his priorities were quite different from those of the cavalry officers who seemed to dominate the army at that time. He became particularly friendly with Bernard Montgomery with whom he shared both personality traits and a similar outlook on many military matters.

Arthur's career in the Air Force progressed during the inter war years, achieving promotion through the ranks of wing commander, air commodore and air vice marshal. He was honoured by being awarded the Order of the British Empire. During this time, he pressurised the senior air force command to have developed large, long range bombers which could carry out raids into Germany. A number of such bombers were produced, including the very successful Lancaster bomber.

At the beginning of World War II, Harris became Deputy Chief of Air Staff and was promoted to the rank of air marshal. It was discovered that only one in three planes sent out on bombing raids came within five miles of their intended target. He was obviously required to improve on this record. Harris was appointed Commander in Chief of Bomber Command and his honour was advanced to Knight Commander of the Order of the Bath,

As a result of the cabinet considering a paper on strategic bombing, many of its members formed the opinion that the war could be won by heavily bombing enough cities to force the enemy into capitulation. Sir Arthur Harris was therefore instructed to carry out an extensive area bombing campaign. When observing an enemy air raid during the London Blitz, Harris commented that the Nazis entered the war, expecting to carry out bombing raids without being subject to retaliatory raids themselves. He then quoted the words of an Old Testament prophet:-

Hosea ch 8 v7 *'They sowed the wind, and now they are going to reap the whirlwind."*

Harris subscribed to the belief that sustained and massive bombing would force Germany to surrender He launched a number of vast bombing raids in line with the directive he had been given. Fleets of bombers numbering as many as a thousand were sent to bomb strategic cities like Cologne and Hamburg. With the success of these raids, Harris predicted that Germany would soon surrender within very few months because German morale would crumble at the massive refugee problem that sustained bombing of cities would create. Churchill found this policy distasteful but the home population was served with the propaganda that only strategic targets were attacked with the regrettable collateral damage of some loss of civilian life. Harris was irritated by Churchill's reluctance to wholeheartedly endorse his bombing strategy but Harris's predictions made early in 1943 proved to be over optimistic as the war continued for over two further years.

 A high level of security clearance was needed to know why certain targets were chosen for being bombed. It was frequently reported on the news that the bombers had been out over Peenemunde and the ordinary British public wondered why this small Baltic seaport had been chosen as a target rather than Berlin. At that time, it was not generally known that this was where the flying bombs (V1's) and rockets (V2's) were being manufactured and stockpiled to launch a vast unmanned aerial bombardment of London, an early application of drone warfare.

Late in 1943, major bombing raids were carried out on Berlin but Harris's success with his Hamburg raids was not replicated. The city was well defended with anti-aircraft artillery. Although severe damage was inflicted on Berlin, the devastating impact which Harris had predicted did not materialise and the allies lost huge numbers of bombers and aircrew.

Before the D-day invasion, Harris was ordered to concentrate his bombing attacks on the French railway network. This was a difficult task which his bombers were not ideally equipped to carry out. After D-day, Harris was commanded to carry out bombing raids which supported Eisenhower's ground offensive. In particular, the bombing of the factories in the Ruhr which produced synthetic oil, This objective was effectively realised as this source of vital oil was destroyed.

Harris was still wedded to the idea that the destruction of German cities would hasten the end of the war and he organised a particularly devastating air raid over Dresden. This raid was probably unnecessary as it was 1945 and the war would very soon be over. The R.A.F. and the U.S.A.A.F. dropped a higher load of ordinance on the city than had ever been used during the entire war, creating a firestorm in the city and killing about twenty-five-thousand of its inhabitants. The raid was criticised for causing such a high mortality rate among civilians while doing very little to further the war effort. A month later, Harris carried out his final air raid over Berlin just before the Soviets entered the city. The final big strategic air raid was the destruction of an oil refinery at Tonsberg in southern Norway.

In the book, 'Bomber Offensive' which Harris wrote at the end of the war, he writes of the Dresden air raid,

"I will only say that the attack on Dresden was at the time, considered a military necessity by much more important people than myself."[1]

Bomber Command's crews were denied a separate campaign medal as they were already eligible for the 'Air Crew Europe Star' and the 'France and Germany Star'. However, Harris saw this as a snub to his men and he refused the peerage which he had been offered, as it had to other war time leaders of equivalent status. However, he was awarded a number of other decorations, both from the British and overseas governments. In particular, he was advanced to Knight Grand Cross of the Order of the Bath, was created a baronet and promoted to Marshal of the Royal Air Force.

Effective as he was in his role of head of Bomber Command, Harris had personality traits which made him difficult to work with. He couldn't see both sides of an argument and would invariably overstress the rectitude of his own case. He didn't take kindly to advice, however sensible and well intentioned it may have been, regarding such advice as interference. He dismissed any evidence which was contrary to his preconceived ideas, as propaganda and any criticism he experienced was not well received. However, it was perhaps important for a person carrying out his particularly difficult commission to have such a personality. There is no doubt that he had determination. Although born in England, Harris regarded himself as Rhodesian rather than English. Towards the end of the war, he was approached by the Rhodesian prime minister with the offer of becoming Governor of Rhodesia. Although he would dearly have loved this post, his refusal to accept the Governorship of Rhodesia is evidence of his loyalty to both this country and to the Royal Air Force.

After the war, Sir Arthur Harris moved to South Africa where he managed the South African Marine Corporation for five years before returning to Britain. He finally settled in a home in Goring-on-Thames, right next to the river where he died aged ninety-one.

Post Script.

As someone who lived out his childhood in London during most of the war, I experienced the effect of German bombing first-hand when a bomb dropped very near to my grandmother's house. She lived twelve doors up in the same street where I lived. Sleeping under the kitchen table in a room which had been reinforced with wooden pillars and a window which had been protected against blast by a wall of sandbags built just beyond the window, the family slept through the blast. We were not aware of the damage that had been done until the following morning when we awoke to discover that every other window in the house had been shattered and that most of the plaster on the walls had been loosened or dislodged. My grandmother who had been sleeping in an upstairs bedroom in her own house was miraculously unharmed and manged to get out of the house in the dark. On surveying the damage which became clear with the arrival of daylight, she declared that she could not have got out of the house, had she been able to see the amount of the debris she would have had to climb through to escape into the street. Her house was so badly damaged that it had to be completely demolished, creating yet another of the bombsites which existed in that part of London.

Later in my life, I found myself spending a large part of my working life in Coventry. Having lived in London through the blitz, I felt a special affinity with the Coventrians who had vivid memories of the Coventry air raid which had occurred very early during the war. At the end of the war, Coventry did not restore the old cathedral but build a new cathedral adjoining the ruins of the old one. The bombed out ruins of Coventry Cathedral, its spire still intact, stands today as a poignant war memorial. I am so proud that the Christians in Coventry decided, even before the end of the war, that Coventry should become a centre for reconciliation after conflict and so it is to this day. The words, 'Father Forgive', are prominently displayed, engraved and gilded into the eastern wall of the ruined cathedral. Nails recovered from the charred woodwork of he burnt out cathedral were formed into a cross of nails and copies of this have been sent to other cities who experienced similar devastation during the war, particularly Dresden. A strong relationship of love has grown up between these devastated cities. More recently, I have been able to visit Dresden and their main church, the Frauenkirche, which has been completely restored to its former glory. A Coventry cross of nails is on display within the church. It is so encouraging that Christians have been able to create a lasting ministry of reconciliation between former enemies out of something so evil and devastating as war.

Viscount Bernard Montgomery

Viscount Bernard Montgomery

Bernard Montgomery was a famous World War II general but had many negative character traits. These undesirable character traits may well be the result of the way he was treated as a child. Bernard was born in Kennington, Surrey, the fourth of nine children. His father, Henry, was an Anglican minister and his mother, Maud, who was eighteen years younger than Henry, was the daughter of a famous preacher. Henry inherited an estate in Donegal on the death of Bernard's grandfather but the estate was hugely in debt and repayment of this was well beyond the means of a Church of England vicar. However, the family's financial prospects improved when Henry was promoted to become Bishop of Tasmania and Bernard spent many of his formative years there with his family.

As a bishop, Henry thought it his episcopal duty to spend as much time as possible with the inhabitants of rural Tasmania and spent very long periods away from his family, visiting his flock in the countryside. Bernard was ignored for most of the time by his mother who was still a fairly young woman and during the short time he spent in actual contact with his mother, he was subject to beatings. This loveless environment resulted in Bernard growing up into a boy who, by his own admission, was a dreadful child whom few could put up with. He became alienated from his mother. In later life, Bernard didn't allow his son, David, to have anything to do with his grandmother and he refused to attend her funeral

The family returned to Britain so that Bishop Henry could attend the Lambeth Conference. Bernard was educated at King's School, Canterbury, but moved to St. Paul's School when the family transferred to London, following Bernard's father being appointed as secretary to the Society for the Propagation of the Gospel. From school, Bernard continued his education at the Royal Military

College, Sandhurst, where he was a rowdy and disruptive student and narrowly avoided being expelled.

On being commissioned, Montgomery saw his first overseas service in India. His battalion moved to Europe with the outbreak of World War I where he saw action at the Battle of Le Cateau. During a counter offensive, he led his men in a bayonet charge to drive the enemy out of their trench but he was shot through the lung by a hidden enemy sniper. He feigned being dead to avoid attracting further sniper fire but one of his men, who attempted to rescue him, was shot and fell dead on top of Montgomery. The sniper fire continued, hitting Montgomery again in the knee but the dead body on top of him took most of the bullets. His company withdrew, assuming both Montgomery and the body on top of him were dead but at night, a stretcher company recovered both bodies under the cover of darkness and found Montgomery just about alive. He was returned to England where it took a year for him to recuperate. He was awarded the Distinguished Service Order for the conspicuous gallantry he had shown in leading his men in the attack on the trench.

On recovery, he returned to the Western Front with the rank of brigade major and took part in the battles of Arras and Passchendaele. He ended the war with the rank of lieutenant colonel. The thing that made the greatest impression on Montgomery during this war was the inadequate leadership displayed by the senior staff officers who remained in safety, well behind the front line where fighting was taking place. While it was obviously sensible for senior officers to remain out of the firing line, this would have been more acceptable had those officers made some attempt to make personal contact with the men doing the fighting and not to assume that they were just there as cannon fodder. Montgomery formed the opinion that a good staff officer should be seen by his men as actually serving the troops under his command and not remaining as an anonymous figure in the background.

At the end of World War I, Montgomery was given command of a battalion of the Royal Fusiliers. The only opportunity for his rising to the senior ranks of the army was to be selected for the army Staff College at Camberley. He hadn't achieved selection by the normal routes but on meeting Field Marshall Sir William Robertson, Commander in Chief of the British Army, at a social function, he managed to persuade him to add his name to the list. After graduating from Staff College, he was appointed to an infantry brigade, fighting in County Cork against the Irish Republican Army. He came to the conclusion that without adopting extremely harsh measures which he knew the British public would not allow, this was a battle the British could not win. He therefore advocated that the Irish should be given some form of self-government. He later returned to the Royal Warwickshire Regiment as a company commander.

His only known courtship up until this time was with a seventeen year old girl, Betty Anderson. He spent much of their time together explaining how he would win a war in the desert as a tank commander, an amazing prediction. Although impressed with his ambition, Betty rejected Bernard's proposal.

Two years later, Bernard met and married Elizabeth Carter, sister of another senior army officer. Elizabeth had already been married and had two children. In view of Montgomery's abrasive nature when dealing with other military personnel, one might have wondered whether he would be able to make a success of the marriage. In fact, the marriage was very happy and the year after their marriage, the couple had a son, David. Sadly, ten years later, Elizabeth suffered an insect bite which turned to septicaemia and she died. Both Bernard's stepsons became army officers. Dick was taken prisoner of war when on a reconnaissance mission after the Battle of El Alamein. To Bernard's delight, he managed to escape the following year during the confusion which arose between the Germans and the Italians when Italy withdrew from the war.

During the decade before the outbreak of World War II, Montgomery became Commanding Officer of the 1st Battalion of the Warwickshire Regiment. He was posted to Palestine and then to India where he became an instructor in the Indian Army Staff College. On his return to Britain, he took command of the 9th Infantry Brigade with the rank of brigadier. The new Commander in Chief of Southern Command, General Wavell, was so impressed with the way Montgomery organised an amphibious landing exercise that Montgomery was promoted to the rank of major general. He took command of the 8th Infantry Division which was serving in Palestine where the British had a mandate. He had to suppress a revolt by the Arabs who were protesting against the immigration of Jews into Palestine. He returned to Britain, the year before the war broke out suffering from a serious illness but one from which he made a good recovery.

On the outbreak of war, Montgomery was posted to France with the British Expeditionary Force. Montgomery was so concerned about the sexual health of his soldiers that he issued a circular on the prevention of venereal disease. This led to a serious clash with his superior officers and the army chaplains. It would appear that the concern of his superiors was not so much that this circular had been issued but that it was couched in what they considered to be obscene language. The support of his corps commander, General Alan Brooke, prevented Montgomery from being dismissed but General Brooke warned Montgomery that he didn't want this sort of mistake to be made again.

Montgomery was not impressed with the preparedness for battle of the division under his command and while the other sections of the British Expeditionary

Force were preparing themselves for defence, Montgomery's troops were being trained for battle. This training proved invaluable when the army moved into Belgium to take up positions along the River Dyle to oppose the advancing German forces. Montgomery's division earned the reputation of being very agile, flexible and versatile and, due to their training, they always seemed to be in the right place at the right time. When the army retreated into France, in preparation for being evacuated from Dunkirk, Montgomery's troops had an invaluable role in maintaining the integrity of the British Expeditionary Force as the Belgian army started to disintegrate. When the army returned to Britain after being evacuated from Dunkirk, Montgomery was made a Companion of the Order of the Bath. On his return to Britain. Montgomery was very critical of the way the British Expeditionary Force had been managed in France. This antagonised the War Office and Montgomery was moved to what appeared to be a less important command.

Montgomery was placed in charge of V Corps which had the responsibility of defending Hampshire and Dorset from being invaded but he didn't get on well with his immediate superior, Lieutenant General Auchinleck. He was promoted to the rank of Lieutenant General in command of South Eastern Command and took over the defence of Kent, Sussex and Surrey. He ensured his troops had the training which would keep them in a high state of physical fitness and organised a number of training manoeuvres. He was ruthless in sacking officers whom he didn't think were up to the job.

The Chief of the Imperial General Staff, Alan Brooke, persuaded Winston Churchill to appoint Montgomery to become commander of the British 1st Army in North Africa. His task would be to prepare the army for Operation Torch, the code name for the operation to expel the Germans from what had been part of the French empire in North Africa but which was now occupied by the Germans. Montgomery commented to a colleague that, after having an easy war, things are now likely to hot up. When the colleague told Montgomery not to be too despondent, Montgomery replied that he was not talking about himself but the German general, Rommel.

Within a week of Montgomery taking command, the atmosphere in the British army greatly improved. He changed from wearing the traditional peaked cap of an army officer to a beret, bearing the badge of the Royal Tank Regiment alongside that of a British general. Montgomery transformed the fighting spirit and efficiency of the army and made a point of being seen by as many of his troops as possible. The army became a hive of activity and Generals Alexander and Brooke were amazed at the transformation they found on their visit. Churchill wanted the British to attack as soon as possible but Montgomery insisted on not attacking until he had prepared his forces into a state that would ensure them of victory. He arranged to coordinate the efforts of the army, navy and air force to optimum effect. When that time came, Montgomery won a decisive victory at El Alamein, the first British land victory of the war. This led to the Germans being driven out of Africa and the allies posed to invade Italy. Montgomery's status as a member of the Order of the Bath was raised to Knight Commander (KCB) and he was promoted to the rank of full general.

The invasion of Italy was a joint venture with the Americans but the relationship between Montgomery and the American generals, George Patton and Omar Bradley, was not good. Montgomery boasted a degree of superiority as, unlike himself, the American generals had not yet been tested in battle and the three of them were likened to squabbling schoolgirls. However, the invasion did take place with Montgomery's British 8th Army being the first to land on the toe of Italy. The American General, Mark Clerk's American 5th Army (which was reinforced with a large number of British troops), landed at Salerno on the heel of Italy. This army faced considerable opposition from the Germans who launched a series of counter attacks to slow their advance but they fought their way through to eventually reunite with Montgomery's army.

The advance into Italy was slow and the army was beset with many casualties. The Germans always seemed to be able to retreat to good defensive conditions. Montgomery expressed dissatisfaction with the lack of cohesion and opportunism among the forces involved in this offensive and was delighted when he was recalled to Britain to command the forces which would be involved in Operation Overlord, the code name for the invasion of Normandy being planned. The supreme commander of this force was the American General, Dwight Eisenhower. Both he and Churchill were finding Montgomery difficult to work with and were considering replacing him with the affable General Alexander. They were dissuaded from doing so by General Sir Alan Brooke who successfully argued that Montgomery was a far better general and should remain in post.

Bad weather conditions delayed the Normandy landings. When they did eventually take place, Montgomery's plan was to take Caen in the east of the bridgehead with Anglo-Canadian troops. This would provide a firm shoulder from which the American troops could advance to the Seine. The capture of Caen took far longer than the two or three days for which Montgomery had planned as the German general, Rommel, realising the importance of this city, sent panzer divisions to defend it. Thus, Montgomery's forces faced a very stiff battle. However, they succeeded in the objective of keeping the German forces occupied which made the advance of the American forces to the Seine much easier.

Meanwhile, the Bletchley Park code breakers had broken the German code. As the French Resistance had destroyed the landlines, the Germans had to rely on radio communication which the British could intercept and decode. Thus, Montgomery became aware that although the Germans still had an operational panzer division in the field, they had no reserves while he had three armoured divisions in reserve. Therefore, Montgomery knew that Normandy had been won. The Canadians finally took Caen in July and Montgomery moved his tanks on to the plain south of Caen, forcing the Germans to commit the last of their reserves to stop the Anglo-Canadian offensive. Hitler refused to allow his troops to be ordered to retreat from Normandy, a disastrous directive, resulting in the Germans suffering catastrophic losses.

The invasion through France continued successfully although not without the occasional dispute between Eisenhower and Montgomery, the most serious of these almost leading to Montgomery being sacked. Montgomery was concerned that the allies should reach Berlin before the Russians and managed to persuade Eisenhower to support his plan, codenamed Operation Market Garden. His plan would facilitate the advance of the allies into the industrialised Ruhr but involved the bold but risky strategy of an airborne strike behind the enemy lines to capture intact road bridges across the Rhine. A massive drop of airborne troops took place at Arnhem, close to the city of Nijmegen, the location of one of the most important bridges. Both Churchill and Montgomery claimed that the operation had been 90% successful but had to admit that it hadn't realised its intended objective. There are many reasons why this operation failed. Nijmegen was more strongly defended than had been expected and it has been suspected that a spy may have become aware of the allied intentions and informed the Germans. Radio communication between the troops dropped in the Arnhem region was difficult because the area was heavily wooded. It took the Canadian army longer than expected to clear the river Scheldt estuary which was important for this operation. Bad weather hindered the attempt of the main army to reach in time the enclave established by the para-troops at Arnhem. There was also difficulty in finding a suitable dropping zone to drop the supplies needed to support the troops. Uncharacteristically, Montgomery admitted that mistakes had been made on his part.

However, in due course, the allies were able to cross the Rhine and push on through Germany until they met with the Russians who had already advanced beyond Berlin, thus ending the war with victory.

After the war, Montgomery was created Viscount Montgomery of Alamein. He became Commander in Chief of the British Army on the Rhine (BAOR), the name given to the British forces occupying Germany. When the North Atlantic Treaty Organisation (NATO)'s Supreme Headquarters, Allied Powers Europe, was formed, Montgomery became Eisenhower's deputy. He continued to serve in this capacity under Eisenhower's successors until he retired at the age of seventy-one.

At the end of the war, some of Montgomery's negative personality traits became very evident. He was overbearing, conceited, loved publicity and had an urge to continually promote himself, claiming more than was his due for success in the war. In his memoirs, Montgomery criticised some of his former comrades in arms in harsh terms, including Eisenhower and Field Marshal Auchinleck. He had to retract his criticism of Auchinleck in a radio broadcast in which he thanked Auchinleck for stabilising the front line at an earlier battle, fought at El Alamein. Montgomery would have been hailed as a hero on his visit to America but was so openly critical of America that he was stripped of the honorary citizenship of Montgomery, Alabama, which he had been awarded earlier. On a visit to El Alamein after the war, he told Egyptian army officers that they would lose any war they fought against Israel, a prediction which later proved to be correct. He publicly supported apartheid, describing Africans as uncivilised savages, incapable of developing their country themselves. After a visit to China, he praised the impressive leadership of Chairman Mao Tse-tung. He was against the legalising of homosexuality in Britain, declaring:-

> *"This was 'a charter for buggery which may be acceptable in France but not here because we're British, thank God."*

Montgomery's life could be summed up as someone who succeeded as a general but failed as a man.

T. E. Lawrence
of Arabia

T. E. Lawrence of Arabia

Thomas Edward Lawrence was born in Carmarthenshire. He was born out of wedlock. His father, an Anglo-Irish landowner, had left his wife, was living with the lady who had been hired as a governess to his daughters. They were living under the pseudonym of Lawrence. Over the next few years, the family moved many times, leaving Wales for the lowlands of Scotland, then to the Isle of Wight and next, back to the mainland where they stayed for a short time in Hampshire. Their next move was to Dinard in Brittany and then on to Jersey. When Lawrence was eight years old, the family finally settled in Oxford where they remained for the next twenty five years. Thomas was educated at the City of Oxford High School. He and one of his brothers were keen members of the Church Lads' Brigade, based at St. Aldate's Church.

Lawrence was very interested in architecture. When in his mid-teens, he and a friend carried out an extended cycle tour of Oxfordshire and Berkshire, visiting almost every parish church and making notes of anything of particular antiquarian interest. In his late teens, he made a similar tour of France where his interest was mainly focused on mediaeval castles. He must have been a gifted linguist because he was frequently complimented by the locals on his excellent French.

From school, Lawrence went on to study history at Jesus College, Oxford University, where he joined the officer cadet corps. He was fascinated by mediaeval history and during his time at Oxford, he toured Syria, visiting Ottoman Castles which had existed at the time of the Crusades. He wrote a thesis on 'the Influence of the Crusades on European Military Architecture' and graduated with a first class honours degree.

Aware of Lawrence's gifts and interests, the archaeologist, David Hogarth, sponsored a scholarship, based at Magdalen College, Oxford University, for Lawrence to join the team of archaeologists working under Campbell Thomson and Leonard Woolley. They were carrying out excavations at Carchemish. While in the Middle East, Lawrence learned Arabic and remained there until the outbreak of the First World War. During his time at Carchemish, Lawrence's team often came into conflict with a German team of civil engineers who were working nearby on the Baghdad Railway. Lawrence disapproved of their attitude towards the locals but the stresses involved in this relationship helped Lawrence to develop in himself, leadership qualities and skills in conflict resolution.

At the outbreak of war, Lawrence and Woolley were co-opted by the British military to carry out an archaeological survey of the Negev and Sinai. The description of this expedition as 'archaeological' was merely a smokescreen. The real purpose of the work was to map out the area. This was strategically important, as the Ottoman troops would have to cross the Negev to attack Egypt. Thus, Lawrence and Woolley provided in their survey the location of all the features such as water sources which would be important for any force carrying out a military operation in the area.

Lawrence did not immediately enlist in the army at the outbreak of war but waited until October by which time, the particular roles which the army needed to fulfil had become clear. Lawrence was commissioned as 'second lieutenant – interpreter' and was posted by his former mentor, the archaeologist, Lieutenant Commander David Hogarth, to the new 'Arab Bureau Intelligence Unit' in Cairo.

At the time, there was a growing Arab nationalist movement, seeking independence from the Ottoman Empire, and the Emir of Mecca was negotiating with the British with a view to gaining their support for an Arab uprising against the Ottomans. He was prepared to throw in his lot with the British provided that they would guarantee the formation of an independent Arab state which included Syria. The British High Commissioner in Cairo sent a letter which basically accepted the Arab proposal with reservations about the land which bordered the Mediterranean, including the Holy Land. Lawrence appreciated this proposal as he had long advocated that the Arabs should have their own autonomous state. However, here we see diplomacy at its worst. In London, a separate agreement with the French was being signed by the government which meant that Britain would recognise Syria as part of the French empire.

Lawrence was sent to Mesopotamia with a view to assisting in the relief of Kut and ferment the process which would lead to the Arab uprising. The Arab revolt began and had a few successes but then ran out of steam, leaving a situation in which it seemed that the Ottomans could retake Mecca. Lawrence was charged with identifying someone who would be capable of leading and sustaining the Arab revolt and his choice fell upon Faisal, son of Sharrif Hussein, one of the Arab chieftain's. Lawrence was a great strategist and together with Faisal, worked out a plan to put the Ottoman railway under threat and to prevent the Ottoman forces around Medina from being a threat to Arab forces. Lawrence was personally involved in many battles and sorties against the Ottoman and German positions, particularly in disrupting rail communications. The German and Ottoman forces, retreating from the village of Tafas, massacred the villagers. In retaliation the Arabs massacred their prisoners. They had Lawrence's approval in doing this.

Lawrence then made a solo three-hundred mile journey across the desert to Aqaba, his route taking him close to some major Arab towns. When near Damascus, he counselled the Arab nationalists to delay their revolt until the arrival of Faisal's forces but he organised an attack on a bridge which would give the enemy the impression that guerrillas were operating in the area. The information he was able to send back to Britain was regarded as extremely valuable and he was considered for the award of a Victoria Cross. However, in the event, the awards he received were the less prestigious honours of being promoted to the rank of major and being invested as a Companion of the Order of the Bath.

Lawrence assessed that the main value of the Arab forces was in guerrilla type warfare as he couldn't see them accepting the discipline which would be imposed, should an attempt be made to organise them on British military lines. Thus, Lawrence continued to work with Faisal as the Arab forces conflicted with the Ottomans. The railway was frequently attacked, requiring the Ottomans to continually divert their resources to keep the line repaired in order to maintain communication with Medina. Lawrence particularly distinguished himself at the Battle of Tafilah in which, what started out as a defensive action, turned into an offensive action and led to a complete rout of the enemy forces. In the official history of the war, this action was described as 'a brilliant feat of arms'. Lawrence's outstanding leadership in this battle was recognised. He was promoted to the rank of lieutenant-colonel and awarded the 'Distinguished Service Order'.

One of the most important actions in the war was the capture of Aqaba, a strategically important town on the Red Sea coast. The Ottomans considered that the city couldn't be attacked from the landward side as it would be impossible for an army to cross the desert which was the city's hinterland. Its defences were therefore organised to resist an attack from the sea. Lawrence and Faisal achieved what the Ottomans considered impossible and led their army across the desert. From there, they were able to enter the city quite easily on the undefended landward side. Lawrence had not informed his high command that this action was planned, fearing it would be opposed, as the capture of Aqaba by the Arabs could be detrimental to French interests.

At the end of the war, General Allenby, who was the Commander in Chief of that particular theatre of war, was unstinting in his praise of Lawrence. He described Lawrence as the mainspring of the Arab offensive which he was able to achieve through his detailed knowledge of the Arab language, their culture and their mentality.

An episode that Lawrence experienced during this campaign may have affected him mentally, perhaps explaining the strange turn that Lawrence's career took at the end of the war. Lawrence carried out a number of solo operations. While fighting with the Arabs, he wore Arab dress and as his Arabic was fluent, he could pass off as a fair skinned Arab. On one occasion, he was reconnoitring Dera'a in this disguise and was captured by the Ottoman military. They had no idea who he was but during the fairly brief period that he was in captivity, he was beaten and sexually assaulted by the Ottoman officer and his soldiers. Lawrence doesn't recount the nature of the sexual assault but he wrote, 'that on that night, my integrity had been irrevocably lost'. This concludes Lawrence's book, 'the Seven Pillars of Wisdom', an account of his involvement in the Arab uprising against the Ottomans,

In writing his book, 'the Seven Pillars of Wisdom', Lawrence was concerned that the public would think that he was taking advantage of his role in the Arab revolt to earn a considerable income. He was determined that this would not be the case and arranged for the book to be sold at one third of its production cost, thus leaving himself in debt.

The climax of the Arab uprising against the Ottomans came with the capture of Damascus. Lawrence was very much involved in the planning and the build up to this but wasn't present at the moment the city finally fell. He arrived a few hours after the first British regiment reaching Damascus, the 10th Light Horse Regiment, had entered the city. Their senior officer had accepted the surrender of the city from its governor. However, Lawrence took a prominent part in the setting up of the newly liberated Damascus as the capital of an Arab state with Faisal as its king.

Two years after the war had ended, the French fought the Arabs at the Battle of Maysaloun and took over Damascus as part of the French Empire in Syria, destroying Lawrence's vision of the establishment of an independent Arabia. During the latter stages of the war, Lawrence had sought to convince the government that the establishment of an independent Arab state was in the interests of the British. However, the government had made a secret agreement with the French, 'the Sykes–Picot Agreement', which was contrary to the promise of Arab independence which Lawrence had made when negotiating with the leaders of the Arab uprising which defeated the Ottomans.

Lowell Thomas, a theatrical impresario, had travelled to the Middle East at the end of the war and had met Lawrence. Thomas realised that the campaign would provide the basis of great theatre and he produced a show entitled 'With Allenby in Palestine and Lawrence in Arabia'. Lawrence assisted Thomas in producing this show which became a great success and raised Lawrence to celebrity status. However, he stated later that he regretted being involved in this presentation.

After the war, Lawrence worked as an adviser to Winston Churchill in the Colonial Office. He campaigned for a political arrangement in the Middle East which reflected his and Churchill's vision of the area. He knew that the Arabs didn't want to be ruled by France and he published his opinions in many reputable British newspapers. He thus earned a negative reputation in France as one who was France's implacable enemy, continually encouraging the Arabs to revolt. This was an unwarranted accusation but the French identified Lawrence as the scapegoat which accounted for their inability to control Syria.

Lawrence hated bureaucratic work and after a year, he resigned his civil service post to make a very strange career move. He had been very impressed with the part the Royal Air Force had played in the war and enlisted as an aircraftman under the assumed name of John Hume Ross. Since his army rank was lieutenant colonel, he could probably have transferred to the RAF with the equivalent rank of wing commander, as his strategical genius in land combat could well have been adapted to air combat. He had some difficulty in being accepted into the RAF as an aircraftman. It was suspected that he was using an assumed name supported by false papers. However, he did ultimately succeed in getting admitted to the air force where he served for several years until the end of his enlistment period. He was responsible for pushing for the service to adopt much more powerful seaplane rescue tenders as the existing ones had proved to be too slow and had failed to rescue crews, downed in the sea. He worked with the 'British Power Boat Company' to develop a boat with a range of 140 miles at its cruising speed of 24 knots and with a top speed of 29 knots.

He declared himself to be very happy during his service in the Royal Air Force and was somewhat regretful when this episode came to an end. In a tribute to Lawrence, Winston Churchill wrote that Lawrence saw as clearly as anyone, the potential of airpower in war. The government was interested in bringing Lawrence into a post where he would be influential in preparing the country to deal with the rising threat of Nazi Germany. However, this was not to be. Tragedy was soon to follow.

Lawrence was a very keen motorcyclist, possessing a number of very powerful motorcycles. One day, when out on his motorcycle, his view was obstructed by a dip in the road and he had failed to observe two cyclists until the last moment. He swerved to avoid them but was thrown over his handlebars, suffering an injury which would prove fatal. Lawrence was six days in hospital before he died. One of the doctors attending Lawrence began to research the causes of death experienced by motorcyclists through head injuries. This research led to the adoption of crash helmets by both civil and military motorcyclists.

Winston Churchill attended Lawrence's funeral and described him as one of those beings whose pace of life was faster and more intense than what is normal.

Reginald Mitchell

Reginald Mitchell

Most of those, who have been identified in this volume as great national heroes or achievers, are well known, indeed, are household names. Reginald Mitchell may not be so well known but he deserves inclusion among this illustrious peer group. This is because of his work on a project which yielded something, without which, World War II might well have been lost. He didn't allow the fact that he had cancer for the latter part of his working life deter him from giving his utmost to the important work in which he was involved. In the end, his cancer proved terminal. However, he lived until just beyond the launching of the plane which he had designed to become an essential warplane in the Royal Air Force's armoury.

Reginald was born in Hanley, Staffordshire. He had two sisters and was the oldest of three brothers. In his family, he went by the name 'Reg'. His father held the post of Headmaster at three different schools in the area we know as the Potteries. During the time that Reginald was being educated at Hanley High School, he developed an interest in constructing and flying model aircraft. On leaving Hanley High School at the age of sixteen, he served an engineering apprenticeship at Kent Stuart, a railway engineering works. On completing his apprenticeship, he moved on to a drawing office and continued his studies at a local technical college where he showed considerable ability in mathematics.

He left Kent Stuart and briefly worked as a part-time teacher. He applied to join the armed forces but was turned down on the grounds that as a trained engineer, he was more important working for the country as an engineer than in the forces. In view of his later career, how wise this decision turned out to be. Reginald might have otherwise disappeared anonymously among the masses slaughtered during the conduct of World War I.

Reginald joined Supermarine Aviation Works in Southampton. This firm was engaged in building flying boats which was very much in line with an interest that Reginald had displayed while at school. In those days, flying was in its infancy. The first powered flight had only taken place a few years earlier in 1903 and major cities had not developed airfields from which planes could take off and land. It was therefore natural that firms, interested in developing aircraft, should specialise in sea planes.

In 1913, Jacques Schneider, a French Financier, had inaugurated a competition to be held annually (later biannually) to encourage the development of civil aviation. In this competition, manufacturers would enter sea planes to compete in a race to determine which was the fastest plane. The competition would end, once a manufacturer had won the race on three consecutive occasions and that manufacturer would hold the Schneider Trophy in perpetuity. A list of winners and the speeds achieved is included with this account. The first winning speed was 45.7 m.p.h. which may seem ridiculously slow but this was achieved within ten years of powered flight being proved possible. Naturally, this was a contest in which Supermarine Aviation had an interest and they won the competition for the first time in 1922. Their plane, 'Supermarine Sea Lion II', achieved a speed of 145.72 m.p.h.

At this time, Reginald would have been learning his craft as an aeronautical engineer with Supermarine Aviation and he may well have been involved in the design of 'Sea Lion II'. His ability and creative thinking was soon recognised by the firm and he received rapid promotion, first to the position of assistant to the works manager and then as chief draughtsman. At the age of nineteen, he married the head teacher of an infant school, Florence Dayson, who was eleven years his senior. It was not long after this that Reginald became Supermarine's chief engineer.

Over the next sixteen years, Reginald Mitchell designed twenty-four aeroplanes. One of his early successes was in response to an Air Ministry competition in which he submitted the 'Commercial Amphibian'. Although this was judged to be the best aircraft in terms of its design and reliability, it was only awarded second place! Mitchell's first design for a land aircraft was called the 'Supermarine Sparrow'. His 'Supermarine Southampton' flew to Australia. It left Felixstowe in October and returned in December. This flight taught Mitchell a lot about the way aircraft operated in the tropics. In 1926, the Air Ministry issued a specification for a fighter aircraft and Mitchell's team came up with a number of designs. The most successful of these was the 'Single Seat Fighter'.

Supermarine now started to move away from wooden amphibious aircraft to planes made of metal for which Mitchell had invented a new system for cooling aircraft engines by mounting a cooling device in the wing. In the 1930's, Supermarine went through a difficult phase when it failed to sell many aircraft but their fortunes revived with orders being place for the 'Supermarine Scarps'. This was a redesign by Mitchell of the 'Supermarine Southampton'. The R.A.F. also ordered some fighter planes, such as the 'Sea Otter', which was a redesign of one of Mitchell's earlier planes, the 'Walrus'.

Mitchell was greatly helped in designing planes by the National Physical Laboratory which had built a wind tunnel. This was invaluable in testing air foils. From wind tunnel tests, Mitchell discovered that the radiators for cooling the engine on a plane he was designing as an entry for the Schneider Trophy, were responsible for a disproportionate amount of drag. He was able to show that flat surfaced skin radiators reduced drag far better than the corrugated radiators favoured by American aircraft designers whose planes often won the Schneider Trophy. Thus, Mitchell was able to redesign the plane to become one which was more streamlined than any other plane then flying. He was also able to reduce the weight of the plane by using the new alloy, duralumin, rather than steel, for the plane's fuselage.

This new plane, the 'Supermarine S5', won the Schneider Trophy in 1927, two of Supermarine's three entrants finishing first and second. This victory broke the dominance of the Italian and American planes which had been entered for the Schneider Trophy in recent years. Supermarine planes, powered by specially designed Rolls Royce engines, won the next two Schneider Trophy races. This meant, by the terms set out for the competition, Supermarine won the trophy outright and brought this prestigious event to an end. As the government had decided not to enter a R.A.F. team for the 1931 competition, Supermarine's final entry, the 'S.6B', was only made possible as a result of sponsorship by Lady Houston, a wealthy philanthropist. The 'S.6B' went on to break the world air speed record by flying at 407.5 m.p.h. Mitchell was awarded the Commander of the Order of the British Empire (C.B.E.) in recognition of his services to aviation.

<u>Winners of the Schneider Tropy</u>

Date	Nation	Plane	Power	Speed
1913	France	Deperdussin Coupe Schneider	120 kW 180 hp	73.6 km/h 45.7 m.p.h.
1914	Great Britain	Sopwith Tabloid	75 kW 100 hp	139.66 km/h 86.78 m.p.h.
1920	Italy	SIAI/Savoia S.12	410 kW 550 hp	172.56 km/h 107.22 m.p.h.
1921	Italy	Macchi M.7bis	190 kW 250 hp	189.66 km/h 117.88 m.p.h.
1922	Great Britain	Supermarine Sea Lion II	340 kW 450 hp	234.52 km/h 145.72 m.p.h.
1923	United States	Curtis CR-3 A6081	354 kW 475 hp	285.46 km/h 177.38 m.p.h.
1925	United States	Curtis R3C-2 A7054	421 kW 565 hp	374.27 m.p.h. 232.56 m.p.h.
1926	Italy	Macchi M.39 M.M.76	600 kW 800 hp	396.70 km/h 246.50 m.p.h.
1927	Great Britain	Supermarine S.5 N220	652 kW 875 hp	453.28 km/h 281.66 m.p.h.
1929	Great Britain	Supermarine S.6 N247	1,400 kW 1,900 hp	528.88 km/h 330.55 m.p.h.
1931	Great Britain	Supermarine S.6B S1506	1,750 kW 2,350 hp	547.30 km/h 342.06 m.p.h.

In 1933, Mitchell underwent an operation for rectal cancer but he was left permanently disabled. However, war clouds were looming and it became vital for Britain to have aircraft capable of defending the country. Mitchell was by far the most able aircraft designer in the world and in view of the national threat, he didn't take ill health retirement but continued working, designing a plane which was the forerunner of the Spitfire. There were serious design faults in this prototype but by incorporating modifications based on successful innovations made in other parts of the world, his final design was a highly successful warplane. Mitchell had merged the innovations he had incorporated into this plane so cleverly that it was able to be improved and modified throughout the war years. Mitchell also designed a four engine bomber, the 'Type 317'.

Surprisingly, in his latter years, Mitchell took flying lessons and gained his pilot's licence in 1934. It was unusual for aircraft designers to actually take to the skies themselves.

In 1936, it became evident that Mitchell's cancer was terminal and he had to give up work, dying the following year. However, his work was accomplished. When war came and the Germans sent armadas of aircraft to bomb Britain into submission, they were met by squadrons of Spitfires, a far superior plane to anything the Germans possessed. Although British aircraft losses were heavy, they were far outnumbered by enemy casualties. When Goering had miscalculated that Britain must be running disastrously low in fighter aircraft, he sent a vast fleet of bombers over the channel on what has become known as Battle of Britain day. Radar had enabled their course to be tracked and they were met by squadrons of Spitfires and Hurricanes, another successful British fighter plane. The German planes suffered disastrous casualties. Goering realised that his tactics were futile and ceased sending over squadrons of bombers to be decimated by the Royal Air Force.

What more can be said of Mitchell? He was recognised as a quiet, unassuming genius who always had an intuitive grasp of essentials. He never sought the limelight and disliked public speaking. He said nothing until there was something worth saying. On the debit side, his son, Gordon, described him as a man who was sometimes difficult to live with. While Mitchell struggled to comprehend the scale of organisation needed in an enterprise like Supermarine, it is not surprising that his personality clashed with Barnes Wallace, inventor of the bouncing bomb which was used to breach the dams enclosing German reservoirs. Barnes Wallace had been sent to improve the efficiency of Mitchell's department but due to his disagreements with Mitchell, he had to be recalled. While irascible towards those he considered were claiming expertise they didn't possess, Mitchell was devoted to his staff at Supermarine to whom he showed kindness and respect. This was returned by their loyalty and affection.

Mitchell is commemorated by a number of buildings named after him. In Stoke-on-Trent, the Mitchell Memorial Youth Theatre (now the Mitchell Arts Centre) was built after money was raised by an immense public subscription. In Hanley, the Hull Lane Junior School was renamed the Reginald Mitchell County Primary School and Hanley High School was renamed the Mitchell High School.

Gladys Aylward

Gladys Aylward

Gladys was one of three children born into a working class family living in north London. On leaving school, she worked as a housemaid but had a strong vocation to become a missionary in China. She was accepted for an introductory training course by the China Inland Mission but she had some difficulty in learning the Chinese language and her course was not extended beyond the initial training period. However, this didn't dampen her ardour for doing this work and in her late twenties, she spent her life's savings on making a journey to China.

She couldn't afford to make the safe ocean journey to China by sea so she travelled via the Trans-Siberian Railway. This was hazardous as at the time, the Soviets and the Chinese were fighting an undeclared war and for much of the journey, she shared the carriage space with Russian troops. She was detained by the Russians but managed to escape with the help of local people who enabled her to make her way to Japan. With the help of the British Consul, she ultimately reached China.

On reaching China, she worked with Jeannie Lawson, an older missionary who ran a hostelry known as 'The Inn of the Eight Happinesses'. These are identified as virtue, gentleness, love, tolerance, truth, loyalty, devotion and beauty. While its primary purpose was to provide hospitality for travellers, it provided an environment where Jeannie and Gladys could recount stories which explained the life and purpose of Jesus.

For a time, Gladys worked for the Chinese government as a foot inspector. This involved travelling round the country to ensure that the new law, forbidding the foot-binding of young girls, was enforced. This was a dangerous task as there was much opposition to changing a practice so long embodied in Chinese culture. Foot inspectors even faced violence but Gladys's gentle but resolute approach to the job made her very successful in carrying out this daunting task.

Gladys went out of her way to provide help to those in need and started an orphanage for the many destitute children she encountered. She advocated reform of the severely outdated Chinese prison system, even intervening to bring calm to a situation where prisoners were rioting against harsh conditions.

In 1938, China was invaded by the Japanese and Gladys realised that she had to take the children to a secure haven away from the path of the advancing Japanese. In spite of being unwell and wounded herself, she managed to lead more than one hundred children, over mountains to a place of safety. This period of her time in China proved specially fruitful in winning converts to Christianity.

Gladys's life was again in danger during the communist revolution under Mao Tse Tsung. Missionaries were being actively sought out by the communist army. Thus, Gladys had to return to Britain in 1949 where she settled in Basingstoke and spent much of her time touring the country and lecturing about her work and experiences in China. When the hostilities in China had ended, she returned to China, residing in Hong Kong which was under British administration. She applied to the Chinese communist government to see whether she could return and continue her work in mainland China but this application was refused. She finally settled in Taiwan where she founded the 'Gladys Aylward Orphanage' and worked there until her death in 1970 at the age of sixty-eight.

A film, 'The Small Woman' has been made about Gladys's heroic life but it didn't meet with her approval. She felt mortified by the way she was depicted. Her struggles to get to China were underplayed and she was cast by a glamorous film star who bore no similarity in appearance to Gladys. To inject a romance element into the film, Hollywood included a non-existent love affair between her and a Chinese Nationalist colonel and she was depicted as deserting her children to be with him.

The ministry started by Gladys in Taiwan continues to grow. Her orphanage has expanded into new buildings to become the 'Bethany Children's Home'. In Britain, a secondary school in London was renamed the 'Gladys Aylward School' shortly after her death.

Significant events in British History

Julius Caesar invades Britain	55 BC
London founded	50 AD
Boadicea's rebellion	61 AD
Hadrian's Wall built	22 AD
St. Augustine arrives in Canterbury	597 AD
Norman Conquest	1066 AD
St. Thomas a Becket martyred	1170 AD
Magna Carta	1215 AD
Battle of Lewes	1264 AD
Battle of Evesham	1265 AD
Battle of Stirling Bridge	1297 AD
Battle of Bannockburn	1314 AD
Arrival of the Black Death	1348 AD
Battle of Poitiers	1356 AD
Peasants' Revolt	1381 AD
Battle of Agincourt	1415 AD
Battle of Bosworth	1485 AD
Execution of Mary, Queen of Scots	1587 AD
Spanish Armada	1588 AD
The Gunpowder Plot	1605 AD
English Civil War	1642 – 1651 AD
The Great Fire of London	1666 AD
Battle of Blenheim	1704 AD
Robert Walpole becomes 1st PM	1721 AD
Battle of Quebec	1759 AD
American declaration of Independence	1776 AD
Battle of Trafalgar	1805 AD
Battle of Waterloo	1815 AD
Stockton to Darlington Railway opens	1825 AD
Abolition of Slavery Act	1833 AD
First postage stamps issued	1840 AD
Victoria Falls discovered	1855 AD
Battle of Omdurman	1898 AD
South Pole reached	1912 AD
1st World War	1914 - 1918 AD
Women granted suffrage	1918 & 1928 AD
2nd World War	1940 - 1946 AD

<u>Roman Emperors during time England was part of the Roman Empire</u>

Julius Caesar	55 BC	(Veni, Vidi, Vici)
<u>Augustus</u>	27 BC–14 AD	
<u>Tiberius</u>	14–37 AD	
<u>Caligula</u>	37–41 AD	
<u>Claudius</u>	41–54 AD	
<u>Nero</u>	54–68 AD	
<u>Galba</u>	68–69 AD	
<u>Otho</u>	69 AD	
<u>Aulus Vitellius</u>	69 AD	
<u>Vespasian</u>	69–79 AD	
<u>Titus</u>	79–81 AD	
<u>Domitian</u>	81–96 AD	
<u>Nerva</u>	96–98 AD	
<u>Trajan</u>	98–117 AD	
<u>Hadrian</u>	117–138 AD	
<u>Antoninus Pius</u>	138–161 AD	
<u>Marcus Aurelius</u>	161–180 AD	
<u>Lucius Verus</u>	161–169 AD	
<u>Commodus</u>	177–192 AD	
Publius Helvius	193 AD	
Marcus Didius	193 AD	
Severus Julianus	193 AD	
<u>Septimius Severus</u>	193–211 AD	
<u>Caracalla</u>	198–217 AD	
<u>Publius Septimius Geta</u>	209–211 AD	
<u>Macrinus</u>	217–218 AD	
<u>Elagabalus</u>	218–222 AD	
<u>Severus Alexander</u>	222–235 AD	
<u>Maximinus</u>	235–238 AD	
<u>Gordian I</u>	238 AD	
<u>Gordian II</u>	238 AD	
<u>Pupienus Maximus</u>	238 AD	
<u>Balbinus</u>	238 AD	
<u>Gordian III</u>	238–244 AD	
<u>Philip</u>	244–249 AD	
<u>Decius</u>	249–251 AD	
<u>Hostilian</u>	251 AD	
<u>Gallus</u>	251–253 AD	
<u>Aemilian</u>	253 AD	

Valerian	253–260 AD
Gallienus	253–268 AD
Claudius II Gothicus	268–270 AD
Quintillus	270 AD
Aurelian	270–275 AD
Tacitus	275–276 AD
Florian	276 AD
Probus	276–282 AD
Carus	282–283 AD
Numerian	283–284 AD
Carinus	283–285 AD

Empire divided int East & West

Diocletian	east, 284–305 AD)
Maximian	west, 286–305 AD
Constantius I	west, 305–306 AD
Galerius	east, 305–311 AD
Severus	west, 306–307 AD
Maxentius	west, 306–312 AD

Empire reunified

Constantine I	306–337 AD
Galerius Valerius Maximinus	310–313 AD
Licinius	308–324 AD
Constantine II	337–340 AD
Constantius II	337–361 AD
Constans I	337–350 AD
Gallus Caesar	351–354 AD
Julian	(361–363 AD
Jovian	(363–364 AD

Empire divided int East & West

Valentinian I	west, 364–375 AD
Valens	east, 364–378 AD
Gratian	west, 367–383 AD
Valentinian I	west, 367–383 AD
Valentinian II	west 375–392 AD
Theodosius I	east, 379–392 AD
	east and west, 392–395 AD
Arcadius	east, 383–395 AD
Magnus Maximus	west, 383–388 AD
Honorius	west, 393–395 AD
Theodosius II	east, 408–450 AD

Constantius III   west, 421 AD
Valentinian III   west, 425–455 AD
Marcian (east, 450–457 AD
Petronius Maximus   west, 431, 455 AD
Avitus   west, 455–456 AD
Majorian   west, 457–461 AD
Libius Severus   west, 461–465 AD
Anthemius   west, 467–472 AD
Olybrius   west, April–November 472 AD
Glycerius   west, 473–474 AD
Julius Nepos   west, 474–475 AD
Romulus Augustulus   west, 475–476 AD
Leo I   east, 457–474 AD
Leo II   east, 474 AD
Zeno   east, 474–491 AD

<u>**Kings and Queens of England**</u>

Saxons

Egbert	802 - 839
Ethelwulf	839 - 856
Ethelbvald	806 – 860
Ethelbert	860 – 866
Ethelred I	866 – 871
Alfred the Great	871 – 901
Edward the Elder	901 – 924
Athelstan	924 – 940
Edmund I the Elder	941 – 946
Edred	946 – 955
Edwy	955 – 959
Edgar	959 – 975
Edward the Martyr	975 - 978
Ethelred II the Unready	978 – 1016
Edmund II Ironside	1016

Danes

Canute	1016 – 1035
Harold I Harefoot	1037 – 1040
Hardicanute	1040 – 1042

Saxons

Edward the Confessor	1042 -1066
Harold II	1066
Edgar Atheling	1066

Normans

William I, the Conqueror	1066 – 1087
William II, Rufus	1087 – 1100
Henry I	1100 – 1135
Stephen	1135 – 1154
Empress Matilda	1141

Plantagenets

Henry II	1154 – 1189
Richard I the Lionheart	1189 – 1199
John I	1199 – 1216
Henry III	1216 – 1272
Edward I	1272 – 1307
Edward II	1307 – 1327
Edward III	1327 – 1377

Richard II	1377 – 1399

Lancastrians

Henry IV	1399 – 1413
Henry V	1413 – 1422
Henry VI	1422 – 1461, 1470 – 1471

Yorkists

Edward IV	1461 - 1470, 1471 – 1483
Edward V	1483 – 1483
Richard III	1483 – 1485

Tudors

Henry VII	1485 – 1509
Henry VIII	1509 – 1547
Edward VI	1547 – 1553
Jane Grey	1554
Mary I	1553 – 1558
Elizabeth I	1558 – 1603

Stuarts

James I	1603 – 1625
Charles I	1625 – 1649

Oliver Cromwell   1649 - 1658
Richard Cromwell 1668 = 1660

Charles II	1660 – 1685
James II	1685 – 1688
{William III	1688 – 1702 }
{Mary II	1688 – 1694 }
Anne	1702 – 1714

Hanoverians

George I	1714 – 1727
George II	1727 – 1760
George III	1760 – 1820
George IV	1820 – 1830
William IV	1830 – 1837

Saxe-Coburg & Gotha

Victoria	1837 – 1901
Edward VII	1901 – 1910

Windsor

George V	1910 – 1936
Edward VIII	1936
George VI	1936 – 1952
Elizabeth II	1952 – 2022
Charles III	2022 –

British Prime Ministers

Robert Walpole,	M.P. for Kings Lynn	1721 – 1742	Whig
Spencer Compton,	Earl of Wilmington	1742 – 1743	Whig
Henry Pelham,	M.P. for Sussex	1743 1754	Whig
Thomas Pelham-Hollies,	Duke of Newcastle	1754 - 1756	Whig
William Cavendish,	Duke of Devonshire	1756 - 1757	Whig
Thomas Pelham-Hollies	Duke of Newcastle	1757 - 1762	Whig
John Stuart	Earl of Bute	1762 - 1763	Tory
George Grenville	M.P. for Buckingham	1763 - 1765	Whig
Charles Wentworth	Marquess of Rockingham	1765 – 1766	Whig
William Pitt, the Elder	Earl of Chatham	1766 - 1768	Whig
Augustus Fitzroy	Duke of Grafton	1768 – 1780	Whig
Frederick North	M.P. for Banbury	1780 - 1782	Tory
Charles Wentworth	Marquess of Rockingham	1782- 1782	Whig
William Petty	Earl of Sherburne	1782 – 1783	Whig
William Bentinck	Duke of Portland	1784 – 1783	Whig
William Pitt, the Younger	M.P. for Camb. Univ.	1783 – 1801	Tory
Henry Addington	M.P. for Devizes	1801 – 1804	Tory
William Pitt, the Younger	M.P. for Camb. Univ.	1804 - 1806	Tory
William Grenville	Baron Grenville	1806 - 1807	Whig
William Bentinck	Duke of Portland	1807 - 1809	Tory
Spencer Percival	M.P. for Northampton	1809 - 1812	Tory
Robert Jenkinson	Earl of Liverpool	1812 – 1827	Tory
George Canning	M.P. for Seaford	1827 – 1827	Tory
Frederick Robinson,	Viscount Goderich	1827 – 1828	Tory
Arthur Wellesley,	Duke of Wellington	1828 – 1830	Tory
Charles Grey	Earl Grey	1830 - 1834	Whig
William Lamb,	Viscount Melbourne	1834 – 1834	Whig
Arthur Wellesley,	Duke of Wellington	1834 – 1834	Tory
Robert Peel	M.P. for Tamworth	1834 – 1835	Conservative
William Lamb,	Viscount Melbourne	1835 – 1841	Whig
Robert Peel	M.P. for Tamworth	1841 – 1846	Conservative
John Russell	M.P. for City of London	1846 – 1852	Whig
Edward Stanley	Earl of Derby	1852 - 1852	Conservative
George Gordon	Earl of Aberdeen	1852 – 1855	Conservative
Henry Temple	Viscount Palmerston	1855 – 1858	Whig
John Russell	M.P. for City of London	1858 – 1859	Whig
Henry Temple	Viscount Palmerston	1859 – 1865	Liberal
John Russell	M.P. for City of London	1865 – 1866	Liberal
Edward Stanley	Earl of Derby	1866 - 1868	Conservative
Benjamin Disraeli	M.P. f. Buckinghamshire	1868 - 1868	Conservative

William Gladstone	M.P. for Greenwich	1868 – 1874	Liberal
Benjamin Disraeli	M.P. f. Buckinghamshire	1874 - 1880	Conservative
William Gladstone	M.P. for Midlothian	1880 – 1885	Liberal
Robert Cecil	Marquess of Salisbury	1885 - 1886	Conservative
William Gladstone	M.P. for Midlothian	1886 – 1886	Liberal
Robert Cecil	Marquess of Salisbury	1886 - 1892	Conservative
William Gladstone	M.P. for Midlothian	1892 – 1894	Liberal
Archibald Primrose	Earl of Rosebury	1894 - 1895	Liberal
Robert Cecil	Marquess of Salisbury	1895 - 1902	Conservative
Arthur Balfour	M.P. for Manchester E.	1902 - 1905	Conservative
H. Campbell-Bannerman	M.P. for Burghs	1905 – 1908	Liberal
H. Asquith	M.P. for Fyfe	1908 - 1916	Liberal
David Lloyd George	M.P. for Carnarvon Bs.	1916 - 1922	Liberal
Bonar Law	M.P. for Glasgow Central	19 22 – 1923	Conservative
Stanley Baldwin	M.P. for Bewdley	1923 - 1924	Conservative
Ramsay Macdonald	M.P. for Aberavon	1924 - 1924	Labour
Stanley Baldwin	M.P. for Bewdley	1924 - 1929	Conservative
Ramsay Macdonald	M.P. for Seaham	1929 - 1935	Labour
Stanley Baldwin	M.P. for Bewdley	1935 - 1937	Conservative
Neville Chamberlain	M.P. for B'ham Edgbstn	1937 – 1940	Conservative
Winston Churchill	M.P. for Epping	1940 – 1945	Conservative
Clement Attlee	M.P. for Limehouse	1945 – 1951	Labour
Winston Churchill	M.P. for Woodford	1951 – 1955	Conservative

BBC Poll of 100 Greatest Britons

1. **<u>Sir Winston Churchill</u>**
2. **<u>Isambard Kingdom Brunel</u>**
3. *Diana, Princess of Wales*
4. Charles Darwin
5. **<u>William Shakespeare</u>**
6. **<u>Sir Isaac Newton</u>**
7. **<u>Elizabeth I</u>**
8. *John Lennon*
9. **<u>Horatio Nelson, 1st Viscount Nelson</u>**
10. **<u>Oliver Cromwell</u>**
11. Sir Ernest Shackleton
12. **<u>Captain James Cook</u>**
13. **<u>Robert Baden-Powell</u>**
14. **<u>Alfred the Great</u>**
15. **<u>Arthur Wellesley, 1st Duke of Wellington</u>**
16. *Margaret Thatcher*
17. *Michael Crawford*
18. *Queen Victoria*
19. *Sir Paul McCartney*
20. Sir Alexander Fleming
21. *Alan Turing*
22. **<u>Michael Faraday</u>**
23. **<u>Owen Glendower</u>**
24. Elizabeth II
25. *Stephen Hawking*
26. William Tyndale
27. **<u>Emmeline Pankhurst</u>**
28. William Wilberforce
29. *David Bowie*
30. *Guy Fawkes*
31. Leonard Cheshire
32. *Eric Morecambe*
33. *David Beckham*
34. *Thomas Paine*
35. **<u>Boadicea</u>**
36. *Sir Steve Redgrave*
37. *Sir Thomas More*
38. *William Blake*
39. *John Harrison*

40.Henry VIII
41.Charles Dickens
42.Sir Frank Whittle
43.John Peel
44.John Logie Baird
45.Aneurin Bevan
46.Boy George
47.Sir Douglas Bader
48.Sir William Wallace
49.Sir Francis Drake
50.John Wesley
51.King Arthur
52.Florence Nightingale
53.Thomas Edward Lawrence
54.Robert Falcon Scott
55.Enoch Powell
56.Sir Cliff Richard
57.Sir Alexander Graham Bell
58.Freddie Mercury
59.Dame Julie Andrews
60.Sir Edward Elgar
61.Queen Elizabeth The Queen Mother
62.George Harrison
63.Sir David Attenborough
64.James Connolly
65.George Stephenson
66.Sir Charles Chaplin
67.Tony Blair
68.William Caxton
69.Bobby Moore
70.Jane Austen
71.William Booth
72.Henry V
73.Aleister Crowley
74.Robert the Bruce
75.Bob Geldof
76.The Unknown Warrior
77.Robbie Williams
78.Edward Jenner
79.David Lloyd George, 1st Earl of Dwyfor
80.Charles Babbage

81. Geoffrey Chaucer
82. *Richard III*
83. *Joanne K. Rowling*
84. James Watt
85. *Sir Richard Branson*
86. *Bono*
87. *John Lydon (Johnny Rotten)*
88. **<u>Bernard Montgomery, 1st Viscount of Alamein</u>**
89. *Donald Campbell*
90. Henry II
91. James Clerk Maxwell
92. *J. R. R. Tolkien*
93. *Sir Walter Raleigh*
94. *Edward I*
95. Sir Barnes Wallis
96. *Richard Burton*
97. *Tony Benn*
98. **<u>David Livingstone</u>**
99. Sir Tim Berners-Lee
100. *Marie Stopes*

The author has restricted the scope of this book to up to and including the second World War.

Of the 100 Great Britons identified in the BBC Poll, the author has selected just 27 for inclusion in this book. These are shown in the list as underscored, bold and in green. Many other names are included in this book which are not found in the BBC list.

Names shown in blue are individuals who might well have been included in this book but whose field of achievement is either, already well represented by other famous names, or who are post-war personalities.

Other names are shown in italics. Sports or entertainment stars whose fame is unlikely to live much beyond this generation are shown in red.

Author Information - Ray Filby

Dr Filby was a scholar at the Royal College of Science, Imperial College, London University from which he graduated with a B.Sc, and a Ph.D. in physics. Later, during his career, he was awarded an M.Sc. degree in manufacturing systems engineering by Warwick University where he was awarded a special prize by the university for his performance on this course.

Ray Filby fulfilled his National Service in the army (R.E.M.E.) which he completed as officer in charge of the garrison telecommunications workshop in Gibraltar. He worked for a time as a development engineer with Hilger and Watts, a London based firm of optical instruments and machines. A large part of his career was spent in education lecturing in maths and physics at technical colleges in Birmingham and High Wycombe before becoming head of the maths and science department at Henley College in Coventry. After fulfilling a short term contract as a technical writer for Jaguar cars, Ray Filby spent the final part of his career working for Severn Trent Water as an information scientist in their water quality department.

Ray Filby has had many years' experience of church life in a number of churches, fulfilling at various times, the roles of Pathfinder Group Leader, Youth Fellowship Leader, Secretary to the Parochial Church Council, Churchwarden and Reader (Licensed Lay Minister). This experience is reflected in the stories he writes which embrace several genres, including historical fiction, short stories, Bible study, murder stories and romantic fiction.

Other Books by Ray Filby

Biblical Fiction

The Sun and the Moon of Alexandria

This is a fictional biopic of Apollos, a missionary saint and one of St. Paul's co-workers. Although mentioned many times in the New Testament, little is known of the life and background of Apollos. Thus, there is scope to create a story which constructs a feasible account of Apollos' youth in Egypt, his journey to Israel, his conversion, his relationship with St. Paul, his missionary work and his marriage. The story culminates in his martyrdom. In situations where Apollos interacts with well-known Biblical characters, the narrative remains faithful to the New Testament account.

The Warrior and the Bride

This work of Biblical fiction is largely set in the period covered by the 2nd Book of Samuel and the 1st Book of Kings. It features Benaiah and Abishag, two characters who had important roles to play in serving King David and his successor. Although a work of fiction, the author has tried to make it consistent with the Biblical narrative and references are provided wherever the story is related to a Biblical event. The author realises that minor inconsistencies occur in the text but then, minor inconsistencies can be found in the Bible itself. There is no indication in the Bible that the two main characters were in any way related but nothing in the Bible specifically states that they were not.

Soldiers, Saints and Sinners

'Soldiers, Saints and Sinners' is a collection of fictitious stories, featuring some of the minor characters whom Jesus encountered in his ministry. It attempts to suggest how their backgrounds might have been important in the way they led to their encounter with Jesus and the way these encounters furthered the progress of Jesus' ministry. Each story is preceded by a modern Biblical translation of the passage which recounts their appearance on the scene where Jesus was ministering and is followed by five questions which are suitable for a person's private devotions or for use in the context of a group Bible study.

Parables, the Greatest Stories ever told – retold

'The Greatest Stories ever told – Retold' focuses on the better known parables of Jesus and rewrites them as situations in modern life which correspond to the situations in Jesus' day, attempting to promote the same teaching that Jesus was giving in the original parable. Each parable is preceded by a modern translation of the original parable and followed by ten questions which are suitable for a person's private devotions or for use in the context of a group Bible study.

Bible Study

An Insight into the Gospels and the Book of Acts

'An Insight into the Gospels and the Book of Acts' is an overview of the themes, contents, emphases, and structure of the first five books of the New Testament. While there is so much similarity in the stories and teaching in each of the gospels, this book contrasts the way each gospel is written and presented. It highlights the quite remarkable differences which exist between each of the gospels as they are directed to different audiences and have different primary objectives. The book is presented with the main content of the book appearing on the right hand (odd numbered) pages and supportive texts placed opposite the relevant passages on the left hand pages.

St. Columba's. its life and its People

Churches are living organisms, each with their own distinctive patterns of life. While their members experience the same ups and downs in life as the population as a whole, their Christian faith results in their reacting to circumstances in a distinctive way.

This book is a set of short stories, some of which trace the unfolding of events which occur as part of church life, and others, which recount the experience of individual church members. Readers are invited to consider the practical or ethical problems which arise in these stories and think how they themselves might have dealt with or reacted to those situations.

Children's Books

The Tasks of Chronavon

When sensible twelve-year-olds, Alfred and Alice meet a mysterious angel called Chronavon in the vestry of their church, it seems someone is playing a practical joke on them. After all, angels don't just pop up in church vestries to enlist the help of two young people to journey back in time to prevent a devilish time traveller from altering the course of history. Yet it soon becomes clear that Chronavon's incredible story is true. As Alfred and Alice are whisked backwards through the centuries, they become immersed in the rich customs and costumes of the past through Henry III's troubled reign, the insecurity of Princess Elizabeth before she became Queen Elizabeth I and the Civil War between the Cavaliers and Roundheads. 'The Tasks of Chronavon' is an exciting, informative tale for young readers which effortlessly weaves fact and fiction with a sprinkling of humour and shows how little human values have changed over time.

<u>The Evil Occupants of **Easingdale Castle**</u>

Teenager, Jason, and his friends, Bill, Becky and Liz, are recruited by an unusual messenger to pit their wits against an international gang of forgers, occupying their local castle. The gang are intent on destabilising the British economy by flooding the country with forged £20 notes which could pass off as the real thing. The gang is well equipped with hi-tech machines.

It remains to be seen whether Jason and his friends, who are also technically knowledgeable, can outwit the gang.

Technology will have advanced since this book was written and young readers are invited to consider whether they could have done better than Jason and his friends with equipment now available.

Travel Novel

<u>**The Evil Emir of** Transoxiana</u>

Becky meets with her special friends, Jason, Bill and Liz, to tell them she is being posted to Transoxiana. She needs to explain exactly where she will be working, that she will be accompanied by Jason and that she will be spending some time with her Kyrgyz penfriend, Askari, and her husband, Temier. During Becky's stay with Askari, Temier falls foul of an extremist Islamic cleric, the self-styled, Emir of Transoxiana. The resourcefulness of Becky and Jason, helped by Bill and Liz who travel out to join them, is needed to keep Askari and Temier safe from the Evil Emir. In spite of the danger being faced, they all manage to have the experiences in Transoxiana which make their stay both exciting and enjoyable.

Historical Novels

The Countess who should have been Queen

Margaret Plantagenet was born near the end of the Wars of the Roses. As the daughter of the brother of King Edward IV, a situation could well have arisen when she or her brother, Edward, had a claim to the throne. Margaret was not ambitious to become Queen but was happy to marry a commoner and settled as an enlightened landowner with her husband in Berkshire. Margaret became Queen Catherine of Aragon's chief lady-in-waiting and was awarded a peerage to become Countess of Salisbury. Margaret faithfully supported

Catherine right through her reign and as far as she could when Catherine was sent to live in isolation after her divorce. One of Margaret's sons, Reginald, became a prominent churchman and angered the King by writing a treatise, heavily critical of Henry VIII, the way he had divorced Catherine and taken over the Church of England. Reginald was living out of reach of Henry on the continent so Henry vented his wrath on Margaret and her family.

The Lady and the Lollards

The story is set in the troubled reign of Henry VI at the end of the Hundred Years' War and the main part of the War of the Roses.

King Henry was a saintly king whose reign was marred by bellicose, ambitious rivals. In spite of serious setbacks and challenges to their rule, King Henry and Queen Margaret leave lasting legacies to the nation which are still part of our national life and institutions in this present age.

Lady Constance and two Lollards, Matthew and Michael, work as agents of peace in a war-torn country, bringing succour to the victims of this war. They find that they are able to perform an amazing act of service to help King Henry and Queen Margaret when their fortunes are at their lowest ebb.

Crime Novels

A Church like Cluedo

After graduating from college as a civil engineer, Annette Owen had hoped to work in the developing world under the auspices of a missionary society. When this door to Christian service was closed, she applied to become an ordained minister but was turned down by the selection committee. She was however able to exercise a very fulfilled ministry as a clergy wife. Unfortunately, her clergy husband had dark secrets in his life of which Annette was totally unaware until a situation arose which resulted in murder being committed. The impact of this had an unexpected effect on the course of Annette's life.

Inspector Sinclair and Sergeant Powers most interesting cases

This account of some interesting cases solved by the detective duo, Inspector Sinclair and Sergeant Powers, is not a normal 'whodunnit' in which the murderer is not revealed until the very end when the detective reveals the clues which he or she alone has picked up to solve the case without sharing their significance with the reader until the very end.

The stories in this book are divided into sections, a list of those involved to help the reader keep track of the characters,

'the Event' which describes the situation when the murder took place,

'the Investigation' which describes the systematic way in which the detectives investigated the case
and

'the Evidence' in which the crucial evidence by which a cast iron case against the murderer was built up, is reviewed.

<u>Consequences of Careless</u> <u>Cyber Crime</u>

Detective Inspector Christine Powers and her partner, Detective Sergeant Bill Matthews, are involved in a missing person enquiry, but this turns into a murder investigation when the missing person is found buried in a shallow grave by a layby. They have their suspicions but no leads on the way the murder was carried out or the motive. However, an unexpected lead does come to light when they start to investigate a cyber crime which proves to be linked with the murder.

<u>Astoundingly Audacious</u> <u>Heists 2023</u>

This series of short stories describes a number of heists which are amazing, not just by virtue of their ingenuity, but because of the high profile nature of the target of the theft.

Even when the identity of the criminals involved is discovered, there is difficulty in bringing them to justice because of the embarrassment that the publicity associated with the disclosure of the heist would cause the establishment figures, responsible for the security of the stolen items.

<u>Science Fiction</u>

<u>Planets, Plagues and</u> <u>Pandemics</u>

Klandacia, a planet orbiting a nearby star, has a technology well in advance of that on earth. A pandemic, similar to the coronavirus outbreak experienced on earth, has caused the death of many Klandacians and is a recent memory to the humanoid population of this planet. As the Klandacians have developed an economy which is cashless, it came out of the pandemic without the economic turmoil experienced on earth as it emerges from the coronavirus pandemic. The Klandacian Supreme High Priest receives a message from God requesting that help should be sent to earth. Although the journey to earth will take many years, four Klandacian astronauts volunteer for the mission, two men and two women.

Romantic Fiction

Consequences of Immature Love

Boy-Girl, Man-Woman relationships cement our society. Because these relationships are seldom straightforward, they provide scope for an indefinite number of works of fiction. In this novel, you are invited to follow the amorous adventures of Georgina Matthews and Arthur Gray from the time they leave school and start at university until they ultimately marry the partner for whom they seemed destined from the outset.

Social Activities

Puzzles, Quiz and Activities Suitable for Social Events – Volumes 1 - 6

These books consist of a set of puzzles, quiz and activities which the author designed for use at a monthly social event organised by St. Michael's, Church, Budbrooke, in the Community Centre in the part of the parish known as Chase Meadow. People who have opted to take part really seem to have enjoyed these activities which are interesting rather than extremely challenging. While a good general knowledge is helpful in completing some of the activities, they are not designed to expose people's ignorance as data sheets and appropriate reference books like atlases are made available to help participants find any information needed. Thus, the activities are educational.